INDIAN RIVER CO. MAIN LIBRARY
3 2901 00559 9783
P9-DDU-863

Indian River County Main Library
1600 21st Street
Vero Beach, FL 32960

THE ADEN EFFECT

THE ADEN EFFECT

A CONNOR STARK NOVEL

CLAUDE BERUBE

NAVAL INSTITUTE PRESS
ANNAPOLIS, MARYLAND

Naval Institute Press
291 Wood Road
Annapolis, MD 21402

© 2012 by Claude Berube

All rights reserved. No part of this book may be reproduced or utilized in any form or by any means, electronic or mechanical, including photocopying and recording, or by any information storage and retrieval system, without permission in writing from the publisher.

Library of Congress Cataloging-in-Publication Data

Berube, Claude G.
The Aden effect : a Connor Stark novel / Claude Berube.
p. cm.
ISBN 978-1-61251-109-2 (hardcover : alk. paper) — ISBN 978-1-61251-110-8 (e-book) 1. Aden, Gulf of—Fiction. 2. Piracy—Fiction. 3. International relations—Fiction. 4. Middle East—Fiction. I. Title.
PS3602.E7693A66 2012
813′.6—dc23
2012020771

∞ This paper meets the requirements of ANSI/NISO z39.48-1992 (Permanence of Paper).

Printed in the United States of America.

20 19 18 17 16 15 14 13 12 9 8 7 6 5 4 3 2

Book design and composition: David Alcorn, Alcorn Publication Design

3 2901 00559 9783

FOR KATE

We should never forget that everything Adolf Hitler did in Germany was "legal" and everything the Hungarian freedom fighters did in Hungary was "illegal."

—MARTIN LUTHER KING JR.,
"Letter from a Birmingham Jail"

PART I

PROLOGUE

TWENTY-TWO DAYS AGO

Western Indian Ocean, 0215 (GMT)

The first rocket-propelled grenade hit the supertanker's bow twenty feet above the waterline. The second hit the superstructure a deck below the bridge. The crew staggered back from their positions, desperate to escape what they knew was coming next, knowing they had nowhere to go.

The *Katya P.* was exactly where Faisal's sources said it would be. His network had told him when the supertanker had transited the Strait of Hormuz, its next port of call, and its course. He had estimated the ship's speed correctly and saw it over the horizon an hour before dawn during the dark blue hour when the sky and seas were still and the only sound on the water was the gentle hum of his own ship's engines.

He ordered the three skiffs manned by six of his Somali pirate-soldiers to be released. Armed with a mix of AK-47s and RPGs, the men were fueled by the kind of courage found only in the effects of the drug khat. They believed they were prepared. They knew they were going to win the day.

Faisal checked the radar and smiled. The supertanker was on course two-zero-zero on its way to the Cape of Good Hope. This job had become far too easy.

"What is it, Faisal?" his helmsman asked. "Why are you smiling?"

"You were just a boy when we started. Do you remember? Only a few years ago the great ships were safe in the Gulf of Aden. Now they fear us."

"I remember. We were all young when you recruited us. You promised that we would be the most powerful force in these waters and that we would no longer go hungry. You have kept your word."

"Yes. Now it is the great shipping companies who go hungry seeking safer waters. But there are none. See our prey there? He avoids the Gulf of Aden and tries to sail around South Africa. He will fail like the others."

The skiffs were away.

Faisal raised the handheld radio to his mouth. "Go faster and get alongside the ship," he ordered.

The skiffs closed quickly on the supertanker, the hum of their motors rising to a crescendo as they chased it down. Through his binoculars Faisal saw that it was riding low and slow, full of oil bound for the great powers. Great white waves rose at the bow as the laden supertanker labored through the ocean, aching to outrace the small boats. The familiar crackling of a ship-to-ship radio confirmed that the ship had seen the pirates and that it was indeed the prey he had waited for.

"Mayday, mayday, mayday. This is the oil carrier Katya P. *Our position is 10° 20′ 3″ N and 58° 5′ 10″ E on course two-zero-zero at fourteen point five knots. We are being approached by pirates and require immediate assistance."*

"Their captain is desperate," Faisal said to his helmsman. "Listen to how quickly he says the words. Listen as he gulps air. He cries out, but no one hears except the ocean and us."

"We are safe for now, Captain?"

Faisal was tired of explaining what should have been so apparent to his helmsman after all these years. But he recruited desperate and hungry men, not the most literate or intelligent; and what small intellectual powers they had were slowed by years of khat use. They were his fodder, and there were enough men in Somalia to fill his crew no matter how many losses he incurred.

"There are two million square miles of our beloved waters and only one American warship," he said impatiently. "We have time."

As the skiffs closed on the *Katya P.*, Faisal heard loud sirens on the tanker and saw the crew scampering to take up antiboarding positions. This was fine. All he could see were water cannons used for repelling boarders. He raised the radio and ordered his skiffs to open fire again. A third RPG struck the *Katya P.*, followed by the familiar staccato of the pirates' AK-47s. He watched as the tanker's crew fell one by one while racing toward the superstructure, which no longer afforded them protection. Pirates from two skiffs continued firing at the crew as the third pulled alongside the *Katya P.* Using an extension ladder and ropes the Somalis deftly made their way up and over the rails.

Within a few minutes the pirates had secured the tanker. The captain and what remained of the crew stood on the deck, their hands behind their heads. Four tall Somalis, clad only in ragged shorts, held guns at the ready should any of them be so foolish as to try to escape.

Faisal's ship pulled alongside the tanker with the other two skiffs in its wake, their crews cheering their leader and their great victory; two of them fired blindly into the sky in celebration until Faisal ordered them to cease. He boarded and approached the prisoners. Most were much smaller than the Somalis. They were the workhorses of the oceans, these Filipinos, whose labor cost the great shipping companies little. One man among them was white and had the fat waist of a Westerner or a Russian.

"You are the captain?" Faisal asked.

"Yes. Captain Ilya Korchenko." The overweight man's belly quivered with each breath.

"Your watch is very nice. Gold?"

"Here, take it," Korchenko said, removing his watch and offering it as a token of surrender before it could be taken from him.

Faisal accepted the watch and examined it closely. "Very nice. This is inscribed. I have not known someone to inscribe their own watch."

"It was a gift," Captain Korchenko said. "From my family."

Faisal smiled wolfishly. "I appreciate their gift. I will put it to good use."

"I will contact my company to ask for your ransom," Korchenko said.

"No. That will not be necessary."

"What? But there has always been—"

"No ransom this time." Faisal raised his own Kalashnikov and fired three rounds into the captain's chest. The other pirates did the same with the remaining crew. Faisal tossed the watch to one of his crewmen.

"Kick their bodies overboard, Saddiq. And send this watch to our friend in America. Tell him the time is coming when I will need him to act."

"Of course, Faisal. Is there anything else?"

"Yes. Do you still have relatives in England?"

"I do, Faisal. Two cousins in Birmingham. They have many friends."

"Birmingham," he pondered. "Yes, Birmingham is far enough yet also close enough. Are they capable?"

"One fought in Mogadishu."

"That does not tell me he is capable."

"For enough money they will do whatever you want."

"Good. There is a man in Scotland I wish them to kill. I will pay them and their friends well."

"They will do it. What is the man's name?"

"Connor Stark."

DAY 1

U.S. Embassy, Sana'a, Yemen 1030 (GMT)

The air-conditioning wasn't working—again. It was the fourth time in two weeks, but with the summer solstice weeks behind them she could at least look forward to shorter days ahead. Caroline Jaha Sumner kicked off her shoes and ran her fingers through her short black hair. They came away wet with perspiration. The light blue shirt and white cotton skirt that set off her dark skin were wilted and damp, but at least she could shed her summer-weight jacket, relieved that she had no meetings scheduled with the locals today.

"Madam Ambassador?" said Lt. Col. Raphael Tyler, drawing her attention away from her discomfort and back to the two men seated in her office. The Marine managed to look stiff and starched even when sitting. "We don't seem to be making any progress in our efforts to stop the violence. If anything, it's worse than it was before you arrived two months ago. Two bombings near the embassy and seven attacks by pirates on the oil rigs. If we can't stop this, the Yemenis are going to run out of oil in four or five years. And then what will happen to this country?"

Sumner rose and walked over to the bulletproof window, wishing she could open it for a breath of air. The view wasn't much, but she could see one of the nearby marketplaces. The booths were shuttered at this hour while the shopkeepers were home for lunch, but the street was still crowded with men in long white robes and shrouded women. The bustling street seemed strangely silent viewed from the confines of the fortified, soundproof office.

Not for the first time C. J. wondered if she had done the right thing in coming here. She had a unique relationship with the administration—with the president—and could have selected other assignments, a subcabinet position at the State Department or a preferred ambassadorship like France. Instead she had chosen a difficult assignment in one of the least stable parts of the world. She brushed away more perspiration and walked back toward her desk, gently sliding her fingers along its polished maple surface. It reminded her of the varnished maple on the back of her mother's revered cello. She curled her bare toes into the hand-woven silk Persian rug and then sat on the front of the desk rather than returning to her chair behind it.

She had faced challenges in the Foreign Service, on Capitol Hill, and in the White House, and had overcome all of them. This assignment was not going to be her first failure. Sumner gently twisted the thin gold necklace she had purchased at the *suk* in Bahrain during the layover on her way to Yemen. The elderly merchant had claimed that she looked like his youngest daughter, like a *habesha* of Ethiopia or Eritrea. Her large, wide-set brown eyes were fringed with long lashes that seemed even more prominent in contrast to her thin eyebrows, small nose, and wide forehead. Her slim build was due to genetics, but the strict exercise regimen she had maintained since she was a high school field and track athlete would have mitigated any weight she picked up—she had surprised more than one man with the amount of food a slender five-foot-tall woman could consume at a good restaurant. She had smiled gratefully at the merchant who knew how to work a customer and paid half his asking price.

"Raphael," she said to the defense attaché. The subtle flattening of the Marine's lips was the only sign of his displeasure with the informality she had insisted on using since she assumed her post. "I think we need to look at the whole picture again."

"Colonel, may I?" asked Bill Maddox.

"Go ahead," Sumner cut in before the Marine officer could respond. Bill was an old friend, and she trusted him to be both objective and supportive.

"Madam Ambassador, we're in for some real challenges in the next few months."

"'We,' Bill? Or your company?"

"'We' as in all of us. You. My company. Our government. Even our military."

She swung her dark, well-toned legs against the desk, her toes brushing across the rug.

Maddox continued. "Maddox International has been hired only to build the oil rigs, and even that has been tougher than expected because of all the attacks on our supply ships. If the Yemenis don't think we can finish the job, they may award the rights to extract the oil to someone else—someone who may not act in the best interest of the United States."

"Bill, when you started arming yourselves a couple of years ago, you should have thought about the consequences—about the way the Yemenis would view it."

"It was my legal right to develop a maritime security firm that would look out for my company's people, platforms, and materials."

"And defense contractors did so well in Iraq with the local populations during the war," she sighed. "I saw the report, Bill. Your security force's attack on the dhows last year is one of the reasons the Yemenis won't talk to me now."

"My ships defend our people and our investments because the U.S. Navy isn't here to do it. The captain of my ship did exactly what he should have done, and as he had done several times before. The pirates approached our oil platforms and started firing at our people. We chased them off, and when the pirates decided to fight, our ship responded in self-defense."

"Perhaps I could interject something here," said the Marine colonel, his eyes coming to rest on C. J. after following the verbal exchange like an observer at a tennis match. "Mr. Maddox is right, ma'am. Central Command has determined that private interests are now on their own to defend themselves for the immediate future. We don't have the soldiers available to do it. And with our recent naval cat-and-mouse games with Iran and North Korea, we don't have the ships or aircraft to patrol this area either. Since the administration decided to reassign all the assets of Combined Task Force 151—the unit that used to combat piracy here—the companies that do business here are SOL. Our primary mission now, ma'am, is to diplomatically engage with the Yemenis to secure continued rights to the oil fields south of Socotra before someone else does."

"I know that," she said patiently. "But part of that is convincing them that we can do the job whatever happens. What if something goes wrong? Or already has gone wrong. What if yesterday's earthquake had affected the offshore wells Maddox International has already dug, Bill? I know we need the oil. But even if we get the rights to pump it, we still have to secure the platforms."

"That's why we need the Yemenis to work with us to secure those waters," Maddox said.

"Reaching out to the Yemeni government hasn't worked, gentlemen. They still won't meet with me. I need a way in." She paused for a moment to think and seemed to come to a conclusion. "Raphael, would you please excuse us? I think Bill and I need to discuss a few things."

The Marine rose and left the office without saying a word.

"He's right about one thing, Bill."

"Only one thing, Madam Ambassador?"

"No one else is in here, Bill. Please drop the 'madam ambassador.' 'C. J.' is fine. It's not like we haven't worked together before."

"That was more than a decade ago, C. J. And it didn't exactly go well, remember?"

She let his comment slide by. "Bill, the fact is, Washington won't do much to help us. Yemen is just one more place that never gets covered by the nightly news. We're on our own, but we can do some good here. It's why I came."

"Maybe, we can do our job better when we *don't* make the news," he said.

She swung her dangling legs against the front of the desk. "So far, we're not doing the job at all. I've tried everything, used every trick I learned on the Hill. And I've gotten nowhere. The one advantage we used to have here isn't currently at my disposal." She stared at him, half-hoping he wouldn't answer.

"Connor Stark will not return here, C. J."

"Maybe not willingly," she fired back with a determined look that Bill Maddox recognized all too well. "I need the agreement, and that means talking to the right people. I read my predecessor's reports. I don't know what the secret to Connor's success here was, but I know he negotiated all the agreements you had with the Yemenis. Can't you ask him to come back?"

"It's not that I can't. It's that I won't," Bill replied turning his back on the ambassador. "He and I agreed that he would set up the maritime security forces for my company and then he was out of here. Once our first oil platform was completed, he was done. And that was before you came on the scene, C. J. There's no way he'd come back if he knew you were here."

"Maybe. Maybe not. We need him, Bill."

"C. J., leave it alone and find another way."

She paused, contemplating the few remaining options open to her. "Too bad," she finally said. "My mission—this mission—takes priority. Thanks, Bill, we're done here. You know your way out of the building," she said dismissively as she reached for the phone.

When the person on the other end picked up, she didn't even bother with a greeting.

"I need a favor."

Northeastern U.S. Air Space, 1130 (GMT)

After speaking briefly with the harried-looking flight attendant, the swarthy, black-haired man took a seat next to a woman in her fifties who could barely wedge herself into the passenger jet's narrow seat. He hated coach class. With packing his few belongings, cleaning out his apartment, and filling out inane administrative forms, he hadn't slept in nearly two days. He sank into the seat and closed his eyes, but couldn't block out the piercing brightness of the sun rising over the Capitol dome. He waved his finger at his seatmate in a motion that suggested she slide the window curtain down. She ignored him.

Ten minutes into the flight, he was still trying to settle in and get comfortable, but in his rush to be seated he had neglected to remove his jacket. It was an annoying blunder for someone so fastidious in his dress. He hated wrinkles. Fidgeting, he pinched the bridge of his aquiline nose, moving his head from side to side in continued disbelief at his bad fortune.

"Ouagadougou," he sighed, more loudly than he had intended. "Ouagadougou."

In his peripheral vision he saw his seatmate's thick neck snap her oversized head toward him and realized that she had heard the words meant only for himself. The concern in her face made it evident that she wasn't curious. No, she was afraid. He had seen it all too often before. His mere appearance was enough to strike fear into Westerners. Before the divorce, his first wife had taken to sneering at his dark skin and well-groomed goatee. That he was of Persian and not Arab heritage didn't matter to his seatmate—or to his wife, for that matter. He suspected the gray-haired woman next to him would have just as easily confused a turbaned Indian Sikh for a Saudi Islamic fundamentalist. Damien Golzari sighed and stood to remove his jacket, forgetting for one crucial moment the shoulder holster he was wearing beneath it.

At the sight of his holstered gun, the woman screamed and began trying to get away from him, an impossible endeavor as she was in the window seat and had nowhere to go. "He has a gun! He was saying something in Arabic!" she shrieked. "Someone stop him!"

His jacket was halfway off and his arms were still in the sleeves when he was tackled from behind by one man and then another. *Damn it, not again*, he thought. The right side of his face met the carpet of the airplane's aisle, grating a layer of skin off his right temple. The first assailant jerked Golzari's forearm behind his back as the second tackled his torso. The first man quickly handcuffed him and confiscated Golzari's nickel-plated gun, in the process tearing the armpit of his British-tailored suit. Golzari made no effort to resist. He had been through this before, as both recipient and contributor.

The speed and expertise with which Golzari's assailants took him down indicated law enforcement training, confirmed when the second assailant gruffly said, "TSA." Golzari sighed and accepted his fate at the hands of the Transportation Security Administration air marshals, hoping the unpleasantness would end soon.

His nose was firmly planted in the cheap, foul-smelling carpet, unable to escape the reeking filth left by thousands of shoes. But that carpet now constituted his entire field of vision. He could only mumble, "Ooo-waa-doo-waa. Ooo-waa-doo-waa!"

The younger of the two air marshals grabbed a handful of Golzari's thick jet-black hair, lifting his jaw off the carpet so they could understand him. "What are you saying?"

"Ouagadougou. It's a city in Africa. In Burkina Faso to be exact. Bloody hellhole. Probably the poorest country in the world. Nothing in it. Nothing near it. I'm condemned to go there on my next assignment. And it's not an Arabic word," he added, punctuating his dry sarcasm with a polite nod toward his seatmate. She sniffed and patted her hair back into place.

"I'm Special Agent Damien Golzari, U.S. Diplomatic Security. I have my badge. You can take it from my pocket if you like, or you can uncuff me and we can have a more civilized exchange." The older air marshal took out the badge and checked the credentials, then released Golzari and advised the flight crew standing around them that there was no emergency.

"Apparently the other flight attendant didn't give you and the crew notice that I am aboard." Golzari looked down the aisle past the still-frightened passengers at the flight attendant with whom he had spoken when he got on the plane.

"Sir, I am so sorry," she said quickly. "We were running late, and I just . . ." she raised her palms helplessly. She was in her thirties and wore a wedding band.

Probably has a couple of kids at home, Golzari thought, *and is just trying to do her job.* Air travel had become an increasingly crowded and rude environment. "It's not a problem, madam," he said politely. "It happens to me all the time. But perhaps you'd be kind enough to find me another seat? I don't think I'm welcome here anymore."

Relieved by his understanding, the flight attendant motioned him forward to First Class.

Golzari looked back at his now former seatmate, widened his eyes, and quietly whispered: "Boo."

DAY 2

Ullapool, Scotland, 1820 (GMT)

Connor Stark wiped the cold rain from his face and leaned over the wheel of his Boston Whaler—a 345 Conquest—straining to see if there was any traffic astern of the large Caledonian MacBrayne ferry off his port bow. One of the ferry's crew recognized Stark and gave him a friendly wave. Stark waved in return, then cut the engine's revolutions to slow his boat until he had a better sense of what lay ahead in the harbor. After a year of working these waters, shuttling back and forth between Ullapool and the training facility, he knew every local craft and most of their owners. He knew their schedules and how they operated their boats. It was the occasional visitor unfamiliar with the local traffic scheme that he had to watch out for.

The rain slowed as he approached the boat slips. To the northeast he could see An Teallach, the mountain's Torridonian sandstone dimmed to brownish gray in the late-afternoon light. A break in the clouds covering the mountaintop exposed the sun, still a couple of hours from setting, and rays of light streamed onto the white stone buildings along the quay. To the west were tall pines, vestiges of the once-extensive Caledonian forest. To the east, the machair plains, filled with yellow rattle and orchids, glowed in the evening sun which momentarily broke through the clouds. The harbor itself was a small inlet on Loch Broom. At dusk on calmer days the whole loch reflected the surrounding hills. Even on rainy days like this, Stark knew of few places as idyllic.

Ullapool, a simple town of fifteen hundred residents, was off the beaten track except for a few tourists passing through on their way somewhere else and the passengers and supplies going out to the Hebrides Islands and Stornoway. The town's few shops didn't exactly flourish, but they managed to get by on steady business; none were open late except the pubs.

Stark pulled into his slip near the fishing boats, tied up, and exchanged pleasantries with the other owners, who were talking about the only news of the day—the arrival of a Ministry of Defence helicopter from the small base at Kyle of Lochalsh. The rain finally stopped as he made his way to the Friar John Cor pub to greet Maggie and enjoy his usual drink.

Stark followed a fellow townsman through the front door. Some of the regulars playing darts or watching the Glasgow Warriors on the overhead television paused long enough to nod his way while he removed his pea coat and placed it on an empty stool. He heard the sound of the fryer sputtering hot oil as the kitchen door swung open.

"Alright, Connor?" said a sweet voice with a Scottish lilt.

He smiled. "Same, Maggie," he said to the red-haired bartender and owner of the pub.

"Sure you don't want a pint of something else, instead?" she said as she slid the dram of single malt across the bar. Before letting go, she hesitated, raised one eyebrow, and looked past Connor. "You have visitors," she said softly.

Stark sipped his scotch and looked at the mirror behind the bar, immediately spotting the two uniformed men seated at a table near the wall. Both rose from their seats and approached. One was a U.S. Navy lieutenant commander in khakis and a black Eisenhower jacket. The other . . . the other took longer to figure out, as Stark hadn't seen the uniform before. Possibly enlisted. Instead of crackerjacks or working blues, he wore a khaki shirt and black pants reminiscent of the early-twentieth-century Black Shirts or Brown Shirts of Mussolini or Hitler. Apparently, the Navy bureaucracy had yet again managed to modify naval uniforms without looking at the history books. He stroked his heavy beard, then took the time to retie his long ponytail.

"Are you Commander John Connor Stark?"

Connor winked at Maggie, picked up his whiskey, and turned to face the two visitors.

"I'm Lieutenant Commander Billings from RAF Mildenhall," said the officer in the black jacket before Stark could reply. Billings handed him a photograph, a full-length portrait of a young lieutenant commander in khakis. The man in the photo had close-cropped, rust-colored hair and a smooth, youthful face. Stark's hair had long since turned darker and was now flecked with gray, and his face was weather-beaten from years at sea. The officer in the picture stood rigidly for a promotion-board photo—a promotion that never came. But that officer was long gone.

"It's Connor, not 'commander.' And I was a lieutenant commander, like you. But that was a hell of a long—" He wasn't allowed to finish.

"I'm sorry, sir, but it *is* 'commander.' We're here to take you back with us," Billings said quietly.

"Back? Back where?"

"Sir, you've been recalled to active duty effective immediately with the rank of full commander. Can we discuss this elsewhere?"

Stark was baffled by this unexpected turn of events. A promotion would have required a Navy board and confirmation by the U.S. Senate, neither of which had happened so far as he was aware. He laughed. "You're kidding me, right? Maggie, another one, would you?" Stark set his now-empty glass firmly on the bar. "We have nothing to discuss, gentlemen."

Stark's rising voice stilled the noise of the bar's other patrons. The two dart players interrupted their game. The only voice that remained was the television announcer's play-by-play of the rugby match.

"Connor, you should want the boys to get rid of these gentlemen?" Maggie asked softly, though loudly enough for the visitors to hear.

"No, Maggie. I'll handle this," he said without facing her. Then he looked around the bar. "I'll pick up anyone's tab who wants to call it a night," he said to the locals, nearly all of whom had become his friends since he arrived in Ullapool and discovered this pub.

One by one, the patrons rose and left. A couple put a reassuring hand on Stark's shoulder as they passed. A few tourists unsure of what was happening quickly downed their drinks and decided to go to another pub.

"Sir, you need to come with us," Billings said when only the four of them remained.

"Thanks, but I think I'll stay here, Lieutenant Commander Billings. Have you seen this town? Pretty, isn't it? Good drinks and good people too," he said as he looked around the bar. "It's quiet, and it's my home now."

"I'm sorry, sir, but that's not an option. You will come with us."

"Look, I've done my duty—although some of the Navy JAG folks might disagree with that—and my departure from the Navy wasn't exactly on the best of terms. Someone in BUPERS must have royally screwed up their database to cut orders for me. I suggest you go back and tell them that."

"There's been no mistake, sir. I can't tell you who or why, because I just don't know, sir. All I know is that I've never seen orders issued this fast. They were requested, issued, and delivered within the past six hours. The direction came from the secretary of defense himself."

Stark frowned in surprise. Had a new secretary decided to rescind the decision of his court-martial and return him to account for his previous actions? "What if I don't return with you?"

"We begin extradition proceedings and you will face incarceration upon returning to the United States."

Stark paused, rethinking Maggie's suggestion and regretting his decision to clear out the pub. "Lieutenant Commander Billings," Stark said, downing his second scotch, "I'm not leaving here unless there's one hell of a good reason."

"Commander Stark, I was told that you are needed for an assignment for which you are uniquely qualified."

Stark laughed. "The hell I am. Give me those orders." He took them and squinted in the pub's fading light, struggling to read the small type. "Yemen?" He turned to face the bar. "Maggie, I may need another."

With a wry look, she set the bottle of Talisker by his glass. For now, at least, he was on his own.

The lieutenant commander looked at his companion and then back at Stark. "We don't have much time," he said to Stark, "but we'll be here until first light. We'll expect to see you at the helicopter then."

Stark nodded. "I'll be there with an answer. That's all I can promise. If it's not what you want to hear, get the handcuffs ready."

"Do I have your word that you won't try to leave this town until then, sir?"

"When Connor Stark gives his word, he keeps it," Maggie said sharply. "Either take a seat and eat something or leave. We don't make money here just talking."

Outside the bar, darkness was setting in early with the rain. The lights from the few streetlights reflected eerily off the misty fog that had settled over the harbor and the town.

"You're not taking those two men seriously, are you, Connor?" Maggie asked long after the two Navy men had eaten and departed for their hotel.

"They have official orders. I could go to prison if I don't."

"But you left that life. It almost killed you. Why go back?" Maggie said plaintively as she turned the key to the final lock on the pub door. The Friar

John Cor was always the last pub to close in Ullapool. She turned to face him, her red hair already beginning to sparkle with droplets of the mist.

"I did my job there. I don't want to go back. But . . ."

"No 'but,' Connor," she interrupted. "I'm not letting you go." She walked a few paces and then turned when he didn't follow. "Are you coming?"

"I need to get something from the boat. It shouldn't take long. Wait here for a few minutes, OK?"

"I'll meet you at home," she answered.

"I'd feel better if you at least carried mace."

"In Ullapool?" she laughed in disbelief.

"You're right. I should be more worried about the other guy." He'd seen her drop drunken sailors at the pub who were twice her size—usually foreign sailors because all the Ullapool men knew better than to mess with Maggie.

"Go on and get what you need from the boat. We'll talk later." Maggie turned and walked away in her determined Maggie walk. Her boots hit the ground hard with every confident stride, her bottom swayed in tight jeans, and her long red ponytail swung from side to side. She turned back only once to give him a quick smile. She always seemed to know when he had lingered to look at her. The sound of her self-assured footsteps faded around the corner; they were the only sounds in the still of early-morning Ullapool.

He pivoted and headed toward the piers.

His boat was near the end of the wooden B Dock. Stark paused to peer out over the darkness that was Loch Broom before carefully climbing on board. Nearly twenty years had passed since a terrorist attack in Italy had given him his first brush with death, but he still hesitated to put his full weight on his bad knee.

He unlocked the fore cabin and stepped down, electing not to turn on the light because he already knew where to find what he wanted. He pushed aside a stack of books and removed the thick envelope from the small storage compartment; he passed his hand over the sealed envelope and then placed it in his jacket.

The unmistakable pattern of a car's headlights dimly appeared in the starboard window, passing from fore to aft. Stark frowned. It was still too early for the fisherman to arrive on the pier and ready their boats. From the direction of the concrete pier, he heard three car doors open; none shut as an engine idled. Deciding it was no concern of his, Stark left the fore cabin and was about to lock it when three men stepped from the pier twenty yards away onto the wooden dock. The idling car's headlights were still on behind them, and he could see only their silhouettes—tall and thin. Another few yards closer and he could tell that they were not Caucasian or Asian. And all held something at their sides—arm-length rods that appeared to be of metal. His heart beat faster as they continued to approach. Only two could walk abreast on the four-foot-wide dock. The third man was behind them.

"Can I help you?" he asked, testing them as well as to buy time. They were fifteen yards away now, and he could distinguish their features. They appeared to be East African. They did not answer him and continued to advance. They had almost reached the boat now, and he had nowhere to run.

Stark grabbed an orange life vest and passed his left arm through its straps, holding it like a shield. He took a long knife from the tackle box with his right hand. The first two men raised their rods like clubs. Standing near the wheel, Stark used his left elbow to press the button for the boat's horn. A loud squeal broke the silence of the night, temporarily distracting his attackers. He leapt up on the boat's starboard built-in external locker and steadied himself. The boat's freeboard was a foot above the dock at high tide; he would have the height advantage that Sun-tzu had advised twenty-five hundred years before.

The first two charged him. One clumsily swung what was now clearly a tire iron. Stark blocked it with the thick life vest and brought the knife up into the East African's chest. The man gasped and slipped backward off the dock, which was still wet from the earlier rain, as Stark extracted the knife and pivoted to face his next attacker. The man was clearly caught off guard by his partner's failure and the splash his body made as it fell into the water.

Stark took advantage of the moment of hesitation with a riposte. Though he wished for one of his old épées or sabers, the fishing knife still found its mark as its tip pierced the East African's eye. When the man dropped his bat and brought both hands up to his face, Stark thrust the knife into his unprotected abdomen. As he buried the knife he heard a snap and saw the glint of metal; instinctively, he held out his shield arm and waited. The life vest could deflect the strike from a tire iron but could only slow the penetration of a knife. The cold metal cut into his left forearm. He tossed the vest aside, and with it more than a few drops of his own blood, and shoved the man with all his strength.

Blinded in one eye and overcome by pain from it and his abdomen, the second attacker lost his footing and fell backward off the dock. Stark heard the unmistakable crack as the man's head hit the transom of the boat in the next slip.

Only one of the three attackers remained, but Stark was injured now. The third man pushed Stark back into the cockpit and climbed on board for his own height advantage in this combat. His furrowed brow suggested a more cautious approach than his fellows had used and concentration on his next move. This man was not an amateur.

Behind him Stark saw a fourth shadowy figure approaching from the pier. The idling car engine and the screams of the second Somali had muffled the footsteps. He knew he had to dispatch the man in front of him before he could possibly handle the fourth.

The third East African drew back his knife and waited. Stark had experienced the pause of combat before, each side waiting for the other to make a move, hoping for a mistake on which to capitalize. His fencing training took over. Stark planted his left foot on the deck, shifting his shoe to create a dryer spot from which to launch his attack.

The East African bent his knees as if to project himself onto Stark and then grunted in surprise when an oar came from behind and hit him square across his legs. His feet slipped on the wet locker and Stark pounced, throwing him hard to the deck. He grabbed the slack of the stern line and wrapped it tightly around the man's neck. The East African struggled and vainly swung his knife, trying to connect with Stark. Stark pulled the line tighter and tighter until the man's arm fell by his side and the knife dropped harmlessly onto the deck. With the remainder of his strength Stark tightened the line one last time. The man's entire body went limp.

"I could have taken him," he said to the figure still on the dock.

"You can't do everything alone," Maggie said.

DAY 3

USS *Bennington* (CG-74), North Arabian Sea, 0342 (GMT)

"Attention in the pilothouse, this is Ensign Fisk. I have the conn. Belay all reports."

Fisk's eyes continued to adjust to the darkness around him and the ambient light from the consoles. Barely a quarter of the four hundred souls on board were awake and attending to their duties. It was oh-dark-thirty, and Bobby Fisk had joined the officer of the deck, a lieutenant junior grade who had been three years ahead of him at the Academy.

"You might want to hold off on belaying your reports, Bobby. It doesn't hurt to reinforce what's going on." The OOD took a sip of coffee and grimaced as he handed another cup to Bobby.

"Thanks." Fisk shuddered at the first sip. "Seaman Grace still trying to figure out the coffeemaker?"

"Yeah, but at least it'll keep us awake." The OOD pointed him in the direction of the port bridge wing and secured the hatch behind them. Both men zipped up their jackets to keep out the cool night breeze. Bobby pulled his ship's ball cap lower on his head to secure it from a sudden gust. The blue cap was embroidered in gold with the *Ticonderoga*-class cruiser's name and hull number, crest, and motto: Vigilant and Victorious.

"Captain gave you double duty, too?" said the OOD. "Not exactly the way you thought you'd join your first ship, is it?"

Bobby shook his head, his round, earnest face solemn. "Six weeks ago I was walking across the stage and shaking hands with the vice president at the Naval Academy stadium and getting my commission. And I'm already in trouble."

"You can't blame yourself for what happened," the OOD said. "Heck, none of us were at fault."

The *Bennington* had been under way from Bahrain for less than twenty minutes when the commotion started. First came the standard intervals of the navigator's recommended course headings and adjustments, essential information even in a familiar channel. Bobby, as the conning officer, repeated the figures to the helmsman, who repeated them back to Bobby to ensure there was no misunderstanding.

The scratchy, high-pitched voice of the five-and-a-half-foot-tall captain had broken in, ordering a course change. The navigator disagreed and stated the proper course. The ensuing countercommands and recommendations reached a confusing intensity. At another command from the captain, the ship jolted with an increase in speed and the port lookout simultaneously sang out a warning. Bobby felt a sudden gut-wrenching slam and heard a noise pitched a thousand decibels higher than the captain's voice, the unmistakable sound of steel meeting steel scraping along the port side of the hull. Bobby dashed out to see what the ship had hit.

Directly beneath him was one of the channel's buoys, passing fore to aft and leaving most of its paint on the *Bennington*.

"NAV, you're relieved. OPS take over for NAV," screeched the captain. "Red mittens! Red mittens for everyone!"

Bobby knew what that meant for NAV, a woman he'd spoken to only briefly in the wardroom. She had tried repeatedly to warn the captain about his ordered course changes; he wouldn't listen. Now her career was effectively over. And it was entirely possible that the rest of the bridge officers wouldn't be far behind her.

All Bobby saw of NAV—or rather ex-NAV—after that was her back as she boarded the helo back to Bahrain with her bags.

The breeze picked up as the OOD lightly tapped his coffee mug against Bobby's cup: "Cheers." After another sip and grimace he continued. "It'll get better, Bobby. This ship's not that different than the old YPs we used to drive on summer bloc, except she has ten times the crew, is three times as long and fast, and has weapons. Just remember what the chiefs of the YPs at the Academy used to say—drive it like you stole it, and park it like you bought it."

Even in the dim light, Fisk could see the wink and grin that accompanied that last comment. He smiled weakly back and felt a little less alone.

After his watch, Bobby stopped by the wardroom to get some water. On his way out he paused at the cabinet devoted to the ship's namesake. Behind the glass was a map detailing a Revolutionary War battle and a portrait of the New Hampshire general who had led his troops to victory there—a stone-faced man holding a musket in one hand; his other arm was raised, commanding his men to follow. Ensign Fisk wondered if leaders like Brig. Gen. John Stark, hero of the Battle of Bennington, still existed.

Antioch, Maine, 1330 (GMT)

"Going to the coroner's office, are we?" asked the police officer emerging from one of the back rooms. He carried a cup of coffee in his left hand and with his right placed a pen in the left pocket of his neatly pressed, short-sleeved uniform shirt. The nametag pinned above the pocket read Hertz. "I'm Tom," he said, reaching out to shake the visitor's hand.

"Damien Golzari," Golzari responded. "Diplomatic Security Service," he added as he held out his identification. Hertz nodded with less surprise than the fat lady on the plane had shown. Hertz led the way outside, where the two men got into the squad car and left the lot.

Little escaped Golzari's sharp eyes, but even a casual observer would have noticed immediately that the few people walking the street on this windy day were dressed in the traditional full-length thobes of the Middle East. Judging by their clothing and features, he guessed they were Somalis. Odd, he thought, for a small town in Maine. "How long have you been with the department?" he asked Hertz.

"Nine years, ever since I graduated from the police academy. I grew up here."

"I used to be a beat cop—in Boston. I miss it. This place looks like it's half a world away from there instead of a couple hundred miles," Golzari said, his eyes scanning the pedestrians and their unusual garb.

Hertz laughed, surprised that this well-dressed government agent with a refined British accent had walked the streets of Boston as a cop. "Two blocks away is 'Little Mogadishu.' I'll give you a little tour." He turned into a blighted-looking neighborhood near the river. "A few years ago, the local politicians brought in a few thousand Somali refugees. It was a nice thought, but there were no jobs. The mills closed down years ago. Life is hard for them, maybe harder because a lot of them haven't tried to fit in. The cops have even been told to overlook certain things here and in a couple of other housing communities."

"What kind of things?"

"Medical issues, for example, like girls being brought into the local emergency room because of botched clitoridectomies. My girlfriend is a nurse at the hospital, and she comes home with some real horror stories. Bankers talk on the QT about seven- and eight-thousand-dollar payments being wired overseas. Lots of other odd stuff. You ready to see the coroner, Damien?"

Golzari's mind had wandered, thinking about the people of this neighborhood and the vast difference between their immigration experience and his own, remembering what people had thought of him as an Iranian immigrant. Hertz's question snapped him back to the present.

"Yeah, I've seen enough here."

As the squad car turned toward Antioch's small downtown, a Mercedes-Benz SUV pulled out behind it. The Somali driving the Benz followed the car at a decorous distance. He relished the thought of killing again. He had already killed three people in America, not nearly as many as he had been responsible for in Somalia and barely enough to keep his skills intact. He took his eyes off the road to admire his image in the rearview mirror, then put a bottle of spray cologne close to his neck and squirted himself several times, breathing in the scented mist.

Ullapool, Scotland, 1350 (GMT)

"Who were they?" Stark asked the detective, giving Maggie's hand another reassuring squeeze. Maggie didn't relax her grip. They had spent most of the night in the pub in a booth overlooking the harbor. Two police cars with their flashing blue lights remained at the pier.

"Still don't know who two of them were," the detective replied. "Not exactly the kind that carries identification, are they. The only name we have is the man who rented the vehicle. His current residence is in Birmingham, but he was born in Somalia."

"Somali?"

"You did quite a job on them, Connor. Three men attack you, three men dead."

"Would you have preferred a different outcome?"

"Alive so they could answer questions would have been nice," the detective grunted. "We need more information. This doesn't seem like a crime of opportunity. We tracked the car to the other towns between here and Birmingham, and there were no significant crimes when they were there."

"Maybe they wanted my boat," Stark said dismissively.

The officer stared at him for a moment. It didn't take a Scotland Yard detective to figure this out. "There were other boats that didn't have anyone on board and were easier targets. Did you owe them money?"

"I told you, I never saw them before."

"Have you ever dealt with Somalis?"

Stark paused. "I've dealt with a lot of people."

"Care to elaborate?" the officer asked.

"No," he said as two men in khaki uniforms entered the pub and strode up to the booth.

"Thought you two were supposed to leave at first light. What happened to Navy punctuality?" Stark said to them.

"We're still waiting for an answer, sir," said Lieutenant Commander Billings.

"It seems everyone is," Stark replied, looking first at the detective and then at Maggie. "Gentlemen, could all of you wait outside for a few minutes?" he asked.

When the last man left, he turned to Maggie, trying without success to mask the resignation clearly evident in his eyes. "We never did have that talk at the house," he said.

She released his hand and touched his face softly, struggling to make eye contact. "Had you already decided?"

"I wasn't sure. I was going to talk with you first."

"And these men you killed changed that?"

"Yes. They changed everything."

Antioch, Maine, 1407 (GMT)

The coroner pulled back the sheet that covered the body. Golzari had seen dead bodies before. Lots of them. Young, old, male, female, intact, dismembered. Too many to let the body of this young man affect him. He reviewed the police report and saw the reporting officer's name—Hertz. He glanced up at the officer who had brought him from the police station before turning back to the report. "John Malesherbes Dunner the Fourth. Age twenty," Golzari said without looking up from Hertz's report. "Sophomore at Antioch College. Hair brown. Eyes brown. Hometown Potomac, Maryland. Clothed body found on the northern bank of the Passamaquoddy River one hundred yards from the falls at 6:45 p.m. by a jogger crossing the bridge into Antioch. No known witnesses. Roommate identified the body."

Golzari set the report aside and looked up. "I know his father." He looked at Hertz. "Have you questioned the roommate yet?"

"No. When I was told you were on your way here, I thought I'd wait."

"Thanks. Dunner's father is on a flight from Mexico and should be here in a couple of hours."

"Can I start the autopsy now?" asked the coroner. Golzari nodded, accepting the silent offer of some Vick's VapoRub for his nose to help mask the stench.

The body was discolored, mottled in a dark green pattern that reminded the DSS agent of Irish Connemara marble. "Did anyone check the temperature of the water?" Golzari asked.

"The normal sixty-six," Hertz responded.

"If he was found yesterday at around 6:45, he would have died about a day ago, give or take a few hours. His blood was reacting to the hydrogen sulfide. Is that right?" Golzari asked the coroner.

The hefty, triple-chinned coroner merely nodded as he waddled to the other side of the table and began to cut. The autopsy showed nothing out of the ordinary until the coroner pried the boy's mouth open with his hands and pulled back his cheeks to get a fuller view. "Hmm," he mumbled.

"Something?" Hertz asked.

"The teeth. Overall they seem very healthy. Basically what you'd find in someone his age and background, though he could have brushed more. Except—strange—they have a slightly green tinge. Almost like he smoked or chewed tobacco, but a different color. Unless this got caught in his mouth while he was in the water, it looks like he chewed whatever it was right before he died." The coroner produced a small, wet leaf that had been lodged between the young man's molars.

"Maybe. Hertz, are these his clothes?" Golzari pointed to a tray to the side.

"Yup. T-shirt, shorts, and sandals. He probably took a walk on that old pedestrian bridge the night before. Options are: one, he lost his footing, in which case it was an accident and this is closed; two, he knowingly jumped, in which case this is also closed; or three, he was pushed, and this becomes a homicide."

Golzari took a breath mint tin from the pocket of the shorts and unscrewed the lid to expose its still-dry contents. "Fancy that." Surely the coroner couldn't be so naïve as to believe that this was chewing tobacco. "Doctor, don't be surprised if his blood sample shows signs of an amphetamine."

"You mean like meth?" Hertz asked, peering into the open can and then staring suspiciously at the DSS agent.

"No, like khat, or cathinone to be precise," he said, turning his back on the body and heading toward the door. "Let's go talk with the roommate."

The dormitory room smelled like unwashed socks, skunky beer, mildew, and leftover pizza. Johnny Dunner's roommate was dressed much as Johnny had been—T-shirt, khaki shorts, and leather sandals. Unlike the clean-shaven Dunner, the roommate sported a sparse goatee on his chin, a mere shadow of Golzari's own meticulously groomed growth.

"Want a seat, guys?" the roommate asked motioning to Johnny Dunner's bed, which was covered with dirty laundry.

"Thanks, I'll pass," Golzari said looking at the pile in disgust.

"I thought all I had to do was identify Johnny."

"Agent Golzari has just a few questions for you," Hertz responded. The roommate sat back on his bed and looked up at the two law enforcement officers.

"Okay. Ask away. Mind if I chew?" He pinched a small wad of leaf from a tin and picked up a cup from his desk to spit in.

"When was the last time you saw Johnny," Golzari began as he watched the young man's jaws move rhythmically.

"Couple of days ago," the boy said matter-of-factly.

"More specifically?"

The roommate's eyes rolled upward as he tried to recall. "About ten o'clock that night."

"Here?"

The roommate, still drowsy after this unusually early wake-up call, was slow in trying to remember. "Yeah, but he left."

"Do you know where he went?"

"No," the boy said, spitting leaf juice into the cup. Golzari had seen it before, of course, but he remained repulsed by the disgusting act.

"Are you nervous?" Golzari asked.

"No," the roommate said slowly.

"Why was Johnny on the bridge at the falls?"

"I don't know."

"Did he regularly go there at night?"

"I don't know."

"How often do you brush your teeth?"

"Huh? What?"

"Simple question. In case you haven't noticed, there's a hint of green on your teeth. Unless you're going for the Saint Paddy's Day look—a few months too late—I'd say it's from something else. Where'd you get the khat?"

The kid nearly swallowed the wad in his mouth. "I-I don't . . ." he stammered.

"That's not Red Man you're chewing there, Sparky. Where'd you get the khat?" Golzari asked again, his friendly smile changing to a menacing glare.

"Do I have to say?" the boy asked Hertz.

"Yes," the officer answered, "you do."

"I don't know if I should. I mean I . . ."

"Look, kid," Golzari said, cutting him off, "I happen to know a few things about khat. It comes from East Africa. Ever been there? No? Well, I have. A lot of people there chew it every day, so the streets look like Zombie-town. Everyone stoned out of their minds—and I don't mean the New England liberal arts college funny kind of stoned out of your mind. Since 1993, khat has been categorized as a Schedule IV controlled substance in the United States. That means you can be fined $250,000 and spend three years in prison just for having some in your possession. And if Johnny had khat just before he died and fell into the river, then we need to know who provided it to him. Was it you or not?"

The roommate spat into the cup again, refusing to raise his eyes from the floor. "No," he finally said. "Johnny gave it to me."

"Where did he get it?"

"From one of the Somalis downtown. But I don't know anything about who. Johnny never told me."

"How long have you been using?"

"Since about a year ago. The end of our first semester."

"Johnny didn't waste any time," Golzari muttered. "So much for staying clean. Was he doing anything out of the ordinary two days ago?"

"He was gone for most of it."

"Where?"

"Every couple of months he went away for half a day. He'd come back with enough khat for us."

"For just the two of you?"

"For a lot of people, but Johnny only kept enough for himself and his friends. The rest went downtown."

"And you don't know who got it?"

"That's what I said."

"Anything different about this trip?" Golari asked as he looked around the room.

"Sort of," the boy replied. "He was pretty quiet when he got back here that night. He gave me a couple of bags, then he was on his computer for a while."

"What was he doing?"

"Searches, I think. At one point he said, 'Holy shit.' He started acting funny and pacing around."

Hertz sat at the desk and turned on Dunner's computer.

"Hey! Are you supposed to do that?" the roommate asked, starting to rise.

"Hey! Are you supposed to do khat?" Golzari retorted, slapping the kid's face for good effect. The kid shut up and sat back down.

"Did he say anything else?" asked Golzari.

"Just that he wanted to call his dad but didn't know if he should."

"Where's the khat?"

The roommate stood and brushed aside Dunner's pile of clothes on the bed, uncovering three packets of khat and an envelope with something written in Arabic script.

"Abdi Mohammed Asha," Golzari read aloud. He opened the envelope, revealing a gold watch inscribed in Cyrillic.

"That's the name," Hertz said without turning around.

"Huh?"

"The last search on Google. 'Abdi Mohammed Asha.' Could be a Somali name."

"What else did he search that night?"

"'Katya P.' and 'Ivan Korchenko.'"

"Any hits?"

"Yup. *Katya P.* is the name of a supertanker apparently taken by pirates about a month ago, although no ransom was asked. Korchenko was her captain."

Golzari looked at the watch again. Though he couldn't read Cyrillic, two capital Ks stood out, corresponding to the ship's and the captain's names.

"One more thing, Damien. Looks like Dunner also got directions to Boston Harbor that day."

"Anyplace specific?"

"A pier."

"We're done here, Hertz." Golzari turned back from the door to add, "Don't go far, kid. Don't talk with anyone about our discussion. And sure as shit don't do any more khat." He seized the bags and strode out of the dorm room.

The freshly mown grass on the quad outside the dormitory was far more aromatic than half-chewed khat or the body of Johnny Dunner. Golzari took a deep breath to clear the smell of dirty laundry from his nostrils. The hum of a large riding mower faded as its pattern took it away from the two law enforcement officers.

"What the hell was that about, Damien? Did this just become option three?"

"The facts are definitely starting to point toward homicide. Drugs and pirates. Something tells me I'm not wrapping up this investigation today. Have a lot of problems with khat here?"

"First I've heard about it," Hertz replied.

When they reached the far side of the quad and the edge of the campus, Golzari put one hand on the hood of the police car to balance himself as he brushed grass clippings off his meticulously polished shoes.

"Do you recognize the name from the envelope?" he asked Hertz.

"Nope. But we have somebody who might. The police department has a liaison to the Somali community." Hertz made a call.

Ten minutes later the gray Mercedes-Benz SUV pulled up next to the squad car. A tall, lanky Somali emerged, smiling at the men as he casually strolled toward them. Golzari looked from the Mercedes to the approaching Somali.

"Hallo, hallo, Officer Hertz!" The Somali shook the officer's hand. "So good to see you. How can I help you today?"

"Just a name, Khalid. Do you know Abdi Mohammed Asha?"

Khalid paused as if in thought and then shook his head without losing his smile. "No. Unless he is one of the new arrivals?"

"I don't know," Hertz said. "I was hoping you could tell me. It *is* a Somali name, isn't it?"

Golzari, standing downwind from the Somali, nearly gasped as he got a strong whiff of the Somali's pungent cologne. He wished he'd used more of the Vick's.

"I will talk to our people and find out for certain, Officer," the man said enthusiastically.

"Thanks."

The Somali left quickly, and Golzari and Hertz got into the squad car to drive to a local diner for breakfast.

RAF Mildenhall, U.K., 1540 (GMT)

"How do the Brits feel about your using one of their helicopters, Lieutenant Commander Billings?" Stark asked as they landed at the rain-soaked airfield. Those were his first words since leaving the pub.

"Reciprocity, sir."

When the flight crew waved an okay, the two Navy officers and Stark disembarked, keeping their heads low as the helicopter blades continued to spin; Stark instinctively grabbed his shoulder-length hair and held it tightly lest it be caught up by the blades.

A waiting vehicle took the three men to a Quonset hut that had not been refurbished since the Cold War. The bleak furnishings suited Stark's mood. What didn't suit him were the uniforms that awaited him on a table set off to the side. All bore his rank and name. Some poor tailor must have worked late to have all this available so soon.

An old metal table with two chairs had been placed in the middle of the otherwise barren room. A slender, blond man in his early thirties was seated in one. He wore a well-cut blue suit and modestly patterned tie.

"I'm Robert Witherfield, sir. Please have a seat."

"You're British," Stark noted as he pulled the chair out and faced the man.

"This is the United Kingdom, you know. I'm with MI5."

"That's internal security. I'm leaving the U.K."

"Correct. I'm here to ask you about last evening's incident."

Witherfield had no paperwork before him. No report. No pen or paper. Just two cold blue eyes focused on Stark.

"I told the local officer everything I know."

"You'll forgive me if I don't believe you."

"You'll forgive me if I don't care."

Witherfield glanced at Billings, who simply shrugged.

"Refusing to help won't get us far, now will it, Commander?"

"Refusing to help would probably get me in an American jail. I'd say that's far."

"You're being difficult."

"You're being nosy."

Witherfield leaned back in his chair. "We aren't getting anywhere."

"Then how about a quid pro quo?" Stark offered.

"What do you want?"

"Tell me why you're interested."

"Very well. We traced one of the men. Years ago he was part of a militant unit in Mogadishu."

"Pity you didn't know that before he entered your country."

"Your turn, Commander Stark," Witherfield said, leaning back and crossing his legs.

"Before I moved to Scotland, I was involved in maritime security. Part of my job was protecting an American firm's assets in the Gulf of Aden. On occasion we exchanged gunfire with Somali pirates. I didn't recognize the Somalis who attacked me last night, but there were a lot of pirates and I didn't always get to see their faces. That's all I know."

"Why would pirates attack you now in Scotland?"

"I don't know. I'll be sure to get in touch if I find out," Stark answered sarcastically. "If there's nothing else . . . ?"

Witherfield looked on impassively as Stark rose and approached the table with the uniforms.

Stark remembered occasions when he'd worn most of them—the standard desert camouflage uniform for Central Command, blue ship's coveralls, dress whites, summer whites. He paused momentarily at the summer whites, recollecting a beautiful day in Naples during his first deployment. He and two other junior officers were sitting at a café laughing and enjoying their first taste of the famed Neapolitan cuisine. Four sailors from the ship were seated two tables over. It was the first port call, a chance to relax away from the ship's rules. The sound of a speeding car broke through the conversations. The car's windows were down. One man pointed a machine gun at the café and peppered the area as someone else lobbed something toward them. There was no escape for those inside the restaurant; most instinctively hit the deck. Stark and another officer dove at the next table, where an older couple sat too stunned to move. The Navy officers knocked them out of their chairs to the ground and covered them in a futile last attempt to protect innocents.

Stark heard nothing when he regained consciousness. People were waving their arms and moving their mouths as they ran about, but silence reigned inside his head. He looked down at his summer whites. One leg was now crimson with his own blood, part of the pant leg ripped away by the blast. Debris covered his shirt—plaster and food and the gray brain matter of one of his friends. *That was nearly twenty years ago*, he thought as he wrenched himself back to the present.

Each of the uniforms before him now bore his Surface Warfare Officer pin and the three rows of ribbons he had earned during his service. The uniforms might fit him physically—that remained to be seen—but the military mentality and pride that went with them were long gone. The uniform of honor he'd worn for so many years had become, with his court-martial a decade after Naples, a cloak of shame. On the final occasion when he removed his uniform he had felt like an animal skinned alive. That skin was gone and could never grow back. But these were not his original uniforms. They were just clothes, and putting them on would be no different from putting on jeans and a sweatshirt.

Billings interrupted him as he reached out for the desert camos.

"One more thing before you put those on, sir."

"No," he said, anticipating what was coming.

"I'm sorry, sir, but you know the regulations," Billings said, gesturing toward the door.

A few minutes later Stark was in a chair in the base barbershop. He looked one by one into the mirrors that surrounded him as the barber took up his clippers and raised an eyebrow. "What do you want off first, the beard or the hair?" When the hairy man seated in his chair didn't answer, the barber shrugged his shoulders and started with the ponytail.

Fifteen minutes later, Connor Stark was looking at his face for the first time in years.

Pirate Mother Ship *Suleiman*, Western Indian Ocean, 1549 (GMT)

"You have not heard from your cousin in England?" Faisal asked Saddiq.

Saddiq said nothing.

Faisal paced around the pilothouse of the *Suleiman*, the mother ship to six skiffs and the flagship of his personal fleet. The *Suleiman* was on a slow, steady course paralleling the *Katya P.* A month had passed since the glorious day of the supertanker's capture. Most of the pirates had expected him to take the prize to the coast of Somalia where all the other ships had been taken. But this one, he had said, had a special purpose and had to be kept away from the prying eyes of foreigners. He walked to the chart table and looked down at the red marks that displayed the positions of his other mother ships. Then he picked up his binoculars and focused on the bow of the tanker. The explosives had been loaded and secured.

"You haven't answered me," Faisal said, still looking at the product of part of his plan.

"We spoke last week. He had an address for the man Connor Stark and was taking his friends to Scotland to kill him as you ordered," Saddiq responded.

"We should have heard by now."

"They were three against one man. They could not have failed."

"You do not know this man."

"How do you know this Connor Stark, Faisal?"

"He is the only American the Yemeni government trusts."

Antioch, Maine, 1612 (GMT)

Golzari met with John M. Dunner III in his suite at the Green Hills Inn, Antioch's best—and only—major hotel. The bags under Dunner's eyes suggested that the elder statesman hadn't slept since learning of his son's death. How could any father? Even so, his shirt and suit were crisp and fresh; his tie maintained a tight knot.

"Mr. Secretary, I'm very sorry for your loss," Golzari offered as Dunner motioned for him to sit across from him.

"Thank you, Damien. It's good of you to be here. I haven't seen you since you were on my detail."

Golzari smiled briefly as he recalled the day he had been assigned to Dunner. It wasn't the first time he had met him. In fact, Dunner was one of Golzari's first impressions of America. Damien was just a few years old when Dunner spirited his father and most of the family out of Iran. As one of the former shah's generals, the elder Golzari would have been a great prize for the Islamists, who had put a large price on his head.

"Yes, sir. It was an honor to serve. If I may, I have just a few questions, sir."

"Of course."

"Sir, we believe your son died the evening before last. When was the last time you spoke with him?"

Dunner's left hand began to tremble. "Last week, unfortunately. I was on a Latin American tour. But he did leave a message for me two nights ago."

"What did it say?"

"Just that he needed to speak with me as soon as possible. I got the message and meant to call him the next morning. I didn't. I thought I was too busy to call my only son. I should have called." Dunner's head sagged briefly toward his chest, then rose.

"Do you have any idea what he wanted to tell you?"

"No. I'm sorry."

"What can you tell me about him? I haven't seen him for several years. What was he like?"

Dunner leaned back and closed his eyes. "Smart. Precocious. You know that he traveled with me when he . . ." Dunner paused as tears welled up in his eyes. " . . . when he was younger, when I was ambassador to Moscow and, of course, in Riyadh, as I'm sure you remember." He took out a handkerchief, wiped the tears away, and regained his composure.

"Did he know Russian and Arabic?"

"Only rudimentary Arabic. A few words, perhaps; but enough of the alphabet to read road signs. He was better at Russian. He could have done so well, but there were . . . problems."

"Can you be more specific, sir?"

"All the moving around. My constant traveling. I wasn't around enough. It happens. When we came back to the States a few years ago, he got involved in drugs. He went to a rehabilitation center for a while, but he was doing so much better at school here."

Golzari hesitated, then forged ahead. "Sir, I hate to say this, but there is some evidence that he may have been under the influence of khat when he died a couple of nights ago."

"Khat? Here in the States?" Dunner was visibly unsettled at the idea that yet another drug was threatening the United States. That it had taken the life of his son seemed not yet to have sunk in.

"Yes, sir. I don't have hard evidence, but I suspect that Johnny's death was not accidental. I have a lead, but I am currently scheduled to leave next week for a new assignment in Burkina Faso."

"Then you'll pass on the investigation to someone else?"

Golzari raised his hands. "I'd prefer not to. My family is indebted to you. We would never have escaped from Iran without your help. I will find a way to continue this investigation to ensure it's done properly."

Dunner leaned forward in his chair and looked directly into Golzari's eyes: "Get to the bottom of this, Agent Golzari. I want to know how my son died, and why. I don't want another family to experience what I have gone through in the past two days. I've trusted you with my life before. Now I'm trusting you with the lives of people we don't even know. I will give you my support from Washington. Here's my number," he scribbled on the small pad of paper provided by the hotel.

"Yes, sir," Golzari answered, looking down at the number as he replied.

As Dunner leaned back, the moment of personal strength and resolve faded. Golzari knew the next question was the one the elder statesman had wanted to ask when he first arrived.

"Can I take my son home, now?"

"The coroner's office has been directed to release your son. Someone from State is standing by to help you."

Leaving his first benefactor to mourn alone for his son until the boy's mother arrived from Washington, Golzari joined Hertz outside at the squad car.

"It's never easy to talk with the family after something like this, is it, Damien?"

Golzari shook his head. "Never. I thought I was done with it when I left the police force." Then he switched the subject. "Did you make the call to Customs?"

"The only ship at the pier Johnny went to that day was a freighter—the *Mukalla Hassan* out of Mukalla, Yemen, with one stop in Southampton, England. She left Boston yesterday for Nigeria. Does that help? Where are you going next?"

"England," Golzari said decisively, "the ship's last port of call. I'm going to London to talk to a friend who might be able to help."

"Can I do anything on this end?"

"No, I'll take it from here, Tom. You've been a big help. Here's my card. Let me know if you hear anything from your liaison about this Abdi Mohammed Asha."

"You'll be the first to know, Damien."

Golzari took the first flight he could find, which happened to be a military flight on its way to RAF Lakenheath, a short way from London.

The domestic dispute call in Little Mogadishu was routine. Hertz was sure it would amount to nothing. They never did. Sure enough, by the time he reached the fourth-floor walkup in the riverside tenement the couple had resolved their argument. As he began walking back down the stairs, he saw Khalid on the second-floor landing below him.

"Any word about that name I gave you, Khalid?" Hertz tucked his pen and notepad into the front pocket of his shirt as he descended toward the tall Somali.

"I may be able to help you and your friend from the college. He was police, too?"

"Federal agent," Hertz replied importantly.

"Ah, I don't think I caught his name, my friend." The wet smacks from Khalid's steady chewing echoed in the stairwell.

"No problem. I can reach him if you have some information." Interference screeched on his radio.

"Is he still here?" asked the Somali.

"No, he left for London." Hertz reached for his radio and adjusted the squelch.

"Ah, well, no matter. I can start with you, Officer." The Somali swiftly pulled out a switchblade and jammed it into the surprised policeman's stomach. Hertz froze just long enough for Khalid to pull out the knife and reach up to slash his throat with it. As Hertz brought his hands instinctively to his bloody neck, Khalid stabbed him again in the abdomen and then pushed his body effortlessly down the stairs.

DAY 4

RAF Lakenheath, U.K., 0845 (GMT)

While waiting for the delayed embassy car that would drive him the seventy miles from Lakenheath to London, Damien Golzari examined the three well-thumbed paperbacks he had just pulled out of his bag, trying to decide whether he would read Plato's *Timaeus*, Euripides' *Daughters of Troy*, or a text on Iranian archaeological sites. He was well prepared for the inevitable delays world travel involved. He had become used to them during his decade as a Diplomatic Security Service agent. DS hadn't been a bad life so far; well, except for the two marriages it had destroyed, though he seriously doubted they would have survived regardless of his profession. He was already an experienced traveler when he came into the Service, having lived abroad during much of his youth.

The job gave him access to some of the best locations in the world—as well as, unfortunately, some of the worst. In working for the government Golzari felt that he was working for stability, something lacking in his childhood in Iran. That appreciation for stability was one of the things that had attracted him to law enforcement. He had started as many of those in his field had done, working for a local police department—in his case, Boston. But the job had proved too confining, too parochial for his thirst to see and know the world. The Diplomatic Security Service gave him a much broader purview. He had protected diplomats and investigated crimes from Paris to Riyadh. London was very familiar ground.

This trip was hardly going to be a holiday, but Golzari was happy to be back in England. Although his father had settled the family in the United States after fleeing the 1979 Iranian Revolution—with the help of then-Ambassador

Dunner—he had insisted on a proper British education for his son. Golzari had always been grateful to the old man for that.

His Blackberry vibrated just as he decided on *The Daughters of Troy*. The message from the Antioch Police Department was terse: Officer Hertz had been attacked and killed by an unknown assailant while making a routine call in the Somali refugee community.

"Son of a bitch," he said aloud. He should have stayed in Antioch and tried to find this Abdi Mohammed Asha. He might have to return. Since he was already here, though, he'd check with his source.

39,000 feet above the Atlantic Ocean, 0850 (GMT)

The Somali emerged from the washroom refreshed. Most men would have found the past few hours harrowing—murdering a police officer, clearing out his living space, and making quick arrangements to flee the country. Abdi Mohammed Asha did not. He had been bullying, intimidating, maiming, killing, and evading the civilized rule of law since he became a soldier at the age of eight. He made his way toward the center of the Brazilian-made Embraer Lineage 1000 business jet and smiled as he sank his lanky frame into one of the comfortable leather seats.

"Why are you smiling?" asked the Chinese businessman seated across from him.

"Because I am no longer freezing in America and living among pigs," he said with his eyes closed, enjoying the scent of the freshly applied Euphoria cologne—his new signature scent. One of his most recent victims in the United States had been holding a full bottle of it when he died.

"You were fortunate that I could extract you."

The Somali shrugged. "I would have escaped. I have several passports. And they still do not know who I am."

"Perhaps." The Chinese man leaned back into the comfortable seat.

"Only three matter," the Somali continued, "and two of them are dead. I killed the Dunner boy and the policeman. When I kill the federal agent there will be no one left who can tie 'Khalid' to anything."

Hu was unconvinced. "How did they discover your real name?"

"I don't know. When the boy returned from picking up the last khat shipment he asked if I knew who Abdi Mohammed Asha was. I told him the name was unfamiliar to me, just as I told the police. When he said that he planned to ask his father, I had to kill him."

"And the police said nothing else?"

"No. But you were right about the boy," Khalid conceded.

"Of course I was," Hu said. "Look at me."

Asha obeyed.

"We invested heavily in Suldaan Yaxye Abokor. It was only luck that saved you when he was killed by a rival. You were to have been killed as well. We sent you to the United States intending for you to stay there until we were ready to send you back to Somalia."

"I know this, Hu."

"I'm not finished. The boy served his purpose, yes. Family members observe and overhear things, and the information you extracted from him will help to expand my country's intelligence network. But we were not yet ready for you to leave the United States," he repeated.

Asha shrugged, deciding to accept the praise and ignore the rebuke. "Yes, it helped that you knew the boy already had a problem with drugs. It was easy to get him to talk."

"But that he discovered your name is worrisome, Asha."

"I cannot explain it, Hu, but I don't think it is a problem. The police had only a name. The man who belonged to that name is gone. If they had anything else, I would know."

"Then why is the agent going to England?" Hu summoned an attendant and held up his glass to be refilled.

"I don't know, unless . . . the ship? The ship stopped in England before Boston. If the Americans know the ship's name and who owns it, then . . ."

"Then the Americans have nothing. When they learn who the owner is, their investigation will stop. They can't afford to accuse him or his family." He reached up to take the glass of Perrier from the flight attendant.

"Of course."

"Follow this agent. Take care not to be recognized." Hu kicked off his loafers and held out his feet as the attendant replaced them with slippers.

"Of course I will. But we only spoke for a minute. He isn't likely to recognize me."

"I want a full report of his activities in London. We will have one of our operatives there to assist you."

"And after that?"

"After that, Faisal wants you to report to him."

"It is time?"

"Almost. Abokor's killer is dead. Soon you will return to Somalia, as we all agreed."

Asha closed his eyes in satisfaction, secure in the knowledge that his exile was nearly at an end. Soon he would become the greatest Somali warlord of them all.

RAF Lakenheath, 0853 (GMT)

Stark had never been able to relax in airports, but this time was much worse than usual. Still agitated at having been dragged from his adopted village, his boat, his pub, and Maggie, he tried to sit quietly and wait. Two dozen people were interspersed throughout the lounge. Some slept; others texted on various hand-held devices. A couple watched a cable news program on the overhead screen. Half were uniformed, mostly Air Force enlisted. The other half wore civilian clothing but were probably military given their short haircuts and youth.

One person among all the others stood out to Stark. His black hair was short and neatly trimmed, though longer than a military man would wear it, but it was the goatee that clearly distinguished him as a civilian. There were dark bags under his equally dark eyes. He was in his early thirties and about Stark's own height of six feet, but he was far trimmer looking, and his head seemed oversized for his frame. He had hardly moved since arriving at the lounge, but his darting eyes continually surveyed his surroundings. His bearing reminded Stark of a jaguar preparing to pounce at the right opportunity.

The man's well-tailored suit almost hid the bulge at mid-torso beneath his left armpit. The suit, the shirt, the tie, even the cordovan shoes—which shone like the corfams military personnel wore for formal dress or inspection—all indicated that the man had enough money to pay for quality clothing. The only thing missing were cufflinks, but perhaps the man was going for understated elegance; and anyway, jaguars don't wear collars and tags. Stark had also spent enough time in the Middle East to recognize someone likely to be indigenous to the region. The man's face and skin color suggested Arab or Persian, with the latter more likely.

In sum, here was a nonmilitary man at a military airfield with a gun concealed beneath his coat. Stark figured him for an agent. Probably not Secret

Service because the man didn't have an earpiece; nor were there any other agents apparent, and advance men rarely worked alone. Probably a military investigator, then, with one of the Department of Defense outfits. Maybe the Navy's NCIS, or perhaps AFOSI, the Air Force counterpart. But DoD agents weren't known for their expensive clothing, and in any case weren't paid enough to indulge in it. That left open the possibility of a Diplomatic Security Service agent. They were everywhere around the world, and as often as not they worked alone.

This guy looked to Stark like someone who worked better alone. His stiff posture and aloof air, plus the thick books at his side, gave him an aristocratic air, as though he had been born into money or had at least gone to school with the rich and knew how to emulate them.

Golzari met the eyes of one of the military personnel in the airport waiting room, a man seated in the corner with his arms crossed. Their eyes locked for a moment, and that was all the time Golzari required to memorize every detail about the man before turning his gaze elsewhere so as not to call attention to himself.

The man was in his mid-forties, about a decade older than Golzari, with brown hair that was graying at the temples. The skin on the lower half of his face was a shade lighter than the upper half, suggesting that the man had very recently shaved off a beard and moustache. He was dressed in desert cammies. Though he was too far away for Golzari to read the nametag or service branch, the man's O-5 collar devices indicated a lieutenant colonel or commander; the distinctive patch above his service tag was proof that he was a surface warfare officer in the U.S. Navy. But a man wearing desert cammies wasn't bound for a ship. This one was heading to the Middle East.

The uniform appeared new. The material was not faded from repeated launderings, and the boots had no scratches or marks. Though fit looking, he was thick-bodied, the kind of thickness not uncommon in former athletes. All the signs added up to a man who had not been in the military for some time, which likely meant he was a reservist recalled to active duty. Judging by the scowl, he was none too pleased about it.

An airman's voice boomed over the loudspeaker: "All personnel en route to Bahrain, proceed immediately to the boarding area." Golzari's subject picked up a fully packed, new green seabag and winced as he placed his weight on his right knee. Golzari's lips twisted in disdain. He had little love for members of the military who seemed so patently unsatisfied with their assignment, particularly reservists who clearly didn't want to be recalled.

Their eyes met again as the Navy commander passed within arm's reach of Golzari on the way to the boarding area. Under other circumstances, Golzari thought, the man might have been an adversary, someone encountered in a cheap Third World bar, perhaps, where a few drinks and a misspoken word would devolve into an altercation. But Golzari was not one to frequent cheap bars.

Stark sized up the elitist fed as he passed by on his way toward the plane and thought that he might have enjoyed kicking the man's ass if they had ever met in one of the many bars he had frequented over the years. But he couldn't imagine the fussily dressed fed walking into a real bar.

U.S. Embassy, Sana'a, 1237 (GMT)

Stark had spent the past few days trying to figure out why he had been recalled. Certainly his work for Bill Maddox's firm had given him some knowledge of Yemen, but there were plenty of active-duty people qualified to serve as defense attachés, and he was pretty sure none of them had ever been court-martialed. Besides, attachés were among the military's elite, subject to months of training in their assigned country's politics, geography, and language, and of course the diplomatic niceties of the job.

Most of the articles that had caught his eye dealt with the deteriorating situations in Iraq, Iran, Afghanistan, and North Korea. His understanding might be at a basic level, but Stark could see that America's focus on the wars and potential wars in the Middle East was having both domestic and international ramifications. Among other things, it had left the rest of the world open to the influence of other countries. Particularly alarming was an article in *The Economist* describing the economic and military aid packages that China had negotiated throughout Africa and Central and South America. It seemed to him that the United States was on the verge of losing its status as the world's only superpower.

A young assistant regional security officer met Stark at Sana'a International Airport and drove him back to the embassy in an armored SUV. Both men were silent for most of the drive. Chitchat seemed inappropriate in an area where the activity on a calm street corner could quickly escalate into a terrorist incident. The city hadn't changed much in the year or so since he'd last been here. But aside from the cars and the neon-lit storefronts, he doubted that much had changed in a thousand years. Taxis sped by erratically, much as in any major American city. The heat from the mid-afternoon sun had tempered much activity. Most of the men he saw on the sidewalks were busy chewing khat, further reducing any productivity. He remembered fewer people idling in the afternoons, perhaps a sign that unemployment was up yet again. Every time the vehicle stopped at a traffic light, a few men paused in their conversation and eyed it warily. He wondered if they watched him out of curiosity or as a potential foreign target.

After the driver dropped him off at the entrance to the embassy, Stark checked in with a man at the front desk and was handed his credentials.

"Welcome to Yemen, Commander," the young man said. "The ambassador is expecting you." He pointed to the stairway behind him. "One flight up."

Still stiff from the long plane ride, Stark winced his way up the stairs. The friendly voice that greeted him as he approached the top made him stop short and look up.

"It's about time you got here, Connor. The golf course just hasn't been the same without you."

"Bill," Stark said, grinning at the man seated against the wall to the left of the receptionist. He shook Maddox's hand and pulled him into a bear hug. "You should be right at home playing in the desert—it's just one big sand trap."

Maddox snorted. "We'll talk about that later. You have to meet the ambassador alone first, and you have to know before you go in that I had nothing to do with this, okay? I advised her against it."

Stark frowned. "Her? What are you talking ab—"

The door to the ambassador's office flew open and a rich soprano voice rang out. "Mindy, I thought you said he was on his way up." Ambassador Caroline Sumner glanced past the receptionist, then smiled. "Oh. You *are* here. Please come in, Commander," she said cautiously.

After a brief moment of shock, Stark moved without a word toward the inner door, only his compressed lips revealing the extent of his anger. He glanced back at Maddox, who simply grimaced and sat back down. "Good luck," he mouthed.

"You've *got* to be kidding me!" Stark said as the receptionist closed the door behind him. "I'm not sure what I'm more surprised at—that you're an ambassador or that you ripped me away from my happy retirement to come here!" He didn't even try to mask the displeasure in his tone.

Although the room was supposed to be soundproofed, the two people in the reception area could clearly hear his booming voice.

"Commander, I—"

"Commander? No. It's Connor. Just plain Connor. At least it was until *you* sent the Navy after me."

"Don't shout at me. I'm a United States ambassador. Show some damned respect, Connor, if not for me than for the office I hold and for the president I serve. Or you'll find yourself court-martialed again."

"Really?" he said in a voice of velvet steel. "If you or the president want me court-martialed, go right ahead. I've been there before," he said, daring her to say something else.

She sank into her seat and paused. "Please, Connor, sit down."

Stark grudgingly complied, if only to substitute the expensive cushioned chair in front of her desk for the memory of the airplane seats he had occupied for the past thirty hours. "Why the hell am I here?"

C. J. swiveled her chair to face the window, giving him only her elegant profile to look at.

"Your predecessor left this morning. He wasn't getting much traction with what we've been assigned to do here. I haven't been in the job long. I want to get this right, but I keep hitting walls. I need someone I trust who can break through those walls."

Connor threw back his head and laughed. "That's a new one, C. J. When did you start trusting me?" He rose from the chair and walked toward the window, back into her field of view.

"I do trust you. Your word is better than any contract." Assuming the full authority of her office, she sat in silence, waiting for his full attention.

Stark stared out the window, allowing the tension in the room to build. In all the time he had spent in Yemen he had never seen the city from this vantage point. At this time of day the market in the street below was full of vendors and customers bickering about the price of items for sale. "That word didn't save me from a court-martial," he said, finally turning to face her.

"You did what you felt you had to do, and what you had said you would do. I did what I could to help. It wasn't up to me, Connor. There were other issues, much bigger ones than you or me."

"Whatever." Connor shook his head. "Why am I here?" he repeated.

"Pirates. The same ones you dealt with until you left last year. The situation's gotten worse in the Gulf of Aden. At this point, the pirates are hitting any ship they want. We have no military support in the region—practically everything has been redirected to the Persian Gulf or the western Pacific. I'm here to get the Yemeni Navy to agree to secure and stabilize the region, including the oil platforms off Socotra. Bill just doesn't have enough assets to do it on his own."

"So, get your agreement. What's the problem with the Yemenis?"

"They're stalling. They have all these boats we gave them a few years ago, but they won't put to sea. We don't know why. And we don't have anyone they'll work with. Someone with a real working relationship with them . . ."

" . . . which I had when I worked for Bill."

"Yes."

"Which is why I'm here."

"Yes."

"And you think I'll help you after all that's happened?"

She shook her head sadly. "No. I don't, really." For a moment she allowed her fatigue and frustration to show.

Stark leaned forward in his chair and felt his shirt stick to his back; the office temperature was approaching that of the outside. "Then why?" he asked. "Why bring me here?"

"I hoped."

"Hope is overrated."

"Not when it's the only option left to you," she said.

"When it's the only option left, it's called desperation, not hope."

"Okay, I'm desperate. Will you help?"

"I haven't yet heard a reason why I should."

"For Bill?"

"Bill hasn't asked me."

"How about for your country?"

"I think I did enough for my country when I was in uniform."

"You're in uniform now," she reminded him.

"This time it's not by choice." Stark removed an envelope from his pocket, the same envelope he had gone to his boat to retrieve before the three Somalis attacked him in Ullapool, and held it up. "This is my general discharge. You want me to help? Change that to an honorable discharge."

"Ok," she said quietly.

"You don't have that kind of power."

"No? I got you recalled to duty and brought here, didn't I?"

"Good point," he admitted. "Let's assume I can do whatever you need me to do. What then?"

"As soon as I have what I want, you can go back to . . . wherever you want to go."

He thought about it for a moment. Until a few days ago he had finally been leading a life of peace and contentment, secure in the knowledge that he had disconnected from his past. And then three Somalis had tried to kill him. They had come to his adopted home, the home of his friends, Maggie's home. Would that threat continue if he made the wrong decision now?

"I'll do this," he said finally. "And if my record is cleared as a result, I'll accept that. But let me be clear—very clear: I'm not doing this for you or your damned president." Stark caught himself. He hadn't been in uniform twenty-four hours and had already violated Article 88 of the Uniform Code of Military Justice—contempt toward officials, namely his commander-in-chief. Fortunately, C. J. was a diplomat and was probably ignorant of the UCMJ. Stark, however, had firsthand experience with it and had violated it in almost every way possible the last time he was in uniform.

"I understand, Connor. Let me know what you need."

"I don't need anything from you. I'll do this my way." He turned away.

"Connor," she said. Stark paused at the door keeping his back to her.

"Your way will be the right way, right?"

"It'll be done."

"Ready for a drink?" Maddox asked Stark as they walked out of the embassy and into the parking lot.

"It's a dry country," Stark reminded him. "The closest liquor store is about a thousand miles away." Stark sighed but then brightened. "Well, not totally dry. I know of one place that might have something decent."

"I thought you might. You always have, Connor."

"We were younger and thinner then. And you didn't have gray hair."

"You're one to talk. I see a few white flecks in that old rusty stubble of yours," he said, offering Stark a cigarette. Maddox wore a white golf shirt that exposed his hairy arms. His fingertips were yellowed by years of smoking, and his voice was raspier than it had been twenty years ago when they were in college. For the first time Stark noticed the dark bags under his friend's eyes. Clearly his work with the oil rigs had taken a toll.

Stark accepted and motioned to Maddox for a light. It was his first cigarette in fifteen years and only the fifth in his life. He had smoked the first four with Maddox, too. The mere act of lighting one seemed to clear his mind.

"How the hell did I wind up here, Bill?"

"I couldn't stop her. I tried. She's headstrong."

"Some things never change. So my job is to negotiate with the Yemenis and get them to send their boats to sea to patrol in the Gulf of Aden and south of Socotra near your oilfields."

"That about sums it up."

"What's the situation there? How much have you managed to get done?"

"We've finished three of the rigs. We don't know when the last two will be completed. We've had a lot of delays. Most of our equipment and supplies are coming through Mukalla. Since the president shut down CTF 151 and redeployed everything to the Persian Gulf and the Pacific six months ago, we haven't had much protection from the pirates. European and Arab naval presence is sporadic at best, so I've had to rely on the small force you set up."

"Last thing I ever expected to do was start a maritime security company." Stark took a long drag on the cigarette as he looked around the nearly empty compound. There were a lot fewer people around than the last time he was here. The walled portion of the compound was topped off by thousands of yards of concertina wire. Aside from the embassy building itself, most of the filth-encrusted structures inside had only one or two stories. The tennis courts on the far side of the lot were empty, the nets ragged with disuse and exposure to the elements. Even the Sheraton a few blocks away had failed to manage a clean façade. A Toyota minivan and a Land Cruiser were the only vehicles in the parking lot.

"You did good—and the folks you hired know their jobs. The *Kirkwall*'s a good boat. The *Deveron* and the *Arnish* don't have her speed, but each of them carries two RHIBs and a helicopter as you recommended. Your instinct was right. The bird does a great job of extending the patrol range, and the inflatables deter the pirates, but the Ali Babas are a lot bolder these days. And I don't have to tell you what all this security is costing me. At some point—and soon—I'll be spending so much on security that any potential benefits from the oil rigs will be negligible, especially since I don't own them outright. Which is why Washington is so concerned about stability and negotiations with the Yemenis."

"I get it, Bill. If they're so concerned, though, why is the embassy understaffed? I've been here for less than two hours and I've already noticed it. No spooks. No regional security officer—how can an embassy operate without an RSO?—only half the number of Marines you'd expect, and no other military staff at all. What the hell is going on here?" Stark took another long drag on the cigarette, enjoying the feel of the nicotine in his system. Bad for him? No doubt. But depressing times called for unusual measures.

"The Yemenis sent the CIA station chief home two weeks ago after someone outed him. State's RSO was recalled to Washington at the same time. The embassy did get two assistant RSOs a few days ago."

"Yeah. One drove me here. He doesn't look old enough to shave."

"Both of them are straight out of training."

"First assignment for both of them? In a critical-threat post? Where's the adult supervision?"

"Who knows? Plus, the ambassador believes diplomacy is the answer rather than force."

"If she doesn't think military security assets are the answer, why the hell did she bring me here? Oh, right: I'm not really military. I'm someone who knows certain Yemenis."

"Bingo. Your predecessor was a good guy. Smart and well trained. But he ran into a wall with the Yemenis—and with her, too. She thinks spit-and-polish is a waste of time."

The two men strolled past the lot to two waiting black SUVs, both part of Maddox's personal security detail, and leaned cautiously against one, expecting the surface to be hot from the day's direct sun.

"Well, I'm here and I've agreed to do the job. Let's go over your show, Bill. What do I need to know?"

"We have one supply boat departing Mukalla every day carrying food, essentials, and crew swap-outs. We're changing out personnel every ninety days since it's a high-threat environment. Ninety days here and ninety days back home. We also have a larger ship that carries construction supplies. Both ships are always escorted—either by the *Kirkwall*, the *Deveron*, or the *Arnish*, or sometimes more than one. The Yemenis are still shaky about them and won't let them enter the harbor, so they wait off the coast and then escort the supply boats across the Gulf of Aden."

"Has there been any change in who owns the supply boats?"

"No, it's still your friend. But we haven't dealt with him directly very much since you left. He leaves most of the day-to-day stuff to his stevedore in Mukalla."

"Ismael?"

"No, Ismael died in an accident. Hit by a car. It's now a knucklehead named Ahmed al-Ghaydah. He's inexperienced. Doesn't know much about operations. We've had a lot of logistics problems in port. He's also tough to reach, and that's caused delays."

"Got it. I'll ask my friend about him."

Maddox nodded. "Thanks, Connor. The supply boats also deliver equipment from the mainland for free along the route. The Yemenis don't invest much in Socotra, and this is one way they provide supplies. Then we continue on around the east side of the island, then south and west to the oil platforms. Lately all three of our security boats have been in the water with very little downtime. Two provide escort duty while the other patrols to the west of the platforms looking for the pirates. How much have you been keeping up with the news?"

"Not much. I thought ignorance was bliss."

"Yeah, right. My people are putting together a briefing packet for you. Three things have changed since you left for Scotland. The pirates aren't just operating around the Gulf of Aden. They're in the Red Sea, off Oman, off the Seychelles, even along the Indian coast."

Stark whistled in disbelief. "Any sign the Indians are concerned about this?"

"I've met the Indian ambassador because about a third of the people working on the platforms are Indian. They're playing it pretty close to the chest about this one."

"They have to. They've got the Chinese knocking on their back door and their front door at the same time. Do you have the name of their naval attaché?"

"Captain Jayendra Dasgupta. I like him. Very professional. He's a ship driver like you."

"Like I *used* to be. I got a message to my friend before I left for Yemen. We're meeting. After that, I want to go down to Mukalla and join one of the resupplies to get a feel for what's going on around the rigs. That okay with you?"

"Sure. But don't you think C. J. will be a little upset that you just got here and you're going AWOL already?"

"She'll get over it. Better to ask for forgiveness than permission. Are you still flying a helo from the rigs to Socotra?"

Maddox nodded as he tossed the remains of the cigarette to the ground. Stark's own cigarette promptly followed.

"Good," Stark continued. "I'll take the boat over, then fly back to the island and hop a puddle-jumper to the mainland. I'll need company communications just in case."

"My company's assets are yours. I'll make sure your old designation is reactivated."

"There's one more thing."

Maddox closed his eyes and shook his head when Stark told him about the attack by the Somalis in Ullapool. "Shit. Did you tell C. J.?"

"No. I need more information first."

"Why would they target you?"

"Guess I'm just special."

Maddox slapped him on the shoulder as his security detail opened the rear door of the vehicle. "That you are, Connor."

The White House, Washington, D.C., 1315 (GMT)

Chief of Staff Eliot Green reached down and grabbed another Coke—his fourth of the day—from the cooler built into his credenza as Deputy Secretary of State John M. Dunner III entered his office. The tall, gray-haired diplomat had a rare untarnished image in the cesspool that was national politics. Political pundits had predicted that he would be President Becker's choice as secretary of state. Becker, on Eliot Green's recommendation, had instead picked a professor of international relations from Harvard with no managerial experience, much less any knowledge of how the D.C. political game was played. She depended on the White House for all guidance—as they had intended her to do. To placate the pundits, Becker and Green selected Dunner as her number two—and the White House treated him exactly like number two.

"Have a seat, John." Green motioned toward the two upholstered chairs stationed in front of his big walnut desk. "Something to drink? Coffee? A Coke?"

Dunner shook his head, slowly walked around the nearest chair, and lowered himself into it. Green couldn't help noticing the heavy bags under his red-rimmed eyes. The man probably hadn't slept at all since he found out that his only son—his only child—was dead.

"Again, John, I can't tell you how sorry I am for your loss," Green said. "And the president too, of course, as I'm sure he's told you. Johnny was a fine young man with enormous promise. I'm sure he would have become a man worthy to fill your shoes." *If he'd ever managed to get away from the drugs*, Green added silently to himself.

"Thank you, Eliot. Visitation will be tomorrow. Elizabeth and I hope to see you there. I wanted to take care of a few things here while I have some time. I've advised Secretary Forth about next month's conference with the Russians, but I'm most concerned about Yemen. I've been in close contact with Ambassador Sumner, and—"

Green dropped the Mr. Nice Guy imitation and reverted to his usual abrasive personality. "You've been in close contact with a lot of people, John, some of whom were not exactly your subordinates."

Dunner looked taken aback. "What do you mean?"

"Let's not play this game. You've been talking to the Hill without our permission. You're not playing with the team, my friend."

"I'm doing my job as I see it, Eliot. Yemen is at a critical juncture. We need that agreement with them, but we're not giving C. J. Sumner the tools or the people she needs to get it done. I checked the personnel records. We've been pulling people out one by one over the last three months and not replacing them. This is a 'critical-threat' post, but they don't even have enough security people to protect the embassy if something should happen. We can . . . I mean . . . don't you see?" The fatigued old man, ordinarily the most eloquent of speakers, found himself at a rare loss for words.

"You're clearly under a lot of stress, John, and the president and I are worried about you. He's wondering if you'd like to step down so you can spend more time with Elizabeth."

Dunner sat straighter, summoning the determination that had carried him through the last few days. "No, Eliot. Absolutely not. I will bury my son. Then I will return to do my duty for my country. Elizabeth will expect nothing less from me."

Fine, Green thought. *We'll do this the hard way.* "John, the president doesn't agree, particularly in light of how your son may have died."

"What does that have to do with my job?"

"I have an initial report from the director of Diplomatic Security, whom I asked to investigate this matter. Apparently, your son was doped up on some drug called khat when he died and was in all probability a drug dealer himself.

Step down now, John. You'll be inundated with offers from universities and foundations. Find a nice teaching position. The specifics of your son's death can remain a private family matter. It would serve no one if this sordid affair became a topic of discussion in the media and the blogs. You don't want that. And I'm sure I don't need to remind you that this is an election year."

"You're a real bastard, Eliot," Dunner said slowly, his voice trembling less from weakness than anger.

"You serve at the pleasure of the president, John. It's his pleasure that you step down."

"I'll write a letter of resignation right away. He'll have it by the end of the day."

"No need to trouble yourself. Here's something I drafted for you. All you need to do is sign it. It's one less thing you need to worry about at this difficult time."

St. James Square, London, 1422 (GMT)

"Welcome back to the East India Club, Mr. Golzari." The front desk attendant spoke in a hushed, respectful tone commensurate with the surroundings. "It is always a pleasure to see you."

"Thank you, Steven, it is always a pleasure to be here," Golzari said, smiling as he handed his leather travel bag to the waiting servant.

"Shall I inform the dining room that you will be coming in for luncheon, sir?"

"No, Steven. I'll be dining elsewhere. I'm expecting Mr. Witherfield to join me within the hour. Please send him up when he arrives."

"Very good, sir."

As on every return, Golzari took a moment to savor his surroundings. With the exception of his two brief marriages and the small studio apartment he kept in Washington, Golzari hadn't had a real home since college. This magnificent building in St. James's Square was the closest thing he had to one. It was, he decided, the only civilized place he had ever lived. The understated elegance and quiet rooms full of history comforted his senses in a way that no other place ever could. The club's dress code of a jacket and tie at all times was a welcome departure from the world of denim jeans, t-shirts, and flip-flops in the United States.

Before it had become the East India Club the building had been home to two centuries of British aristocrats. King George IV, while still Prince Regent, had famously received news of Wellington's victory at Waterloo while attending a dinner party here. The club counted among its notable members Admiral Lord Mountbatten and the American jurist Oliver Wendell Holmes. During the war it had witnessed the frantic activity that surrounded Eisenhower's headquarters at Norfolk House diagonally across the square.

Golzari's club membership was effectively the only thing he hadn't lost in either of his divorce proceedings—not that his wives wouldn't have tried to take that too had it been possible. Even now, though, early in the twenty-first century, ladies were not allowed to join. On the other hand, he mused, neither of his ex-wives was a lady. He turned toward the hallway, pausing slightly as he noted, not for the first time, the large wood-and-brass plaque on the wall memorializing all the members who had lost their lives in England's wars. He stopped by the bar to pick up a drink and then made his way to the one-man elevator at the rear of the building.

Once in his room, he checked the windows and closet, the inevitable habit of a perpetually security-conscious DSS agent. He made a local call to his old friend Robert and then sipped at his drink as he checked for new messages on his Blackberry. Glancing through his email, he was disappointed to read that Deputy Secretary Dunner had resigned. There were too few good people in government, he thought, and Dunner's departure was a loss for wisdom and decency in an administration sorely lacking in both. His debt to Dunner remained, however, whether he was in the government or not.

"Posh Robert!" Golzari said, extending a hand to his former partner as he opened the door.

"Damien!" Robert Witherfield replied warmly, returning the handshake while keeping a firm grip on the briefcase in his left hand.

Golzari stepped back to allow Witherfield to enter the room. "It's been awhile, Robert."

"Too long. Welcome back to the world's finest city."

"Yes, indeed. I've always thought that Hubert Robert was really thinking of London when he painted *Gallery of the Louvre as a Ruin*."

"Good lord, Damien, will you never get off that depressing Rococo trash? God knows our art instructor tried to broaden your horizons. In any case, Hubert Robert's work is all in the Louvre. They have all the bloody garbage we didn't have room to store. You need to spend time in British museums again to refresh your education—unless, of course, we pop off to Paris. Do you have time?"

"I wish I could, Robert. I remember our last trip there with particular fondness, although I'm not sure they'd let us back in France yet."

"Too right. Well, how about a drink and dinner then? There's a smashing Indian restaurant on Shaftsbury that I want you to try."

"Why do you never suggest going to a 'smashing' British restaurant?"

"Didn't you know? That's why the British Empire expanded. We were looking for a decent meal."

"Then business before pleasure. Have a seat, Robert," Golzari said, gesturing to the chair closest to the window. Witherfield sat down, opened his briefcase, and pulled out several folders. "Well, Damien, will you have the good tnews first, or the bad news?"

"Let's start with the good, shall we?" Golzari suggested, sipping his Bombay Sapphire and tonic.

"This is completely off the record, of course?"

"As it always is with us—with everything," Golzari returned.

Robert raised an eyebrow and smiled. "Good. Here are the files. I made no copies, so you'll need to look these over while I'm here. And, of course, I was never here." Witherfield winked.

Golzari chuckled. "You've been watching too many James Bond movies, Robert. Or should I say Austin Powers?"

"Are you implying that I have bad teeth?"

"No, just bad clothes."

Witherfield adjusted his impeccably knotted silk tie. "You really know how to hurt an ally."

Golzari started reading while Witherfield continued to talk. "I wish I had had more time to gather material for you on Abdi Mohammed Asha. He's a bit of a problem child."

"Ever cause any problems here, Robert?"

"Not directly, no. But he'd have been right at home with the 'Mad Mullah' back in the day. Of course, back in those days we actually mounted campaigns against people like him, even if it was in British Somaliland—or Somalia, if you will. Coincidentally, Asha belongs to the Mad Mullah's clan—Dhulbahante."

"Wait a minute." Golzari stopped reading and looked up at Witherfield. "That can't be right. The Somali refugees he was living among in the States are all Bantu. A Dhulbahante wouldn't go to the other side of the world to live with Bantus—not in a society as strongly tied to clans as Somalia's still is."

"I'm not sure I have an explanation for that, Damien, but we do know that Asha is not a simple refugee. He was a soldier with strong connections to the power structure in Somalia. The only reason he came to our attention is because we were tracking his boss, a warlord named Suldaan Yaxye Abokor—a particularly nasty fellow. Asha was one of Abokor's lieutenants."

"Nasty how?"

"He took the Islamic law of *hirabah* to heart. Anyone he saw as creating disorder had their opposing hands and feet amputated."

"Of course. And he represented the order. What happened to him?"

"Ironically, another warlord found Abokor's activities to be disorderly. Abokor and some of his people were massacred about a year ago. Asha happened to be in Yemen at the time."

Golzari read his way down the third sheet. "And Asha disappeared after that. Has the new warlord lived happily ever after?"

"Not really. He and several of his top people were killed two weeks ago."

"By another warlord? Or al-Shabaab?"

"Neither, actually. They were your chaps."

"Ours?"

"I'm afraid so. The media didn't pay much attention to it because it happened to coincide with a North Korean missile test. The United States issued a press release afterward saying that an al-Qaeda base in Somalia had been destroyed by three U.S. Tomahawk missiles."

"So that's what that was about. And the new warlord wasn't tied to al-Qaeda?"

"Not a chance, my friend. Al-Shabaab isn't the only organization in the area. The fight nowadays is between the old warlords and the Islamists. The terrorists just stay under the radar to train. But it's not like the Somali communities elsewhere have been quiet. In fact, I've been investigating three Somalis from Birmingham who attacked a Yank."

"In Birmingham?"

"No, Scotland, actually. The Yank killed all three of them, though MI5 says he got some help from a Scottish woman."

Golzari raised his eyebrows. "Lovely. Were the Somalis tied to al-Shabaab?"

"No, but one of them had fought in Mogadishu."

"That's damned odd. Why would expatriate Somalis attack an American in Scotland? Can I interview the American?"

"He was snatched up by your Department of Defense."

"Under protection?"

"No, I believe under the guise of employment."

"This gets odder and odder. Are you sure he's not CIA?"

Robert laughed. "Definitely not. He's a rough one and a renegade."

Golzari shrugged and changed the subject. "What can you tell me about the *Mukalla Hassan*?"

"It's there in the material I gave you. To summarize, she's a fifteen-thousand-ton freighter. Never been tied to khat before. According to our customs officials, she delivered a cargo of dates and vegetable oil in Southampton."

"Who owns the ship?"

A knock at the door stopped their conversation. Golzari readied his weapon before looking through the peephole. He signaled okay to Witherfield before opening the door to admit a servant carrying a tray. Golzari took the single item from the tray, thanked the servant, and placed the Bombay and tonic in front of his friend. Robert lifted the glass in appreciation and continued.

"The company is owned by a brother of the Yemeni president."

"Hmm." Golzari sat quietly for a moment. "I had planned to fly back to the States and check for new leads in Antioch, Maine, but I've changed my mind. Asha was in Yemen right before he came to America, and Johnny Dunner's khat was on a boat from Yemen. I don't think there's anything left for me in Maine." He nodded. "Yemen is my next stop."

"You don't plan on speaking with the ship's owner, do you? I hardly think that would be wise."

"We both know there are other ways to get information, Robert. You chaps in MI5 have taught me a few tricks over the years. I really wish I could stay here longer, though."

"Why is that, Damien?"

Golzari grinned. "The food's better even in London than it is in Yemen. Many thanks, Robert."

"My pleasure. We have to help you Yanks once in a while so you don't mess up the world too much."

"We're just cleaning up the imperial mess you left behind, you know."

"I don't recall the headmaster tolerating such rudeness when we were at Cheltenham."

"The headmaster never knew half of what went on within those walls."

"And a good thing that was. Now, how about that Indian restaurant? Your treat, of course."

"Consider it payment for services rendered, courtesy of the petty bureaucrats in Washington."

The taxi's light indicated that the driver was off-duty. The Chinese man behind the wheel had driven this cab for months, but to date the on-duty light had never been on and he had never carried a fare. He took orders only from his superiors, and those orders so far had involved driving around the city conducting surveillance or accommodating the occasional in-cab meeting. Today his orders were to play host to a Somali.

Asha sat in the passenger seat waiting for the American federal agent to exit the exclusive club in St. James's Square.

"How long has he been in there?" he asked the driver.

"Since fourteen thirty-two hours," the Chinese driver replied with stoic efficiency.

The taxi was parked in a spot on the south side of the tree-filled commons of St. James's Square with a direct view of the club. Asha ordered the driver to meet him later and climbed out of the cab, walking around to stretch his legs while continuing to watch the entrance. The American agent finally left the building in the company of a tall, well-dressed blond man. Allah had not given him the opportunity to kill the man in Maine. Here in London he would have another chance. He decided that the blond man would die too. Asha could not take action against both of them at the same time, but he could follow them and wait for an opportunity.

USS *Bennington*, Indian Ocean, 1427 (GMT)

The *Bennington* approached a small ship that looked barely capable of floating, much less moving. Ens. Bobby Fisk, on duty as the conning officer, tracked it on radar, noting that it was responding to the *Bennington*'s movements, veering away as the American warship moved closer.

"Conn, bring us parallel to that dhow and keep two hundred yards to her starboard," the OOD said to Bobby.

"Aye, sir." Bobby checked the course and speed of the dhow, then issued a series of minor course corrections to the helmsman. He ordered increased speed as he felt the top-heavy cruiser's deck shift from the maneuvering. Almost immediately there was a clamoring up the ladder behind the pilothouse door and the helm announced: "Captain on the bridge!"

"What's going on here? OOD, why is the ship shaking?"

"Sir, I ordered a change in course and speed to parallel that ship," Bobby answered, pointing to the small boat and offering binoculars to the CO.

The captain shoved the binoculars away. "I don't need those. Why?"

"They've been intentionally avoiding us, sir. This is a good target for the VBSS team. They haven't had many chances to board and search."

"I don't think so," the captain replied peevishly. "Those people just want to stay out of our way. Any course corrections other than patrolling in our box, you contact me or the XO, you understand? If you can't manage to do that we'll take you off the watch rotation and give you some responsibilities elsewhere."

Bobby took a deep breath as the captain left the bridge. The OOD ordered a course change away from the foreign ship. As Bobby gave the command he looked through his own binoculars to see several men on the dhow making rude gestures at the departing warship. They were cheering. Bobby and the OOD were not.

Bobby was in a bad spot on this ship, and he knew it. Challenging one's commanding officer was mutiny, but he'd been in the *Bennington* long enough to know that the command structure on the ship wasn't working the way his instructors at the Naval Academy had said it would. He didn't know whether the captain was sick, burnt-out, crazy, or just incompetent, but the *Bennington* was not a functional ship. There had to be another way.

The operations officer (OPS), Bobby, and the weapons officer (WEPS) were smoking cigars after dinner when Air Boss—the pilot in command of "the Lost Boys," the ship's helicopter detachment—joined them. OPS had a year's seniority over Air Boss, so the cigar cabal deferred to him.

"You heard what happened on the bridge this afternoon, OPS?" Bobby asked. He wasn't sure whether the sweat trickling down his back was due to the stifling heat or nerves; probably some of both. The extra pounds he had put on since boarding the *Bennington* didn't help.

"I heard," OPS answered. "This is the first deployment I've ever been on when we've actively avoided the ships we're supposed to inspect." He shook his head in disgust.

"He won't listen to us," WEPS complained. "We cruise around and around inside our box. You know damn well some of those dhows are pirates, but we just let them go by. There has to be something we can do about this. What about Fifth Fleet? He has to listen to them."

"I'll email a buddy there and see if they can issue a directive to provide reports on inspections," OPS said. "Maybe that'll work."

"What if it doesn't, sir?" asked Fisk.

OPS looked around the circle. "Gentlemen, clearly we've been neglecting young Ensign Fisk's education. Bobby, there's a book in the wardroom that should have been required reading for you at the Severn River Trade School."

"Oh? Which one?"

OPS smiled. "*The Caine Mutiny*."

London, 1959 (GMT)

Asha waited for two hours outside the restaurant. From his spot diagonally across the street he could maintain a direct line of sight on the American agent. Although two tables near the large window had been free, the swarthy American and his dinner companion had taken a table on the far side of the restaurant. Clearly the man had worked in foreign countries before—car bombs detonated on a busy street could shatter windows into a million pieces that could shred the flesh of those nearest the impact. Even though car bombs seemed to be a thing of the past in the United Kingdom, the American was being careful even here. Asha felt a glimmer of professional respect for this American agent; he would enjoy defeating him.

As dusk approached, Asha shifted away from the lamppost he was leaning against and began pacing back and forth on the city block, never letting his gaze wander far from the door of the restaurant. Occasionally he caught site of the American's blond dinner companion. Asha took a free paper from a newsstand and moved his eyes horizontally from left to right, pretending to read it so as not to be conspicuous. Not that the people on this busy street would notice one more black foreigner as they hurried from Piccadilly Circus toward the restaurants here and the residential areas behind him.

Asha tried to determine the relationship between the two men. Was it personal or professional? He was certain that the American agent had come to England because of the death of Johnny Dunner. That meant his priority would be professional. But an agent with a clandestine service would be unlikely to discuss an investigation in an open environment such as a restaurant. The blond man had, of course, been inside the East India Club for some time before he and the American left for the restaurant. If the man was a British official, the two could have easily discussed the investigation inside the club and then gone to dinner. Did that mean they had both personal and professional relationships? Asha smiled. It didn't matter. Both men would die tonight.

Asha came to attention when he noticed a waiter nod to the American and then carry away a leather notebook that almost certainly contained the tab. His heartbeat quickened. He tucked the newspaper under one arm, walked toward a crosswalk, and began to cross the street. His finely honed killing instincts were sharpening his senses—eyes, ears, nose—readying him for what lay ahead. His heart nearly leapt from his chest when the car horn blared out from the right. Accustomed to American traffic patterns, he hadn't even thought to look in that direction before crossing. He calmed his thundering heart and made his way to the storefront next to the restaurant. If they returned to St. James Square and the East India Club, as he expected them to do, then they'd head in the opposite direction and he could simply follow them, lost among the many other pedestrians going that way.

As he anticipated, the two men emerged from the restaurant and immediately turned their backs to Asha, laughing and talking about some school. *Spoiled Westerners with too much money*, Asha thought with contempt. He slipped the switchblade from his pocket and concealed it beneath the newspaper in his left hand, then moved in closer. Now only a few steps away from them, he kept his head down, focusing on the pattern of their stride in case they changed direction and he needed to do the same. Darkness had fallen over London now. He had never failed in killing a person after dark. He tossed his newspaper aside. The evening breeze separated the pages as it fell to the ground.

"After-dinner drink?"

"Absolutely. My flight isn't until the morning. Where do you suggest, Robert?"

"There's a spot just up here that will do nicely."

In front of them was a *paifang*, one of the Chinese archways common in the restaurant districts of most cities with a Chinese population. As Robert pointed to a second-floor jazz club, the breeze at their backs freshened. Recognizing a familiar scent, Golzari's senses came to full alert.

"Do you smell that?" he said softly to Robert.

"Yes, bloody awful," the Briton replied as the scent of Euphoria became more pronounced. "Really, some people have no taste at all."

Golzari whipped around to locate the source of the scent he had last encountered in Antioch. The man right behind him was forced to stop and look up. Golzari recognized him instantly: Khalid, the police liaison. Golzari heard the metal snap of a switchblade. Khalid whipped it upward, but the Diplomatic Security agent's reflexes were too quick. He brought up his left forearm to stop the knife from reaching his torso. The blade cut through the jacket and sliced his arm.

Asha brought his knee up hard into Golzari's groin. Golzari grunted in pain and doubled over, helpless for the moment. Robert lunged for the attacker but was a step too far away to catch him. Asha began to run across the side street but in his haste again forgot the British traffic pattern. A Mini that had just turned the corner lifted him into the air. Asha nimbly rolled over the hood and landed upright on the far side of the street, where he paused for a moment to glare at the American agent.

Golzari held Asha's eyes as he pulled the gun from his shoulder holster. "Come on, Robert. I'm okay," he said, struggling to catch his breath and ignore the pain.

The attacker turned and ran down Shaftsbury, and Golzari and Robert followed. The Somali was already half a block ahead of them, dodging past pedestrians and pushing aside those he couldn't avoid. Golzari and Robert did the same, unable to gain any ground on him.

When the Somali reached the bright lights of Piccadilly Circus a few blocks later, he realized that he had erred. Without the dark of a side street to conceal him, he was clearly visible to his two pursuers. He looked carefully to his right, having finally learned his lesson about the traffic pattern, then darted across the street to the closest Tube station and jumped over the turnstile. When the policeman standing in front of the station tried to stop him, Asha turned around just long enough to stab him. The officer folded his arms across his stomach and fell to his knees.

As Robert and Golzari charged in and made their way over the turnstile a few seconds later, Golzari paused long enough to check the downed officer, shouting, "Law enforcement!" as he displayed his badge. The officer waved him forward toward the escalator and struggled to his feet to follow, reaching for his radio.

Robert raced down the long escalator only twenty feet behind the Somali with Golzari approaching rapidly from behind. The wounded police officer was valiantly trying to keep pace.

Golzari didn't bother ordering Khalid to stop. It would have been a waste of breath that he badly needed. Khalid leapt from the final steps of the escalator, taking in the two Tube entrances while he was still in midair and choosing the entrance to his right. He darted past a group of teenagers as lights flashed along the platform, signaling the imminent arrival of the next train. One of the teenagers screamed when she saw the bloody knife in Asha's hand. The Somali grabbed her and threw her toward Golzari. Robert pressed forward and tried to knock away the switchblade. The Somali planted a fist in Robert's sternum and then pushed him off the platform into the path of the oncoming train. Robert's head hit one of the rails as he fell. He lay helpless across the tracks as the train approached the station.

Golzari finally managed to free himself from the hysterical teenager. He grabbed Khalid with one hand and pointed his gun at Khalid's head with the other. Khalid made no attempt to pull away. He simply smiled and inclined his head toward the tracks below the platform. Golzari only had a split second to act, and he didn't need even that long to make his decision. He released Khalid, jumped onto the tracks, and pulled Robert's body between the rails, pressing his torso down as the oncoming train's horn blared. There simply wasn't enough time to heft him back onto the platform. Sparks flew as the screeching brakes desperately tried to stop the lead car. Golzari flung himself against the far wall, hoping he had done enough to save his friend.

Asha watched as the train moved over the body lying between the tracks, then spun about on one foot and pushed his way through the cluster of horrified teenagers toward the exit, pausing to smile and wave his knife at the wounded police officer, who had finally made his way to the scene. Then he raced out of the station.

The train stopped in front of the stunned teenagers and the doors opened. An automated female voice came over the speakers: "Mind the gap!"

DAY 5

London, 0431 (GMT)

Damien Golzari closed his eyes and sank back into the soft chair beside the hospital bed. He hadn't slept during the surgery and had allowed himself to relax now only because Robert was no longer in critical condition and had regained consciousness long enough for the doctor to tell him how lucky he was to be alive; it was an attempt to temper the news that he had lost part of his right arm.

"Damien?"

The slurred voice brought Golzari out of his drowsy state.

"Right here, Robert."

"Where's the bastard?"

"He got away."

"You saved my life."

"It's my fault that it needed saving. I shouldn't have drawn you into this."

"We have both been in this a long time. We know the risks," he said weakly, though he couldn't hide the pain in his face.

"How do you feel?"

Robert looked down at the bandages covering the spot where his arm had been amputated. "Like Horatio Nelson after the Battle of Santa Cruz."

Golzari smiled at Robert's courage.

Robert fought to stay awake as his eyes began to close. "What now?"

"I'll stay as long as you need me, Robert."

"Bollocks. Go get the bastard."

U.S. Embassy, Sana'a, 1500 (GMT)

If only she had more people working for her, C. J. thought, she'd have been able to keep Connor Stark on a much tighter leash. She hadn't brought him halfway around the world just to have him disappear.

"Going to have dinner with a friend," read his cryptic email. "Back soon." *Going to have dinner with a friend, my ass, she fumed.*

She knew he wasn't with Maddox. And she'd checked with the head of the Marine detachment—Stark had signed out an SUV and left the compound alone. *Damn it, he knows there have been attacks around here. Damn stupid-ass stunt. She pedaled faster.*

The gym in the basement was empty save for her. The stark white room was nothing like the posh facility she belonged to at home, but for the moment it was all hers. She'd decreed that only she had access to it whenever she worked out, much to the consternation of the embassy's Marines, who believed that total access to gyms was not only a necessity but a birthright. Every ten minutes a Marine would look through the window to see if the coast was clear. She could see the annoyance in their faces that she—not just an outsider, but a civilian—had invaded their space.

"If Connor gets killed, it's his own damned fault," she said aloud as she pulled harder on the oscillating handles. She hadn't noticed on the display that she'd already burned eight hundred calories in forty-five minutes.

Still with energy to burn, C. J. slowed her pace, removing her hands from the machine's arms and continuing to power it with only her legs as she picked up the towel draped over the weight machine next to her and wiped the sweat from her dripping face. The television screen mounted on the wall in front of her played one of the twenty-four-hour cable news channels. In forty-five minutes of watching, the only news she'd gotten was from the ticker running along the bottom of the screen; the anchor and the various commentators had spent the entire time focused on the latest antics of a blond pop star she'd never heard of. Nothing about Iraq, Iran, Afghanistan, or North Korea. Nothing about the activities on her beloved Capitol Hill, where she knew every senior staffer and could always predict which senators could be turned on key votes—where she'd worked with Connor Stark all those years ago. "Damn him," she said again, wiping the sweat from her forehead and neck.

For at least the fiftieth time since she had arrived in Yemen she questioned her sanity for choosing this post over the more desirable ones she had been offered. In the end, it came down to her passionate desire to change the world for the better and her conviction that she could. The privileged child of parents famed in the music world, she had spent the last two decades of her professional life looking for opportunities to do that. After graduating from Georgetown, summa cum laude, she had entered the Foreign Service. Junior employees seldom got plum assignments, and hers had been one of the worst. After two years in the Foreign Service—two years of wasting her time on diplomatic make-work and dissimulation—she decided that she could do more good elsewhere and got a job on Capitol Hill. In comparison with her present situation, though, the two years in Haiti had been a piece of cake. But then she hadn't been the ambassador, only a junior employee at an embassy during an era of relative peace. Here she sat on the periphery of a maelstrom with an apparently insoluble problem: How could she convince the Yemenis to help oppose the pirates? What could she do to motivate them? Perhaps most important, how could a woman—a young black woman—earn the respect necessary to do her job in a notoriously male-oriented culture?

In the women's locker room, C. J. slipped off her sneakers, removed her sports bra and shorts, and made her way to the farthest of the three shower stalls. It wasn't the high-tech Mandarin Oriental spa she regularly frequented in D.C., but at least the showers worked today.

She entered the stall and turned the showerhead to "pulsate," letting the hot water massage her back and shoulder muscles. *People are the same everywhere*, she thought. *On Capitol Hill and here in Yemen. Everyone can be motivated by the right cause or the right price. I can do this.*

She just needed to figure out what the Yemenis wanted. She'd tried approaching their foreign minister, but after a single meeting at which she presented her credentials he had been "too busy" to see her again. Some days she thought that nothing had changed since her time as a young staffer on the Hill when U.S. policymakers refused to take her seriously, figuratively patting her on the head dismissively whenever she had an idea (and sometimes literally patting her on the behind, whether she had an idea or not). Although she was the official representative of a superpower, the Yemeni Foreign Ministry still treated her as a second-class citizen. She couldn't twist their arms—especially since she couldn't even extend her arm to them without causing offense. She had tried bartering with them for oil rights. She had gotten the Department of Defense to send the Yemenis new patrol craft but received nothing in return. Bribery hadn't worked. She offered more foreign assistance; they politely refused. That left only one option: constituent influence. And in a country where democracy was as foreign as she was, that seemed unlikely to work. This government wasn't about to empower its people lest a greater insurgent movement than had already emerged in a few cities sweep it from power.

She turned around to rinse off the cheap liquid soap the General Services Office provided to the embassy. As she reached up to adjust the showerhead she remembered another shower in Eastern Europe. She had been on a CODEL—congressional delegation—trip years before, escorting her boss. She and Senator Hamilton Becker of Massachusetts had both had just enough to drink when she quietly joined him in his room and went from adviser to very private girlfriend. He was the inconsistent constant in her life.

She shook her head and opened her eyes. *Focus*, she told herself. *There's no time for memories.* She tilted her head back and enjoyed the feel of the water pounding on her eyelids. She opened her mouth, and let the water pour in, allowing most of it to fall over her lower lip. Constituent influence might work, even in a nondemocratic country. People wanted governments to take action, didn't they? And she could use Connor to do it. But how to handle him? Connor Stark despised being handled; he had hated it even when he was in the Navy. He had to do things his own way. That could work. All she had to do was give him a well-defined job, point him in the general direction, and let him be Connor Stark. He knew the Yemenis and they knew him, and she had to trust that he could arrange the access she needed. She just hoped he wouldn't make the same type of poor decision that had destroyed his Navy career a decade before.

Stark had been correct back in her office: she really had to be desperate to place her expectations for success on someone who had never been able to do things through the proper channels—a man who in the past had taken on a terrorist cell without the authority of the U.S. government behind him and had undiplomatically challenged an allied nation. Would he plunge this country into further turmoil or help secure U.S. national security interests? She wished she knew.

Sana'a, 1510 (GMT)

Stark knew exactly where he was going when he pulled out of the U.S. embassy's compound onto the streets of Sana'a. Little had changed since his last visit. A few more barricades had been added to protect the embassy from car bombs. Otherwise, the city looked much as it always had. The brick buildings with their unique patterned designs still crowded up against the streets. Slender minarets still pierced the skyline. The buildings packed within the ancient walled city were home to nearly two million people, but few of them were out at this time of day. He had traveled less than a quarter mile when the rearview mirror showed that a car had begun to follow him.

He had driven through the city center before and knew it to be the most direct way to the restaurant, but instead he chose to wind his way through various side streets—a counterterrorism measure the embassy advised all personnel to follow. The other car stayed with him.

He parked in front of the red awning that shaded the entrance to the restaurant and checked the odometer before exiting the SUV and handing the car keys to a valet—along with a generous sum of Yemeni riyals to ensure that the vehicle remained dent-free. He walked cautiously into the restaurant, well aware that he would stand out as a foreigner. Most of the men inside wore the traditional long white robe and *mashadda* headdress. Even had he tried to dress like a local, however, no one would mistake him for anything other than a Westerner. He appeared to be the only foreigner in the restaurant.

"Mutahar," he said quietly to the maitre d' who greeted him. The man silently motioned for Stark to follow. Conversations came to a standstill as each head in the restaurant turned to follow the American's progress through the room. Stark seemed not to notice the stares as the maitre d' led him through the heavy smoke and the enticing aromas of lamb, coriander, garlic, and cumin to a large room in the back.

Two men stood in front of the heavy damask curtains that guarded the entrance. Stark had no way of knowing whether they were private or state security. It hardly mattered. They scrutinized him carefully before separating the curtains to let him through.

Five men sat against the cushioned back of a large semicircular booth, all dressed like the other patrons in the restaurant. The man in the center had a thin black moustache and a close-cropped beard. He said something in Arabic to his companions when he saw Stark standing in the entrance, and the other men immediately stood and left the room. Stark's host rose as well and came around one side of the table with his arms outstretched. His potbelly pushed against the front of his loose white robe. He was clearly a man who enjoyed his food.

"As-salaam alaykum, Connor!"

"Alaykum as-salaam, Mutahar!"

The two men kissed on each cheek, then embraced. Mutahar led Stark by the arm back to the table. "Come and sit down, my brother."

"I am honored that you could meet me on such short notice," Stark said as he lowered himself onto a plump cushion.

"And I am honored by the gifts you have sent to me every month since you left my country," Mutahar replied, punctuating each word with his index finger as if accusing Stark. "I have a private collection that no one within a thousand miles can rival." He smiled. "Someday I really must visit Scotland."

"If you enjoy the cold, the damp, and the rain but find comfort in a warm fire and the warmth of open-armed friends, then Scotland and I would welcome you. Your business is good?"

The first course appeared through the curtains as Mutahar shrugged. "It could always be better."

"Of course. May Allah always bless you, your family, and your business."

Mutahar lightly struck his breast to signify his appreciation of the thought. A server poured tea redolent of spices.

"I miss your beard, Connor. You look less . . . Arab!"

"The Navy lacks your fine taste!" Stark settled into the banter, knowing that this would not be a quick meal, not if he were to extract the information he needed. The two men chatted casually for more than an hour—friends catching up with their lives. When Mutahar expressed his surprise that Connor was now on active duty with the U.S. Navy, Connor seized on the subject.

"Your ships are still operating out of Mukalla?"

"Yes, most of them."

"That is good. Our mutual friend Bill Maddox has always relied on your business to support the oil platforms. I hear that you now have more ships."

Mutahar beamed with pride. "I have been fortunate. I have over sixty dhows carrying cargo throughout the Indian Ocean, the Red Sea, and even the Persian Gulf. I also now have twelve large freighters that go to India, China, England, and the United States."

"You are blessed by Allah, praised be his name," said the atheist Stark. "I was saddened to hear of Ismael's death. Hit by a car?"

Mutahar shook his head. "Run down in the street like a dog. Ismael deserved a better ending. He was a good man, a hard and loyal worker, and devoted to his children. He often worked late. He was crossing a street in the dark. The police never found the car that did this. A witness saw a truck but nothing else."

"That's unfortunate for his family."

"Yes, but I am taking care of the family now. They will not want for anything. I owe that to him for his service," Mutahar said.

"He was a good stevedore. When I worked for Maddox there were never problems at the pier. I understand Maddox has some concerns about the new man, Ahmed al-Ghaydah."

Mutahar sipped his tea slowly. "He is still new. Young."

"You are a good businessman, my friend. You must have great trust in him."

Mutahar shrugged. "His family is very powerful in that region. Sometimes business decisions must rest on matters other than efficiency and trust."

"Indeed. His name tells me he is from the Al-Mahrah Governorate to the east. But you also have a powerful family in this beautiful country."

"Connor, al-Ghaydah's family has been powerful since the time before Yemen was reunified, when the Russians controlled that part of the country. When they had the tanks and the . . . 'Scoods'?"

"Ah, Scuds. The missiles. Yes. The family approached you about giving him a job?"

"No, after Ismael died al-Ghaydah approached my son and asked for the job. He mentioned his family, as if we did not know who he was."

"This specific job?"

Mutahar nodded.

"How long ago?"

"Two months."

"I see. This is a difficult time not to have a good man like Ismael in that position, especially with the pirates becoming bolder every day," Stark commented, eating more lamb and tearing more *taboon* to dip into the sauce.

"The pirates have been with us for many centuries," Mutahar noted.

"Yes, but they are busier now than before." Stark drank some tea.

"And we have other challenges as well," Mutahar said.

"I have read about them. We live in interesting times." Stark referred obliquely to the growing unrest among the population. Water was becoming scarce in Yemen. People can survive without many things, but water is not one of them. But this was not the place to discuss politics, particularly volatile issues such as this one. He needed to shift the conversation before he lost Mutahar.

"Your firstborn. He is well?"

"He is." Mutahar's face reflected pain and embarrassment. "You saved his life from the pirates, Connor, my brother. You risked your life and the lives of your crew to save men you did not know. I remember this. My family remembers this. We speak of it sometimes, though not with him. You did that and much more for my family. Always you have acted to earn our trust and friendship."

"Your son and his crew were on the sea. Their ship was in ruins and sinking; some of the crewmen were hurt. I was obligated to help him—as I would help anyone in distress."

"Perhaps obligated, yes, but many people are obligated and yet take no action. You took action—at the risk of your life—for strangers. That spoke well of your character. It is a character that I have learned runs strong and true." Mutahar paused to drink more tea, then continued in a muted tone. "You knew of the hashish that was on his dhow when you saved him?"

"It would have been difficult not to see it or to mistake it for anything else, my friend."

"Yet you said nothing to the authorities or to me."

"I was not in uniform. I was helping someone under attack at sea. I was concerned with lives; the drugs sank with his boat, so they hurt no one. I can only hope he learned from that incident not to transport hashish again. Besides, if I had told the authorities, you would have one less son, and we would not be sitting here now as brothers."

Stark watched Mutahar contemplate that last statement. "Yes, and sometimes our children disappoint us. But what are we to do, *Allah subhanahu wa-ta'ala*?"

Stark decided the time was right. "Mutahar, your eldest brother is the ruler of this nation and your younger brother commands its navy and coast guard. My government would seek your family's help."

"This goes beyond our friendship?"

"No, nothing goes beyond that. But we must come to an understanding."

"If I speak to you as a Navy officer, you will report what we say to your superiors."

"I am a Navy officer," Stark agreed. "But I have not always done exactly as my superiors wished me to do." Mutahar smiled at Stark's defiance. "I am also your brother, Mutahar. As your brother, I give you my word that I will not share what you tell me with anyone unless you wish it, but I must know some things so that I can do the job I have been assigned."

"Then we will talk, but not here. You will come to my house in a few days. Then we can speak freely. You will be welcome for many days. I have new horses for you to ride. My people still talk of your skill with horses."

"You and your people are too kind."

"Before you leave, Connor, there is a package for you." He pointed to a wrapped box on a small table to the right of the door.

"Mutahar, you are gracious indeed, but no gift is necessary. To see my friend again—that is enough of a gift."

The Yemeni businessman threw back his head and laughed. "No, my brother. I merely wish to share one of the many gifts you have sent to me since your departure. Sometimes my country's rules are difficult for you, yes? You would not have been able to bring this into Yemen yourself."

Stark realized what his friend was saying and laughed heartily, the kind of laughter he reserved for his few close friends. He retrieved the box—and the bottle of scotch it contained—and turned to leave the room. For the first time since arriving in Yemen, Stark felt at ease.

Sana'a, 1512 (GMT)

Golzari's rental car from Sana'a International Airport didn't have air conditioning, an inconvenience in the middle of summer. He was sure the rental agents had done it on purpose when they saw his American diplomatic passport, but he chose not to argue. In any event, daytime temperatures in Sana'a were relatively moderate even in the summer because of the city's altitude, and dusk and cooler temperatures were approaching.

As he walked into the parking lot he mentally counted the number of Middle Eastern countries he had visited on an investigation or security detail. *Oman twice; Saudi Arabia seven times; Bahrain—do I include every time I passed through that airport? Qatar once; Pakistan six . . . no, seven times—Edita made that point just before she kicked me out; Djibouti four times; Yemen . . . hmm, Yemen—three times, including this one.* He checked the car for signs of tampering or new wiring before even opening the door. When he turned the key in the ignition he held his breath just in case—though he doubted holding his breath would be particularly helpful if a bomb went off beneath him.

Golzari was still deeply troubled by the attack on Robert. While Robert was still unconscious after the surgery, Golzari had stared at the bandages covering the amputated arm, the same arm that had held an épée in their fencing matches at Cheltenham. But he told himself that a man as tough as Robert could get by with half a right arm. And at least he was alive.

Before leaving London Golzari had contacted the Antioch Police Department with a request for additional information about Khalid. All they knew was that he arrived a year ago and disappeared right after Hertz's murder. He had been a helpful liaison between the community and the police for the past few months. That meant Khalid had arrived in Antioch about the same time that Abdi Mohammed Asha disappeared from the Horn of Africa. Hertz had been killed after asking Khalid about the name Abdi Mohammed Asha. If Khalid was Asha, as Golzari's gut told him he was, then he had positioned himself perfectly to gain access to police investigations and protect himself.

And now the Somali had once again disappeared. MI5 had found no trace of him at the major airports, harbors, or even the Chunnel. He had either gone underground in England, as he might easily do, or covertly left the country, as he apparently had done from the United States.

If Asha had been in Yemen before arriving in America, then Yemen was the place to look for him now. Golzari was on his way to the U.S. embassy in Sana'a to ask for help with that. He had been to Yemen before and was not unhappy to be back. It was better than Burkina Faso, and archaeologically and historically Yemen was a treasure trove. He had been to the port of Aden and to Sana'a and had driven the road in between, and everywhere history lay heavily on the land. The region now known as Yemen was once the Sabaean Kingdom, a state founded more than four thousand years ago that had lasted almost two millennia. Yemen had been conquered or controlled by empire after empire—the Romans, the Egyptians, the Ottomans, and the British. Aden had been a vital port for the British Empire, supporting trade with the Middle East and, later, providing access to the Suez Canal. The British had taken Aden as a colony in 1839 and didn't give it up until 1967—well after they had ceded control of larger possessions such as Canada, India, and Australia.

The country had been divided into North Yemen and South Yemen after that, and had reunified only in 1990. The religious practices of its people still reflected that former division. There were Shia Muslims to the north and Sunnis to the south. And like most other Middle Eastern countries, Yemen's economy depended on its oil. Currently, Golzari reflected, that was something of a problem. He had read a recent *Wall Street Journal* article indicating a steep decline in production and the government's hope to see a reversal with new fields discovered to the south of Socotra. The current government's continued well-being probably depended on that.

Golzari slowed to a crawl when he was a couple of blocks away from the embassy. It was dangerous to approach an embassy in Yemen at a higher speed. He noticed a standard State Department–issue SUV pulling out of the compound. It turned away from him, headed toward the city's center. Before Golzari was close enough to show his identification to the gate guards, another vehicle caught his eye. An older Mercedes-Benz with tinted windows had pulled away from the curb and was following the embassy car. It might have been a coincidence, but Golzari's alarm sense tingled. And he didn't believe in coincidences. If he stopped to inform the embassy guards inside the gate, he'd lose them. He locked his eyes on the two cars in front of him and joined the parade.

When the embassy SUV stopped in front of a red-shaded restaurant, Golzari slowed to watch. He was still too far away to see the driver, although the man's clothing suggested an American. The driver handed the keys to a valet and then . . .

What the hell! Golzari thought. *There's only one person in that SUV. One guy out on the town with no protection, and he just handed his keys to a stranger who's going to take the vehicle somewhere out of sight*! This was either the world's biggest dumbass or someone who hadn't paid attention at his security briefings.

The valet drove the SUV around the next corner, with the Benz still following. As Golzari turned the corner to follow them, another vehicle pulled in front of him, its driver clearly in no hurry. Golzari could only fume as the two cars disappeared from sight. Unwilling to let the fool inside the restaurant meet the end his stupidity deserved, Golzari decided to find an inconspicuous parking spot and wait outside. He hadn't been prepared for this stakeout, and he had to piss. He pulled an empty plastic water bottle from his bag and considered its narrow neck, which was too small to ensure a tidy release. He pulled a penknife from one of the bag's pockets and widened the opening, then filled the bottle to the brim, furious when an errant drop landed on his trousers. He considered the full bottle he now held. Having cut off the top, he had no way to close it. Unwilling to open the car door and dump its contents lest he call attention to himself, he tried to secure the full open bottle in the car's cup holder. That idiot in the restaurant would pay for this, if someone else didn't get to him first.

Two hours later—two hours of sitting in a stuffy car with a bottle of stinking piss—the American finally emerged, escorted into the evening by a Yemeni man. They kissed on both cheeks and separated. When Golzari finally saw the American's face in the light of the lamp beneath the restaurant's awning, he almost lost control of himself. It was the Navy commander he'd seen at RAF Lakenheath. *A stupid damned reservist wandering around alone in a dangerous city. I am going to have his ass.* He was about to get out of the car to get the sailor and take him back to the embassy in his own car when both the SUV and the Benz approached the front of the restaurant. The commander quickly got in the SUV and drove away. The Benz followed again. And still the idiot driver hadn't caught on. Golzari switched on his own car's ignition and followed.

The Benz was close behind the SUV. That meant there was probably no car bomb, unless whoever was in the Benz wanted to be a martyr. He also noticed another unusual thing about the Benz—it didn't have tags. No diplomatic license plate, no Yemeni license plate. Golzari made up his mind and decided to preempt whatever the occupants of the Benz were up to.

He sped up and passed to the left of the Benz. When he was just behind the idiot commander's SUV, he turned hard right and hit the brakes, causing the Benz to T-bone his car's passenger side. He quickly got out of the car and pulled out his 5.56-mm Sig, facing toward the Benz jammed against the side of his car. Behind him he heard the SUV come to a screeching halt. What was that idiot commander doing now? The driver and passenger doors of the Benz swung open and two men emerged, weapons drawn, and took cover behind the doors.

"Hey!" he heard from behind him. The Navy commander was trying to get his attention. Golzari ignored him and remained focused on the Benz gunmen. He shouted, "Drop your weapons," in Arabic. No response. He was about to fire on the man closest to him when he was tackled from behind. He hit his head against the rim of the car's roof as his gun flew out of his hand. It was the idiot—now about to be dead—Navy commander.

"What the hell are you doing?" Golzari yelled, this time in English, wiping away the blood that was trickling into his eyes. "Get off of me, you bloody troll!"

Connor Stark recognized the face from Lakenheath. "You?"

The other two men raced around each side of Golzari's car, keeping their guns trained on him.

Stark loosened his grip on Golzari and picked up the gun he had dropped. "A Sig 228? What agency are you with?"

Golzari, now leaning against the car, pulled out his badge. "Diplomatic Security."

At Stark's nod the two men reholstered their weapons.

Stark handed the Sig back stock first. "Can you drive half a mile?"

"Yeah."

"Good. Let's get back to the embassy before the police show up." Golzari nodded in agreement.

Stark looked over to the two men. "I'll contact you if I need you again. Thanks for your help."

"Anytime, sir," responded the driver.

The four men returned to their respective vehicles, the Benz going in a direction that was definitely not toward the embassy.

Golzari shook his head, wishing he had just turned into the embassy compound in the first place and minded his own business. He was doubly pissed off because the steering wheel of his rental car was now covered with his blood and his pants were soaked with urine from the water bottle that had broken free during the collision.

USS *Bennington*, Indian Ocean, 1527 (GMT)

"I'll have a salad." Bobby Fisk was sitting at one of the three smaller tables along the bulkhead rather than at the long central table where the captain and executive officer traditionally sat with most of the other officers. He waited for the dinner ritual to begin.

"I'll have a salad" had quickly become the most despised words in the wardroom—the signal that the captain had arrived and that all normal conversation had ended. The only discussion from that moment forward would be the captain's doltish questions. First he would ask the chief engineer how much fuel they had.

"CHENG, what's our fuel status?"

And that, thought Bobby, sealed their fate for another day. Fuel status. That meant the CO would continue to issue his standard order: "Trail shaft," the operating condition that maintained maximum fuel efficiency. The cruiser would run only one of its four turbines to turn only one of its two shafts and propellers. The other shaft would remain unengaged, its prop spinning freely by virtue of the ship's speed.

Bobby knew the CO's next question would be about the ports they might visit, though they had yet to make a single port call. The crew had started to refer to this as the "Flying Dutchman" cruise, after the ship of legend that never made it to port.

Bobby finished his dinner just in time for the CO to ask the next question on his unvarying list: when was the *Bennington* scheduled for its next underway replenishment (UNREP). During that process the cruiser and its supply ship would match speeds and courses and run parallel, close enough to throw a baseball from one to the other.

"Tomorrow, sir; 0900," OPS said simply before viciously stabbing the pork chop on his plate.

When he initially arrived aboard the ship, Bobby had thought dinners in the wardroom would be a real-world continuation of his education at the Naval Academy, where his course subjects had ranged from international relations to low-intensity conflicts, from the theories of Mahan and Corbett to ship architecture. He had hoped to take advantage of the senior officers' experience and knowledge. At this point, though, even a simple discussion about baseball scores would have been a welcome break to the monotony of the nightly wardroom script. The change of seats hadn't helped.

Bobby had had enough. A ship's officers were supposed to converse over dinner, sharing ideas in a civilized manner. It was a navy tradition—or so he had been led to believe. He spoke up, his fair skin flushing in embarrassment when every face in the room turned toward him. "Sir, Admiral Zumwalt advocated a high-low mix of ships for twentieth-century warfare. Shouldn't the Navy consider this for the twenty-first century too? What about using small coastal patrol boats for dealing with pirates, sir?"

The wardroom fell silent. The only sound came from the galley, where the mess specialist was working furiously with a metal spatula scraping the remnants of the meal from the grill.

The CO looked across the room at Bobby, who until then had always sat toward the bottom of the long center table, and offered a simple and final answer: "No." The CO then turned to the supply officer. "Make sure we get enough fresh vegetables this UNREP." And Bobby, as the *Bennington*'s other officers had done before him, decided never again to utter a word about naval strategies or force structures in the wardroom. Lacking the appetite for dessert, he stood with the obligatory "Excuse me, Captain," and promptly left the wardroom.

"Hey, Bobby. Nice try. Join me for a smoke in five minutes," said OPS, who had followed him out into officers' country.

They met at the only space on deck where smoking was allowed. OPS, a lieutenant commander on his fifth deployment, handed Bobby a cigar and a lighter. He then reached back and retrieved a book that had been tucked into his khaki belt at the small of his back.

"This is the book I mentioned the other day. Check it out. It'll give you something else to think about when you go off duty."

Bobby took the book and turned it over to read the cover. "Thanks."

"What's your duty station tomorrow during the UNREP?"

"I have to be in the landing safety officer shack during ops on the VERTREP for one of my quals," Bobby replied. The VERTREP—or vertical replenishment—transported pallets of food and material from one ship to the other using helicopters. Bobby was required to participate in at least three VERTREPs on this deployment in order to complete part of his qualifications as a surface warfare officer.

OPS grinned. "Great. You'll have a perfect vantage point. I want you to pay really close attention to the third trip our helo makes to the supply ship tomorrow. Do not take your eyes off that helo. And don't say anything about it to anyone. Got it?"

"Got it, sir."

Bobby shaded his eyes against the brilliant sun as he walked toward the LSO shack the following morning. The heat was already ferocious. He greeted the LSO and picked up a headset. The ship's SH-60B helicopter—call sign Batwing 57—had already completed two VERTREPs carrying heavy pallets from the supply ship to the *Bennington*. Batwing 57's pilots had demonstrated their skill on this difficult evolution. The skies were clear and the water calm, but even a slight breeze or shaky handling of the dangling packet could set it swinging, sometimes to such a degree that it could take a helicopter down.

On his headset Bobby heard Batwing 57 report that it had secured pallet number three and was en route to the *Bennington*. Midway across, Batwing 57 announced to the LSO and the bridge: "The load is unsteady . . . very unsteady . . . we are cutting the load."

The aircrew on Five-Seven pulled the manual release that opened the cargo hook and released the pallet, which fell eight hundred feet until it hit the water and broke apart. Bobby heard a commotion somewhere on the ship, then a voice from the bridge over comms.

"LSO, Bridge. What was on that pallet?"

"Bridge, LSO. SUPPO listed that cargo as fresh produce."

The LSO put his hand over his microphone and turned to Bobby. "The captain's salad," he said in mock sadness.

For the first time in days Bobby smiled.

U.S. Embassy, Sana'a, 1650 (GMT)

C. J. reviewed her notes as the technician prepared the feed to Washington. He muttered something that she ignored as she continued to rehearse the request she was about to make. She had worked with Eliot Green when he was Becker's chief of staff in the Senate. Speaking to him now, however, was like addressing the president himself. She checked her watch: 9:50 a.m. in D.C. The technician muttered something else, which shook her out of her distraction.

"I'm sorry, what?"

"We're ready, Madam Ambassador," he said, "The feed is live. The White House will initiate."

A few seconds after the technician left the room the screen crackled to life. "C. J."

"Hello, Eliot." The fat, pockmarked face of the White House chief of staff topped by his receding red hair appeared larger than life on the screen in front of her. She wished she had a smaller screen.

"We only have a few minutes, C. J. I wanted to speak with you before the president's press conference on the Middle East. We expect the questions to be on Iraq, Iran, and Afghanistan, but on the off chance there's one on the situation in your region, I wanted to check with you. Oh, and one administrative note: Deputy Secretary of State Dunner tendered his resignation earlier today."

"I know," she answered. "I saw the communiqué."

"The death of his son has been extremely difficult for him, so he decided to spend more time with his family."

"I understand. I'll miss him."

"What about the oil rights?"

"They're a problem. I'm still trying to work some angles with the Yemenis."

"How long have you been there now, C. J.?" Green barked. "You wanted Yemen, you got it. You told us you could make things happen there. The president's still waiting."

"It takes time just to get a meeting here, Eliot. I'm setting it up."

"Wrong answer. We need to move things along or get someone in there who can."

"Eliot, I've got one hand tied behind my back on this. We're operating with about half of the normal embassy staff. Things take longer. I spoke with John Dunner about that. He agreed with me and was trying to get more people assigned here."

"Dunner is gone. You're speaking to me now. We'll send people as they become available."

Eliot Green, who had spent most of his career bullying people on Capitol Hill, briefly thought about how the president should give a non-answer should a question about embassy staffing arise. That was unlikely, but contingency planning was an important part of his job. *That's an excellent question, Chuck. The men and women who staff our embassies are some of the finest public servants in the world. We devote significant resources to the process of selecting the right people for those jobs, and I'm confident that the teams we have in place do their jobs well, in the finest tradition of the State Department. Next question.*

"C. J., really. You need to think about this. We can put you in Belgium. Luxembourg is also available. The president can't keep his eye on every detail in every single country. Can you or can't you do this?"

"It would be easier with more personnel, but I'm pursuing a couple of promising avenues. I called in a favor at the Pentagon, and I have a new defense attaché who knows the Yemenis extremely well." She regretted mentioning that as the words came out of her mouth.

"Where in the Pentagon did this attaché come from?"

"Not the Pentagon proper. He's former Navy, recalled for this job."

"From where? DATT jobs take months of selection and training. Does he have that?"

"He's been living abroad. He knows what he's doing." C. J. was anxious to close the door she had mistakenly opened.

"Okay. I need to get on a conference call to Afghanistan now. I want you to email both Helen Forth and me every day with your progress. And it better be progress, C. J." The screen went blank.

What would be worse, she wondered: failing in Yemen or Eliot learning that Connor Stark was working with her again? *Eliot's a busy man,* she thought. *He'll probably forget all about this.*

When the screen went blank on the Washington end of the call, Eliot Green turned to his aide. "Call the Pentagon. I want to know who the hell they just assigned as the defense attaché to Yemen."

A couple of hours later, C. J. was curled up on a comfortable sofa in the ambassador's residence trying to read a local newspaper printed in Arabic. A knock at the door interrupted her fierce attention.

"Come in," she barked.

Gunnery Sergeant Willis, the head of the embassy's Marine detachment, poked his head in the door. "Madam Ambassador, you asked to be notified when Commander Stark returned. There's someone with him as well."

She stood and slipped on her shoes. "Bring them in, Gunnery Sergeant."

Stark entered first, followed by a well-dressed Middle Eastern man in his thirties who was sporting a large gash on his forehead and carrying a bloody handkerchief in his left hand. He also appeared to have soiled himself. She rose and tried to conceal any revulsion her face might betray to this . . . guest.

"Commander, what's going on?"

"There was a little accident down the road."

She stiffened. "Was it an attack?"

"You could say so." Stark aimed a look of disgust at his companion.

"I was doing my job, Madam Ambassador," interjected Golzari, aiming a dark look at Stark.

"Interfering was more like it," Stark retorted. "This is Diplomatic Security Service Special Agent Golzari. He intentionally collided with the vehicle that was escorting me back from a meeting at a restaurant."

C. J. raised an eyebrow. "Escorting? I was told you left the compound alone."

"That wasn't an embassy-issue vehicle escorting you, Commander," Golzari chimed in. "Those weren't Marines, and they sure as hell weren't DSS agents."

"Madam Ambassador, please let me explain," Stark began, ignoring Golzari. "It was important that I reestablish contact with some people here in order to comply with your request. Overt protection would have interfered with that. Plus, we are currently short on Marines as well as an RSO. Who was

I supposed to take? The two new assistant RSOs would be more hindrance than help."

"No RSO?" Golzari asked in disbelief. "There has to be . . ."

C. J. stopped Golzari with a raised hand. "We have a significant personnel shortage here, Special Agent. Commander, who exactly was protecting you?"

"Highland Maritime Defense. Most of their people are with the boats off Socotra, but Bill Maddox always brings along several when he's in town to conduct business."

"Wait a minute," Golzari interrupted, dabbing at the blood trickling more slowly now from the gash on his forehead. "You're an officer assigned to the embassy and you hired a private security company detail? What kind of operation is this?"

"Agent Golarzi . . ." C. J.'s voice was dulcet sweet as she turned her gaze from Stark to him.

"Golzari, Ma'am."

"My apologies. Agent Golzari, help me understand your role in this. Why are you here?" Her voice rose slightly. "And why did you create a public disturbance?"

"I'm here as part of an investigation into a murder in the United States and an attack on an allied operative in London. As I arrived, I saw an embassy SUV being tailed. I believed the vehicle was without protection, so I followed to ensure that the situation remained secure. I saw Commander Stark enter a local restaurant alone, leaving his car without protection. It appeared to me that he was in danger, so I followed and at an appropriate time took action."

"Agent Golzari, my apologies for the confusion," C. J. said. "See the staff nurse about that cut. Let the consul know if you need any assistance from us in your investigation. Gunnery Sergeant Willis can help with any immediate needs you have—perhaps a change of trousers?"

As the three men turned to go, she added, "Commander, please stay a moment. We have other matters to discuss."

"Thank you, Madam Ambassador," Golzari said stiffly. He turned and followed the gunnery sergeant out of the room without acknowledging Stark.

"Let me guess," Stark said when the door had closed behind them. "You wanted to chew me out again?"

"No, Connor," she sighed. "I'm not going to chew you out." She sounded tired and discouraged. "I'm not going to get into the legalities or the inappropriateness of having private security escort you, even if you didn't technically hire them, though I expect the judge advocate would disagree. We'll deal with that later. How did your meeting go?"

"Fine."

"That's it? One word?"

"Really fine?" he offered.

C. J. groaned even as she cracked a smile.

"I know you want to know what I'm up to, C. J. Here's what I can tell you: I had dinner with a friend who is closely tied to the Yemeni government. I couldn't ask too many specific questions because it's been awhile since we've seen each other. They don't work that way. Every transaction is built upon trust. And trust, as you are no doubt aware, takes time."

She returned to the sofa and removed her shoes again. She motioned to him to take a chair near her, and as he did he smelled the distinct but subtle scent of her perfume: fresh, light, floral, and vastly different from the restaurant's heavy aromas and the fetid smells of the city outside the embassy compound.

"You can't leave me in the dark, Connor. I can't operate that way, and Washington is breathing down my neck."

"Let me find out what's going on first, and then I'll tell you as much as I can without violating any trusts."

"What about violating the trust of your government?"

"It's not my government anymore."

"Are we going to get past that?"

"I don't 'get past' humiliation and dishonor."

"So you've just stewed for the last ten years?"

He shrugged. "I've done other things so that I wouldn't have to think about it."

"Then why didn't you say no when the Navy found you in Scotland?"

"Because they told me I'd go to jail if I didn't come."

"Huh, you're rusty," she laughed. "You used to recognize a bluff when you heard one. I told the Navy that if you refused to cooperate, they should just leave you alone. No prosecution."

Stark glared at her. "You what?"

She shrugged, trying not to look pleased that she had outfoxed him. "I'm giving you an opportunity to clear your record, like you asked."

"What if I decide that's what I no longer want?"

"Then you can go."

"Just like that?"

She nodded. "Just like that."

He eyed her warily.

"I'm sorry about our exchange earlier, Connor. I'm sorry about how I spoke to you. And I'm sorry about recalling you. I'm sorry about . . . well . . . the court-martial. I should have done things another way then. If I had, things might have been different—then and now."

Stark was startled by the unexpected apology and angry with himself. He had indeed gotten rusty. His career and promotions had never been of primary importance to him; those were simply reflections of what he wanted to do—to serve, to protect, to save. He hadn't been able to protect his friends from terrorists in Italy early in his career, but he'd fought back in another country and toppled another terrorist organization in Canada. That episode had cost him the chance to wear his country's uniform. It had been his choice, no one else's. Now it was Ullapool that had been desecrated by an attack, and his friends there who might be subject to further intrusions. What if they tried to hurt Maggie? The fear of that haunted him.

"I'll stay," he said quietly with a hint of deference to the person he now recognized begrudgingly as his superior in the chain of command, "so long as I have some latitude. I'm leaving first thing in the morning for a couple of days."

"Where are you going?"

"I'm going to Mukalla to board one of Bill's security vessels and go out to the oil platforms. I'll chopper back to Socotra and then fly back here. I need to see the situation on the ground myself to get this done."

"I don't like it, but I'll authorize it."

"I'm not getting the sense that you have a lot of support here," Connor noted.

"We have no support. Nothing from Washington. Nothing from the Yemenis. Just pirates to the south of us, terrorists everywhere else, and the Chinese a shadow growing longer each day."

"Shadows are longest with the sunrise or sunset," he said, unusually pensive. "Have you seen much of the Chinese here?"

"No, but my sources say they have a lot of access to the Yemeni government."

"Good sources?"

C. J. paused. "The Indian ambassador. Gavaskar."

"How well do you know . . . him? Her?"

"Him. We've met several times. At first he was cautious, as if he was assessing my reaction to everything he said. He didn't have much to say in our first few meetings, but then he started to offer up more information than I'd asked for."

"Is there a reason for that?"

"I've corroborated everything he's told me. If he's trying to pull one over on me, he's doing a damn good job. No, I think he wants to work with us somehow but is waiting for the right moment."

"What would they gain by working with us here?"

"The same thing the Chinese are after, probably—oil."

"I don't know, C. J. It's not called the Indian Ocean for nothing. Bill said the Chinese have been active all over the place. Maybe Ambassador Gavaskar is looking for an ally to fend them off."

"I've thought of that. We don't have any assets here that they could use. Maybe they're setting the stage just in case there's an opportunity." Her voice trailed off as she contemplated the possible chess moves on an imaginary three-sided board. Then she changed the subject. "Connor, I want to run something else by you. I want to conduct a humanitarian assistance operation. Not just an American effort, though. I would contact every NGO I know to bring people together for this."

"Here?"

"No. Socotra. An earthquake did a lot of damage to some of the towns along the island's northern coast. It wasn't a big enough catastrophe to merit attention internationally—only a few deaths—but as I understand it the Yemeni government isn't doing much to help. We could bring medical staff, construction aid, supplies. What do you think?"

"That depends," Stark mused. "Are you asking from a political or a security perspective?"

"Well, politically, we'd have to run it by the Yemenis, of course. If we propose this publicly, it would be like telling the Socotrans—and mainland Yemenis too—that the government is either unable to address their needs or doesn't care. That would risk a destabilized government with possibly regional implications. The ruling family isn't held in terribly high regard as it is. But it's the security aspects I'd like advice on."

Stark thought for a moment and then said doubtfully, "Honestly, from a security standpoint it would be a nightmare. If we can't protect our own assets with what we have now, how can we put humanitarian workers at risk?"

"You're right. I've been thinking the same thing. But there has to be some way to do this. It's important."

Connor couldn't mistake the focused look in her eyes. She'd looked the same way when she was about to conduct a legislative end-run in the Senate for their old boss. She wasn't going to give up on this idea. "I'll put out some feelers to the Yemenis and work on the security issue. If we can find a way around those two things, then I'm in."

"Promise?"

"Yeah. 'I'm from the government and I'm here to help.'"

"Damn, now I know we're dead in the water," she said with a grin. Connor responded in kind and rose to leave.

"Connor?"

"Yeah?"

"Are we on the same team?"

"No," he curtly replied as he left the room.

Mukalla, Yemen, 1751 (GMT)

Abdi Mohammed Asha looked forward to relaxing in the seaside hotel in this pearl of a city on the Yemeni coastline. Mukalla reminded him of the home he missed—far from the ragged city of snow and the Americans and the Bantu émigrés he had left behind in the United States. There was a reason Bantus were shunned in Somalia, and even here in Yemen. They were beneath him, beneath his clan. But they had had their uses. And Asha had made good use of the skills he had learned from his former warlord. That economically battered American city had welcomed the Bantus with open arms and open wallets, and when he arrived he took what little money they had. He threatened the men, he threatened the women; and every one of them paid a protection fee. One of the Bantus had tried to resist early on by threatening to report him to the authorities. His body was found in the river the next day. After that the Bantus paid him without question.

His distaste for the Bantus ran deep, but the people he truly abhorred were the do-gooder college students at Antioch College who tried so hard to help the Bantus assimilate into a culture that hadn't asked for them and didn't want them. The Antioch students, spoiled children of soft Americans, were so easy to manipulate, so gullible. They wanted to know about Somali culture, history, and language. They wanted to know what it was like to live under cruel warlords. So Asha told them. He had been just a simple fisherman, he told them. And the bad warlords took his fish, his boat, and his nets, leaving him with nothing. The students cried for poor Asha, so happy that he was now living in Antioch—not that a single one of *them* would ever deign to live there. After four years they drove off in the BMWs provided by their parents and fought for economic justice. In the meantime, they talked to him and he quietly sold them khat. He took particular pleasure in using the boy whose father ran American foreign policy, a foreign policy that hurt the Somali warlords and the people they called "pirates," as his mule.

The luxurious hotel pleased him. He was a man of power again, and such men deserved the very best. Mukalla had once been a powerful city, the capital of the governorate of Ghaydah, and young Ahmed al-Ghaydah himself had reserved this spacious room overlooking the Gulf of Aden. Asha was safe here. Once Hu's plane had taken him from England to Yemen, Asha had taken no chances, used no credit cards. No one would find him. He would travel between Yemen and Somalia only by boat.

Asha admired his image in the mirror as he rubbed Euphoria into his face and neck. Then, locking the door carefully behind him, he went to Ahmed's house in the city, where they smoked apricot-flavored *shisha*, an indulgence he had greatly missed in his exile. Asha exhaled, producing a great cloud of smoke. "Excellent, Ahmed, Allah be praised."

Al-Ghaydah leaned back against his cushion. "Faisal's plans are going well, Abdi Mohammed."

"Do we have enough people now?"

"Yes, yes," al-Ghaydah nodded. "They have been gaining experience. They tested two bombs near the U.S. embassy. One nearly killed our own deputy foreign minister."

"If he is killed with the Americans, then *inshallah*."

Al-Ghaydah agreed. "*Inshallah*."

"When is the next attack?"

"Faisal has told them to try again in two days. The ambassador seldom leaves the compound now, so opportunities are few."

"Then how do they know when to attack?"

"She asks for meetings to express her government's concerns about the oil fields and the pirates." They both laughed. "Alas, the Foreign Ministry is a very busy place, and meetings are very difficult to schedule. Tomorrow, she will receive an invitation to the foreign minister's office. She will have to leave the compound to attend this meeting."

"Allah be praised. I will go to Sana'a to watch this."

"They will be honored if you join them. What else is required of us, Abdi Mohammed?"

"That is for Faisal to say."

DAY 6

USS *Bennington*, East of Socotra Island, 1032 (GMT)

The Seahawk helicopter—Batwing 58—had been hovering for ten minutes when the bridge ordered Bobby Fisk's VBSS team away. Visit, Board, Search, and Seizure teams had operated for years in the Persian Gulf and Indian Ocean, but this would be the first VBSS launched from the *Bennington* during this deployment. Bobby was feeling a range of emotions—excitement and pride to be part of the team, and just a bit nervous too.

Boarding ships in the region to search for illegal cargo was one of the *Bennington*'s duties, by authority of a United Nations resolution. Despite the cruiser's time on station, though, it had stopped no ships at all before this one, suspicious or otherwise. The OD had several times spotted a suspicious dhow and asked the captain if he wanted to send the VBSS team out on an RHIB—a rigid-hulled inflatable boat—to conduct an inspection. The CO's responses were as formulaic on the bridge as they were in the wardroom: "Not this time. They don't look suspicious." In each case, the ship in question had been several miles away. Bobby had concluded that the CO had excellent vision.

The *Bennington*'s patrol area was a hundred miles east of Socotra. Radar spotted the first ship of the day as the crew was eating lunch on Slider Tuesday—"sliders" being the well-earned Navy slang for greasy hamburgers. The ship was an old Offshore Supply Vessel (OSV) with a distinctly high forward superstructure and a flat stern section for carrying supplies. Batwing 58, flying at five thousand feet, had observed the ship making wide, slow turns at less than six knots. With Five-Eight's fuel running low, Batwing 57 was rolled out to protect what was expected to be the first boarding of the deployment.

The VBSS team found a compliant target. The suspect OSV's crew of eighteen was huddled at the bow watching the menacing helicopter that hovered broad on the starboard bow, its GAU-16 .50-caliber machine gun trained out toward the ship in order to provide the boarding team overwatch and, if necessary, fire support. Bobby was third over the side and onto the main cargo deck, which was packed with dozens of oil drums. Bobby motioned to two of the team members to check the drums while he went forward with an Arabic-speaking team member, glad that Fifth Fleet—or perhaps more accurately a friend at Fifth Fleet—had issued a directive that an Arabic speaker be present on the boarding team.

Bobby and the translator took each member of the OSV crew aside individually for questioning. No one knew anything about the ship's destination or about the drums of fuel on its deck. After finishing with the last crew member, Bobby checked his watch. Fifth Fleet orders specified a minimum of two hours for each boarding. Only twenty minutes of those two hours remained. He knew the captain would not allow the inspection to go on any longer than the bare minimum required.

Bobby summoned most of his team members aft to coordinate their findings. Half of the fuel drums were full. The ship carried far more food stores than a crew of eighteen could possibly need, even if they stayed at sea for a month. There was no paperwork on the ship. It all looked very suspicious to him. He radioed his findings to the cruiser.

His earpiece came alive. "Hessian, Hessian, Batwing Five-Seven. Be advised of a fast-approaching skiff approximately one-six nautical miles to the east." Bobby stood by for orders from the *Bennington*. There were only two reasons for the skiff to be heading this way. Either it was a pirate skiff looking for a victim to attack, or—he looked at the oil drums and thought of the food—this was a mother ship, a mobile base of operations that allowed small skiffs to operate hundreds of miles offshore. Air Boss had explained some of the methods the helos could use against suspected pirate skiffs. This was going to be a perfect opportunity to witness them.

But he had heard nothing from the cruiser. The sound of Batwing's rotors faded as it moved east to investigate. Soon the skiff would see the cruiser's silhouette and speed away.

"*Bennington*, Batwing Five-Seven. Skiff has turned south and is moving off at high speed. Requesting permission to pursue and stop."

The captain's voice rang out almost immediately. "All units are ordered to return to base pursuant to higher directives."

"Well, sure," Bobby said to himself. "The damn skiff would be a new boarding and we'd have to start the time clock again. And the captain would have to waste two whole hours more of fuel." Midway through the final word of the sentence, Bobby realized that his mike was on. *Oh, shit!* He braced for the reaction.

"All units, return immediately. Hessian team leader, report to me on arrival." Bobby suddenly felt ill. The slider and creamed spinach he'd eaten for lunch were on their way back up. He leaned over the leeward side of the ship and vomited as the OSV's crew laughed. The chief petty officer of the boarding team patted Bobby on the back. "Don't worry about it, sir. Sometimes the sea gives to us, and sometimes we give to the sea. Sometimes it's not pretty either way."

Suleiman, East of Socotra Island, 1140 (GMT)

Faisal could not believe his good fortune. Allah had indeed blessed him and his crew. The stupid Americans had boarded his ship and had seen the fuel drums but had not discovered the weapons hidden in a submerged tethered container. He had spoken only in Arabic to the translator when questioned and feigned ignorance of English as well as of regional pirates. Then he heard them called away and watched the officer vomit. Had the young officer disappointed the father of the ship? *Disappointing one's father can be daunting,* he reflected, *sometimes a life-changing thing.*

Faisal well remembered being his father's pride, the beloved firstborn son—before his younger brother had come along. Faisal had never understood how he had so suddenly lost favor to the mewling newborn Ali. As the years passed, it was always the perfect son Ali who received more attention. Ali, everyone said, was destined to surpass his older brother and lead their family in the future. They said his visions for the future would heal the country and make it prosper. Faisal's hatred grew with each word of praise for his brother.

One day when Faisal was fifteen, he was in the offices of his family's business in Aden while his father was negotiating with some American and British officials. His father called Ali, still just a toddler of four years, into his private office. Faisal watched through the office window as his father picked up Ali and kissed him, beaming with pride. The Americans and British shared the father's joy in his perfect son. Wasn't Faisal also perfect? Had he not tried to please his father? The resentment had risen in his belly like the lunch the young American officer had just lost over the side of Faisal's ship. The Westerners' loud voices had carried clearly through the thin office walls. They spoke about port visits and said that the American Navy ship now in the harbor, USS *The Sullivans*, and the next visitor, the USS *Cole*, would bring money to Aden and its people.

Faisal had stormed down to the docks, trying to escape his humiliation, and had come across a few men loading boxes into a skiff. His imam was with them. Startled, they hastily threw a tarp over the deck.

"What do you want here?" one of the men asked. "Who is your family?"

"I am Faisal," he declared proudly. "I require no family." The men laughed at the boy's childish defiance.

"Welcome, Faisal," said the imam, who introduced him to the men. "Would you like to help us?"

Pleased to be asked, Faisal said, "What do you wish me to do?"

"You see that American warship anchored in the harbor?"

"Yes. Who could miss it? The Americans should not be here; nor should the British. They bring us nothing but shame. I wish they would all go away."

"You will have your wish, young Faisal," the imam said. "That ship is one of their most powerful warships, and we are going to make it go away. Cast off that line for the men."

Faisal did as he was asked and watched as the overloaded skiff pulled away from the pier. After going only a few meters it swamped and sank in the calm water. The men swam back to shore, and it was Faisal's turn to laugh as they tried to wring out the excess water from their thobes.

"You are fools," Faisal scoffed at the men, careful not to include his imam. "Do you think you can destroy a warship with a leaky rowboat?"

"We will try again," the imam said. "And we will have a better boat next time, but we must know when the American ships will be here in Aden."

"I will get you this information. I know of another American warship that is coming soon. I will tell you when and I will help you prepare, but this time you must listen to me."

"You are just a boy," said one.

"You are men, and yet you failed. I know the sea. I know boats." He drew himself up proudly. "I know many things; I hear and see many things. I know when warships will come to Aden. I can sink them." He wanted to kill them when they laughed at him.

"Faisal is correct," said the imam, admonishing them. "He can help us. The family he claims not to need has just what we want."

The men consulted one another for a moment and quickly agreed. The boy's forceful personality, the timing of his appearance, and the imam's vote of confidence all seemed to suggest that Allah had sent him to help them.

As Faisal promised, the team succeeded in their attack on the American warship. Two of his team members died in the attack; the others were imprisoned. Faisal paid off the prison guards and engineered the men's escape, and with their help he founded his own business, making hashish runs in the Arabian Sea, the Gulf of Oman, and the Gulf of Aden. He watched warship patterns and noticed the decline in the number of American warships as America's priorities shifted away from the area. Their absence gave Faisal the opportunity to organize other insurgents and pirates.

When the Chinese approached him, Faisal immediately saw the opportunity to expand his business and his influence. He was patient and methodical in his plans as he worked with the Chinese businessman who introduced him to Abdi Mohammed Asha. Just as Asha would someday return to Somalia and become a great leader, when the time was right Faisal would lead an army of men and rise to power to rule Yemen. His father and brother would bow before him. It was his birthright.

DAY 7

McLean, Virginia, 0208 (GMT)

Hu visited him only in the evenings, after the sun had set. Eliot Green unbuttoned his too-tight blazer and groaned in relief as he sat in one of the chairs next to the couch where Hu had taken his usual seat. Green pushed an ashtray toward Hu, who pulled a cigarette from a silver case. The trousers of his silk suit made a whispering noise as the businessman from Beijing crossed his legs. As always, Hu wore a black suit, black socks, and polished black shoes. His hair was black, as were his eyes. He had worn no other color in the half dozen years Eliot had known him, with one exception: the man had an endless supply of pastel shirts and subtly patterned ties.

Hu was taller than most Chinese Green had known. Green had read in an intelligence report that South Koreans were generally several inches taller than North Koreans because the dietary conditions in the capitalist country were vastly better than the decades-long near-starvation levels to the north. In the same way, Hu's height, if not genetic, suggested that he had always been part of the privileged class in China—even during the strictly communist era, party members had always had access to an improved quality of life.

Hu took a long, slow drag on the cigarette, blowing the smoke out his nostrils like a storybook dragon. His black eyes never left Green. He said a word in Chinese that Green had come to understand as "leave us." At his command, the two dark-suited men who had accompanied him inside left the room. One always waited outside the door, the other in the car. Once, Green had glimpsed a shoulder holster when one of the guards opened his jacket. Green knew of few businessmen who required armed bodyguards in the United States.

Getting the men's arms into and out of the country wasn't a problem because Hu never used commercial airports. His company owned at least one private intercontinental jet—and a very plush one at that. Green and President Becker—before Becker was president or vice president, of course—had traveled in Hu's aircraft, and fondly remembered the fine food and even better female entertainment their host had provided.

"You have news for me about Yemen." Hu wasn't asking a question; he was demanding an answer.

"Hu, you know these things take time." Green shifted his bulk and reached for the Jack Daniels he'd poured for himself earlier.

"Indeed. I also know that you and I have invested time and resources into this project."

Green tried to recall if the stone-faced Hu had blinked at all since arriving. Nope. Those damned eyes just sucked in everything around them like two black holes. "I've tried everything I can think of to hurry this along, Hu."

"Tell me what you have tried. Perhaps I can offer further suggestions."

Hu's silky voice gave him the creeps. Green gulped at his whiskey and leaned forward, grasping the glass with both hands as he looked toward the coffee table. "The Department of Defense has transferred all antipiracy assets away from the area except for that one cruiser—and we've essentially defanged it to prepare it."

Hu gave the merest of nods.

Green hurried on. "I ordered the State Department to stop transferring personnel to the embassy, especially security and intelligence elements. And Dunner was starting to ask questions, so I convinced him to resign."

Hu smiled. "Very good. What of Ambassador Sumner?"

"She has no clue what's happening." He took another gulp.

"But she isn't stupid."

"No," Green chuckled, "she isn't." He stuck his finger in the Jack Daniels and swirled it around, clinking the ice against the glass. "She may eventually figure it out, but I'm keeping her busy for now. She's holed up in the embassy trying to get the government to talk to her. Without success," Eliot grinned.

"So the Yemeni government will have no formal contact with her, and she won't be able to complete her assigned mission," Hu said, asking and answering his own question.

"If she becomes a problem, I'll make the proper arrangements," Green assured him. "Hell, I didn't want her there in the first place; she just stepped into it."

"Is Becker concerned for her?"

Green chuckled. "We both know the president, Hu. He's concerned for himself. She doesn't know about his other women, and he knows where his real loyalty lies. He knows you have been a strong supporter since his first Senate race."

"Ah, good, Eliot. We already have plans for that oil. We would not wish to lose it to an American company." Hu paused, his obsidian eyes narrowing. "On another matter, the president is sliding in the polls. Should we be concerned?"

"We'll be fine. The party convention is in a couple of weeks. The incidents your friends are helping with will generate public outrage and support for the president just in time for him to give the speech of his life. We'll win this election, Hu. No problem."

"Very good. The money will be deposited tomorrow—the standard amount, of course."

Hu said something in Chinese so quietly that no one outside the room should have heard. Eliot Green knew what that meant: Hu had a direct wire to his men. Green once feared that Hu might also be recording their conversations but had decided that he probably wasn't. If such a recording ever became public, the Chinese businessman and his associates would also be implicated, which would complicate their plans. Green heard the front door open. The bodyguard stood at the entrance to the living room.

Hu rose quickly and gracefully, and Green struggled to follow suit.

"We will be successful, Eliot," Hu said firmly.

"Who the hell can stop us?"

PART II

DAY 8

M/V *Kirkwall*, Gulf of Aden, 0600 (GMT)

"Commander Connor Stark to see Captain Johnson," Stark shouted from the bobbing whaler to a deckhand. "Request permission to come aboard."

"Permission granted, sir."

Once he was on deck, the transport boat sped back to the pier at Mukalla.

"Welcome back to the *Kirkwall*, Commander," said the skipper. She shook his hand and then hugged him.

Jaime's eyes were the same robin's-egg blue that he remembered so vividly from his first sight of her fifteen years earlier. "No gray hairs from the responsibility of command?" he joked.

"I dye them," she said, pushing back an errant strand of blond hair. "You should do the same."

"Bill says you're doing a fine job, just as I expected. I wouldn't have hired you as my replacement if I didn't think you could do it."

"The money didn't hurt, especially when that son of a bitch left me and the kids. C'mon up to the pilothouse. I just made a fresh pot of your second-favorite beverage."

Stark followed her up the ladder toward the aroma of rich, dark coffee. She handed him a royal blue coffee mug imprinted with the security company's logo and name.

"How's business?" he asked, taking an unsweetened gulp.

"Busy. We could use another hand around, but I see you've been co-opted. I was surprised when Bill told me you were back in uniform."

"No one was more surprised than I was. Defense attaché is the last job I figured I'd ever hold."

"Too bad. You were a great CO on the *Cyclone*. We all wanted to be part of your wardroom when you got a destroyer or a cruiser."

"If that had happened, you'd have been my first choice for XO." He surveyed the familiar pilothouse. It had become better organized and more efficient looking during the last year—the result of Jaime's meticulous work.

"It was family over career back then, Connor. At least he didn't fight me for the kids in the divorce."

"How are they?"

"Growing by leaps and bounds. How can I not miss them during my ninety days on?"

Stark looked out through the pilothouse windows at his former command. The *Kirkwall* was an old British *Seal*-class long-range recovery and support craft. It was small—only 120 feet long—and displaced 160 tons. Twin Paxmans, built by the same company that produced diesel engines for the *Cyclone* class, powered the steel hull. It could do twenty-three knots on a good day, which meant the *Kirkwall* could outpace and protect any of the supply boats it was escorting; any ship slower than fifteen knots was vulnerable to pirate attacks.

A voice crackled over the radio. "*Kirkwall, Kirkwall*, this is the *Mukalla Ismael* in company with the OSV *Endurance*. We are under way and expect to arrive at the prearranged coordinates for escort, over."

Jaime picked up the microphone. "*Mukalla Ismael*, this is *Kirkwall*. Message received. Copy all. *Kirkwall* standing by channel one-six. Out." She replaced the mike and picked up the shipboard announcer. "All hands, this is the captain. Stand by to get under way for escort duty in twenty minutes; that's two-zero minutes." She turned back toward Stark. "I told the boss that we need to think about replacing this boat with one that has a helo and RHIBs like *Deveron* and *Arnish*."

"It's that bad?"

"The pirates are just adapting too fast. I've turned back seventeen attacks against the supply ships. But we could always use more boats. And a real U.S. Navy presence around these parts wouldn't hurt."

"What's here?"

"The closest thing to a Navy ship would be the *Bennington*. I heard her over comms last night, so she's somewhere nearby in the Gulf. Hey, isn't she named for your great-great-great-granddaddy's battle?"

"Yup. General John Stark. He led a New Hampshire regiment and defeated the Hessians at Bennington. What do you mean by 'closest thing'? She's Navy, right?"

"Well, more or less. I got some gouge on her when I heard she was in the Indian Ocean. I know someone who served under her CO during his last command. Not exactly the best and brightest. Plus, the ship's old and coming out of service soon, so no one's willing to put any money into it."

"How'd he get command?"

"His uncle is chairman of the Senate Armed Services Committee and his cousin is a three-star admiral."

"Jesus. We're not that much different from the Yemeni ruling family. How about the pirates? Are they still driving skiffs around?"

"Yeah, but there are more of them now. They pretty much stay away from our client ships after so many failed attacks; they want the low-hanging fruit, the commercial freighters that don't have any protection."

"What else have you learned about them?"

"Nothing since the president shut down CTF 151. Only a few people are tracking what's going on. This is the Wild West, Connor. A couple months ago we did pick up a Somali kid in a skiff that had run out of fuel and was never found by its mother ship—the guy carrying their satellite phone was high on khat and dropped it in the water. All the others on the skiff had died from exposure, and the kid was pretty close."

"What authorities did you release him to?"

"Neptune and Davy Jones. He died a few hours after we picked him up. Our medic was able to speak with him through the interpreter first, though."

"Did you find out anything?"

"Not much, except that the rumors of a pirate king are true. The kid said that the clans aren't in charge of the pirate boats anymore; almost all of them take their orders from a guy called al-Yemeni."

"He's not Somali? Great. Now we have both sides of the Gulf of Aden to worry about."

Two ships coming up astern caught his eye. "Looks like we're ready to go," he said.

"Toss your pack below. Stateroom 3 is yours. Grab some chow. Chef's waiting for you and said he has your favorite."

He moaned. "Haggis? Oh, boy. Thanks for the hospitality, Jaime."

U.S. Embassy, Sana'a, 0620 (GMT)

Golzari was apoplectic. The Navy commander had gone against regulations by driving alone in Yemen. He had almost certainly violated some other rule by using private security people, even if they weren't being paid. And because of Stark, Golzari was going to have a scar on his forehead and had been forced to throw away a good pair of trousers.

With the gunnery sergeant's help, Golzari set up shop in the spartan RSO's office. He waited impatiently while the information technology staff set up his access to the classified networks he needed to search for Abdi Mohammed Asha and the police liaison Khalid, who apparently were the same man. Was Asha/Khalid still in England? Had he gone on to his native Somalia? Or could he be here? Johnny Dunner's khat, which had been shipped to Asha in Boston, had come in on a ship out of Mukalla. It was Golzari's only lead.

Golzari swirled the cup of black tea he'd gotten in the embassy mess as he considered the situation. He had promised John Dunner that he would find out what really happened to his son. Aside from his family's debt to Dunner, Golzari had become personally fond of the man during his time on the assistant secretary's security detail. The old man was quiet and considerate of those who worked for him, quite unlike the harpy from Harvard who until recently had been Dunner's boss. Diplomatic Security agents, like the Secret Service, got a unique perspective on what public officials were really like when the cameras were off. Protectees were generally accompanied everywhere except the restroom and the bedroom, and agents were often posted outside those within easy hearing range. The charges took a while to get used to the twenty-four-hour protection, but they eventually forgot about it and let their guard down, showing their true selves. And in most cases, that wasn't a pretty sight. Golzari had often wondered if Rome's Praetorian Guard had felt the same way. That was probably why so many of them eventually turned on their emperors.

Golzari sipped his tea and nearly spit it out. This country was known for diverse and flavorful teas, but the embassy had none. General Services had no soul. Setting down the cup, Golzari turned back to the problem at hand. Abdi Mohammed Asha was Somali. Golzari knew his tribe and the town where he lived. That was a start. Would Asha return there? If he did, Golzari wouldn't be able to follow him; no Americans were allowed into Somalia.

If Asha was in Yemen, he was still within reach, though the authorities probably couldn't—or rather, *wouldn't*—help Golzari with an investigation:

Asha wasn't Yemeni, but he was more like them than Golzari was. He knew the creed: *My brother and me against my cousin; my cousin and me against my town; my town and me against . . .* The best-case scenario would be interminable delay. *We will help you as much as we can, inshallah, but . . .*

The best lead he had on Asha and his ties to Yemen was the series of small khat shipments transported on the *Mukalla Hassan*, which was owned by the Yemeni president's brother. Certainly the Yemeni police would be anxious to help with that one, Golzari thought wryly.

The graying gunnery sergeant looked in the open door. "Sir, anything I can do for you?"

"Yeah, Gunny, I need a good tailor, a hard drink, and a soft pillow."

"In this country, sir?"

"Good point. How about you just keep lunatic Navy commanders at least twenty yards from me?"

"I haven't formally met any recently," the sergeant replied in a heavy southern drawl, "but from what I hear, he won't be around long. He and the ambassador have had some heated discussions since he arrived. Some walls just ain't soundproof enough."

"They don't get along. What a surprise. Why do I get the feeling this guy wouldn't get along with us good people either, Gunny?"

"Don't judge him just yet, sir," came the raspy reply. "Scuttlebutt is he's here under some unusual circumstances." The sergeant stepped further into the little office. "Mind going on a drive with us tomorrow?"

"Where to, Gunny?"

"The foreign minister's office, sir. Ambassador Sumner received a call inviting her to meet with him."

"A phone call?"

"Yes, sir. That's what I understand."

"She's going?"

"Yes, sir. At zero nine hundred we leave the compound in two vehicles. We're short, so we could use the extra firepower."

"How long have you been assigned here, Gunny?"

"Almost eighteen months. I roll out in six more."

"Have you been here longer than the ambassador?"

"Sure have, sir. She's been here only a couple of months."

"How often has she gone to the foreign minister's office in that time?"

"Just once, sir. When she presented her credentials."

"How many times has she been invited?"

"This is the first time." The sergeant narrowed his eyes. "Do you think something's up?"

"I'm not sure, but standard protocol between diplomats is that invitations are on paper and hand-delivered. Never telephone calls, especially in the Middle East."

"Do we advise against the meeting?"

"No, I could be wrong. But let's take some extra precautions just in case. Can you pull the list of all incoming and outgoing embassy calls and emails from the past seventy-two hours?"

"I'll have it to you within the hour."

Gunny was as good as his word. An hour later Golzari stroked his goatee as he read down the list, cross-referencing all incoming and outgoing embassy calls against a list of the names and U.S. residences of the remaining embassy personnel. The list confirmed that the embassy did indeed receive a call from the foreign minister's office and that the number matched the known office number. That ruled out the likelihood that the invitation had been issued from a different location, but it didn't exclude the possibility that someone within the Foreign Ministry was collaborating with a terrorist group. Golzari leaned back in the old creaking chair that the General Services Office hadn't replaced since the 1960s.

The email list revealed a few anomalies. Two emails from the embassy to the White House in as many days filed at the same time as emails to Secretary of State Helen Forth. Both came from Ambassador Sumner. Why would Sumner copy the White House? Only State should determine if an issue merited informing the White House, and then it would come directly from the secretary of state's office, not the ambassador. Golzari could have asked the information technology office for the content of the emails, but he didn't see the need for it just now. He wasn't supposed to be investigating anything other than Abdi Mohammed Asha, and even if he did have authorization to review other emails, wasting time to do so meant that much less time to find Asha.

He walked down to the senior Marine's office. "I'd be happy to join you tomorrow morning, Gunny, but I'd like to try something different than you've planned."

"What do you have in mind?"

Suleiman, Gulf of Aden, 0625 (GMT)

While his crew ate their meal on the fantail, Faisal checked his watch and then tapped a cigarette from the pack and lit it, his second of the day. He propped his bare foot on the starboard rail as he inhaled and looked down at the choppy sea.

"How many times have you checked your watch, Faisal?" asked his helmsman, Saddiq.

"I must call Ahmed al-Ghaydah at a specified time," Faisal responded.

Saddiq looked at him knowingly. "You don't like him."

"Why should I? He's incompetent. He got the job because of his name, not his ability. His family is still powerful, but not as powerful as when the Soviets supported their region."

"It is true that Ahmed has no interest in business," Saddiq agreed. "Only for obsolete Russian weapons that he barely knows how to shoot and Ukrainian whores he knows even less about how to handle."

Faisal ignored the off-color joke while admitting to himself that it was almost certainly true. "He is useful to us. That is all that matters. Let him complain that the job is beneath him. I care only that he does it properly. He won't be there long anyway."

"Ah, but does he do it properly?" Saddiq returned. "I hear what the cargo captains in the Gulf are saying. They all complain about him too. He ignores them and doesn't respond to their complaints."

"He only ignores the ones he is supposed to ignore," Faisal said. "All that matters is that he helps those I tell him to help—the ones transporting hashish and khat. At least he manages to give me a daily report on ship movements."

"Why is it so important that you speak with Ahmed now, Faisal?" Saddiq asked as Faisal checked his watch yet again.

"Hu called me yesterday to say that there is a new American military adviser in Sana'a. He is out on a boat today. He will be an easy target." He tossed his still-burning cigarette into the water, switched on the satellite phone, and impatiently pecked at the numbers.

Ahmed was slow to answer. Finally, "Yes?"

"Ahmed? It's me."

"Yes?"

Damn that idiot, Faisal thought. *His speech is too slow. He probably has another wad of khat in his stupid mouth.* "Give me the information, Ahmed."

"The ships are leaving now for the Socotran platforms."

"How many?"

"Two. One offshore supply vessel. Name is, uh, name is, ah, *Endurance*. One freighter. *Mukalla Ismael*. Five thousand tons. They will arrive in twenty-four hours. They are being escorted by the Highland Maritime Defense ship *Kirkwall*."

"The one without a helicopter. Have the security ship sunk."

"What? Why does this matter? What has changed? It will cost a lot of money to make such arrangements so quickly," Ahmed whined.

"It matters because I say it matters." Faisal turned off the phone. "Stupid fool," he muttered as he walked over to one of the AK-47s and inspected it, making sure it was clean and loaded. "Come, have something to eat," Saddiq said, hoping to calm his captain's anger.

"Tell me, Saddiq, have you heard from your cousin in England?" Faisal demanded, still holding the AK-47.

"No, Faisal."

"Then Stark is not dead."

"I fear not. I would have heard by now. I am sorry, Faisal."

Faisal raised the weapon and pointed it at Saddiq's chest. "You will go back to the *Katya P.* and wait for my orders there. Do you understand?"

Saddiq stepped back and nodded in fearful compliance.

M/V *Kirkwall*, Gulf of Aden, 0707 (GMT)

Connor was back in the pilothouse in time to watch Jaime Johnson brief the two helmsmen, who would each stand four-hour watches.

"The two supply boats will track to us. *Endurance* has been directed to be on station eight hundred yards to our port bow, and *Mukalla Ismael* will be on station eight hundred yards to our starboard bow. This will be a very tight formation, so make sure you keep a close eye on the radar as well as using the Mark I Mod I Eyeball."

The helmsmen grinned at the Navy-ized term for a simple sensory organ. Most of the *Kirkwall*'s crew were former Navy or Coast Guarders who appreciated the old joke. The operators—the shooters—however, were a mix of former special forces both American and foreign, with a few tough Nepalese Gurkhas thrown into the mix.

"We will remain on heading one-zero-eight at one-five knots for approximately twenty hours until we hit the only waypoint here"—they watched over the captain's shoulder as she pointed on the map to a spot just east of Socotra Island—"at 12° 34' 11" N and 54° 38' 37" E. At that waypoint we will then turn on a heading of two-one-nine for two hours until we reach the primary oil platform. Let's go."

Stark leaned against the aft bulkhead in the pilothouse. The sea was calm, and only minimal haze obscured the horizon. Absent any breeze he smelled the diesel fuel that hung heavily in the air. The pilothouse was largely silent except for the occasional commercial radio traffic.

"Over here, Commander," Jaime said quietly. "What do you see on the radar?" In calm seas, a person didn't have to speak loudly to be heard.

Stark concentrated on the green luminescent screen as the radial arm swung around the circle clockwise in synchrony with the navigational radar above the pilothouse, painting a new picture of the environment within their line of sight every few seconds. At sea level, line of sight was about three miles; after that the earth's curvature prevented a person—or radar—from seeing farther. But the ship's radar was mounted high enough to give them a forty-mile picture. Navigational data such as their ship's longitude and latitude appeared at the edge of the screen.

The radar showed two long lines of blips. Connor fine-tuned the resolution. "Hell, there must be more than twenty ships there. Convoy?"

"Give the man a cigar. They started running them a few months ago with some escort ships. In a minute you should see something else. Get a pair of binoculars out of that pocket there," Jaime suggested.

"Ready, Captain."

"Hold it. Hold it," she said scanning the horizon. "There they are: twenty degrees off our starboard bow, just to the left of the *Ismael.*

Stark saw them immediately. Two warships. They were too distant for him to determine their markings, but he had never seen anything like them. "Those are not U.S. destroyers."

"What you're seeing are two of China's latest and greatest destroyers."

"Chinese? The last I knew they were buying old Soviet *Sovremenny*-class ships. When did they start building their own? And are they really escorting convoys here?"

"It's a strange new world when the USA isn't the protector anymore. We're stretched too thin, and the Chinese are exploiting it. The Indians are desperate to catch up," Jaime said, returning her attention to her notepad.

"When a maritime power no longer has fleets of commercial ships or a naval force to protect the few it does have, it is no longer a maritime power," he lamented.

"It's just a matter of time, Connor. The Navy you and I grew up with is starting to fade away. There's a new kid on the block."

"China's no kid. Hell, Jaime, what are those idiots in Washington thinking?"

"That's a lot higher than my pay grade," she said. "But at least Highland Maritime is here to help out. Helm, you've got it from here. We should be clear for the next couple of hours while we pass aft of the convoy. I'm going to email my kids and then take a swing around the ship to see how everyone's doing."

The three ships—*Kirkwall* and the two ships it guarded like a mother bear protecting her cubs—moved along at a steady fifteen knots, barely sufficient speed to evade the pirates who were sure to be waiting.

When dusk approached ten hours later, Jaime had been back in the pilot-house for hours, double-checking equipment, keeping her eye on the radar, and paying particular attention to any commercial traffic that might interfere with the job. All of her attention was drawn suddenly to one blip on the radar—judging from its size and speed, a small boat with a single engine. The radar had difficulty picking up small craft at longer ranges, particularly between wave crests. Simultaneously a watch-stander shouted a warning. Jaime picked up the ship-to-ship mike.

"*Endurance, Endurance*, this is *Kirkwall*. There is a small boat approaching you at high speed from three-four-zero degrees of our position, approximately five nautical miles." She then grabbed the ship-wide mike: "All hands to stations. One high-speed craft approaching CBDR," she said loudly, emphasizing those four letters and the danger they spelled. CBDR—Constant Bearing, Decreasing Range—meant an eventual collision if neither of the two factors changed.

"Wait a minute. That boat's on a CBDR with us, not with one of the supply ships," Stark noticed from the radar.

Jaime Johnson had just come to the same conclusion when the ship-to-ship blared out.

"*Kirkwall, Kirkwall.* This is *Endurance.* We see the small craft now. It is going to pass astern of us."

That confirmed it. The private security boat was the target, not the unarmed supply ships.

Stark noted another change on the radar screen. "Captain, two more approaching craft, both CBDR. Wait, one is breaking off going afore *Endurance.*

Dammit, there's another one coming from the same direction. Jaime, they're all targeting us."

"All hands, Alpha fire team prepare for direct attack from the port side. Bravo fire team to the bow," the *Kirkwall*'s captain ordered.

On the ship all around him Stark heard the methodical movements of professional soldiers preparing for battle. He also heard something else and stepped outside the pilothouse to check—the distinct sound of a helicopter.

The captain returned to the ship-to-ship comms: "Unidentified craft approaching three peacefully transiting ships. You are on a collision course with us. Veer off or we will defend ourselves. Oh, screw them," she said as she set the mike back into its cradle.

The craft were converging on the *Kirkwall*. The first one, only ten meters long and now less than one thousand yards away, was heading directly toward them.

"Alpha fire team, weapons free. I repeat, weapons free." The port side of the boat erupted with multiple flashes of gunfire trained on the incoming craft. Stark took his binoculars and focused on the craft, and then tried to shout a warning. "Captain, the . . ."

The boat exploded four hundred yards away with more force than a fuel tank alone could have generated.

"Jaime, that boat was unmanned," Stark called to her, "and probably loaded with explosives."

"What? Helm, all engines ahead full, right full rudder. Come to course zero nine zero." The helmsman dutifully repeated the command as he carried it out.

Bravo team was now firing from the bow.

"Get a weapon, Connor, and help Bravo team." Stark grabbed one of the guns from the rack in the pilothouse and had just leapt down the starboard ladder when the small boat shook from above. Had he not had one hand on the railing, the explosion would have blown him overboard. He raced back to the bridge to find smoke, shattered glass, and open air. Half of the port bulkhead and hatch had been shorn away.

"Jaime!" The captain lay facedown on the deck. He turned her over and cradled her in his arms, brushing away the hair and blood on her face. One of her arms fell limply, bonelessly back to the deck. He checked for signs of life; she still had a pulse. He didn't have to check the helmsman's pulse—his brain matter was all over the deck and a piece of jagged metal protruded from his chest. Connor gently laid Jaime down and picked up his weapon in time to see two RPGs on one of the manned boats pointing toward the *Kirkwall*'s stern. They attackers fired just before Alpha team's sharpshooting Gurkhas gunned them down. The Gurkhas were themselves quickly felled by the grenades, their limbs torn away by the blasts as their torsos were strewn about the deck or blown overboard.

Stark picked up the mike, relieved to find that the radio still worked, and issued a mayday with the ship's coordinates, hoping someone else was out there to hear it besides the pirates.

The second small boat made its run and a grenade arced toward the stern. Stark swore and braced himself for the impact.

USS *Bennington*, North of Socotra, 1732 (GMT)

"*Request immediate assistance . . .*"

The OOD called the captain and explained what the bridge had just heard. "Sir, Batwing 58 is up and to the east with thirty minutes of fuel. I spoke with the tactical action officer and Air Boss, and I recommend closing the datum at flank speed. The winds are favorable to recover Five-Eight while we close, refuel her, and buster"—the brevity codeword for 'proceed at maximum speed'—"her up to the area of the distress call . . . yes, sir, but best speed should be . . . sir, best speed is . . . aye, sir." The officer of the deck gently replaced the phone, but he was clearly livid. Bobby knew the conversation hadn't gone well.

"Conn, come around, course two-seven-zero. Stand by for flight quarters." The OOD stared out the window, his fists clenched behind him and jaw muscles jumping.

"Helm, right standard rudder, come to course two-seven-zero. Speed, OOD?"

"Trail shaft." The OOD left the bridge for the port bridge wing and slammed his fist down on the railing. Bobby followed him out.

"OOD, that'll take twice as much time for us to get there."

"I know that, Bobby. Hell, we probably couldn't get there in time anyway. But instead of two hours we'll be there in four. Maybe the Lost Boys can do something from the air."

Northwest of Socotra, Gulf of Aden, 1755 (GMT)

The shock of the explosion briefly knocked Connor unconscious. The ship was listing badly when he awoke.

"She's sinking," he heard a distant voice yell out.

Dragging himself to the bridge wing, Stark saw water flooding over the *Kirkwall's* transom. Daylight was fading fast to the west, but the silhouettes of the two supply ships heading southwest to Somalia were still visible. They had been taken.

He took stock of the situation, frantically considering options. Alpha team was gone, dead to a man. A few crewmen from Bravo team had been blown overboard, but several remained. Stark reentered the pilothouse and checked the radio, hoping to get out one last mayday; the cordless mike led to a shattered box. He picked up two life preservers and hoisted Jaime over one shoulder.

Again he heard a helicopter, but it was moving away. As the sound of the rotors faded he heard shouts in the water. He looked toward the lifeboats, still in their davits, in time to see the funnel collapse on top of them.

He shouted as loudly as he could: "Kirkwalls! This is Connor Stark. I have the captain with me. I'm on the port side midships. Follow my voice." The last vestige of daylight faded from lavender to black. The stars shone brilliantly in the cloudless, moonless sky, their reflections in the water the only light.

"Here!" he shouted again. "Follow my voice." He was encouraged to hear multiple splashes coming around the bow. The calm water amplified sounds in the still air. He heard water lapping against the aft topside compartment and even closer over the side. There was no time to work the lifeboats loose. Securing life preservers on himself and Jaime, he slipped her over the side and then lowered himself down. He pulled her limp body close with one arm and kicked away from the sinking ship before it could drag them under with it.

His body remembered his years of swimming laps in Olympic-sized pools training for Seoul, but his heavy, wet coveralls and steel-toed boots made maneuvering difficult. He moved doggedly on, dragging Jaime, keeping her face above the water, farther and farther away from the boat.

Every few strokes he yelled out, "Kirkwalls, follow my voice!" He swallowed water and gasped for air. He felt the sea trying to pull Jaime away from him, but he never let go of her. The survivors, almost all younger than he, were finally approaching. Four crewmen made it to him before, in the otherwise silent sea, they heard the *Kirkwall* slip beneath the water.

"Everyone, stay close." Only then did Connor Stark realize how cold nighttime water could be even in the Gulf of Aden. He experienced his first shiver and rubbed Jaime's unbroken arm, hoping to warm her.

His water survival training kicked in, and he directed the crew to huddle to limit the loss of body heat. They kept their injured captain in the middle of the pack to reduce the shock sure to follow her injuries. The crew took turns speaking to keep their minds alert and prevent the delirium and numbness that would eventually overcome all of them if they were not rescued.

"Stay close," he told them above the silent waters. "We're all going to make it. Do you hear that Jaime? All of us."

Time passed and the stars wheeled above them. Stark treaded water with Jaime and the four other survivors, remembering every exercise he'd used in those training pools—trying them all. Jaime's pulse was weakening. A few times she appeared to wake only to fall back into unconsciousness.

Stark's extremities started to feel the cold water's effects. The muscles in his fingers and toes contracted. The others were also experiencing the first signs of hypothermia. Their feet and hands cramped up and stiffened, then their joints. Two of the Kirkwalls began to garble their words.

Suleiman, Gulf of Aden, 1820 (GMT)

Faisal shivered slightly in the cool night air as he placed the call to Mukalla.

"It is done," al-Ghaydah said.

"Give me the report from my ships," Faisal said harshly.

"It was very costly. They were very well armed."

"What else?"

"We lost four boats."

"Yes, yes. That was expected. What of the security ship carrying the military adviser?"

"It was their smaller ship. One of our new unmanned boats got through and damaged it, and our RPGs killed most of the crew. Any that survived surely died when the ship sank. They are all dead, Faisal, just as you ordered."

"You did well, Ahmed. Did the ship call for help before sinking?"

"One distress call went out, but there was no one to respond. The Chinese ships were too far away with their convoy. The only other warship was the U.S. Navy one—the one that boarded the *Suleiman* and then ran away."

Faisal al-Yemeni laughed.

Northwest of Socotra, Gulf of Aden, 1940 (GMT)

Stark heard a helicopter in the distance, but it wasn't the small helicopter he had heard during the attack. This one made the distinct thumping sound of a U.S. military helicopter—a Seahawk. The only surface ship he knew to be operating in the area was the *Bennington*, and every cruiser had Seahawks. The surviving crewmembers, hopeful again, used their waterproof flashlights to signal.

The Seahawk drew nearer. If the survivors in the water were lucky, the helicopter would have a harness to haul them up, but with three crewmembers already aboard, the craft would have space for only a couple of extra bodies. Even that would depend on how much fuel was available. Every pound mattered. How far had the Seahawk already flown? How close was the *Bennington*?

The helicopter's wash created concentric waves around the six survivors as its searchlight picked them out of the darkness. All Connor could see were the craft's green and red running lights and the massive searchlight.

He could feel Jaime's body constricting, succumbing to the cold and shock. "C'mon, Jaime, stay with us. Please. You have to try."

"My babies, my crew," she whispered.

"You're going home, Jaime. Just hold on."

USS *Bennington*, Gulf of Aden, 1942 (GMT)

"*Bennington*, Batwing Five-Seven, over," the co-pilot's voice crackled in the Combat Information Center over HAWKLINK, the secure data link from the helicopter to the ship.

"Go ahead, Five-Seven."

"Six survivors found at datum, all in life vests; no life raft. One survivor appears to be unconscious. My intentions are to lower the rescue swimmer, pick up as many survivors as possible, and return to mom to drop them off and refuel before going back for the rest.

"Copy all, Five-Seven. Six survivors, no life raft. We are passing this information and your intentions to bridge and CO."

Bobby stood close to the OOD as they listened to the exchange. He felt a bit breathless from the tension and excitement. Both men were about to be relieved by the next watch, but neither wanted to leave. With the OOD's permission, Bobby called down to the officers' quarters and told them what was going on. The captain, XO, Air Boss, and OPS all arrived on the bridge within a minute. The OOD briefed them on the situation.

OPS noticed the ship's speed on the indicator. "Helm, confirm our speed." The young sailor complied. OPS quickly went to the chart table between the chief quartermaster and a third-class boatswain. With seemingly blinding speed, he calculated the time to reach the survivors. "Captain, with OOD and NAV's concurrence, I recommend we proceed on course two-six-zero at *flank* speed, recover Five-Seven, have her drop off survivors, refuel her, and relaunch her toward the datum. We will continue closing the position at flank. We should also ready the RHIBs for launch in case we need to pick up the remaining survivors once we arrive at datum." OPS spoke as quickly as he had made the calculations.

Bobby watched the captain's face in the ambient light; he seemed confused by the rapid-fire information directed at him.

"We'll be burning a lot of fuel, and we don't know when we'll rendezvous with an oiler," he said doubtfully.

"Sir," the XO interjected, "this situation is grave. There are six individuals in the water; one is unconscious. Water temperature is," she checked the console, "sixty-two degrees. They've got a couple of hours at best. We need to get there now!"

The CO frowned at his executive officer. "Who are these people anyway, XO? Why are they out there?"

"*Kirkwall*, sir. She's a U.S.-owned ship that protects private U.S. assets."

"A mercenary ship protecting American assets? The U.S. Navy does the protecting out here, missy. Are we clear on that?"

The XO overlooked the "missy" for the moment. "Sir! That's not the issue. Those are lives. We don't have a choice. We *have* to help!" She tried to think of some way to push him without angering him. "The U.S. Navy *always* answers the call, sir. And we need to act now."

Air Boss weighed in as well, trying to appeal to whatever logic the CO might listen to: "Captain, I concur with OPS' plan. At flank speed the ship would arrive in two hours. Given the time/distance problem, the helo should be able to rescue several survivors and return to the ship twice prior to *Bennington*'s arrival on-scene."

Everyone on the bridge held their collective breaths while the captain paused to absorb the multiple streams of recommendations.

The XO cautiously added an extra nudge. "Captain, recommend we go with Air Boss' idea and upon rescue proceed to Djibouti for transfer of the personnel and refueling."

That seemed to reach the captain. "Hmm, refuel at Djibouti. I've never been to Djibouti."

Bobby fumed silently while the captain dithered. He could feel his face flushing with the anger that threatened to explode from his mouth.

After a full minute the captain finally responded. "Okay. OOD, make course two-six-zero, flank speed. Contact Batwing 57 and advise them of our intentions."

Datum, 1948 (GMT)

The helicopter crew kept the survivors in sight through the FLIR and night vision goggles as they prepared to conduct the rescue operation. When the pilots, hoist operator, and rescue swimmer were ready, Batwing 57 passed above the survivors and turned downwind to a point twelve hundred yards in front of them. The co-pilot pressed the automatic approach button on the Automatic Flight Control System (AFCS) control panel and the aircraft commenced a computer-assisted "automatic" approach that resulted in a gyro-stabilized hover, the AFCS computer keeping the helicopter over a fixed geographic position eighty feet above the survivors. A crewmember started the winch that lowered the rescue swimmer into the water.

Fighting the waves and sea spray kicked up by the Seahawk's wash, Stark grabbed the wetsuit-covered rescue swimmer's forearm and placed it on Jaime Johnson's limp body. The rescue swimmer nodded rapidly. He quickly hooked Jaime to his Tri-SAR harness and then spoke into the radio at his right shoulder. The hoist cable went taut, and the rescue swimmer and Jaime Johnson rose out of the water and into the night sky. In another ten minutes the rescue swimmer was back in the water hooking himself to the next survivor. Each time the swimmer was lowered, Stark passed the harness to another Kirkwall. As the swimmer hooked himself to the last of the Kirkwalls, he shouted to Stark that Batwing 57 was at capacity and would have to return to the ship. Stark nodded his understanding.

With all the survivors save one safely aboard and the cabin secure for flight, the pilot depressed the automatic depart button and Batwing 57 began the 120-knot arc back toward the rapidly closing *Bennington*. As the sound of the Seahawk's giant rotor died away, Stark wondered whether the ship would arrive in time. For the first time he doubted his survival.

Stark thought he was hallucinating when the helicopter returned. He lacked the strength to help the rescue swimmer hook him into the harness or even to hold up his head. As he rose into the air his eyes remained on the water below. An iridescent rainbow glittered in the helicopter's spotlights, the remains of fuel leaked by the *Kirkwall*. The lights revealed no other sign of the ship and those who had given their lives on it. Someone from the helicopter was shouting down at him, but the numbness had finally won. The adrenaline needed to save Jaime and lead the others was gone. He hung limply in the sling, oblivious to the sounds above him as he used his remaining energy to keep his eyes on the watery grave.

Stark had been on a cruiser only once before—when he was a young ROTC student on a summer midshipman cruise. The Aegis-equipped cruisers were still new then, with only a few in the fleet. Now they were practically obsolete. With a corpsman on either side supporting him, he joined the rest of the Kirkwalls in sickbay, where a senior corpsman was attending to Jaime Johnson.

"Is she alive?" Stark croaked. He felt the ship begin to shudder, the unmistakable feel of a steel hull accelerating through the water. The bright lights of sickbay faded into black before he heard the answer.

DAY 9

USS *Bennington*, Gulf of Aden, 0330 (GMT)

"Commander? Commander Stark?" He woke to see a woman with red hair hovering over him. At first he thought it was Maggie. But she didn't wear a naval uniform. Did she?

"Sir, I'm Lieutenant Commander Marla Lorenski, the executive officer."

Stark fought his drowsiness and pulled himself up to a sitting position. "Thank-you for coming, XO."

"Our pleasure, sir. It's zero-six-thirty. I realize you haven't had much rest, but the chief here says it would be okay to ask a few questions. Actually, they're Fifth Fleet's questions."

"Something for the morning brief, huh?" Stark took in the two other people crammed into his sickbay cabin—a corpsman and a specialist.

"Our intelligence specialist here will ask the questions," the XO said. "It shouldn't take long. After that we can go to the wardroom and get something in your system."

"The *Kirkwall*'s crew, the captain?" Stark turned toward the others.

"Just the six of you, Commander," responded the senior chief corpsman. "No other survivors or bodies that we found. The captain is one tough lady, sir."

Stark felt as if a weight had lifted from his shoulders. "Is she awake? Can I see her?"

"No, sir, she won't be talking for a while. The doc said she had the worst of it and needs a lot more attention than he can give her. Broken arm, shock, cracked ribs, head injuries. It was a very near thing with her being in the water so long. We're going to medevac her to a French military hospital in Djibouti as soon as our helo is within range.

Stark nodded his thanks and turned to the lieutenant commander. "XO, I need to get back to Sana'a."

"I'll talk with Air Boss and the CO to see if we can accommodate. Now I'm going to leave you in the specialist's hands for a debriefing."

Still dazed, and suddenly overwhelmed with hunger, Stark struggled to recount every detail he remembered from the attack—the types of boats, the number involved, and especially the helicopter he had heard before the first blast shook the *Kirkwall.*

When he finally limped into the wardroom, the senior officers and a few junior ones were just finishing breakfast. He stood dutifully at the end of the table and recited the traditional request.

"Commander Connor Stark. May I join you, Captain?"

"Please do," the captain nodded. Only once in Connor's own career had he seen the senior officer present at the table reject the request. He was an ensign in an old *Perry*-class frigate. The skipper had just found out that his wife had slept with his chief engineer. The captain maintained a cool professionalism elsewhere on the ship, but he refused to allow the CHENG to eat at the same time as he did.

"Thank you, sir," Stark replied as he took an open seat opposite the captain. He nodded at the other officers present at the table. A very young-looking ensign gave him a shy smile.

One of the mess cranks asked Stark his preference for breakfast.

He didn't hesitate. "Coffee first and then everything else you have."

The captain cleared his throat and assumed a severe expression. "What were you doing out there, Commander?"

"I'm the new defense attaché in Sana'a, sir."

"Defense attaché?" the captain asked. He looked confused. "I was told you were on a mercenary ship."

"Sir," Stark replied, "the *Kirkwall* is—was—a privately owned armed escort vessel employed by Highland Maritime Defense to provide security to the oil platforms and supply vessels operating near Socotra. It's part of my job to understand all activity in Yemeni waters related to U.S. interests. I was on my way to visit Maddox International's new oil platforms."

"There's nothing out there that hasn't been here for two thousand years," the captain said dismissively. "You should have stayed at the embassy. I haven't been to Yemen. Is it worth a port call? Perhaps the *Bennington* should visit."

Stark almost said that the murder of twelve, and very nearly eighteen, people ought to qualify as something new when he realized that the captain had lost interest and had returned his attention to his breakfast. He was astonished that a man so vacuous commanded a U.S. Navy cruiser. "I appreciate the ship picking us up, sir," he said instead. "Glad you were nearby."

The captain glanced up but didn't reply.

Stark spoke again, hoping to get some idea why the Navy had virtually abandoned the waters of the Gulf. "We sure could use some more ships out here to keep things settled."

"Why? The Navy has more important things to deal with elsewhere." The captain took a piece of toast off the small rack and nibbled on it like a rabbit.

Bobby Fisk had given up all thought of his own breakfast and was paying rapt attention to the exchange.

"But, sir," Stark continued, "this would be a perfect time for us to have a lot of small boys out here to cover more territory. I used to command a PC and . . ."

The captain interrupted him without pausing to swallow his toast. "I don't see the need, Commander. Small boats only waste vital resources. CHENG, how are we doing on fuel? Are we going to make it to Djibouti?"

Bobby waited hopefully for Stark to continue, but the visiting commander gave up just like everyone else did.

Stark downed the rest of his coffee, pushed back his chair, and stood. "Excuse me, Captain," indicating he wished to leave. The captain waved him away.

Stark didn't envy the XO or crew of this ship. Until he met the CO, the ship's crew had seemed first-rate. But he knew that a bad captain could demoralize even a first-rate wardroom and crew. The small man seated at the middle of the long wardroom table was clearly such a captain.

Stark looked at the XO and nodded slightly toward the door, signifying that he wanted to talk outside. He left the wardroom to the sound of the chief engineer's report on the significant loss of fuel sustained during the previous night's high-speed operation. The other officers who had been seated at the table, including the XO and the cigar cabal, rose and followed him out.

"Commander," the XO said quietly in the passageway, "I spoke to the captain. No go about your flight."

"XO, I trust you to look after the *Kirkwall*'s captain and crew. Now I need to get to Sana'a and report on this."

"Air Boss, are you okay to fly up there?" the XO asked.

"Not a problem. Once we're further west, it's a straight shot up."

"OPS, do you think we can help the commander here?"

The operations officer sighed. "I guess so, but the well's starting to dry up."

Stark watched this byplay, not certain what was going on but well aware that a smart crew could almost always find a way to get things done.

The XO smiled. "It's a plan."

"XO, are you and the others okay on this ship? Does Fifth Fleet know about the situation here?" Stark asked, expecting a vague response that would not be seen as potentially mutinous.

To his surprise, the XO gave him a forthright answer. "Commander, what you've just experienced is only a taste."

"I don't have many strings to pull, XO, but these are dangerous waters. If there's anything I can do to help, I'll do it. We were armed and well trained, and they hit us hard. I can't imagine they'd target a cruiser, but those unmanned skiffs and the helicopter have taken things to a whole new level. You didn't see anything in the air?"

"Our SPY-1 radar has been down for months—no spare parts to any ship except those in high-priority areas."

"Sounds like someone's forgotten about this ship, XO."

"Commander, it's why one of our nicknames is the 'island of misfit toys.'"

"I haven't seen any misfits." *Except for one* he added to himself instead of breaching protocol. "Let's keep in contact and see how we can help each other."

"Much appreciated, sir. As soon as we get authorization from Fifth Fleet, we'll get you in the air."

Sana'a, 0330 (GMT)

Two hours before Ambassador Sumner was scheduled to leave the embassy compound, Golzari drove again along her intended route looking for anything that seemed unusual or out of place. It was a game he and his father had played when he was a child, after they fled Iran. The Ayatollah's minions might well pursue the shah's former general and his family even in a foreign country, so Damien Golzari had learned the game. He had continued to play it in all the years since, honing his skills while walking down city streets as a beat cop, in grocery lines, and in airport lounges like the one where he had first spotted Connor Stark. The game had saved his life several times in his work as a

Diplomatic Security Service agent—most recently in London when the scent of cologne had alerted him to imminent danger. It had long since stopped being a game.

Two of his weapons were out and at hand on the front passenger seat. The first was his Sig 228 5.56-mm pistol, standard State Department issue. He would be issued a new pistol when State changed over to the 229, which was a little beefier than the 228 but still used NATO-compatible ammunition.

His second weapon was an M4, a carbine variant of the military's M16 with a shorter 14.5-inch barrel and collapsible stock. He had strapped two extra magazines of M4 ammo to the gun, and his go-bag with eight more magazines on a bandolier was within reach on the floor. That should be more than sufficient to get him through a firefight.

He noted some changes on his final pass. Three men standing next to a parked moving van on a dusty street corner caught his eye. They appeared to be taking a cigarette break. One of the three did not look Yemeni. He was taller and thinner and much darker skinned than the two Yemenis. Golzari didn't slow down. After two more blocks he turned down a side street and circled around to park just a block away from the van on the opposite side of the main thoroughfare.

The three men were standing casually, laughing as they smoked. Golzari took a hard look at the one who was not a Yemeni. He appeared to be East African. When he turned so that Golzari could see his face, Golzari went rigid; it was Khalid—or, as he now suspected, Abdi Mohammed Asha. The two Yemeni men climbed into the van's driver and passenger seats while Khalid continued to smoke and talk with them through the open driver's window. Periodically he looked casually down the street in the direction from which the ambassador's car would be coming. He never looked in Golzari's direction.

Golzari had a fleeting doubt. Was he sure about this? Or was the van just a moving van and the men just friends chatting during a work break? *Damn that Stark*, he thought. The little incident with the private security guards had undermined his confidence. He had to decide. Gunny and his Marines would be leaving the embassy compound with the ambassador in just a few minutes.

"Bloody hell," he muttered, holstering his pistol and covering his M4 with his go-bag. He got out of the rental vehicle and locked the doors. In the window's reflection he saw Khalid shake the driver's hand and wave to the passenger. Golzari turned and started walking quickly toward the van. Khalid was crossing over to Golzari's side of the street, moving nonchalantly toward a café that hadn't yet opened. Suddenly he turned abruptly right toward the street. Even when he could see nothing but the man's back Golzari had no doubt that this was the same man he had met in Maine and tangled with in London. He spoke quietly into the microphone: "Code Black. I repeat, Code Black," signaling the ambassador's convoy to take an alternate route immediately and return to the relative safety of the compound.

Less than twenty seconds later he saw the Somali put a cell phone to his ear, listen for a moment, then start back across the street, waving at the van.

Thirty yards away now, Golzari reached for his Sig. Taking a chance, he said out loud: "Abdi Mohammed."

Asha froze and looked back at Golzari, confused that anyone but the terrorists would know his name. When he saw the familiar face, he moved forward a step to attack, then saw the Sig in Golzari's hand. Lacking a comparable weapon, he turned and ran down the street in the opposite direction.

"*Kaf* (Stop)!" Golzari yelled in Arabic. As Asha continued away from him, Golzari heard the moving van's engine rev up as the vehicle pulled away from the curb. Golzari continued to chase Asha even as he knew that he couldn't outrun the van behind him. He pivoted toward the vehicle, which was now less than a block away and headed straight for him.

Light from the sun at Golzari's back reflected off the van's aluminum mirror protectors, and the driver held up one arm to shade his eyes from the glare. The passenger was jogging the driver's other arm and screaming at him, further distracting him. Pedestrians on both sides of the street darted back into the recesses of storefronts, giving Golzari more freedom of movement and minimizing the possibility of collateral damage. He planted his feet firmly as he aimed his Sig at the driver, ignoring the passenger, who was now leaning out the window with a weapon.

The van closed the distance. The driver was now clearly centered in Golzari's sights. He fired three quick rounds. At thirty feet, he couldn't miss. Two shots hit the driver in his chest; the third exploded in his throat. The van continued advancing, veering slightly away from Golzari without a driver to steer it, and missed him by a few feet. The passenger, who had been unable to get off a shot with his AK-47, was trying to turn around in his seat to aim again, but Golzari had two clear shots at him once the van had passed. The other Yemeni slumped forward to the floor as the van continued its momentum, stopping only when it slammed into a storefront and exploded. The force of the blast lifted Golzari into the air.

His father's bodyguards would have been proud of him. Two terrorists dead with a total of five shots. As he brushed dust and debris off his jacket—*another suit ruined, damn it*—Golzari reflected that it was better to kill terrorists than to take them into custody and risk their acquittal in a long, drawn-out trial. Better all around that they die in their final battle. Fewer loose ends. Less paperwork.

Golzari spun around searching for a sight of the Somali man he now knew to be Abdi Mohammed Asha, but he was long gone.

U.S. Embassy, Sana'a, 0642 (GMT)

C. J. Sumner brought a hand towel with her when she emerged from her private bathroom. Golzari had seen the signs before. The hair around her face was still wet from the cold water she had splashed on it. The hand holding her towel was shaking, and she wobbled slightly in her high heels. She had removed her suit jacket, and deep circles of perspiration stained the armpits of her yellow silk blouse. She intentionally avoided the window, even though its frames and panes were specially reinforced to stop bullets. She sat down and rolled her chair close to her desk, her eyes darting toward the window. Clearly she didn't feel safe even in her own office in the embassy compound.

She took a deep breath. "Special Agent Golzari, I want to express my gratitude for what you did this morning. You saved a lot of lives."

"Thank you, Madam Ambassador, but the important one got away."

She shuddered, then squared her shoulders. "I haven't given you a chance to tell me the details of your investigation and why it brought you here."

"It started when I was in the States investigating the death of Deputy Secretary of State Dunner's son. He apparently fell off a bridge in Antioch, Maine, and drowned. It's standard procedure that someone from Diplomatic Security be sent to investigate cases involving the families of personnel under our protection."

"How is the death of a student in Maine related to Yemen?"

"The boy was a khat user. A Somali refugee known in Antioch's refugee community as Khalid was apparently his provider. The evidence indicates that the most recent shipment of khat—which Johnny Dunner had picked up in Boston the day he died—had come in on a Yemeni ship that ported in Southampton, England, en route. I met Khalid during the investigation in Antioch because he claimed to represent the refugee community. I didn't know at the time, of course, that his real name is Abdi Mohammed Asha. Khalid apparently killed an Antioch police officer who was investigating young Dunner's death, and afterward fled the country. By that time I was in London talking to a colleague in hope of getting more information on the Yemen connection. Khalid turned up there as well. He attacked and permanently maimed an MI5 officer. So I came to Yemen trying to follow the connection."

"Go on," Sumner said, her shakiness gone.

"This morning I saw Khalid—Abdi Mohammed Asha—speaking with two men standing next to a moving van parked on your expected route. It was a short step from there to deduce that the two men were terrorists and that the moving van was packed with explosives."

She leaned back and thought it out. "Why did you think someone who might have given khat to Dunner's son was involved in a terrorist attack against me in Yemen?" she asked Golzari.

"Terrorists worldwide have connections with the drug trade," he explained. "Drug money can buy a lot of high explosives. It's possible that Asha's appearance here is a coincidence, but I'm inclined to believe it isn't."

"Are you aware that Deputy Secretary Dunner has resigned?"

"Yes, ma'am, I saw the message. Was a reason given?"

"I was told it was because of his son's death. It's a huge loss for the embassy here. The deputy secretary saw that we were undermanned and was pushing to get us back up to full strength." She shook her head as if to clear it. "That's past, though. What do you plan to do next?"

"I have some leads, but I'm scheduled to go to Burkina Faso as the RSO." The distaste in his voice when he said that remote country's name was unmistakable.

She brought her hand to her chin and smiled. "Who did you piss off?"

Golzari smiled back in spite of himself. Perhaps this ambassador was different from the others he had met.

"Not a fan of Ouagadougou?" she asked.

"Of course I am, Madam Ambassador. It's a charming little town well known for its fine cuisine. And who could pass up the opportunity to represent the only law enforcement within five hundred miles in a nation of abject poverty poised to explode into violence?"

"Actually, Agent Golzari, there are some lovely French restaurants in Ouagadougou. You'd be surprised. I'll make a deal with you, though. I'm without a regional security officer at the moment. If you can pull double duty, I'll have you reassigned here until your investigation is complete."

"I'm not sure if I can do that, Madam Ambassador. I seem to have gone through my entire wardrobe, and there isn't a decent tailor in town."

C. J. smiled at the sarcasm. The Persian-born agent had a certain charm. "I'll see what we can do about that. Again, you might be surprised. I'll call your director this afternoon to inform him that you'll be staying here."

"That's very kind of you, ma'am. It might be best if you left out a few details, if you know what I mean."

"I do indeed, Special Agent Golzari. I'm fully aware that tact and discretion are undervalued commodities in D.C."

The ambassador's intercom buzzed. "Yes, Mindy," she said.

"Madam Ambassador, the White House has scheduled a video teleconference for 11:30." Both Golzari and Sumner made a quick calculation and came to the same conclusion: it was far too early in the Capitol for normal business.

"Do you mean 11:30 a.m. our time?"

"Yes, ma'am," came the disembodied answer.

"Who do they want to talk to?"

"Just you."

"Thank you." She released the intercom button. "Special Agent Golzari, I'll let you go about your duties."

"Yes, ma'am. I'll go and find that tailor."

C. J. was already preparing for the VTC by the time Golzari closed the door behind him. She turned to her computer and checked news sites for anything that might be related to Yemen or the surrounding countries. Nothing. The White House situation room must have heard about the planned attempt on her life. That had to be it.

She donned her suit jacket and looked cool and composed when Green's unattractive image appeared on the screen. "Eliot. A little early in D.C., isn't it?"

"We heard about the attempted attack. How are you?"

"Fine. Everything is under control. We have good people here. A visiting DSS agent broke up the attack and has provided a full account to the Yemeni authorities."

"Right. Make sure you tell Helen. She's worried. You're okay, though?"

The solicitousness surprised her. She had never known Eliot Green to be a warm and caring person. Quite the opposite, in fact; he had a reputation for ruthlessness in his pursuit of results. Something was up.

"You're not calling to check on me, are you?"

"No. There was an incident off the coast," he said. She braced herself. "We only have a few details. Three ships departed the port of Mukalla yesterday morning and were attacked by pirates. One of the ships, a private security ship—the *Kirkwall*—was attacked and sunk. The other two ships were unharmed but have been taken into Somali waters."

C. J. struggled for control. She was not going to show her grief, especially not to Eliot, who had never liked Connor. A knot developed in her stomach. She had managed not to lose her breakfast after the attack; she felt no guarantee now. "Lives lost?" she managed to ask in an even tone, anticipating the worst news. If Green knew that Connor had been on the ship, he'd probably take delight in telling her.

"Yes. As far as we know there were eighteen individuals on board. Twelve are missing and considered dead. A U.S. Navy cruiser picked up the other six."

She let it sink in. Six survivors out of eighteen. There was a 66 percent chance that Connor was dead. She had forced the system to recall him. Had she killed Connor Stark?

"Things seem to be picking up in that part of the world. We're thinking about ordering an evacuation of the embassy."

"No," she said adamantly. "Please don't. I want to stay. We should stay. We can't back down."

"Embassies are evacuated on a regular basis when the threat level gets too high, C. J. Make no mistake, if that happens, I will advise the president that the time has come to pull you out."

Green was a pro at pretending to be concerned, but pretense was all it was. C. J. knew him too well to be fooled. He wanted her out of there, she realized. He wanted her to fail.

"No," she said stiffly.

"It's hard for you to be objective when you're part of events. You may not know what's best. And you might put more people at risk." Did she detect a smirk? "The president will make a statement about this later today," he continued. "We'll pass along the time so you can watch it with your staff. Again, I want to say that the White House is glad you were able to avoid a tragic incident."

C. J. rested her head against the back of the chair as the face of Eliot Green faded from the screen. The rest was all too short.

"Madam Ambassador?" her secretary called again on the speakerphone.

"Yes, Mindy," she said without lifting her head. "What is it now?"

"The embassy has been asked to process an emergency flight request. It's a helicopter from the Navy cruiser USS *Bennington*. They have one passenger—our defense attaché."

Golzari frowned intermittently as he typed out the incident report for headquarters. He had long ago decided that filing reports was the worst part of being a beat cop or a federal agent. He was relieved that the situation here seemed to be under control. The Marines had come to full alert, and the Yemeni government had posted extra security guards outside the main gate.

"Gunny." Golzari acknowledged the grizzled Marine who had just entered the office. He looked back at his computer just in time to watch the screen go blank. The realization that he hadn't saved the report came shortly afterward. "Shit!" He pounded the CPU tower with his fist. "What else can go wrong today?"

The Marine shook his head to signify his disagreement. "Things went right today, sir. You caught an attack before it started and you x-ringed the two drivers before their explosives were able to do serious damage—except, of course, to that store."

"I want that son-of-a-bitch, Gunny."

"Are we talking about the terrorist that got away or your friend the Navy commander?" he joked.

"Priorities, Gunny. I get one, then I get the other. Where the hell is he anyway?"

"You didn't see the email from the ambassador?" Gunny realized his mistake as he looked at the stricken computer. " . . . well, it's in there somewhere. The commander was riding on one of the oil platform supply ships last night—actually he was on the escort ship."

"The merc ship?"

"They like to think of themselves as private security specialists, sir."

"Ever known one who wasn't a merc?"

"I think these people may be the exception, sir. They seem different from the mercs I saw in Iraq. Mr. Maddox doesn't hire them out to the government like the PSCs in Iraq do. They just protect his ships and assets. That's how Commander Stark set it up for him."

Golzari sat up straighter in his chair. "Stark set it up?"

"Yes, sir. When I first got here Connor Stark was a civilian with a big, bushy beard."

Golzari's mind brought up an image from the RAF Lakenheath airfield lounge. One of the first things he had noticed about Stark was the lighter area of his tanned face where a beard would have been.

"The gouge I got was that Stark and Maddox are old college buddies. When Maddox got permission to explore the oil fields and the pirates started hitting them, Stark acquired the first security ship and trained its crew. Did pretty well on the water, from what one of the other security guys told me. He even stopped an attack on a Yemeni cargo dhow. The Yemeni government formally commended him for that one."

"That seems a bit excessive."

"Not when the captain of the dhow is related to the ruling family."

Golzari was trying to process the information Gunny was handing out. Maybe Stark wasn't a complete idiot. "Swell. So Stark's a merc himself. I wonder why they brought him back on active duty. Any gouge on that?"

"No sir. As far as I know he was through with that kind of work, so it must be something big for him to be brought back, especially in uniform."

Shaking his head, Golzari gave up. "What did I miss in the email, Gunny?"

"Commander Stark was on the escort ship when pirates attacked it midway to the Socotra oil platforms. The ship was sunk and twelve of the eighteen onboard were killed. He survived."

"Jesus. I'm surprised the media hasn't picked this up."

"There is no media here, sir. The government keeps a pretty tight lid on what gets out."

"What else did the email say?"

"Five of the survivors are en route to Djibouti for medical attention. Commander Stark is flying up here on one of their helos. We were advised to prepare the landing pad for them. ETA is," he looked at his watch, "about twenty minutes. Actually, I better get up there in case they get here early."

Golzari leaned back to do some thinking as the Marine turned to go. "Thanks for the decent tea, Gunny," he called after him.

"Anytime, sir. My people really appreciated what you did out there."

Golzari's computer flashed suddenly back to life, and he started to retype his report. But he kept losing his focus. Stark was once again being an inconvenience. Instead of looking for more information on Asha, Golzari felt compelled to find out more about the growing enigma that was Connor Stark. Within minutes of logging in he had all the information on Stark that the Department of Defense personnel system had to offer. That consisted entirely of Stark's commissioning date and the date he left the service—not left, was discharged. It was neither a standard honorable discharge nor a dishonorable discharge. What the hell was a "general discharge"? The final line added a bit more information: "Court-martialed. Subsequent general discharge." When Golzari tried to access Stark's court-martial proceedings through the Judge Advocate General's computer system, all he got was a response that said "proceedings closed and sealed by order of the court."

Fascinating. For some reason Golzari's thoughts drifted to the fall of Rome. When the Roman Empire became too rich and too bloated for Romans to defend, Rome contracted out its security and warfare to border tribes. That cost the empire dearly. Visigoth leaders such as Alaric served under Roman commanders and then turned on their masters. Golzari liked to think of himself as representing the modern Praetorian Guard designed to protect the emperor and government. That would make the mercenary Stark the new form of Visigoth. Alaric was the first barbarian to sack Rome, in AD 410, but he was not the last. The empire whose borders shrank as Roman beltlines expanded lasted another six decades. Was the United States another Rome, doomed to suffer a similar fate? Would Washington be sacked from without or from within? Would barbarians like Stark lead the way? Mercenaries were, after all, loyal only to their current employers.

He chided himself for letting his thoughts wander again and redirected them to their proper course. Abdi Mohammed Asha was no longer simply a name. He was the tie to khat in Antioch, had probably murdered Dunner's son and Officer Hertz, and, of course, had attacked Robert. And now he was right here in Yemen and had been in the company of two men who were planning to kill the U.S. ambassador. That deserved Golzari's complete and undistracted attention, and yet he was wasting time thinking about Stark. *Damn that Stark*, he thought. And then, *Speak of the devil.* Above the sound of the embassy's stuttering and unreliable air conditioner he heard the faint but growing sounds of a helicopter. The mercenary Commander Stark was back.

Mukalla, 1040 (GMT)

Asha pulled out a wad of khat, pushed it inside his mouth, and leaned on the railing of the balcony overlooking the harbor. No one had followed him here from Sana'a; of this, he was sure.

"He called you by name?" asked Ahmed al-Ghaydah.

"Yes, yes. He said 'Abdi Mohammed.' He knows my real name."

"How would he know it?"

"From Dunner's son. In America. It must have been from him. When he came back from Boston with the khat, the boy asked me who Abdi Mohammed Asha was."

"But where did he learn your name?"

"I don't know. Perhaps he overheard it on the ship when he picked up the trunk of khat. It's possible."

"Oh, no," Ahmed said.

"What? What is it?"

"I was the one who had the trunk put on the *Mukalla Hassan* to be delivered to you."

"What of it?"

"Faisal's ship had captured a supertanker."

"So?"

"He killed the captain and crew. He sent back the captain's gold watch with Saddiq and told me to send it to you with the next shipment. I put it in an envelope with your name on it and put it on top of the khat bags in the trunk."

"You stupid *faq'haa*!" Asha leapt at Ahmed and grabbed his throat, nearly pushing him off the balcony before he threw the boy back inside the room.

"Stupid child," he yelled at him, kicking him in the abdomen and groin as Ahmed vainly tried to protect himself from the blows.

"You can't treat me this way!" Ahmed shrieked as he tried to crawl away from the Somali's attack. "My father—"

"*Us kut! Nikkabuk*!" Asha swore. "You wrote my name on an envelope? For anyone to see?"

"Stop, Abdi, I beg you. I didn't think anyone would see it but you."

"I never received a watch or the envelope, you idiot. There was nothing in the trunk but khat."

"But . . . but . . . I sealed the trunk with my own hands. It must have been inside the trunk when you got it."

"The trunk was not sealed, you fool. The Dunner boy opened it before he delivered it to me at the waterfall so that he could take some khat for himself."

"Then, the envelope and the watch . . ."

"Clearly he took the envelope as well, fool." Asha kicked Ahmed again and began to pace the room like an enraged lion. "I searched his car after I killed him. I would have found an envelope. There was nothing. That means he stopped somewhere before he delivered the khat."

"Where?"

"Probably his room at the college. There was nothing else in the envelope?"

"No. Only the watch. I put it in there myself."

"Don't remind me, stupid child. The boy saw the envelope. He read my name. And then he left the envelope where someone else found it. The envelope with my name on it. Idiot! And what of the watch? Was there something special about the watch?

"It was gold. What else would you have me say?"

Asha kicked him again and Ahmed al-Ghaydah recoiled.

"There was also writing on the back of the watch. I couldn't read it. It wasn't Arabic or English."

"What language? Think!"

"It was like the lettering on my Russian pistol."

"What was the name of the ship Faisal captured?"

"*Katya P.*"

"A Russian name. The ship was owned by Russians?"

"Yes."

"Then perhaps the writing on the watch tied the captain to the ship. And the ship would have made news. That was why the Dunner boy seemed frightened when he asked me who Abdi Mohammed Asha was—he connected that name with the pirated ship."

"But Abdi, the boy is dead. What does it matter?"

"Shut up! I met the police officer and the federal agent outside the college. They must have found the watch and the envelope in the boy's room. That is why the officer asked me about Abdi Mohammed Asha also. Get up, Ahmed. I am done beating you—for now."

Ahmed scurried to the bathroom to clean the khat juice from his face and clothing.

So the federal agent was not killed by the train in London and is now in Sana'a, Asha thought. *If he is following the khat shipment, then his next stop will be here in Mukalla. I will be ready for him.*

U.S. Embassy, Sana'a, 0815 (GMT)

The walls of Ambassador Sumner's office trembled and the portraits, diplomas, and photos with politicians came dangerously close to falling from their hooks as the Navy helicopter landed on the roof. C. J. peered out the window and saw the hovering helicopter's shadow on the compound below.

She's overcome her fear of exposure, Golzari thought. *Or is it that something—or someone—makes her forget that*? Golzari had found the American businessman Bill Maddox already present in C. J.'s office when he answered her summons. They shared a seat on her sofa. Golzari sat straight, his face impassive.

"Bill, do you still fly your own helicopter?" C. J. asked without turning from the window, trying to make conversation.

"No. I don't have time anymore." He leaned forward at the sound of a light knock at the office door.

The ambassador's secretary opened the door, and Connor Stark walked in wearing a Navy shipboard blue coverall uniform. He looked older than he had just two days before, the lines in his face deeper.

Stark went straight up to Maddox. "Bill, I'm sorry. We lost twelve people in the fight. The pirates have the other two ships."

"Jaime?"

"Being treated in a French military hospital in Djibouti. Her injuries were serious, but the corpsman on the ship thought she'll be fine."

Maddox nodded at that bit of good news. "They released one of the supply ships a few hours ago—the *Mukalla Ismael*. What the hell happened?"

They released the other ship so quickly? Golzari thought.

Stark recounted the story—the prelude to the attack, the tactics of the assault itself, and the aftermath, including the heroism of the four remaining crewmembers and their captain, and the sight of the two captured ships steaming off into the distance. When he was finished he asked the ambassador for permission to sit.

"C. J. . . . Madam Ambassador," Maddox corrected himself, remembering that the DSS agent was in the office with them, "oil prospecting off Socotra is no longer a viable practice for my firm. Without U.S. forces to protect my people, I relied on my own security measures. They failed. I knew the people who were lost last night. I'm the one who has to make the calls to their families. And those will be the last calls I'm going to make because I'm pulling all of my people out of here—off the escort ships, off Socotra, off the platforms."

C. J. was stunned. Her plans couldn't succeed without Maddox. "Bill, you can't do that," she begged.

"The hell I can't. I made an agreement with the Yemeni government to explore for oil and set up the platforms. We're almost done. They can finish the damned thing. We've already lost too much to continue. Connor, do you agree?"

Stark looked at C. J. "It's not my call, Bill."

Maddox's look took in both of them. "This isn't Canada, and we're not the same people we were back then. I'm finished."

C. J. pressed on her upper lip with one finger, furious at Maddox's slip of the tongue in front of the DSS agent. Their common past was none of Golzari's business.

Golzari was intrigued by Maddox's revelation of the relationship between these three seemingly disparate people—the political appointee, the businessman, and the merc. So they had all known each other in Canada. Would that have been about the time of Stark's court-martial? He promised himself another look into the records.

"Let's stick with the matter at hand and not get into ancient history," C. J. said, trying to get the discussion back on track. "How many people does your firm have out there now, Bill?"

"Nearly three hundred Americans and about a hundred Indian citizens. It's going to take some time to shut down the operations safely and evacuate everyone."

"How much time can you give me before you evacuate?" she asked.

"Time to do what?"

"To get the Yemenis to help with security out there. At least until you complete the last platforms."

"What makes you think you can get them to send their boats out against the pirates?" Maddox asked calmly. "They haven't been willing to lift a finger so far."

"I think I can help with that, Bill," Stark spoke up. "I've seen what's out there. I might be able to help with the security situation."

"If I may," Golzari broke in politely, "perhaps I should be the one handling security. I'm the embassy's RSO." He looked at Stark. "This isn't part of the commander's job and he doesn't have the expertise required."

"What do you mean I don't have the expertise, Golzari? I was here years ago before you showed up."

"Being a merc at sea doesn't count, Commander, especially one who worked for the company in question here. You're a walking conflict of interest."

"'Merc'? You're calling me a 'merc'? Listen, you prick," Stark's voice shook the walls almost as much as the helicopter that brought him had done.

"'Prick'? I don't think name-calling is necessary, Commander. Can't we be civilized?" Golzari said rather pompously.

"I don't give a shit about civilized, Golzari . . ."

Spoken like a true barbarian, thought the agent.

"The ambassador, Mr. Maddox, and I are talking about people we know, about a mission that must succeed, and we sure as hell don't need to include you in this conversation."

C. J. sat back and allowed the tension to escalate.

"Maybe you would be better off now if you *had* brought me into the conversation, Commander," Golzari said. "I know security. I've never lost anyone under my charge. Can you say the same? Never. And that includes this morning."

Stark abruptly stopped his move toward the agent when he heard the last statement.

"What happened this morning?"

C. J. spoke. "I was going to the foreign minister's office and Special Agent Golzari detected and thwarted an attack on me, as I'm sure he'll be happy to explain in a civilized tone. Am I correct, Agent Golzari?"

"Of course, Madam Ambassador."

Golzari recounted the entire incident, then looked smugly at Stark awaiting the praise and admiration he was sure would follow.

"You suspected an attack, you didn't tell the ambassador, *and* you let her out of the compound?" Stark shouted in response. "What kind of idiot are you? What the hell would have happened if there had been more attackers? Or if you hadn't seen them at all?"

"I wasn't certain an attack was going to take place," Golzari answered. "You may recall an incident a couple of days ago in which I thought a member of this embassy was about to be attacked and it turned out the individual was simply being followed by a couple of mercs. Plus, we're a little short-handed here. I had to handle it myself because you were out on a privately owned security ship playing Stephen Decatur and the Barbary Pirates. That was most helpful. You have the thanks of a grateful nation."

Stark hit Golzari square in the nose with a quick jab, then followed with a left hook, his meaty hands dropping the unsuspecting federal agent.

"You're under arrest for attacking a federal agent," Golzari said from the floor, hands at his profusely bleeding nose.

"That is enough! Both of you!" C. J.'s scream achieved a pitch a Wagnerian soprano would have envied. "Get up, Agent Golzari. And then have a seat. Everyone sit down," she ordered as they obeyed like disciplined schoolboys. "Listen to me very closely. As far as I am concerned, Agent Golzari did a fine job today. So did Commander Stark. This is serious business, gentlemen. You will stop this infantile pissing match this instant. We will not fail at this mission. Do I make myself clear?"

C. J. paused until she had nods from Stark and Golzari. "Good. Agent Golzari, I want you to continue your investigation. You will be consulted about security arrangements. Commander Stark, I want you to press the Yemenis to get their boats to sea—now. Mr. Maddox, I'm asking you to plan for evacuation only as a final contingency and to continue working on those platforms until we have an answer one way or the other. Bill, I need you to give me a week on this."

Before Maddox could answer, Mindy's voice came through the intercom. "Madam Ambassador, Ambassador Gavaskar and Captain Dasgupta just entered the main gate."

"Thank you," C. J. said, slamming her palm on the mahogany table. The three subdued men didn't move a muscle. Closing her eyes, she breathed deeply and engaged in a tried-and-true calming ritual. The first few chords of Handel's Concerto Grosso in C Minor flowed into her head. She knew by the second how much time elapsed as she slowed her heart rate and brought herself back from the precipice by reverting to the simple *tock-tock-tock* tempo of the pendulum metronome in her mind as one chord followed another. "Please have them escorted to the conference room, Mindy," she added softly, "—and bring refreshments for them. We'll be there in a few minutes." Sumner took a deep breath and opened her eyes. "Well, Bill?" she asked. At his reluctant nod she rose.

"Agent Golzari, have your nose attended to," she calmly ordered. "Bill and Connor, I need you to join us in case they wish to discuss their citizens working on the oil platforms."

"Yes, ma'am," Maddox replied.

"Commander, I'm sorry to ask this of you so soon after last night, but could you quickly change out of that coverall? This will be a short meeting."

"Aye, ma'am."

"Ambassador Gavaskar! It's a pleasure to see you again," C. J. said fifteen minutes later, offering her hand to the Indian ambassador standing in the conference room.

"Thank you, Madam Ambassador," he said, "it is likewise a pleasure to see you. We were deeply troubled when we heard about the attempt on your life this morning. I believe you have already met my naval attaché, Captain Jayendra Dasgupta?"

Dasgupta bowed.

Stark was struck by the difference between the two Indian men. In fact, Gavasakar and Dasgupta could not have been more different. The ambassador was relatively young—possibly in his early forties—with a smooth, thin face and thick, black hair accentuated by a few stray grays. He was as tall as Stark though not as heavily built. His naval attaché was half a foot shorter, with thinning hair and a lined, weathered face. His uniform showed him to be a surface warfare officer, as Stark had once been.

"My defense attaché, Commander Stark," C. J. said, motioning to Stark. "You know Mr. Maddox. Shall we sit?" C. J. took her place at the head of the table and placed Stark and Maddox to her right and Gavaskar and Dasgupta to her left.

"We know you are very busy, Madam Ambassador," Gavaskar said, "but we wish to convey concern about the unfortunate attack on Mr. Maddox's ships as well. We have a warship approaching the Gulf of Aden, but it was too far away to render aid last night. Had we been closer we most certainly would have provided assistance."

"Thank you, Mr. Ambassador. Your kindness is greatly appreciated by my government."

"As you of course know, we are also concerned about the pirates. We have citizens working for Mr. Maddox. We know that he has been a good and generous employer, and we have always had a good relationship, but our primary concern must be the safety of our citizens. We must consider options."

"Would you like to share those options?" C. J. asked with a smile.

"Yes, I would indeed; however, as you are no doubt aware, I require authorization from my government before discussing such confidential matters," he responded, returning her smile.

She nodded. "I understand."

"I can say that we value America's friendship . . . particularly when the security of both our nation and yours off Socotra and throughout the region is being challenged."

"Then, Mr. Ambassador, may I propose that we continue to meet and identify common ground—or common water, as it were—where we can work together to achieve positive ends for both our peoples?"

"We would be pleased."

A visit to the gym for a light workout might have seemed counterintuitive for most people in his situation, but Connor Stark didn't look at it that way. This place offered a temporary respite from the madness that had surrounded him, or perhaps more accurately had come from him, over the past few days.

The deaths on the *Kirkwall* and the near-death of its captain were never far from his thoughts. As for Golzari, Stark was surprised at himself. He had never been a bully, but his recent behavior made him realize that he wasn't the naval officer he had once been, either—a man who sought to establish peace through strength. C. J. had seen Connor in action in Canada, but that had been a case of justified force to stop terrorists. The attack on Golzari had been an unnecessary act of violence.

Connor considered the high-tech machines dotting the gym, most of which he had no idea how to operate, and opted instead for the free weights along the far wall where two of the younger Marines were doing arm curls with dumbbells. He joined them for small talk, jokes, and a friendly competition on the bench press. They were half his age and accustomed to daily workouts. Stark struggled to match their weights until the previous night and his age finally caught up with him. "I give up, gentlemen. Thanks for letting me join you." He shook their hands, and they congratulated the "old man" for putting on a good show.

He envied their youth. The injuries his body had sustained in the course of several violent incidents had long ago ended his days as a competitive athlete.

He envied their innocence, too. They were young, still unstoppable, unaware of their limitations. But they were Marines. They would learn about battle and death.

As he pulled off his sweat-soaked shirt he thought again of the moments before the attack on the *Kirkwall*. He had stepped outside the pilothouse a mere second before it exploded. Not for the first time in his life Fate had intervened to save him but had taken others around him. He had never been one to believe that an outside force was controlling his life. But if Fate really existed, he planned to challenge it.

For the first time in his life, exercising failed to clear his mind.

Few people used the sauna attached to the locker rooms. Embassy staff could get plenty of heat by just stepping outside. Stark was glad for the solitude. He poured water on the heated rocks and leaned back against the paneled wall to soak in the steam and think. Maddox's mention of Canada earlier in C. J.'s office had brought back unwelcome memories of his second experience with terrorists.

Most Americans would consider Canada an unlikely place for terrorism, if they thought about it at all. He had stumbled on a terrorist cell by accident there when he was working on Capitol Hill as a military fellow to Senator Padraic O'Rourke. And when friends were murdered and the U.S. government refused to act even after he had presented irrefutable evidence to his chain of command, Connor had taken action on his own to prevent the deaths of other innocent people. He paid a high price for doing it. The Navy had charged him with violating just about every rule in the Uniform Code of Military Justice: conduct unbecoming an officer, being absent without leave, failing to obey orders or regulations, disobeying orders, reckless endangerment, and murder. He avoided a long jail sentence only because people in Washington wanted the incident kept quiet. He still didn't know who those people were.

He poured more water on the rocks and inhaled deeply as they hissed at him. He massaged his stiff shoulder and arm, the arm that had held Jaime Johnson upright for hours until the helicopter arrived.

Bill Maddox had said that the pirates released the *Mukalla Ismael* within a few hours of its capture. Why? Mutahar's offices wouldn't have opened until midmorning, and that was the earliest an intermediary could have called with a ransom demand. He shook his head and dismissed the matter. He had enough to do without trying to figure it out. The pirates simply must have realized it was a locally owned ship and turned it back.

He needed sleep to clear his head and heal his wounds. The events of the previous night had left him exhausted, and Bill's reopening of the Canada affair added to the confusion whirling in his head. Of one thing he was certain: his actions back then were still generating consequences. They had nearly cost Jaime Johnson her life. If he hadn't bypassed his chain of command and his government ten years ago, he'd still be in the Navy, and Jaime Johnson might have been as well. And the *Kirkwall*'s crew would still be alive today because Highland Maritime Defense wouldn't exist.

The preset twenty-minute timer rang.

Damien Golzari changed into a T-shirt and shorts as he prepared for a run on one of the gym's treadmills. When the man emerged from the mists of the sauna, Golzari had only one thought: what kind of idiot uses a sauna in the Middle East during the height of summer? Of course. He should have known—an idiot like the mercenary commander.

Stark saw him but said nothing as he opened the locker two down from Golzari's and reached inside. Taking care not to stare, Golzari took in the commander's physique. Stark was surprisingly solid for someone who hadn't been in the military for a decade. He didn't have the lithe figure of a runner. He looked more like a quarterback who had played fifteen long seasons and had been knocked around a fair share. The long, deep scar on Stark's forearm and a longer one across his chest were clearly the result of knife wounds. His knee bore the scar of an operation. Also conspicuous and unmistakable were the old bullet scars—four of them. Golzari had seen them often in his career. One appeared to be no more than a year or two old. The criminal investigator in him judged that the three others—one on his arm, another on his abdomen, and a third on his buttocks—were more than a decade old. So Stark hadn't spent his Navy career on the water far from the hazards of land-based operations; clearly he had experienced battle conditions firsthand.

A decade or so would coincide with the court-martial date in Stark's personnel file and, based on what he heard in the ambassador's office, would tie Stark, Maddox, and Sumner to something that happened in Canada. Damien was in school in England at the time, but he had certainly heard about the very brief period in the mid-1990s when Canada almost had a civil war. It had something to do with elections and a Quebec independence movement.

He couldn't remember much about it, but there had been some violence before the disturbance ended with a deposed provincial leader. Canada had never held much interest for Golzari, until now.

As Stark walked toward the showers, Golzari went into the main workout room to the treadmills. The two young Marines working out with weights came over to congratulate him on the foiled attack that morning. They wished Commander Stark had been there too.

"The 'old man' has heart," one of them said, describing his bench press competition with them.

Golzari didn't want to hear any more about Stark. He still had to find Asha.

The White House, Washington, D.C., 1631 (GMT)

"Ladies and gentlemen of the press, my fellow Americans. It is with deep regret and great sadness that I report the deaths of our ambassador to Yemen, Caroline Jaha Sumner; the U.S. embassy's defense attaché; several courageous Marines; and individuals employed by an American firm. In what appears to be two coordinated attacks, our ambassador and Marines were killed by a car bomb near the U.S. embassy; the defense attaché and private individuals were killed by pirates in the Gulf of Aden. I have known Ambassador Sumner since she was a young staffer on Capitol Hill, and I can say unequivocally that America has lost one of its finest public servants.

"These attacks represent an unexpected and unwarranted escalation in regional violence. This also appears to be the first time that terrorists and pirates have coordinated their attacks on U.S. interests. Because of this, I have ordered a carrier strike group to the Gulf of Aden to protect U.S. citizens in the area and to seize and safeguard the oil platforms off Socotra. It is imperative that we ensure that no terrorist or pirate organization has access to these platforms, from which they could cause incalculable environmental damage if left unchecked.

"I have also directed the secretary of state to issue a formal protest to the government of Yemen and . . ."

Eliot Green shredded the lousy first draft of the speech he had written by hand two days ago. He tapped his thick lips with his forefinger. The terrorists and pirates had just missed two good opportunities. More important, the foreign policy plans of the Becker administration had taken a hit. Still, he could work with this. C. J. might still be alive, but other Americans were dead. As one of his predecessors used to say, "Never let a good crisis go to waste."

U.S. Ambassador's Residence, Sana'a, 1640 (GMT)

"This is a surprise," C. J. said when she opened the door. "I was sure that you and Agent Golzari would be walking ten paces on a dueling field by now."

"Dueling is antiquated."

"Didn't you fence in the Olympics?"

"*I'm* antiquated. I come bearing a gift." He nodded toward a decorative box under his left arm.

"Well c'mon in."

The residence was surprisingly sparse for someone of C. J.'s tastes, though the labeled boxes stacked along one wall suggested that she still hadn't unpacked some of her personal belongings. Stark knew that someone with an ambassador's rank would have an aide to do that kind of thing, but he also knew that C. J. was too independent and meticulous to let anyone else unpack for her.

The three candles scattered around the apartment—one in the kitchen, one on the dining room table, and another on the coffee table—provided sufficient light to see, but he suspected they served another purpose. Their scent provided aromatherapy that gave C. J. some mental respite.

The walls above the stacked boxes were bare except for a large print of her father conducting an orchestra while her mother played the cello as featured soloist. This wasn't a place C. J. would entertain guests, Stark decided. She was too private for that. He wondered if even he should be here.

She sat at the end of the sofa and curled her legs beneath her, as she always did when she was relaxed.

"Sit your antiquated ass down here, Stark." She loudly patted the cushion, allaying his concern about intruding.

"I will, but I'm on a mission first." He headed straight for the small kitchen, found two glasses, and filled them with ice. Only when he had handed her one of them did he accept her invitation.

"Why do I sense this is trouble?" she asked.

"Trouble? Not at all, Madam Ambassador." He opened the box. "Cask-strength Highland Park," he boasted. He filled her glass and then his own. The rich golden liquid danced in the candlelight. "How could this elixir be trouble?"

"Maybe because alcohol is illegal in this country?"

"Stupid rule."

"How the hell did you get that into Yemen?"

"I didn't. It was waiting for me. I have friends here, remember? Namely, one very special friend."

"How special?"

"Special enough that I've been sending him a case of whiskey every month for nearly a year. Every month he gets one from a different distillery."

"Are you bribing him?"

"Certainly not. I'm just maintaining a friendship. When I got here a few days ago he was kind enough to regift me with a bottle."

She raised her glass. "Then, Connor, a toast: May all Connor Stark's Yemeni friends be as generous."

He raised his own glass. "And may we never forget the sacrifices of the fallen."

"Amen." They drank simultaneously and then sank back together against the couch. Connor closed his eyes, savoring the distinct smokiness associated with the island malts.

C. J. moaned in pleasure. "So this is what good stuff tastes like."

"It's been a long day for both of us. I thought we deserved it."

"Again I say 'amen.'" She knocked back the rest of the drink as he did the same and then poured them both another.

"I'm surprised at your music selection," he said of the smooth jazz playing in the background, a trumpeter and singer.

"Why?"

"You were always partial to classical music."

She smiled and sipped her whiskey. "I like to mix it up."

"That's Chet Baker playing."

"You introduced me to his music," she said. "Remember?"

"Oh, yes." A single whiff of her perfume brought it all rushing back. The years hadn't tempered his memory of this particular fragrance, with its hints of roses, vanilla, and honey. He remembered the lavender dress that left her arms bare and exposed most of her back. Her hair was up, back in the days before she had started cutting it close to her head. They had danced to Chet Baker that night. C. J.'s perfume lingered in his nose then and long after.

"Are you awake?"

He quickly opened his eyes at her question. "I was just appreciating the aroma . . . of the Highland Park."

"You must miss Scotland."

"It's my home now."

"Did this assignment take you away from anything? A job?" She hesitated. "A relationship?"

"I made enough money working for Bill not to have to worry about a job. As for relationships, there is someone, but this Navy business may be too much for her. I've called her three times since I was yanked away, but she keeps hanging up on me. She's a strong-willed woman, and she isn't happy about this. How about you?" he asked. "Being an ambassador in Yemen can't be easy on a woman's private social life."

"Same as the old days. I work long hours." She sighed and ran her fingers through her short hair. "There is someone, sort of. He travels a lot, works a lot too. We rarely see each other. I don't even know what to call it. He's in Washington. I'm not."

"You could have stayed there."

"I wanted to do something more than . . . than . . . just being there. I really want to do this humanitarian operation, Connor."

"Okay."

"Okay? That's not what I expected to hear."

"I'll save the security objections for Golzari. I'm not going to fight you, C. J. If this is what you think should be done, we'll figure out how to do it."

She hugged his arm. "Thanks."

"Will you give me some flexibility?"

"With what?"

"I spoke with my friend."

"The mystery friend."

"His name's Mutahar. One of his brothers is head of the Yemeni Navy."

"Oh."

"An uncle is the foreign minister you've been trying to get an appointment with."

"Wait, the foreign minister's nephew is the president of Yemen. That would make your friend one of the president's brothers." She leaned away and sized him up. "My, my, you do have friends in high places," she said, finally recognizing the extent of Connor's influence with the Yemenis. She finished her second drink and poured the next one herself. "Should I ask how you know him?"

Stark realized he was already one drink behind C. J. Nothing ever changed. He had lost count of the Capitol Hill bars they had closed together. "It was over two years ago. I was here commanding the *Kirkwall*. We were off the west coast of Socotra when we heard a distress call. Two skiffs were closing in on a dhow when we intercepted them. They had already done a lot of damage. The dhow was sinking. We took out one of the skiffs. The other one escaped. A couple of us were hit. We took the three survivors of the dhow aboard, including its captain—who was Mutahar's older son."

"So that's how it is."

"It's as simple as that. Mutahar and the family were grateful. They took me in as one of their own. We enjoyed one another's company and became friends. They trust me. I can work through them, but I need to know what I'm authorized to do and say. I'd take you along, but . . ."

". . . but they don't even let female family members eat with them. I know." She paused to reassess her strategy. C. J. couldn't waste words with the Yemenis. Whatever Stark said, the request had to be simple, direct, and achievable.

"Their boats have to come out of the port, just to make a small show of force. I want the pirates to think twice, and I want other governments to think we're finally making inroads here. And I want a meeting to discuss an agreement about the oil."

"I'll see what I can do. It may not be the way you would do it."

The last time Stark had said that, Quebec terrorists had died and he had been court-martialed, though C. J. and the others involved had been saved from the consequences.

"Why have you always been such a rebel?" she sighed.

"I never was until I met you."

Chet Baker played a trumpet solo.

"Is that my problem with men?"

"Why is that a problem?"

C. J.'s Blackberry buzzed on the kitchen counter. She ignored it. "Because it's not right to be a rebel. That's why there are rules."

"Caroline Jaha, sometimes you have to be a rebel to do what's right. Sometimes you have to make things happen. Sometimes you have to be Fate instead of letting Fate control you." That sentiment had resulted in his court-martial, he realized. Had he just doomed her to something similar?

She sighed in resignation. This had to be done. It was why she was here. She hoped that Stark could pull it off this time. She had already expended her one silver bullet for him. Even now, with her rank in the State Department, she might not have the power to save him from the consequences again.

"Just get them to help. I trust you. I'm tired of this uphill battle against them and Washington and the terrorists and pirates. I'm tired of doing this alone."

"You're not alone anymore. But you're the boss, C. J. You have the authority, and you have the assets here to do it—not as many as you'd like, but we have to conduct operations with the assets we have at our disposal, not the ones we'd like to have. You know how to take command. You have the ideas and know what needs to be done. You took charge in the office with me and Golzari."

She moved to nestle her head against his thick shoulder. "Only after you punched him . . ."

"Why did you let things escalate to that point?"

"You needed to get it out of your system, and he crossed the line with you. Plus, he needed to realize that you're his equal. He's arrogant, and he's pretty full of himself after stopping that attack. Once you calmed down and he shut up, the situation improved."

She was right, he thought. "I'll help you."

"No rebelling?"

He chuckled. "No rebelling. I'll do whatever you want." Connor put his empty glass down on a side table and cupped her cheek as his thumb caressed it. She moved closer to him.

"We'll succeed?" she asked.

"We'll do what has to be done," he said quietly.

"Regardless of the cost or the consequences?"

Chet Baker finished his last song and the room went quiet. The only sound C. J. heard and felt was the adagio tempo of his heartbeat. She tapped her forefinger on his bicep to its constant rhythm—the human metronome she needed to pace herself on this path. She tilted her head up toward his and closed her eyes.

Connor lifted his chin at the last moment and lightly kissed her forehead. "So how are the Washington Nationals doing this year?" he whispered.

She dropped her head back against the sofa and laughed.

DAY 10

U.S. Embassy, Sana'a, 0600 (GMT)

"Gentlemen," Sumner said to the two men who stood in front of her desk. "Commander Stark has requested permission to leave the embassy compound for two days. I've granted it. Agent Golzari, you will accompany him as his protective detail."

Stark bit off his objection before it passed his lips; he had agreed to do things her way.

"Madam Ambassador, may I remind you that I am still conducting an investigation and that you ordered me yesterday to find Asha," said Golzari.

"I don't need a reminder," she responded curtly. "I am not rescinding those instructions, Mr. Golzari, but right now this has a higher priority."

"Madam Ambassador, I'd like to remind you that this is a critical-threat post and that—"

"Actually, Agent Golzari, I don't need you to remind me of that either. I'm very much aware that this is a critical-threat post."

"Madam Ambassador, I really must protest . . ."

C. J. held up a piece of paper and said, "This fax arrived overnight from the director of Diplomatic Security approving my request to temporarily assign you here as our RSO. You may protest to a limited extent, but keep in mind that I now own you."

"Welcome to the club," Stark whispered to Golzari.

Golzari looked at Stark without changing his expression, then turned back to the ambassador. "May I ask where Commander Stark is going? The last time he went somewhere things went very wrong. I would like time to prepare for any contingency."

Stark answered him. "We're going to Mar'ib. It's east of Sana'a, about a ninety-minute drive from here."

"Good luck, gentlemen," C. J. said briskly. She flicked on the intercom. "Mindy, I need to meet with the gunnery sergeant." She looked up. "Gentlemen, you're dismissed."

Golzari tossed his overnight bag in the back seat of the SUV next to his larger go-bag. Stark arrived a few minutes later wearing a white cotton shirt and khaki pants similar to those Golzari—and most foreigners in Yemen—wore. Stark carried two bags as well, including one that appeared to be a go-bag. He donned a pair of Oakleys to shade his eyes from the bright midmorning sun.

"What's in that?"

"Probably the same thing as in yours."

"I doubt that. What the hell's in the bag?"

"Emergency kit, a 9-mm, and a few clips."

Golzari snorted. "That popgun will do you a lot of good. Here. I picked up an extra rifle," he said, handing one to Stark. "Ever handle one of these before on a ship?"

"This? On a ship? No."

"Well try to figure it out, Stark, and don't point it toward me. If the shit goes down, I won't be able to help you."

"Golly gee. And I thought you were assigned to protect me. Let's see," Stark said as he held up the weapon. "Hmm, M4A1 carbine. I'm glad you didn't bring the semiautomatic-only option like the M4. Full-auto option is a waste of good ammunition, but it's good to have just in case. Six pounds empty. Shorter stock than the M16 variant. I'd prefer the M16 since the M4 is shit beyond three hundred yards, but I don't expect we'll have to worry about that kind of distance if we're in a firefight, now will we, you presumptuous *prick*?"

Stark punctuated the last word by chambering a round.

Gritting his teeth, Golzari merely uttered, "Get in. I'm driving."

Neither occupant said anything until they saw the signs that told them they were approaching Mar'ib.

"You ever been here before?" Stark asked.

"Mar'ib? No. It's always been on my list of places to visit. Mar'ib is one of the region's oldest cities. It was the capital of the Sabaean Kingdom. Legend says it was founded by one of Noah's sons. Some of the ruins go back three thousand years. There's a temple here. What the hell was name of it? Oh, yeah, Bar'an." Golzari was speaking more to himself than to Stark.

"This is where the Queen of Sheba ruled," Stark commented while gazing out the side window.

"A Greek historian wrote about the Roman prefect in Egypt who was lured here to his death," Golzari added, refusing to be topped.

"Strabo."

"What?"

"Strabo. That was the Greek historian who wrote about that campaign. It was led by Aelius Gallus. He was betrayed by a local guide. The Romans had their asses handed to them. You never know who you can trust," Stark explained.

If Golzari was surprised by Stark's familiarity with a weapon no naval officer should know—except a SEAL—he was downright shocked that the man he had dismissed as a barbarian knew about a relatively obscure historian, much less the name of an even more obscure Roman leader. This made two unexpected revelations in less than an hour.

"How the hell do you know that?" Golzari asked.

Stark raised his eyebrows. "I read."

"Where exactly are we going?" Golzari asked in mounting frustration.

"A friend's."

"Does this friend have a name?"

"Mutahar."

"And what does this friend do for a living?"

"He's a businessman."

"Why are you going to meet with him?"

"He invited me."

"What kind of businessman?" asked Golzari.

"How about we stop playing twenty questions?" Stark shot back.

"I'm supposed to protect you. I need information to do that properly."

"I didn't ask for your protection, Golzari. That was an order from higher up. But if you have to know, Mutahar owns a shipping company and he's involved in some other businesses. Some I know about, some I don't." Stark wiped sweat from his forehead. A year in Scotland had made him more susceptible to the Yemeni heat.

"How long have you known him?"

"A few years. Look, Golzari, he's a friend. He's not a terrorist. I'll be safe at his place."

"There are no safe places in Yemen, Stark."

They were silent again until Stark pointed out the final turn. "His estate is just up the road."

"His estate?" Golzari said sardonically. "How awfully grand. How rich is this Mutahar?"

After a slight bend in the road Mutahar's home came into view atop a hill in the distance. Golzari had to admit that Stark had been correct. This was no simple house. It was a palace with gleaming walls of adobe and coral, and a well-guarded one, at that. A series of one-story arches accentuated the front of the main three-story building, with a three-story arch in the middle. As the embassy SUV came closer, Golzari could see that these weren't simple arches, they were *iwans*—soaring vaulted doorways that opened into a central atrium. Above the middle arch rose a tower two stories taller than the rest of the house. At each corner of the tower was a minaret-like structure that stretched another sixty feet or so into the desert sky. Intricate latticework adorned the edges of every wall and window opening. A large rose-patterned medallion of stained glass glowed above the central arch. The sections on either side of the tower extended backward in graceful curves.

A thick two-story wall with inset guard posts protected the entire complex fifty yards out from the palace, enclosing some smaller single-story buildings within its confines as well. Armed guards patrolled a barbed-wire fence two hundred yards farther out.

Golzari couldn't distinguish the plants at this distance, but the grounds inside the inner wall were green with lush gardens and extensive grasslands. He stopped the car.

"What are you doing?" Stark said.

"I'm waiting for information. No bullshit, Stark. Who the hell is this guy?"

"I told you, a friend. I had dinner with him the day you followed me. He's a member of the ruling family."

Gunnery Sergeant Willis' story about Stark saving the life of a member of the ruling family popped into Golzari's mind. He also knew, based on the report Posh Robert had let him see in London, that Abdi Mohammed Asha's khat had arrived in Boston on a ship owned by a member of the ruling family. Stark had friends in high places, all right. And maybe, just maybe, this Visigoth had stumbled onto or was part of something important.

Golzari had to agree that Stark was safe inside the estate. He was a guest in a well-protected enclosure, and Arab hospitality was legendary in this region of the world.

"Let's go, Golzari. And remember, I can still defend myself. Three Somalis in Scotland could attest to that if they were still alive," Stark snapped. "With your mighty protection added in," he added sarcastically, "I'm invincible."

Something else clicked in Golzari's mind. "Wait. Three Somalis from Birmingham?"

"Yeah, at least one was. How did you know that?"

"From a source who was apparently referring to you. I just now made the connection. Do you know anything about them or why they attacked you?"

"Not specifically. But I've been in this region before. It might have been a hit."

"Ordered by the pirates? Why you?"

"There's a top Ali Baba. Some people refer to him as a pirate king, but that's probably not an accurate interpretation. I thought a lot about it on the helicopter ride back to Sana'a. The attack the other night wasn't on the supply ships—it went directly after the *Kirkwall.* Why mess with an armed ship when there are other unprotected boats out there ripe for the taking? The pirates haven't bothered any of Maddox's boats since he started using armed guard ships."

"What was different?"

"Nothing, except that I was on it. I figure they were after me, just like in Scotland. Which means someone knew I was going to be on that ship at that time and got word to the pirates."

"We've got a leak, then. It could be someone in the embassy, in Maddox's company, or the Yemenis."

"You're right. It's going to take some time to pin down, though."

Golzari had an idea. "You don't want me to protect you, and I don't want to protect you, right?" he said.

"Brilliant observation."

"And you're safe with your friend Mutahar?"

"Of course."

"All right. I'm dropping you off and coming back tomorrow."

"Where are you going?" Stark asked.

"Sightseeing," said Golzari.

"The ambassador won't like it if she finds out we split up."

"Does she have to find out?"

"Not unless something happens to one of us," noted Stark.

"Then let's make certain nothing does, shall we?"

"It's a deal."

Mukalla, 0644 (GMT)

Faisal al-Yemeni was the first person off the *Suleiman* after it tied up at the pier. Still smelling of sweat and diesel fumes, he wore the long white cotton shirt and baggy brown pants torn at the knees that he had worn for the entire voyage. The money he had made from piracy—not to mention his family's wealth—would have purchased fine clothes, but Faisal eschewed such luxuries. Money spent on frivolous clothing or fancy cars was money he could not use for more important things.

"Welcome back!" Ahmed al-Ghaydah said, dropping his arms as soon as he realized his embrace was not being returned. "Asha al-Antoci is here at the hotel, Faisal."

"Take me there."

The hotel was only a short drive from the pier. Asha wasn't there when Faisal entered the eighth-floor room, so he showered and put on one of the spare sets of clothing he kept at the hotel. The arrangement worked well. He and those who worked for him always paid the hotel in cash so there was no way to trace them. Every member of the concierge staff was paid well to notify them if any questions were asked about them.

When Asha returned from an Internet café half an hour later, he found Faisal on the balcony, staring at the ocean.

Faisal embraced him and kissed him on both cheeks. "It has been too long, Abdi Mohammed."

"It is good to be here. Hu put me in a cesspool of a city that was as cold as the Americans' hearts."

"Does your return mean that Hu is ready for you?"

"You don't know? Ahmed al-Ghaydah didn't tell you?" Both men looked at al-Ghaydah, who sat on one of the room's double beds chewing khat like a sheep. He raised his shoulders and shrugged.

Asha and Faisal exchanged looks of disgust. Faisal closed the door to the balcony so that al-Ghaydah couldn't hear them, and the men caught up on events that had transpired since Asha had been spirited away to the United States.

"So neither of our attacks worked," Asha said when he had finished telling Faisal of the foiled attack in Sana'a.

"Not completely," Faisal said, "but we had some success. We sank one of their well-armed mercenary ships and killed the Americans' military adviser. They fear us now even more than before, and they know that their navy cannot protect them. They will not stay here much longer. And then we will have won."

"*Inshallah*, Faisal, *inshallah*," Asha said. "But al-Amriki told Hu that the military adviser and others survived."

"Al-Amriki! American pig! Why trust a man whose face I've never seen? It's foolish to think an American would help us, Asha. If it were not for Hu I would have nothing to do with him."

"I know what he looks like," Asha said.

"How do you know? Have you seen him, then?"

"Hu told me. When we were on his plane after leaving America. He wouldn't give al-Amriki's name, but he said that it disgusted him to have to work with a fat American barbarian with hideous red hair and a name like a color. He said the man holds a very powerful position and will help us reach our goal."

"I'm surprised Hu said even that much. Perhaps he was misleading you," Faisal offered.

Asha shrugged. Hu was a mystery to him. All Chinese were. Soon, *inshallah*, he would be back in Somalia among people he knew and understood. "Perhaps. But tell me more about how you sank the Americans' ship."

"I used the new remote-controlled skiffs loaded with explosives. I tell you, Abdi, they are going to change the face of the Gulf. Everyone will fear us."

"But you said your ship stayed a long distance away. Don't you have to be close to operate the boats?"

Faisal grinned. "Yes, but that is our secret weapon. We have a small helicopter that we keep in the Chinese compound on Socotra. The controller is in the helicopter. This was the first time we used it."

"When did you develop this system?"

"Recently. The Chinese helped us. One of them told me that they like to test their products in various parts of the world. We are happy to help them do that. But what of the American agent you spoke of, Abdi, who followed you from America to London to Yemen? He stopped an attack that should have been successful. He is a threat to us all."

"He recognized me," Asha said. "He is indeed a threat."

"You also recognized him," said Faisal. "And so we will kill him when the opportunity arrives." He opened the door into the hotel room and motioned Asha inside. "Come. We will eat. After that, I will return you here and leave for my father's home. I will be there for two days. He is having a big meeting and wants both of his loving sons there." He slipped on a new pair of sandals and walked toward the door.

"I will go with you," Ahmed al-Ghaydah said, rising from the bed. "I'm hungry."

"You will go nowhere," Asha admonished him. "You will stay here, out of trouble."

"Yes, Ahmed," Faisal agreed. "Stay here. My bag is there. Take it back to the office with you tomorrow. I will pick it up there when I return. Try not to do anything wrong."

Ahmed pouted and stuck another wad of khat into his mouth.

After they were outside the room, Faisal turned to Asha and whispered, "Our business with Ahmed is almost done. We will draw lots tonight to see who has the honor of killing the fool."

Socotra, Yemen, 0645 (GMT)

Bill Maddox was waiting for C. J. Sumner and her three Marine escorts at the Hadiboh airfield on Socotra.

She smiled and gave him a quick hug. "Thanks for your hospitality, Bill."

"My pleasure, Madam Ambassador. Hop in. These two SUVs are the best rides on the entire island."

The Ford Explorers left the airstrip and drove into the middle of the town, although such a small place hardly merited that title. Hadiboh was more a cluster of huts and superficial structures than a real town. A rundown building served as a primitive hospital. C. J. led the way inside and looked around for someone to give permission to speak with victims of the earthquake.

All twelve of the beds the old facility could accommodate were occupied. Mats had been placed around the beds for other patients. On the nearest slept a young girl who looked no older than ten. With no one she could identify as medical personnel in sight, C. J. knelt next to the girl, who awoke at her presence.

"Hello," C. J. said in English. When the girl just looked at her she tried a greeting in Arabic. Still nothing.

"She does not understand Arabic," a baritone voice behind her said in heavily accented English. "She does not understand it because what is spoken on the island is not Arabic but Socotri." The owner of the baritone voice, a tired-looking man of perhaps forty, then said something to the little girl, who struggled to reply.

"She says that her family was killed. A neighbor found her and brought her to town."

"Is she being treated?"

"The doctor is away treating victims elsewhere. These people were told to wait."

C. J. brushed the dirty, sweaty hair away from the girl's face. "Can you find some clean water and a towel?" When these appeared she soaked the cloth and gently cleaned the little girl's face. The child smiled, and C. J. felt her heart melt. When she stood and looked around at the other patients, she saw that some were young and some were old, but all had the same look of despair. "I should have come here before," she whispered, more to herself than to the others.

The group drove from the hospital to a spot outside the town where Maddox stopped the vehicles again and told everyone to get out. C. J. walked up to stand beside him. "This is the new development you told me about, Bill?"

"I'm afraid so, C. J."

Before her stood a *paifang*, a smaller version of the Chinese archways she had seen in Washington's Chinatown and many other parts of the world. The *paifang* was clearly of recent construction. Its paint—shocking red, vibrant gold—was still pristine.

"When did the Chinese get here?"

"A small ship arrived offshore a couple of weeks ago bringing people and supplies. They're operating out of an old Soviet base down the road."

"The Soviets really did have a base on Socotra? I thought that was just a rumor."

"Connor could tell you more about it. The Soviets maintained an airfield near Qadub on the western side of the island during the Cold War. They used the base to refuel and resupply."

"How many Chinese are here?"

"We figure about two hundred. They're mostly construction workers, as far as we can tell. They have easy access to any part of the island. It's only about seventy-five miles long and twenty miles wide."

"This archway with the Chinese calligraphy has other script. Socotri?"

"According to our interpreter, the Chinese calligraphy says the same thing: *From your friends of the People's Republic of China, for ever-lasting bonds with the people of Socotra.*"

As the group toured the island, C. J.'s commitment to play an active role here grew even stronger. She saw a world she had never imagined—umbrella-shaped dragon's blood trees that bled blood-red sap when their bark was injured, cucumber trees with fat trunks and branches, monkeys, and birds found nowhere else in the world. She was enchanted. The Galápagos of the Indian Ocean was an apt description.

Their last stop was at the top of a mountain on the south side of the island overlooking the Indian Ocean.

"Gunny, there's no one around. I think Mr. Maddox and I will be fine out there."

"Aye, ma'am, but we'd like to stay close anyway, if you don't mind."

"Sure. Bill, let's take a walk."

The sea breeze dried C. J.'s sweat and blew away the dust that her clothing had picked up in the lowlands. She reached out and stroked the trunk of a cucumber tree. The photos hadn't prepared her for the unique beauty of this place. On the distant horizon she saw five metallic objects rising out of the water that reminded her of the Martians from H. G. Wells' *War of the Worlds*. "How dangerous will those be to the coastline? I mean if anything goes wrong."

"Nothing is likely to go wrong with the equipment. I've incorporated every precautionary device that exists into these platforms. The most likely source of environmental damage would be caused by an attack on the oil rigs."

"I see." She bent down and scooped up a handful of Socotran dirt, then let it slip between her fingers. "Between the Yemenis who won't negotiate with me," she thought out loud, "the terrorists who are trying to kill me, the pirates who are attacking us, and now the Chinese who are doing—whatever the Chinese *are* doing—I feel boxed in. We may need to rethink our strategy here."

"Any specifics?"

"Some ideas. I'd like to wait until Connor reports back on his meeting."

Mar'ib, Yemen, 1650 (GMT)

"Mutahar, I know that I eat too much when I visit your home, but I simply can't resist food this good." Connor dipped his bread in the *hilba* and savored the distinctive flavors of lemon, coriander, cumin, mint, and other spices he couldn't identify.

"I am glad that you have come here today, Connor."

"I am glad, too, Father!" said a much younger voice belonging to a slender boy with dark eyes fringed by long eyelashes.

The boy's father smiled indulgently. "Why is that, Ali?"

"Because Uncle Connor is teaching me to fence!"

"You learn too quickly, Ali," Stark laughed. Soon I won't be able to fend you off. You're quick and smart."

"Uncle Connor, I have something to show you." Ali motioned, and someone brought a model of a building set on a coastline and set it on a table next to the wall.

Connor rose from his cushion and walked over to look at it, followed by the boy's father. "What is this?"

Ali beamed with pride. "I am building this. It will bring water to our land and help feed our people. After you told me of the great desalination plant in Jebel Ali I studied and learned. Our people need water for their crops. This will help all of us."

"You are building this?" Connor asked Ali but looked at his father.

"Yes, Uncle, with the oil money. I am going to build three plants on our coast. They will bring many jobs for our people."

Stark slipped an arm about Ali's shoulders and gave him a quick squeeze. "Ali, you're very wise for your years."

"I only learn from those who are wise, Uncle Connor," the teenager said before returning to his meal.

"This is your doing, Connor," Mutahar said warmly. "I am very proud of my son." And then more softly, below the hearing of the others in the room, "Ali is our future. He has the vision, the strength, and the purity of heart to solve our problems. Of this the family is convinced. Our people view Ali differently than they see my generation." Mutahar was sharing intimate knowledge reserved for close family—but Mutahar considered Stark family.

"But the money this country gets from oil . . ."

"Much will go to the desalination plants and other projects Ali hopes someday to build."

"Ali is surely a wonderful boy, Mutahar, but . . ."

"Believe me, Connor, my brother. Ali will do great things. We risk everything by placing our hopes in the boy. You know the challenges we face. In a few years, without the water or the oil or the jobs, we will face a rising tide that will undermine stability here and in this entire region, even more than it threatens us now. Who knows what would follow such instability."

"I understand. Tell me how I can help."

Mutahar motioned toward the table. "Begin by eating and listening tonight."

Stark gladly returned to his cushion and ate more *ful* and *salta*.

The dozen or so Yemeni men who sat around the table said little as the meal continued. That they were assessing him Connor had no doubt. Most wore the traditional *jambia*, a curved knife, hanging from their belts. Stark had no weapon—his go-bag was in the vehicle with Golzari, wherever he was—nor did he feel that he needed one. Mutahar would never allow harm to come to a guest in his house.

"Yes, Connor," Mutahar continued the conversation so that everyone present could hear. "This young one is very smart. Perhaps one day I will send him to Oxford or Cambridge."

"Either of those esteemed universities would be fortunate to have Ali, Mutahar."

One of Mutahar's cousins asked, "You are not insulted that he will not go to an American school like Harvard or Yale?"

"Why should I be offended? I have a great admiration for the United Kingdom. Their schools are among the finest in the world. Ali and his family will decide what is best for him. Why would that insult me?" Stark slowly sipped his cup of tea.

"You do not think American schools are the best? That Ali would learn more there?" the cousin said. Connor sensed this line of conversation was a test and was glad for the opening it gave him. Without the help of these men, he had no hope of completing C. J.'s mission.

"They are the best for some people, just as the British or French or Yemeni schools are best for some people. They are all different, and Ali could get a good education at any of them. The more important question to ask is what the schools could learn from Ali."

The cousin smiled slightly.

"My friend," Stark continued, "Ali is smart and will do well at any school lucky enough to get him, but can you imagine how an American school would benefit by having Ali there? What could we as Americans learn from him about his rich heritage and culture? Too few Americans have visited this country. Too few have seen its beauty or experienced the hospitality of its people, as I have witnessed here in the home of Mutahar, may Allah always bless him and his home."

Mutahar nodded to acknowledge the sentiment.

"It is unfortunate that certain . . . conditions . . . have prevented more Americans from visiting as tourists. They would understand and appreciate Yemen better if they did. And perhaps Yemen could likewise learn from us."

Several more men nodded. The cousin remained noncommittal.

"My cousin the admiral tests you, Connor!" Mutahar laughed.

"How so?"

"He hasn't told you that he is a graduate of one of your best schools!"

"Oh? Which one, Admiral?"

"The United States Naval Academy, Class of 1978," the cousin said proudly. "I was one of forty-three international graduates that year."

"Several of us at this table attended your American schools, Connor," said Mutahar. "Some of us have lived in the United States for some time. And yet Americans don't understand us."

"Understanding takes time. You and I have come to understand one another, but that understanding developed over several years. If Ali studies in America, perhaps a new generation can build on what we have started."

"You speak well, Connor," the cousin continued, "but you are also an American naval officer."

"I am a naval officer, yes, but I am many other things too. I believe in the ideas on which my nation was founded. I am a friend to this home. I do not see a conflict among any of those, so long as I speak the truth to you—and continue to enjoy Mutahar's fine food!" All the men laughed at that, including the cousin.

"Yes, Connor, you are a friend of this house," Mutahar said amid the laughter, "and our cook is now your friend, too!"

"Then I am fortunate."

"Your country is not so fortunate these days, Connor," said the foreign minister, who sat across the table from him.

"I am not a diplomat and do not speak for my country. My ambassador could enlighten you on that subject."

"Ambassador Sumner is not here. You are."

"Then I will say we have concerns. We wish to talk more. I know my ambassador hopes to speak with you."

"She is a woman."

"It would be a mistake to underestimate her," Stark cautioned. "She is a woman, yes, but she is formidable—more so than many men I have known. In truth, she has many of the same traits as your own Queen Arwa bint Ahmed, who ruled this land a thousand years ago."

Mutahar laughed. "So you did read the history books that I sent you!"

The foreign minister pondered the analogy for a moment. "If you think so highly of this woman, then perhaps we will meet with her."

"I do, sir, and I am honored that you consider my opinion worthy. In the meantime she has agreed to let me speak on her behalf about certain issues of concern to both of our nations and how we might work together."

"It is late," Mutahar interrupted. "We will talk again of this tomorrow. It is time for Ali to sleep and for us to smoke the *mada'a* together."

Mukalla, 1829 (GMT)

While Connor was enjoying Mutahar's hospitality, Golzari had driven not to the local ancient ruins he had allowed Stark to believe he planned to visit, but southeast to the port city of Mukalla. Along the way he stopped and changed into a plain gray short-sleeved shirt and a *futah*—the patterned sarong Yemeni men wrap around the lower body—along with sandals and a *mashedda*, the scarf used to protect one's face from the elements. He strolled through the town, familiarizing himself with the streets and buildings, until it got dark enough for him to stake out the shipping company's office on the quiet waterfront.

When the office had remained dark for half an hour, he donned latex gloves to avoid leaving fingerprints and set to work picking the lock. His father's bodyguards, members of the feared Savak—the shah of Iran's secret police—had taught him many tricks of the trade as part of his survival training.

The lock presented no problem, even in the dim light, and Golzari soon entered the outer door to the building and then the inner door to the Mar'ib Shipping Company. The office in which he found himself had six desks; beyond them was another office, likely belonging to the supervisor, Ahmed al-Ghaydah.

The dim light reflecting off the harbor lights was sufficient to guide him around the furniture. He entered the supervisor's work area and closed the venetian blinds before taking a small red-filtered flashlight from his bag.

He leafed through notebooks that looked like the ship schedules and logistics needs that a dockmaster would normally have. Several of the ship names on a recent list had checkmarks next to them. Three particularly caught his attention: *Kirkwall, Endurance,* and *Mukalla Ismael.* He found several entries for the *Mukalla Hassan* but no checkmark next to it. He noted the names of the checked ships and continued searching the desk.

Another pad of paper had names and phone numbers that he recognized as belonging to satellite phones. One name was "al-Yemeni," another was "al-Antoci." The latter name intrigued him. Arabic names often include the person's home region, and al-Yemeni was far too general to be of any use, but al-Antoci? His gut told him this was an important number—the number for Abdi Mohammed Asha, who had lived in Antioch, Maine. He memorized the names and numbers as well.

The rest of the desk contained little of interest except for the lower right-hand drawer, which held only two items. The first brought his eyebrows up to his hairline. He had seen only one like it before. It was a 5.45-millimeter PRI automatic pistol used by the Spetsialnoye Nazranie, the old Soviet Union's Spetsnaz special forces. How the hell had al-Ghaydah come by such a treasure? Golzari decided to save him from arrest for possessing contraband and slipped it into his bag.

The other item in the drawer was a standard hotel keycard inside a paper envelope with a room number on it. Apparently, big-city-hotel security measures hadn't caught on in Mukalla. Ahmed al-Ghaydah, Golzari reasoned, would live in a house or apartment. Either he needed a hotel where he could whore around, not unusual for an Arab man, or the key belonged to a room where visitors—people like Abdi Mohammed Asha, for instance—could stay. The hotel was only a few blocks from his current location. He'd noticed it during his earlier stroll. Golzari opened the blinds and left the office.

"Yes?"

Golzari saw the peephole darken as an eye peered through it.

"Mutahar sent me. It's very, very important." The khat-filled al-Ghaydah was in no condition to question how Mutahar would know his current location. He opened the door.

"Peace be upon you, brother," Golzari said brandishing his Sig-Sauer handgun as he burst into the room.

The drugged Yemeni was still trying to process this intrusion when Golzari slipped an arm around his throat from behind. "Be quiet." Golzari checked the bathroom and the closet. "Where is Abdi Mohammed Asha?"

"Abdi? Who are you?"

"It doesn't matter who I am, Ahmed al-Ghaydah. Where is he?"

The overmatched boy, his hands raised and eyes bloodshot, responded, "He left for dinner."

"Where?"

"I . . . I don't know. They didn't tell me."

"Who are 'they'?" Golzari asked, reinforcing the question with the barrel of his pistol against the younger man's back.

"One other person. Please, no."

"Give me a name."

"No."

Khat or no khat, Ahmed showed some resolve when it came to naming Asha's companion. His face reflected the terror he felt.

"Whose bag is this? Yours?"

"No, it belongs to a friend."

"Who? Asha? Or al-Yemeni?"

Al-Ghaydah was too numbed by the khat to pretend he didn't know that name.

Golzari followed up on his advantage, keeping his gun trained on Ahmed as he upended the bag. The cheap, dirty clothing that fell out reeked of diesel fumes and sweat. "Who owns this bag? I will not ask again."

Al-Ghaydah darted unexpectedly toward the balcony and closed the glass door behind him, then pulled a plastic chair to the edge and tried to reach the balcony on the floor above him. The chair wobbled as he struggled to maintain his balance. Golzari slid the door open and lunged for him. Al-Ghaydah managed one brief look behind him before losing his balance. Golzari reached out but could do no more than grasp a sleeve as al-Ghaydah slipped away and fell eight stories to the concrete below.

Golzari stared after him for a moment, then gathered the contents of the bag, stuffed them inside, and put it back in its place. He pulled the *mashedda* up to cover his face and left. When he was safely outside the hotel, he strolled casually back to his car and left Mukalla. On the long drive back to Mar'ib he considered the new connections he had uncovered—and the paperwork that would be involved if State found out he had been responsible for a foreigner's death.

DAY 11

Mar'ib, 0630 (GMT)

Stark swam laps in Mutahar's Olympic-sized pool early the next morning. Swimming—when it was not for his life—was a favorite pastime long neglected. It stretched out his muscles and gave him time to think. No one willingly swam in the cold waters around Scotland. In fact, the last time he had swum laps was here in this very pool.

He had succeeded at last night's dinner with the first step in his plan—getting the foreign minister to agree to meet with C. J. She had a chance now. Next up was to get those Yemeni ships out to sea to deter the pirates.

He pulled himself over the rim of the pool and sat there for a few moments, breathing deeply, until approaching footsteps drew his attention.

"Uncle Connor," Ali shouted. "Look who is finally home!"

Stark stood and grabbed a towel before shaking the hand of Mutahar's eldest son. "It's good to see you, Faisal."

"And you, Connor, in whose debt I remain."

"You owe me nothing, Faisal. I had the honor of being of service and gained the friendship of your family. I could ask for nothing more."

"You continue to be a gracious man, Connor," Faisal said politely.

"You are late," Mutahar said from the doorway in his slow, deep voice.

Faisal turned at the sound of the voice. "I am sorry, Father."

"Uncle Connor," Ali interrupted excitedly. "Watch me, please, and tell me if it is the right way for the butterfly. I have been practicing the stroke just as you showed me"

"Very good, Ali," his father replied, approaching the pool. "Go ahead. We will all watch."

Mutahar briefly embraced Faisal and then turned to watch Ali with unconcealed pride. "There is an ancient fable in my land, Connor," he said without looking away from his youngest son. "A wealthy man died and left two sons but no instructions on which would inherit his wealth. A wise sheikh tested them. One of the sons passed the test. The other did not because he had shamed his father."

Stark could feel Faisal stiffen beside him, and he sympathized with the young man's hurt and embarrassment. Hearing such a deeply personal remark from father to son made him uncomfortable, whether or not he was considered a member of the family.

"It is good to be home," Faisal finally said agreeably. "But I see so many surprises. I barely recognized Connor without his beard."

"Do not tease our friend. He is very upset that the American Navy made him shave it!"

"The Navy?" Faisal smiled at Stark though his eyes remained cold.

"Yes. Connor has been returned to active duty. He is the American embassy's new defense attaché."

Faisal's eyes widened fractionally. "You are now the military adviser for your ambassador?" He paused for a moment as if seeking words. "You are to be congratulated on gaining such a post, Connor."

Stark casually patted at the water on his neck and head. "I am the new defense attaché, yes, but my role is more diplomatic than military."

"Come, my son," Mutahar said abruptly. "We do not discuss such matters today. We will talk later. For now, our family is together. Go and swim with Ali. Perhaps he can teach you the new stroke Connor has taught him. Connor, the front gate informed me that your driver has arrived."

"Thank you, Mutahar. I'll get dressed and bring him in." His peripheral vision caught Faisal's wary stare as he walked away.

"Thank you, I'll escort him from here," Stark told the guards before walking around to open the passenger door of Golzari's vehicle. He automatically looked at the mileage indicator as he entered and noticed that it was several hundred miles higher than it had been yesterday.

"How was the sightseeing, Golzari?"

"Lovely," Golzari replied with a wide smile. "I can't remember when I've enjoyed a trip more."

"Where did you go?"

"I'll tell you later."

"Don't play Secret Squirrel with me, Golzari. Where did you go? You can do a lot of sightseeing in three hundred miles. You could have gone all the way to the coast and back." Stark didn't fail to notice Golzari's slight jerk at those words.

"You get a gold star for observation, Stark. I'll tell you when we're headed out of here."

An attendant took the car keys when Golzari stopped at the main entrance to the house. Golzari took his bags from the backseat and followed Stark into the grand atrium. The multicolored light that passed through the stained-glass medallion high above danced off the marble floor tiles, creating a dazzling display. He thought for a moment that he had entered the treasure cave of Ali Baba's forty thieves. The five-story atrium rose all the way to the top of the tower.

"Business has been good to this man," observed Golzari.

"He has done very well," Stark agreed. "He's smart, and he doesn't screw people. He and Maddox are alike in that regard. Shipping isn't Mutahar's only business. He owns a very successful construction firm at well. Hell, he's built some of the towers in Dubai and has worked on upgrading ports in Oman and Djibouti."

"Impressive. But, as you say, he is a member of the ruling family."

"Connections only get you so far. At some point you have to prove that you're worthy of the largest projects, especially the ones outside the country. And Mutahar has proven that in the business world."

"Umm," Golzari said, taking in the examples of Mutahar's taste and worth that surrounded him. "Nice columns."

"Yeah, nice colors."

"They're Connemara marble, Stark. Do you know how expensive and rare that stuff is these days?" Golzari was reminded of the last time he had seen the distinctive Connemara marble pattern—it was lying on a coroner's table in Antioch, Maine. "And he has two Aldo Luongos? Phenomenal," Golzari said as he moved closer to examine the paintings.

"Aldo who?"

"Aldo Luongo. Argentinean painter. A soccer player turned artist. Wow, these are really fantastic. They aren't on the same level as his work on the tango, but I can't imagine that a Muslim house would display a portrait of a suggestive dance."

"Can we get your bags to your room, or are you going to gawk at everything?"

Golzari gave the Visigoth an annoyed look and picked up his bags. The room assigned to him overlooked the stables. "Nice view," he said sarcastically.

"You're supposed to be my driver. You're lucky you're not staying *in* the stables instead of looking at them. Speaking of driving," Stark added, "where the hell did you go yesterday?"

"Sorry, old man," Golzari repeated as he checked the lock on his window. "That has to wait until after we've left this compound. How long are we here for, anyway?"

"Another day, at least. The big dinner this afternoon should give us an idea. It's at two. C'mon, I'll show you around the place. You can look at more art."

The more he looked, the more impressed Golzari became. He had seen palaces in Saudi Arabia that couldn't match this grandeur. Mutahar had to be one of the wealthiest men in Yemen, if not the entire southern Saudi peninsula.

The tour ended at the stables, where Stark and Golzari found Mutahar and Faisal watching Ali mount his favorite horse, an elegant Arabian stallion. The boy began a slow gallop around the practice ring, his equitation faultless.

Mutahar leaned on the railing and turned to Stark as he approached. "He is good, isn't he, Connor?"

Faisal, meanwhile, eyed Stark's companion. The man's bearing and self-confidence marked him as more than an embassy driver.

"He has had good teachers," Stark replied, "including you. Come here, Ali," he shouted. Ali expertly galloped over to the railing and brought the Arabian to a perfect halt—not so fast as to risk injury to his horse, but fast enough to show a little panache. Stark reached out and stroked the horse's head, admiring the delicate bone structure.

"You see, Uncle Connor," Ali beamed proudly, "you were right. I am good! Shall we have another fencing lesson this afternoon?"

"Yes, Ali, before we eat. And I won't go easy on you, either."

Golzari followed this conversation carefully. The commander was truly beginning to fascinate him. He knew about guns no naval officer should know, he gave riding lessons to a young princeling, and now fencing? Fencing had been his own sport at Cheltenham. He intended to watch the fencing lesson to see just how good this Visigoth was.

"Someday," Ali said before galloping away again, "I will be an Olympic athlete like the great Connor Stark!"

Olympic athlete? Golzari hated to be wrong. But every additional fact he learned showed this man to be less and less the Visigoth. Fencing, riding, and shooting were three of the five events in the modern pentathlon. What other surprises did Connor Stark have to offer? He made another mental note to look a bit deeper into Stark's background when he returned to the embassy. At that moment, he realized that Mutahar was speaking to him.

"You are Connor's driver."

"Yes, sir," he said humbly.

"Where are you from?"

"The United States, sir."

Mutahar looked at him in disbelief. "You don't speak like an American," he pointed out, "and you don't dress like one either."

"America is a land of great diversity, sir," Golzari replied. "I'm as American as the good commander here."

Mutahar tapped the railing as he looked back and forth between Stark and Golzari.

"I am a good judge of men," he said finally. "And I believe there is more to you than meets my eyes. But let it be as you say—for now. You are here with Connor, and you are my guest. Welcome to my home. May I present my oldest son, Faisal," Mutahar gestured to the young man standing beside him.

Golzari and the young man exchanged cordial nods. Golzari knew that Mutahar had pegged him as being from the Middle East. People here could tell the difference between Saudi, Iraqi, Omani, and others as easily as an American could tell the difference between southern, West Coast, and New England accents. So Mutahar almost certainly knew that he was of Persian descent as well.

At that moment Faisal's cell phone rang. He excused himself politely and walked away from the others as he answered it.

Although he made no attempt to listen, Golzari could hear Faisal's part of the conversation quite clearly. "Yes? . . . Was it you? . . . What time did it happen? I see. No, no, I will go there. I will call you when I arrive." He flipped the phone closed and returned to the group. "I am sorry, Father, but I have to return to Mukalla. There has been an accident."

"Oh? What is it?"

"Ahmed al-Ghaydah is dead. He fell off a hotel balcony last night."

"His family, peace be upon them, will be grieved. But I cannot say that I am surprised. He indulged too much in khat and foreign women and paid too little attention to his job. I hired him only as a favor to his father." He reached out to embrace Faisal. "Go now. See his father and tell him that we are very distressed and offer our support."

"Farewell, Father." He nodded at Golzari. "Connor, we will see each other again?"

"I hope so, Faisal."

Faisal smiled. "As do I."

U.S. Embassy, Sana'a, 1500 (GMT)

C. J. was surprised to see Eliot Green's face next to Secretary of State Helen Forth's image on the VTC. "Eliot is joining our conference because of the level of interest at the White House on your status, C. J.," the secretary said. Green nodded without changing expression. Forth looked away from the camera and toward some papers—probably Eliot's standard talking points, C. J. thought. Eliot always demanded structure in meetings, his structure.

"Madam Secretary, thanks for taking my call." A formality since C. J. doubted Forth would have allowed the call without Eliot's permission. "I expect to have good news from the Yemeni government very soon. They've indicated that they're ready to talk about the oil agreement. There's another initiative I'd like to discuss with you today, though. If it works out, I hope it will bolster Yemen's willingness to work with us in other areas."

"Oh?" Helen Forth's face expressed interest. Green's remained wooden.

C. J.'s voice was alive with enthusiasm as she began describing her plan. "I just returned from a one-day evaluation trip to Socotra. I'm not sure whether you're aware of the earthquake that recently damaged the island's villages. It didn't make a lot of headlines. The people there are suffering, though, and I think we could do a lot of good if we were to conduct a small humanitarian operation. Any assistance we provide will be helpful and will create goodwill. You should also know that China has already begun such an effort."

"What kind of aid do you want to provide?" her superior asked.

"Simple things. Medical supplies and personnel, food, water, clothing. If this works and the Yemeni government sees firsthand our sincere desire to help, then we can expand our effort by working with them."

"C. J.," Green chimed in, "just hang on here. Some of those things might be possible, but medical personnel have a higher priority in Afghanistan. And I can't begin to say what we'll need if the naval blockade of North Korea isn't successful."

"How do you suggest carrying this out if we do approve?" Forth asked.

"There are two possibilities: airlift or sealift. The island has a small airport, but we'd have to charter something larger and faster than the embassy plane here in Sana'a. Round trip for our plane is more than five hours, so using that isn't practical. Ideally, we could purchase the materials here in Yemen, supporting the local economy, and transport them on an American ship. Bill Maddox has a few support vessels in the region, and I'm sure he'd be willing to help. Even one shipload would be beneficial. And I'm not requesting military medical personnel, Eliot. I can get civilian volunteers from some of the NGOs."

"Eliot?" Forth asked, seeking direction as usual.

He looked unconvinced. "It's a bit risky given that the piracy situation hasn't abated. Maddox's firm probably can't get a ship safely to Socotra."

C. J. crossed her fingers and took a chance. "I'm convinced that the Yemeni Navy will provide escort ships."

"Well, that's a change," Secretary Forth said.

"Yeah." Eliot leaned forward into the camera, as he often did when trying to make a point—his point. "What's changed?"

"There are new negotiations which I am convinced will be fruitful."

"C. J., does this have anything to do with your new defense attaché, Commander Stark?" Green drew out the last name.

"It does, yes. He is currently speaking with people in the government. I'll have a report for you later today." She was buying time with that last statement, hoping that Stark would indeed show up with good news.

"No." Green's voice indicated a final decision. "It's not a good idea."

C. J. refused to give up. "Eliot, I can do this."

"Your friend Stark is an incompetent troublemaker. He'll fail."

"He won't," C. J. insisted. "Not this time."

"Why are you so sure?"

"Because the Yemeni government will talk to him."

Green flipped his fingers as if swatting away a fly. "That's not enough."

"If the Yemeni Navy agrees to escort Maddox's supply ship, will that be sufficient for you?"

Eliot's eyes suddenly narrowed as an idea came to him. "No. If we—the president—decides aid to Socotra is a good idea, and if the Yemeni government agrees, I'll have a U.S. Navy ship assigned to assist you. The *Bennington* is in the region." Green smiled and looked down at the papers he was shuffling on his desk. "Once Secretary Forth and I read your report, we'll reevaluate. Madam Secretary, does State concur?"

"State concurs," she responded obediently.

"Thank you, Helen," he said. "I wonder if you'd give Ambassador Sumner and me a moment now?"

The feed from State cut out, leaving only Green and Sumner.

"Okay, C. J. Let's talk about your pal Stark. You never told him the full story of that court-martial, did you?"

She inhaled deeply. "No. There was no reason to."

"It would be a shame if he found out the truth after all these years."

C. J. clenched her fists helplessly as Green's face disappeared from her monitor. She wished Eliot Green would disappear altogether.

Mar'ib, 1620 (GMT)

Servants removed the remnants of the meal as the men sat back and smoked. Mutahar licked the last of the honey cake from his fingertips before one of the women brought out wet towels for those who remained. After dessert, Mutahar excused everyone from the room but Stark, his cousin the Yemeni Navy admiral, and his older uncle, the foreign minister. The security guards remained outside the closed doors.

Stark cleaned his hands and face and again praised the food of the house of Mutahar before turning to the business at hand. "Gentlemen, I am always honored to visit Mutahar. He is among my most valued friends, and he knows that I would do nothing to dishonor him, his house, or his family," he punctuated the latter with a nod especially to the foreign minister.

"Connor, please do not take this as an insult," the foreign minister began. "You are an American, and you are also an officer in the U.S. Navy. Mutahar has told us that we can discuss anything with you as you are a brother of this house, but I believe that we should also establish rules before we begin. Are you agreeable to this?"

"Yes, of course," Stark answered. "May I suggest we try the simple approach and offer one another complete honesty?" Stark displayed open palms as he said this.

"Connor, I have been the foreign minister for some years now. One thing I know is that you are required to report to your ambassador and also to your Defense Department." He inhaled deeply from the water pipe.

"That is true, I suppose. But I have never been a defense attaché before. I was returned very quickly to active duty here without formal training. So perhaps I never learned what's expected of bureaucrats?"

The three other men sitting at the table laughed heartily, the foreign minister loudest of all.

Connor continued. "Gentlemen, I have assured Mutahar that nothing you say will be reported back to my government unless you wish it. I need the information I seek now so that I can know how to advise Ambassador Sumner. She wants to work with you. And as I said last night, she is very capable of doing that."

"Very well, Connor. Only that which is explicitly agreed upon will be shared with Ambassador Sumner."

"Thank you. First, Ambassador Sumner has always had an interest in helping victims of disasters. She believes it is her responsibility and her privilege as ambassador to provide assistance when it is needed. The recent earthquake affected many people in Socotra. They are in need of supplies. We would like to provide medical assistance along with food and water for the victims, all in accordance with Islamic law and with your approval, of course. Ships owned by the firm operated by Bill Maddox could carry the supplies."

The foreign minister pondered this offer. "So long as it is not too much American presence. Representatives of our government should be there with you under our flag, as they are with our Chinese brothers who are also offering assistance on the west coast of Socotra. Tell Ambassador Sumner we will grant this."

"Thank you, sir. I will inform her of your benevolence for your people and work out the details. Perhaps the admiral would be an excellent representative of your government. It would be a good opportunity to exercise your ships, and we could use the protection from the pirates."

The elder statesman leaned back and chuckled. "Connor, it is well you are not a businessman—you would give even Mutahar strong competition in negotiations. Ambassador Sumner has been trying since she got here to have our ships patrol. I see what you are doing!"

"I am not asking for the admiral to patrol, only to escort. That is a great difference," Stark explained, dancing around the central issue.

The foreign minister turned to his cousin the admiral. "What do you think?"

The admiral paused to consider the question. "My ships have not been to Socotra in some time. Perhaps Connor is correct. This would be a good opportunity to practice with the new ships."

"Would you then also consider providing escorts for ships resupplying the oil platforms to the south?" Stark knew he was entering more dangerous waters here, but he would have only one shot at this.

The admiral didn't even pause to think about that question. "This would not be possible. Such daily runs would cost too much. As well, the pirates have become extremely aggressive. We heard what happened to your security ship. I'm not convinced that our forces are sufficiently well armed—not yet."

"Admiral, no one knows better than I what the pirates are capable of. I have been surprised at their advanced tactics and aggression as well. I also know what will happen if they are not stopped. The Quran speaks of crimes against order—*hirabah*. What are these men but *hirabi*—creators of disorder?"

"You speak the truth. They are criminals. But there are too many of them."

"If we work together, we can challenge them. We might be able to provide ships and aircraft in the future to help you dispose of them."

"This is a more difficult issue," the admiral admitted. "We know your government would like to establish a permanent base on Socotra. Please understand that that is not possible."

"Please tell me your concerns. Perhaps there is common ground," Stark said.

"Connor, are there other requests you were sent here to make?" the foreign minister asked.

"Yes. Maddox, with great and efficient support from Mutahar's ships, has met every one of Yemen's development requirements. His men are close to completing the last two platforms. We hope for a decision soon about awarding that contract and the rights to the oil."

"We know this," the elder statesman said slowly in his deep voice. "We will tell you this now, Connor. There is no reason for an American base because the United States will not be considered for the oil production contract."

Connor kept his face expressionless. "May I ask why?"

"It is not a personal matter. We like Maddox. He and Mutahar have worked well together. We do not, however, wish to expand our business interests with the United States."

"I'm not sure what to say, Abdul. I am an American and you deal with me. Maddox is an American and you deal with him."

"You are both individuals. Neither of you makes policy for your country. Our government has not benefited from our relationship with America; it has only been . . . damaged. Yemen has suffered since your country's ship was attacked in Aden, even though we were not responsible. Al-Qaeda attacked it. Al-Qaeda continues to attack us as well. They try to turn our people against us. Several years ago when we allowed America's Predator drones to kill al-Qaeda leaders in Yemen, we were promised that the circumstances would not be revealed. It was only to be said that the Yemeni government had ensured justice against the criminals. The United States broke the agreement and boasted of its achievement through leaks to your media." The foreign minister raised his chin in Connor's direction. "After that, many of our people and those from other countries began to oppose us and call us a tool of the United States. We have had problems to the north. One of the old families to the east has been gaining more power and challenging us."

Stark assumed he meant the al-Ghaydah family.

"No, Connor," he repeated. "There will be no oil for the United States."

"Should I ask what will happen to it?"

"Other countries need oil, other countries whose intentions we do not distrust and whom al-Qaeda does not attack. Those countries have money to buy our oil as well." Finished speaking, Abdul reclined again and smoked.

"You would prefer to ally yourselves with the Chinese?" Stark boldly asked the foreign minister.

"We prefer to work with countries that will act in our interests as well as their own," he responded.

"And India?"

He shrugged. "Our historical ties with India extend for centuries. We have no quarrel with India."

Connor knew when he had lost an argument. "Gentlemen, you have been gracious in giving the ambassador the opportunity to serve the people of Socotra and to enjoy the protection of your navy. Aside from the situation to the north and east, is there anything we have discussed this afternoon that I cannot share with Ambassador Sumner?"

Abdul blew a long puff of smoke and leaned toward Stark. "Yes. Do not tell her how good Mutahar's cook is."

Mukalla, 1840 (GMT)

"He just fell off the balcony?" Faisal asked the hotel clerk as Asha paced back and forth behind him.

"The police say he had too much khat," the clerk replied.

"This happened how long after I left?"

"One hour. Maybe two."

"Were there any calls to the room?"

"No. And he made no outgoing calls."

"There was no sign of forced entry?"

"None. No one saw anything."

Faisal swung the swivel chair to face the harbor.

"Does the hotel maintain security tapes?"

"No. But I assure you, no one saw anyone unusual. No Asians, no Africans, no Westerners."

"Was there someone who might have looked Iranian who came into the hotel after I left and came out after Ahmed jumped?"

"There were several. One wore a scarf around his face. He was thin and maybe six feet tall. But many people like that come through the hotel."

"Leave us now," Faisal said, locking the door behind the clerk. Then, turning toward Asha, "I wonder . . ."

"What?" Asha asked.

"At my father's I saw someone I knew. He is the new military adviser at the American embassy."

"You know him?"

"I didn't know his current position until then. I knew him from before."

"He is the man you wanted killed?"

"Yes."

"Do not be troubled. I will see that it is done."

"There was another man with him—his driver. He looked Iranian. Thin. About six feet tall. He arrived after I got there," Faisal said.

"This is the American agent who has been following in my footsteps?"

"It must be."

"Then we have a chance to kill them both. They will certainly leave your father's estate together. One of your guards can tell you when that happens."

"I must call Hu and tell him about these developments," Faisal said. "Abdi, you must go now. Go and kill them both once they have left the safety of my father's estate. Take enough men to be certain. I need to put to sea again to finish preparing the tanker. Can you do this?"

"Of course I can."

U.S. Embassy, Sana'a, 1843 (GMT)

C. J. paced around her office as Rachmaninoff's Prelude in C-Sharp Minor played quietly in the background. If she could have brought one luxury item to the embassy, she often thought, it would have been her baby grand—the beloved piano on which she had learned to play all of the masters. Learning to play had been easy for her, the child of talented musicians. A composer writes music following precise mathematical rules. Any competent musician can read a score and play the notes. But the interpretation . . . that had taken time and thought and growth. A very good pianist brings a musical composition to life in new and vibrant ways. She excelled at that. She controlled every note, manipulated every chord, and took old pieces in new directions. She had once planned a career as a professional musician, had dreamed of thrilling the world with her passion and skills. Considering her parents, it was the natural decision. But a life of service—of helping people—held an even greater attraction.

In some ways foreign policy was like a musical composition. The policymakers wrote the score; the Foreign Service officers and ambassadors could either make the policies come alive or repeat them by rote, without inspiring their audience. They sometimes even missed a note.

C. J. was glad to get the call from Connor telling her about the inroads he had made with the Yemenis. He had done far more in a few days than she had been able to do during her entire tenure here. He had done exactly what she had asked of him and what he promised to do. It was always like that with him. His arrival had buoyed her spirits and given her new confidence.

It was too late in D.C. for her to share the good news with Helen Forth and Eliot, so she decided to cable them instead. They would be happy to hear that the Yemenis had approved an assistance operation and that the Yemeni Navy had agreed to escort an American ship. The question was how much more than that to tell them. Standard procedure dictated that she tell her superiors that Yemen would not consider the United States for the oil rights once Maddox's people had finished the platforms, or give permission for a U.S. military base on Socotra. If she didn't pass that information on to State and the White House, she'd be in conflict with her duties. If she told them, though, Eliot would have the president yank her out of Yemen for failing to achieve her primary mission.

Rachmaninoff ended and the exuberant thunder of Chopin's "Polonaise Militaire" filled the air. C. J. decided she would tell them of the primary mission's failure. She also decided to submit her resignation after the successful completion of the humanitarian mission. But that could wait. State and the White House did not control her fate. She did. If she could at least save the life of that little girl in the hospital, the tradeoff would be worth it.

DAY 12

Mar'ib, 0302 (GMT)

Stark and Golzari said their good-byes to Mutahar and Ali as servants stowed their bags in the embassy SUV. The walls surrounding the estate glowed like molten gold in the dawn light. Only they, their hosts, and the guards were outside at this hour to see the breathtaking sight.

"Two days with Connor, Ali. Has this made you happy?"

"Oh, yes," the boy answered. "Time spent with Uncle Connor is always a pleasure. Next time you are here, Uncle, we will have another match, and I will do even better."

"Yes, Ali. I look forward to it. Keep training. I am honored that you allow me the privilege to train with you."

"Peace be upon you, Uncle Connor."

"And you, your father, and your house, Ali," Stark said, shaking the boy's hand, as fond and proud of him as an uncle would be. He turned to embrace Mutahar.

"Thank you for teaching him again, Connor," Mutahar whispered in his ear. "Next time, we will not have so many people here so we can break out the scotch."

"Then I must return soon."

One of the estate's guards approached Ali and escorted him back to the stables.

As soon as they were in the car, Stark asked the question he had not forgotten. "Where did you go?"

"Mukalla. I broke into the shipping company's office, pocketed a hotel cardkey, went to the hotel, and scared Ahmed al-Ghaydah so much that he lost his balance, fell off the balcony, and died. Is that sufficient? I'd just as soon not file a written report and have to explain all that to my supervisors."

"What the hell, Golzari?" Stark exploded. "Are you nuts? That guy worked for Mutahar! If the past two days haven't given you a clue, I happen to have a relationship with him and his family. Plus, I'm in the middle of negotiating with them. They are integral to the success of the mission. Idiot."

"Listen, Stark, I wasn't careless. They don't know I was involved."

"You can't be sure of that."

"I'm a professional."

"Yeah. So professional that you accidentally killed a guy."

When Golzari ignored him, Stark showed rare restraint and opted against continuing the argument.

Golzari was the first to break the silence. "I fenced at school in England."

"Jolly good for you," Stark retorted sarcastically.

"I watched you work with Ali. You knew what you were doing. What was that comment he made about the Olympics?"

"It's one of those 'long time ago, long story' things."

"It'll be a quiet ride otherwise."

"Okay. I competed in modern pentathlon. It's not that popular anymore. People are more interested in extreme skateboarding."

"You really were in the Olympics?" Golzari was getting accustomed to impressive revelations about Stark, but he refused to be impressed. Even barbarian Visigoths had been trained for the ring as gladiators.

"Only in '88. I was training for the '92 Olympics but got sidelined by an injury."

"Sorry to hear that. What happened?"

"My ship made a port call in Naples. I was in a café with friends. The Red Brigade saw U.S. Navy targets of opportunity and opened fire on us. Wrong place, wrong time."

They were now approaching the outskirts of Old Mar'ib, one of the region's most ancient cities. The dirt road wound up and down the sloping hills that surrounded the ruins. Stone blocks strewn about like an earthquake had struck the area were all that remained of ancient structures ravaged by time and the wars that have always plagued the region. No one lived here anymore. Stark became aware that the vehicle had begun slowly accelerating and then decelerating, and he saw that Golzari's eyes darted back and forth between the odometer and the rearview mirror.

"Problem?" he asked the DSS agent.

"I think so. Car back there has been following us for about ten minutes. They're keeping pace with our speed." Stark reached behind him to pull his Beretta from his go-bag as Golzari hit the accelerator.

"Let's see if he wants to keep up with me," Golzari said as the speedometer hit seventy, eighty, and then eighty-five miles an hour. The other car kept pace.

Stark looked ahead and saw a truck stopped in the middle of the road. Two people were inside and two were standing outside. One of the latter held a long tube to his shoulder.

"Shit, it's an ambush! Golzari, slow down!"

"Bloody hell," Golzari said, decelerating to sixty miles per hour. Force protection rules dictated more speed, but if the men ahead had what he thought they had, the embassy SUV wouldn't make it through. A quick survey of the almost barren land around him left only one choice for cover—the ruins on the hill. Years of training took over. "Grab the go-bags," he said calmly to Stark. His own M4 had been at his side with a chambered round since they left the estate. He left the road and sped toward the closest hill. The men waiting in ambush quickly got into the truck and followed, tires throwing up sand and dust. The pursuit car was nearing but still remained a quarter mile behind them.

If they were going to make a stand anywhere, it would have to be the hill, which offered the highest ground and, with the large rocks and oversized building stones, the best protection. Golzari hit the brakes, simultaneously turning the steering wheel so that the vehicle would skid and present its full length to the attackers and offer a possible barricade for defense. He slammed the SUV into park next to a long slope that rose two hundred yards to a cluster of stone blocks the size of refrigerators. A few old columns still stood proud and tall against the azure sky, but most had fallen and crumbled through the long years. "Go!" he directed Stark, who grabbed both bags and leapt from the vehicle.

The loose dirt, pebbles, and stones on the hillside forced Stark to keep a cautious pace. He made a break for an opening between two clusters of ruins and set up a defensive position behind one of them.

Golzari followed Stark out the passenger-side door and trained his M4 on the pursuit car, now only a hundred yards away. He quickly adjusted the rear sight, then took two shots at the driver. One hit, and the car veered away and slowed. Golzari continued to fire rounds into the car and saw a second man slump from sight. The truck came into range, and Golzari emptied his clip toward it, hoping for a lucky shot. Nothing doing; it was time to get under cover.

As he started up the slope, gunfire erupted from the ruins above. Stark was laying down suppressing fire. A few rounds from the attackers kicked up some dust nearby, but Golzari reached the stones unhurt. Stark had discarded his peashooter and was standing ten yards away with his M4, resting it on a shoulder-high stone for stability. When he saw Golzari safely behind a large stone to his left, Stark reached down, retrieved Golzari's go-bag, and tossed it toward him.

"First car is to the right about three hundred yards," Stark called out. "Two men up with rifles. I've got them. You get the other two. The truck is four hundred yards down and to the left. Four men. I think two have RPGs. What's the range on those?"

"Paint a bull's-eye here."

Stark dropped down and rolled to the right side of his shelter to get a clear view of the slope below. None of the six men—plus the first he'd injured—were moving.

"What do you see, Stark?" Golzari yelled as he reloaded his weapon.

"One of the RPG guys is up and he's . . . shit! Incoming!" Stark rolled back against the rock and opened his mouth to minimize the change in pressure from the imminent explosion.

Golzari did the same just before dirt and debris rained down from the ruins uphill. Golzari peered around just long enough to see that the embassy vehicle was a smoking shambles. "They got our SUV," he yelled to Stark. "Give me some suppressing fire again on three. Ready? One-two-three!"

Stark came around on his good knee and began firing to cover Golzari, who popped up from behind his stone to take a shot at one of the truck crew. His aim was off. The man recoiled with an arm wound, still alive. Golzari hoped that would be enough to take him out of the action.

Stark dove back behind cover, but not before he saw the RPG belch flames again. "Incoming!" he shouted again to Golzari.

Golzari hit the ground just as a rocket-propelled grenade destroyed half of the rock sheltering Stark, covering both men with gravel. He dusted himself off and took stock of the situation. "You okay, Stark?"

"Yeah, just give me a minute."

"We don't have a minute." Golzari looked around again to fire his weapon.

"What are they doing?" Stark asked.

"Three firing from the car, two from the truck, plus two injured. They're not moving away yet. One more thing. They all look like Somalis."

"Pirates? Here?"

"That's my guess. That could be good for us. If they were soldiers, they'd know what they were doing."

"We're still outnumbered three to one. Feels like the Alamo," said Stark.

"Or the Knights Hospitaller and the Siege of Malta in 1565," Golzari countered.

"What's the difference?"

"The Knights got out."

"I like that better. How many grenades do you think they have?"

"I don't know, but it looks like they're reloading now. Let's put another few rounds into the truck. Ready on three." On "three," both men stood and emptied their magazines at the truck. Another truckbound Somali went down with Stark's shots. The one Golzari had shot earlier was still flailing about on the ground, holding his arm. The attackers responded with another round. Puffs of dirt exploded up the slope until one found its mark.

Golzari yelled and dropped to the ground, leaving his M4 resting on the rock above him.

"Golzari?"

When the DSS agent didn't respond, Stark fired a few rounds toward the car and then dropped behind the rock. For the moment, at least, the Somalis had stopped firing.

"Golzari?"

"My arm. Those bastards hit my forearm."

"How bad?"

"I've got a kit in my bag to treat it, but I won't be able to aim the M4."

"Too bad. Why don't you use your Sig or my Beretta? Or can't you fire a peashooter?"

"Screw you."

"Tsk, tsk," Stark shook his head. "Did you learn that kind of language in your posh English school? Treat it. I'll cover for a while." He popped back up and fired a few more rounds.

Golzari slapped a trauma pad in a bandage around his forearm as Stark kept firing, moving toward the row of columns on his right to get a clear view of the truck. The Somalis had tried to get the truck up the slope, but it had stalled after a few yards. The men were outside it now, sheltering behind the truck body, but their calves and ankles were visible beneath it. *A body shot would be better,* Stark thought, *but they're not going to go anywhere without legs.* He took the shots. Two Somalis formerly confident of their cover began rolling around in pain.

That meant there were only two left behind the car, though only one was firing. Stark checked to make sure his 9-mm was still secure in his belt, then crouched and peered around further to the right. The missing Somali was running up the far side of the slope, hoping to come up behind Stark and Golzari and put them in a crossfire.

Stark fired another quick burst at the car and then ran toward a ruined column that would give him some cover as he tried to locate the other Somali. As he moved on toward the next column in the line he heard Golzari's Sig, which both men knew was relatively useless at this range against the remaining Somali at the car. At least Golzari was still firing. Stark bent his head toward what he estimated to be the new position of the running man and, seeing nothing, bounced behind the third column.

"Stark? Where the hell are you?" he heard Golzari call. Stark made his way to the fourth column and peered out again. His target was now crouching behind some rocks. He was looking toward Golzari's position but still lacked a clear view. He hadn't seen Stark yet. The Somali moved up another few paces as he continued to exchange fire with Golzari. Thirty yards separated Stark and the Somali. Stark pulled up his Beretta and rested it on the column, using both hands to aim it. He fired one shot, then two more in quick succession. The first shot grazed the Somali's temple; the second two found their mark and he fell dead.

Stark picked up the M4 and made his way back to the redoubt, signaling Golzari that one more attacker was down. A few bullets hit the stones, their vector indicating that they had been fired from the direction of the truck. At best estimate, two from the car were unharmed and three were dead while three who had been with the truck were injured plus one dead. Injured or not, they were clearly not yet out of the game.

"How do you want to handle this, Golzari?"

"Do you have any clear shots?"

Stark stood and again settled the M4 on the stone, sighting the truck. "One of the downed guys is against the far tire. All I see is a foot. Two are crowded behind the other one." He shifted toward the car. "Shit, one of them is getting in the car." Stark took aim from 350 yards at the front right and rear right tires, flattening them as the car limped away. He fired at the rear window, shattering it, but the car continued. He didn't have another clear shot at the driver. The five surviving attackers were waving their AK-47s after the retreating car.

"You were right," Stark said; "they're not professionals. One of them just drove away and left the others behind. I managed to hit a couple of tires."

"It's better than nothing. We can't advance on these guys without cover." Smoke was still billowing from the shattered embassy SUV, but in the still air it offered no smokescreen to give them cover.

"That smoke should tell folks we're here, anyway," Golzari said. "Or maybe it won't. There don't seem to be many people out here, and the ones who are all want to kill us."

"Do you think we can hold them off another twenty minutes?"

"We've done pretty well so far, haven't we?"

"Maybe. Can you fire your M4?"

"Not accurately."

"I don't need you to be accurate. Hold on."

From his own go-bag Stark retrieved his satellite phone and a map of the area.

"This is Highland One Bravo, request immediate emergency extraction. Condition two. Repeat, this is Highland One Bravo . . ." He added map coordinates and then turned off the phone.

"If you can cover me, Golzari, I can get a better view of them. Just keep them thinking."

"Ready when you are."

"Go!"

Golzari began firing toward the truck in two-round bursts a few seconds apart, ready to reload when needed while Stark advanced toward the remains of the embassy vehicle, pulling up his shirt to protect his mouth and nose from the noxious fumes. Stark moved diagonally downhill toward the truck, keeping his weapon in firing position.

The men's voices grew louder as he closed on their location. He crouched low to the ground looking for an opportunity and a line of fire. The change of location was beginning to make a difference. He could see more of their lower limbs. They weren't returning fire, just trying to figure a way out. He continued to crawl and advance on them, going straight downhill now.

After another forty yards he stopped and waited for one of the Somalis to make a mistake. He didn't wait long. One of them leaned down below the truck to see what was happening. Stark, without any cover at all, was clearly visible.

That sight was the last thing the Somali saw before one of Stark's bullets took out half of his skull.

Two scampered for the rocks, offering Stark larger targets. With four more shots the Battle of Bar'an Temple was over. The Knights Hospitaller had won.

Golzari descended to the truck as Stark ensured that all the remaining Somali attackers were dead. "Nice work," he admitted. It was the closest to a thank-you he could generate at the moment. He searched the bodies for anything that might identify them. There was nothing but some money.

"Anything?"

"Small currency. The one who drove away? It looked like Asha."

"Asha seems pretty central to all this."

"It was just an accident that I was able to tie him into it." Golzari was looking over the truck one more time.

"What do you mean?"

Golzari decided it was time to confide in Stark and told him the whole story of his investigation.

Stark was an interested audience. "How many kids go to that college?" he asked.

"About two thousand."

"Is it just a coincidence that Asha became involved with the deputy secretary of state's son?"

"Not likely." Golzari rechecked the currency the Somalis had been carrying and this time noticed foreign currency mixed in. "Russian rubles, Chinese yuan, Indian rupees, Philippine pesos. Want to guess why they're together?"

"Easy. Those are the most common nationalities at sea—and the ones most commonly taken by pirates."

Golzari pulled a gold watch from his pocket. "This is the piece that sent us down this path. This is what Johnny Dunner found in the container of khat he picked up in Boston: a watch belonging to a merchant captain whose ship was taken by pirates. It was in an envelope addressed to Asha."

"This attack certainly fits the pirates' MO," Stark noted. "An ambush using a couple of vehicles. A couple of RPGs, some AK-47s, but not the smarts to finish when someone actually fights back."

"I don't like the way this is shaping up, old man. Asha and al-Ghaydah, a guy who works—worked—for your friend, Mutahar."

"Correction. He used family influence to worm his way in. Mutahar never wanted him."

"Any chance Mutahar is al-Yemeni?"

"None. He could have had me killed anytime and anywhere. Even on the estate."

"But in the Arab culture you don't mistreat a guest."

"Let's assume that. Why would he have invested in the meetings with the other officials?"

"To find out what you know?" Golzari probed.

"I don't know anything."

"Hmm, I'll leave that one alone for now. Maybe it's someone else, someone using the biggest shipping company in Yemen to secure knowledge of port activity. Here's a copy of the list of ships that had checkmarks next to it that I took from al-Ghaydah's office. You'll note that they're all ships that were attacked by pirates."

"Including the *Kirkwall*," Stark commented as he scanned the list.

"The *Kirkwall* and the two ships it escorted," Golzari corrected. "Al-Ghaydah was tipping off the pirates. He knew the cargo, time of departure, and next port of call for each."

"The only time they ever attacked a security ship, though, was when I was aboard."

"That's the only variable that I can think of, too."

"Scotland, the *Kirkwall*, and now here. I've been the target all along."

"Defense attachés have always been targets, Commander. The terrorist group November 17 in Greece killed a couple of DATTs awhile back."

"They didn't attack my predecessor. And in Scotland I wasn't the DATT yet . . . actually, that's not entirely right. I had just gotten my orders to return to duty."

"Do the other factions in Yemen know about your close relationship with the ruling family?"

"Probably. It's no secret."

"Maybe they just wanted to make a point to the U.S. government and take out someone in the military."

That's when it struck Connor. "No, not just military. The military adviser."

"You have something?"

"Mutahar's firstborn, Faisal. He showed up at the estate before you, so he didn't know you would be there, and he left after getting the call about Ahmed's death. Before you arrived, while we were watching Ali swim, he called me a military adviser."

"He could be al-Yemeni," Golzari said. "He has ties to the shipping company. You said he used to run drugs on his own boat."

"But he was attacked by pirates," said Stark.

"Was he attacked, or was it a drug deal gone wrong?"

"If he is al-Yemeni, why would he do it? He's a member of the ruling family. His father is one of the richest men in the country and he's the oldest son, meaning that he will inherit it all someday. He certainly doesn't need the money. Unless he has some other motivation . . ." Stark stopped for a moment's reflection. Then he continued slowly. "I'm remembering another Yemeni son. His father was a rich man who built things for the Saudi royal family. He took a different path and decided to destroy rather than build. He became a terrorist and started his very own worldwide network."

"Bin Laden?"

"Bin Laden."

"All right, then, Commander. We have work to do. We need to get back to the embassy. We can take this truck."

"We have help arriving soon, and it'll be a lot safer and quicker in the air."

"Who did you call?"

"Mercs. You know, people like me."

They limped back up the hill together as the familiar *thump-thump-thump* of a helicopter's rotors sounded in the distance.

"You did well, Commander," Golzari said as he picked up his bag.

Stark extended his hand, "Connor."

Golzari returned the gesture with his good arm. "Damien."

Their clasp grew firmer in a final competition of wills.

Mar'ib, 0307 (GMT)

As Ali entered the stable, one of the estate's workers emerged from a stall and walked directly toward him. In his hand was a piece of cloth. Ali sensed something wrong and took a step backward against his bodyguard. The bodyguard grabbed Ali's arms and held him. Before the boy could scream, the other man was upon him, pressing the chloroform-soaked cloth against his face. Ali struggled for a few moments, trying not to inhale, but inevitably he did.

"Quickly," the worker said to the bodyguard, "put him in the trunk when I back up to the stable. If anyone sees us, we will lose our heads."

PART III

DAY 12 (cont.)

U.S. Embassy, Sana'a, 0831 (GMT)

Sighing in disgust, C.J. shook her head at the two dirty, dusty, bloody men who stood in front of her desk. "It certainly hasn't been boring since you two arrived. Think either of you can make it a couple of days before getting attacked again?" She pointed at Golzari's bandaged arm. "Are you responsible for this, Commander Stark?"

"No, ma'am. Not this time. Special Agent Golzari was wounded in the course of a firefight outside Mar'ib as we were returning to Sana'a."

"Commander Stark is correct, Madam Ambassador. Eight men, probably Somalis, ambushed us. We killed seven of them. The eighth got away. Commander Stark is largely responsible for stopping them because I was wounded almost immediately."

"Special Agent Golzari doesn't do himself justice," Stark interjected. "Had he not found high ground and cover and taken out two of the attackers immediately, we would have been vastly outnumbered and in a poor tactical position. It was due to his quick thinking and professionalism that we were able to defeat them."

C. J. leaned back in her chair and marveled at the change in their behavior. It was the first time she heard them use official titles. They were treating one another with respect. And they were fighting other people now rather than each other. She could work with this. "Sit down, please, gentlemen, and tell me exactly what happened. No, wait." She held up her hand and spoke into her intercom. "Mindy, please bring a first aid kit and some water." She looked from one man to the other. "Special Agent Golzari, why don't you tell me about the ambush."

After Golzari had described the ambush and Stark had added further details of his meetings with the Yemenis, she gave them her own news. "We're a go for Socotra from the White House," she began, "so we can get this operation under way." She turned to Stark. "Commander, I'd like you to take the lead on organizing the mission."

"Yes, ma'am."

"I saw Bill Maddox on Socotra—" she added.

"You went to Socotra without me, ma'am?" Golzari interjected.

"Don't worry," she said, raising her hands in mock self-defense. "Gunnery Sergeant Willis and his Marines provided excellent protection throughout. Agent Golzari, I'd like you to work with Commander Stark on the mission's security," she continued, then stopped and thought for a moment. "Wait a minute. Let's go back to the ambush. Did you say Asha was among the Somali attackers?"

"I believe so," the agent said.

"Why would a Somali drug-runner ambush U.S. embassy personnel? Do you have any ideas?"

"Just a tie to a shipping firm, and possibly to the ruling family, Madam Ambassador."

She inhaled. "How much of a tie, Agent Golzari?"

"Perhaps the good commander should answer that one."

"We're not sure," Stark said. "We think my friend's son may be involved, but we haven't had time to confirm that yet."

"What if he is, Connor? What then? I can't negotiate with the Yemenis if one of them is involved. We have to know. Can you talk to your friend?" she asked.

"Okay. I'll see what I can find out. But I'll have to do this very carefully."

USS *Bennington*, Djibouti, 0950 (GMT)

Bobby Fisk stood on the quarterdeck wiping sweat and sand from his face as he tried to breathe without singeing his lungs. The humid, oven-hot air of the port off the Bab el Mandeb at the juncture of the Red Sea and the Gulf of Aden felt like heated sandpaper as it scraped against his throat. He watched as crewmen escorted the last of the *Kirkwall* survivors off the ship and into the van that would take them to Camp Lemonier for a final checkup before they were flown back to the States.

The *Bennington* was scheduled to be in port only half a day for refueling, but at least Bobby was looking at dry land. The high-speed dash across the Gulf of Aden to rescue the *Kirkwall*'s survivors had depleted too much fuel to let the ship continue on patrol. Maybe the captain would enjoy himself so much that he'd let the ship make more port calls in the future. Bobby smiled at the thought.

OPS rounded the corner. "Bobby, have you seen the skipper or SUPPO?"

"He and the XO left here about five minutes ago."

"Well, I have good news for you. It looks like we'll be here overnight after all."

"Problems?"

"Nope. We just got orders from Fifth Fleet to load up on medical supplies, food, and extra water."

"For what?"

"We're directed to support humanitarian operations on an island a few days from here. We'll deliver the supplies and then be on our way. Nothing exciting."

Suleiman, South of Mukalla, 1400 (GMT)

Faisal lit another cigarette as the ship's twin diesel engines drove it through the waters off Mukalla toward the island of Socotra. His crew of ten worked swiftly to secure loose objects on the deck and below in case they ran into inclement weather on the way. "Be sure to secure those skiffs," he commanded from his spot three decks above. The crew hurried to obey. A mother ship without its skiffs was no mother ship.

Another sixty Somali pirates and Yemeni soldiers augmented the ship's regular company for this voyage. When the battle came, some would crew the skiffs while the others would defend the ship. All who survived would be well paid for their service.

Faisal paced back and forth, ignoring the man climbing the starboard ladder to meet him.

"My people are ready, Faisal, and look forward to this mission."

Faisal was silent.

"What troubles you, my friend?" Asha asked, tapping out a cigarette from his own pack.

"The military adviser."

"Don't worry, we will kill him."

"You said that once before, Abdi Mohammed, and you failed to kill him."

"I admit I did not take my best men. I took many men instead, thinking their numbers would overpower the military adviser and the agent. The Americans were lucky. They will not be lucky again." He inclined his head politely. "Perhaps you should have killed him when you had the chance at your father's house."

Faisal took a long drag on his cigarette. "Had I killed him then, I would not be here now."

"He is an American," Asha said contemptuously. "They are for killing."

"My father considers him a brother because he saved my life."

Asha laughed. "Yes, from a former rival pirate clan who turned on you in a deal. But you survived because of him and now command these waters. No merchant ship is safe from your fleet. He is not worth your attention."

"Yes, perhaps," Faisal responded, unconvinced. He dropped his cigarette and ground it out beneath his sandal, then glanced up to watch a couple of his men performing maintenance work on the large circular helipad forward and above the pilothouse. The pad was empty, but not for long. "At least my men now have Ali," he said with satisfaction.

"When do we get the helicopter?"

"Tomorrow. It will fly from Abdul Kori Island to meet us."

"Good. Then you will take us to Socotra before the Americans get there. We will be ready."

"Ready for what, Abdi?" Faisal said sarcastically, "to fail again?"

"You insult me, Faisal? I should kill you for that." Abdi whipped out his knife but froze when a gunshot rang out behind him. He dropped the knife and turned to see two of Faisal's men. One was lowering his gun after firing a shot into the sky. The other was pointing his weapon directly at Abdi Mohammed Asha.

Faisal motioned Asha away. "Do what you are assigned to do, and I will do the same. In the meantime, on my ship, these two men will be at your side to ensure your success."

U.S. Embassy, Sana'a, 1555 (GMT)

After dinner Stark joined Golzari in the RSO's office with an open bottle of scotch. Golzari's actions at Old Mar'ib had dispelled Stark's first assessment of him at RAF Lakenheath as an elitist wimp. His appreciation for good whiskey completed Stark's about-face. For his part, the uptight Diplomatic Security Service agent had loosened his tie and rolled up his sleeves enough to reveal his bandaged forearm.

"Can you still shoot with that injury?" Stark nodded at the forearm while he sipped his Highland Park.

"As well as you can, I'm sure. Sometime when things calm down around here we should go down to the range in the basement and have a little shoot-out."

Stark raised one eyebrow. "At each other?"

"Maybe we'll settle for fencing," Golzari amended.

"That sounds a great deal more civilized."

Golzari was amused to hear the man he had characterized as a Visigoth talk of being civilized.

"Should we talk about this upcoming op?" Stark suggested.

"While we're drinking?"

"We really haven't started drinking yet," Stark said. "Just the basics for now. We'll go over the details tomorrow once we've seen the six Yemen Navy boats that will be escorting us."

"Is a grand plan really necessary? The pirates aren't likely to attack a boat escorted by six Yemeni warships."

"They attacked the *Kirkwall*," Stark pointed out.

"With due respect to the *Kirkwall* and her crew, that was one ship, not half a dozen."

Stark shrugged and changed the subject. "So, how does someone go from a British public school to the U.S. Diplomatic Security Service?"

"It's the only job I've found that allows me to combine my two great interests. My family are naturalized American citizens, but my father insisted on a British education. After Cheltenham I went to George Washington University with a double major in criminology and archaeology."

"Interesting combo."

"Actually they're very similar. In each you look for evidence to put a case or a story together."

"You like working at State?"

"The world needs stability, and protecting diplomats helps to ensure that state-to-state communications continue." The chair squeaked as he slowly rocked while sipping the scotch.

"To stability," Stark said, raising his glass.

Golzari raised his glass in reply. "What about you?"

"Boston University, Navy ROTC. I expected to have a full career." He drank more than a sip of whiskey recalling what might have been.

"What happened?"

"I took an assignment on Capitol Hill because I was promised that it would help my career. It didn't."

"You can never trust those folks on the Hill."

"Mmm, actually O'Rourke was a good man. A real gentleman."

"Senator Padraic O'Rourke?"

"Yeah, why?"

"Didn't the ambassador work for him once?"

"You're quick. We were there at the same time. She worked on foreign affairs and I worked on armed services."

"During the Canada incident," Golzari suggested nonchalantly, hoping for an opening into that long-lost secret.

Stark raised his chin and stared at him.

"Sir?" Gunnery Sergeant Willis said from the doorway.

"Saved by the bell," Stark said. "Pull up a chair, Gunny. It's after hours and the bar's open."

"Thank you, sir. I normally would, but I still have to show a few of our young'uns the proper way to PT tonight. You wouldn't believe how puny the weights they lift are."

"What do you have there, Gunny?" Golzari asked, motioning to a red-striped folder under the sergeant's arm.

"You asked about any intercepts that might be related to the attacks in Yemen and to track down some phone numbers."

"I remember."

"NSA said they couldn't get to the intercepts for a while, but I tracked down a Marine at NSA who helped. I'll leave the folder here for you." He slid the folder across Golzari's desk.

"Thanks. Are you sure you won't have just one with us?" Golzari asked.

"Another time, sir, if you'll save some of that for when we finish this operation." Gunny left and closed the door behind him.

Golzari took out the two sheets and read them. "Shit. That's interesting."

"What?"

Golzari slid the sheets across to Stark, who spent a few minutes trying to extract the information from the clutter. It had been awhile since he'd seen classified documents. When he finished, he read them again. "No access to the phone numbers. The phones they use are a new type of Chinese manufacture. Perfect."

"Not to worry," Golzari said. "It looks like our intelligence friends did confirm something I found earlier—a reference to al-Amriki. 'The American.'"

"And?" Stark asked.

"The intercept references a military adviser aboard the Highland Maritime security ship and notes that al-Amriki wants the ship sunk and the adviser killed. Apparently our late friend Ahmed al-Ghaydah called a friend of his on a regular line and mentioned al-Amriki, saying that the adviser and ambassador were both targets."

"An American is behind all this? And the message was before the attack on us?"

"Yes."

"But we should assume that the order still holds true."

"Absolutely. They'll keep trying."

"If that's the case," Stark mused, "this al-Amriki is trying to undermine our negotiations. If he takes me out, that breaks the embassy's closest tie to the Yemeni government."

"Now you see why I'm worried, old man?"

Stark nodded emphatically. "I see it. It's not just a little khat or piracy that we're dealing with. The cell is trying to drive a wedge between the United States and Yemen, or at least to prevent us from getting closer. Why?"

The two men looked at each other. "Oil," they said simultaneously.

"Okay, let's figure this out," Golzari said, rising to stand before a whiteboard on the office wall. "First, suspects." He drew a rough map of the Gulf of Aden with Socotra in the middle. "First possibility, Somalia," he said, writing down the name.

"Which we can strike from the list," Stark replied from his chair. "Even if they had some right to the oil, they have no operational government; Somaliland and Puntland are self-governing territories, but they don't have the reach, resources, or stability. The warlords certainly couldn't develop it either."

Golzari drew an X over "Somalia" and continued. "Second possibility, Yemen."

Stark shook his head. "Based on my conversations with them recently, I don't think it's them. They already have the power to deny us rights to the oil. There's no reason for them to initiate or escalate any violence."

"What about internal factions?" Golzari said.

"It's possible. The average Yemeni agrees more with al-Qaeda in Yemen than with the government, but even they would know that the government doesn't trust or like America and isn't likely to let us have the oil."

"Then let's go beyond the Gulf. India? Russia? China?" He wrote the names on the whiteboard.

Stark nodded in agreement. "All candidates. India and China especially need oil. How do we link them or any other suspect to the pirates?"

"We just have to pay more attention. The evidence will surface. Even in archaeology it happens."

"But in archaeology you have to wait centuries or millennia," Stark said. "We don't have that kind of time."

Golzari tapped the marker against his desk. "There must be more information out there. If we had full access to other intelligence communities' resources we might be able to find it. If this embassy was fully manned that wouldn't be a problem."

"Wait a minute," Stark said. "Let's go back to the internal factions. Al-Ghaydah's family and Mutahar's family are major rivals."

Golzari tapped faster. "What if Mutahar's son Faisal is working with the other family?"

"That wouldn't make sense. If Faisal wants leadership, he'll probably eventually get it within his own family."

"Probably?" Golzari asked.

"Faisal has been in trouble before. He's smart but he has run drugs. Not legitimate commerce like his father. Plus, Mutahar favors Ali. Mutahar did say that Ali was the family's and the country's future. No mention of Faisal."

"So if Faisal wants to be in power, he has to make a deal with the devil—in this case a rival family like the al-Ghaydahs?"

"Yeah," said Stark quietly. "And Faisal brought in one of the al-Ghaydahs to the family business when Ismael—the stevedore—was killed.

Finally Stark rose. "How about we both get some sleep and take this up early in the morning when our minds are clear?"

Golzari dropped the marker. "Agreed. Thanks for the scotch."

DAY 13

The White House, Washington, D.C., 0214 (GMT)

The Fist of the Senate. That's what they had called him when he was chief of staff for Padraic O'Rourke, the senator with the longest record of service in the history of that august body—longer than Ted Stevens and Strom Thurmond. Even Robert Byrd never broke O'Rourke's record. No piece of legislation was unknown to Green, no tactic undefeated, and no dalliance undetected. Some argued that he held more power than the majority leader himself, a fact not lost on the majority leader, who knew that he owed his position to the Fist.

He, Eliot Green, had engineered the selection of young Congressman Becker to replace the deceased Senator O'Rourke, over the outraged cries of half a dozen more senior politicians in Massachusetts. Then, when the party powers said Senator Becker was too young to be on the national ticket, Green persuaded them that he wasn't. When Becker assumed the presidency at midterm, they had no choice but to embrace him. And Eliot Green—the Fist—was there every step of the way to pound the opposition into complete and utter submission. Now, with the general election just around the corner, Green faced the supreme test of his career in getting a full term for Becker. He had handpicked the campaign manager and senior campaign staff. They were loyal to him, not the president. They did what he ordered, not Becker. Green wanted to do what no one but Reagan and Nixon, both members of the other party, had ever done before and win in a sweep of at least forty-nine states. All he needed was a bad opposition candidate and a national crisis to rally the country around the fallen, the flag, and Hamilton Becker.

The White House staff had all left for the day, and the West Wing tours had been canceled for the evening. Tonight inside the closed and secure Oval Office, it was just President Becker and the Fist.

"I thought the polls would be better by now, Eliot."

"We've been in Afghanistan too long. People understand that it's not your war, but they also expect you to finish the job."

"Finish the job. People don't even know what the job is," Becker complained.

"We know. We'll make them understand, and we'll show that we can do it cheaply and quickly," Green said.

"Eliot, the cost of a war I inherited isn't going to change. We both know we're going to be there a long time, regardless of what we tell the public. And now there's North Korea and Iran to deal with."

"We can ignore Iran."

"The oil?"

"We replace it."

"From where? Alaska? The Gulf of Mexico? I've already promised the environmentalists that I won't authorize new drilling."

"That's why we need to look at Yemen again."

"Are the Yemenis willing to negotiate now?"

"No."

"Then what's changed?"

"Opportunity."

"What kind of opportunity?"

"The kind that comes only once every twenty years. C. J. has been attacked a few times, as has her new defense attaché, Connor Stark."

"That name rings a bell."

"He worked for O'Rourke as a national security fellow on loan to us from the Navy. I released him just before you came to the Senate."

"Why?"

"He was a problem. He asked a lot of questions. Now it turns out that C. J. may have been involved. The secretary of defense told me that she specifically requested that he be returned to active duty to serve as her new defense attaché. Her reports indicate that he has been of great assistance and comfort to her."

Green had eased the president into this discussion. Now it was time for the Fist. "Ambassador Sumner has asked permission to mount a small humanitarian aid operation on the island of Socotra. I spoke with Helen Forth and approved it."

"Why?"

"Because this is an opportunity to show the world the benevolence of the United States as it showers gifts on a village no one has ever heard of."

The president shrugged. "So what? We do that all the time. It doesn't buy us anything."

Green laughed. "This time it will. This is going to win you a second term. A couple of months ago, I informed the Pentagon that we have a new policy in the Gulf of Aden. The Navy is operating only one ship there—the *Bennington*, a low-morale cruiser with a candy-ass captain. Fifth Fleet was told to redistribute most of the ship's defenses to other ships operating in the Persian Gulf. Now I've arranged for Fifth Fleet to order the ship to load up on humanitarian supplies. It's going to pick up Commander Stark in Aden and then go to the north side of Socotra to distribute the relief."

"Again, Eliot, so what? Why are you wasting my time with unimportant details?"

Green looked dispassionately at Becker. He really wasn't aging well. The thick brown hair was thinning, and the lean face was getting jowly. "It *is* important," he explained patiently. "It gives us leverage with the chair of the Senate Armed Services Committee."

"That bastard? He's been a pain in my ass since I was a junior committee member. How would this help with him?"

"His nephew commands the *Bennington*. He's an embarrassment. According to my sources at the Navy, the flag community doesn't want to promote him to admiral because he's incompetent. The ship is going to be attacked and sunk by pirates. He's going to die a hero. Then we're going to send in a quick strike force to Somalia and tell America that we exacted justice."

"Then what?" asked the President, seemingly unconcerned that his chief of staff was proposing to sink a U.S. Navy ship and kill an unknown number of its crew.

"Then," Green continued, "comes the big payoff. In a couple of weeks you walk into the party convention to give the speech of your life and coast all the way to victory in November."

"What about the oil?" the President asked naively. "Didn't you say that C. J. can't get the Yemenis to give us the oil rights?"

"We negotiate with the Chinese to take the oilfields without Yemen's approval, on the grounds of national security. Then we split the oil with China. Yemen can't stop us."

"And you can make all this happen, Eliot?"

"Don't I always?"

"Okay. What about C. J.?"

"What about her?"

"Will she get hurt?"

Green assumed a serious and sympathetic face. "It's not enough for American sailors to be lost in battle, Mr. President. We need civilian casualties too if we're to make the biggest possible impact on the American public. The senator's nephew will be our military hero, and C. J. and the other humanitarian aid workers will become saints."

"Okay, Eliot," the president said, already thinking of the cheers that would greet him from the adoring convention crowds as flags waved and balloons and confetti fell from the ceiling. All for him.

U.S. Embassy, Sana'a, 0715 (GMT)

Stark had waited as long as he could to place the call to Mutahar, but events were spinning up, and he was out of time.

"Connor. I had hoped to hear from you sooner." Mutahar sounded weary.

"Hello, Mutahar. I'm sorry, I should have called earlier."

"I do not have much time at this moment. Why is it that I found out about the attack on you from others?"

"I didn't want to worry you, my brother. The attack failed. I lived. They did not."

"I should have had my security forces escort you. These are difficult days for us all. Ali is missing."

Stark was stunned by this unexpected development. "When?"

"Sometime after you left. A stable hand and Ali's bodyguard are also missing."

"Tell me how I can help."

"You cannot. This is for my family to do. Our people are searching for him. Whoever did this will not live long to regret it."

Stark scrubbed a hand over his face. "Who did this?"

"There are many possibilities—al-Qaeda, other families, the insurgents."

"Have you told Faisal?"

"Faisal is at sea. He cannot help us in the search. Indeed, we rarely see him. He spends much of his time with his own merchant ventures now."

"Mutahar, I ask you as my brother. Is Faisal in trouble again?"

"What do you mean?"

"Is it possible he is tied up with the pirates?"

"Connor, we do not discuss such things—anywhere."

"I apologize, but there has been some . . . curious . . . activity, and I have reason to believe that he is involved. I approach you as my brother. I do not wish ill for him or for you, and I will do anything in my power to prevent dishonor on your family."

"What is it that you know, Connor?"

After explaining what he had learned, Stark continued. "There is something else that troubles me, Mutahar. Only Bill Maddox and you knew where in Scotland I lived. You both swore not to share that information with anyone. Is it possible that Faisal learned of it in your home?"

There was a long silence. And then, wearily, "Perhaps I have betrayed you. Last month Faisal was home on a day I received one of your packages. Faisal saw it before I did and read the label. He asked me about it and I said only that it was from a friend. I am sorry to tell you this."

"Then it was I who betrayed myself, Mutahar. I fear that Faisal arranged for people to find me and attack me in Ullapool."

"Are you certain?"

"I can't be until I speak with him. I must find him immediately."

Mutahar sounded old. "It is possible that I don't know how far my own son has fallen. Connor, is it also possible that Faisal had something to do with Ali's disappearance?"

"Neither of us hopes that is true, my friend."

U.S. Embassy, Sana'a, 0741 (GMT)

C. J. Sumner had used her organizational and political skills, not to mention her boundless energy, to pull off a minor miracle; if she had slept more than four hours during this period her staff would have been shocked. In the thirty-six hours since Washington had approved the humanitarian aid operation she had gone back to her contacts on Capitol Hill and convinced nearly sixty nurses, doctors, and carpenters to drop what they were doing and devote a week of their lives to help an unknown town on the other side of the world. With their help plus the equipment being provided courtesy of the U.S. Navy via Djibouti, she was set to go. She looked forward to telling Stark and Golzari that security would be a cinch because the humanitarian personnel would be traveling on a Navy warship.

This operation was small, but for the first time since she had been named ambassador C. J. felt that she was finally contributing by reaching out to the people who needed help the most. She was descending the embassy's central staircase when she saw Stark emerging from the conference room in company with a dark-skinned man wearing a foreign military uniform. When Stark saw her approaching, he came to attention.

"Madam Ambassador, you remember Captain Dasgupta, India's naval attaché?"

"A pleasure to see you again, Madam Ambassador."

"The same, Captain. Please extend my best wishes to Ambassador Gavaskar."

"I will do so, Madam Ambassador. May I say that he was very impressed by your comments when you last met. I believe he will contact you soon to arrange an embassy-to-embassy dinner. Events promoting cooperation between our two peoples are always appreciated."

"I could not agree more, Captain."

Dasgupta nodded at C. J. and then turned back to Stark and shook his hand.

"We have an understanding then, Captain?" Stark said.

"I believe so, Commander. I will discuss this with my superiors."

"Thank you, Captain. That's all I ask."

"What was that about?" C. J. asked after the attaché had taken his leave.

"Reaching out, Madam Ambassador. Isn't that part of my job as defense attaché?"

She had seen that look of mischief before. The half-smirk on the left side of his face always indicated that he had something unique in play. She narrowed her eyes and looked at him suspiciously. "I thought you didn't want this job."

"It's grown on me."

"In two weeks?"

He smiled. "It's actually good to be back in uniform, C. J. I guess no matter how it happened or why, I appreciate the opportunity to serve again. Captain Dasgupta is a first-rate officer. It's my job to get to know him better." Stark neglected to add that he and Dasgupta, because of the number of Indian employees working on the oil platforms, had agreed that it would be a good idea to have the Indian ship in the area. Dasgupta himself would be aboard in case any questions arose.

C. J. nodded, thinking that Stark's whole demeanor had evolved in the last two weeks. He was once again the professional officer she had known and admired in Washington. He even looked younger, the years wiped away by a renewed purpose. Maybe that was true for both of them. The last vestiges of guilt over a high-handed political maneuver gone bad had finally trickled away. She felt her spirits rise.

At that moment, Damien Golzari approached them at a pace quickened by his long strides. "You wanted to see me, Madam Ambassador?"

"Actually, I wanted to see you both. Let's talk in here," she said, entering the conference room. "There's been a slight change of plan," she added after Golzari had closed the door behind them.

"Are we still doing the op?" Stark asked.

"Yes, but D.C. has decided that since there's a Navy cruiser in the region, it might be best from a security standpoint if it conveyed the people and some of the materials."

"Is that the *Bennington* they're talking about?" Stark's mischievous look was replaced by concern.

"Yes it is, Commander. Is that a problem?"

"I'm not sure. I was aboard for only a few hours after they picked us up, but I wasn't exactly impressed by its captain."

"Oh? Well surely an American naval captain can manage an operation as simple as this one. The ship will make port in Mukalla early tomorrow morning and pick up the fifty-seven aid workers already en route to Sana'a as well as you, me, and Agent Golzari. It's already carrying some of the humanitarian supplies, but it will also escort the *Mukalla Ali*, which will carry the construction materials. The agreement you had with the Yemeni Navy will still hold, won't it, if a U.S. Navy ship is involved?"

"I'm not sure. They're expecting an unarmed supply ship, not a cruiser, but I think I can work it around to make them see the advantage. Joint operations like this are rare. It will be good practice for them," Stark responded, not entirely convinced of his own argument. "One more thing. The cruiser has berthing for four hundred. Another sixty will make things awfully tight."

"Fifth Fleet has already considered that. When the ship arrives, they'll select sixty sailors to disembark. The chartered plane flying into Aden today with the humanitarian workers will pick up the sailors and take them to Bahrain until the operation is finished."

Stark was even more concerned by this news. "That's a lot of crew to lose."

"I'm sure it will be fine, Connor. Really, I thought you'd be happy at the news."

"There is a security issue I'd like to discuss, ma'am," said Golzari. "Commander Stark and I went over some communications intercepts. There's no doubt that the terrorists targeted you and him specifically in the two attacks. If they *do* plan another attack, we may want to consider giving them fewer opportunities to get at you. Staying apart from one another might help."

"So once the ship arrives at anchorage, we should separate?" she asked.

"I suggest that, yes. Perhaps Commander Stark could remain with the ship. It's my duty to remain with you."

"Commander?" she asked her attaché.

"What Agent Golzari says is sound advice."

"Very well, gentlemen; that's the way we'll do it."

DAY 14

USS *Bennington* en Route to Socotra, 1440 (GMT)

"How's our fuel, CHENG?" the captain asked in his high-pitched voice.

Stark ignored the dinner conversation among the senior staff in the wardroom, initiating conversations instead with OPS and Air Boss, who were seated near him at the end of the table. The young ensign who had been present at his last meal in the wardroom was seated to his immediate right. Stark was trying to keep his mind off the disappearance of Ali and focus on the job at hand. Air Boss was picking at his cake while OPS used a spoon to play with his quivering Shivering Liz. Tonight's Jell-O flavor was lime.

After swallowing a scoop of his own Shivering Liz, the ensign turned to Stark. "Excuse me, Commander, I was wondering if you'd answer some questions about the humanitarian mission we're going on."

"Sure, Ensign . . . Fisk," Stark said, looking down at the gold-lettered name on the stocky young officer's blue coveralls.

"I took a course on this at the Academy, and we talked about the type of platforms that would be needed. I was wondering if you thought—"

"Ensign," the captain interrupted, "The commander has a great deal of work to do to prepare for tomorrow's operations. Don't you have some qualifications to work on before your next bridge watch?"

"Aye, sir." Bobby Fisk stood behind his chair and asked to be excused.

"Commander, join us for a cigar?" the OPS officer asked Stark quietly as the captain returned to his customary "twenty questions" dinner conversation. When Stark nodded, he said, "Meet us near the LSO shack in ten minutes."

They excused themselves as Stark doubled back to the galley and asked the generous culinary specialist for unsalted crackers and pickled ginger root. The specialist smiled in sympathy as she put a plate in his hands.

"How's the ambassador, Damien?"

"Still sick as a dog."

The two men stood in the narrow passageway outside the quarters assigned to DESRON—the squadron commander—and VIP guests.

"Should we check on her?" Stark showed him the plate of crackers and ginger. "The crackers will put something in her stomach, and the ginger will help with the nausea."

After knocking and hearing a loud moan, they entered the dayroom and then the stateroom itself. C. J. was curled in a fetal position on the bed, her head next to a conveniently located wastebasket.

"Your manservants have arrived, Madam Ambassador," Connor said, receiving only a groan in reply.

"I'll leave this here for you, C. J. It'll settle your stomach. Eat it all. You need to be up and running tomorrow morning, okay?"

Her response of a dry heave could only be interpreted as a "maybe." They left her to her own discomfort.

"Are you going to stay outside her stateroom all night?" Stark asked. "You need to get some sleep, too. Tomorrow is going to be a long and busy day."

"Don't worry, the sheriff of this ship is going to relieve me in a couple of hours. We'll go two on, two off tonight. I'll be fine."

"Do you need me to take a shift?"

"Would I pay your commander salary or your merc salary?"

"This one's free."

"Thanks, but it might be too tough on your constitution, old man."

"Not as tough as my fist on your nose, Damien," Stark warned.

The two lieutenant commanders were already puffing on their cigars when Stark joined them near the LSO shack. The only light came from the green bioluminescent trail in their wake. The weapons officer showed up soon afterward, and the *Bennington*'s officers vied with one another to tell the most outrageous stories about their CO.

"I'm surprised there hasn't been a mutiny," Stark said after hearing a few. "Should I be worried about this operation?"

"That's a loaded question, sir," answered OPS. "He'll follow the letter of the law, but he won't go one bit further than he has to. As for the rest of the crew, some will do whatever's necessary to make this mission a success; others won't."

As the discussion wound down, WEPS broached the subject none of them had dared mention before. "Commander, you ought to know something about that night you first joined us."

"What's that?"

"Best you see it for yourself, sir," WEPS said, stubbing out his cigar. "Go to the bridge after twenty-three hundred. The CO does his final quick walk-through on the bridge at twenty-two hundred and then hits the rack."

"What should I look for on the bridge?"

"Check the deck log from that night. Check it really closely."

The cryptic suggestion piqued Stark's curiosity, and twenty-three hundred found him in the company of six other crew members on the bridge—the OOD, Ensign Fisk as the conning officer, two men working at the chart table, a short female helmsman, and an OS2 at the radar repeater on the starboard side of the bridge.

"What's your first name, Ensign?"

"Bobby, sir."

"Play any sports at the Academy, Bobby?"

"Started out playing baseball but wound up on the pistol team. I never shot before I got there. I spent a lot of extra time at the shooting range to catch up to the other mids on the team." Bobby chose not to mention getting cut from the baseball team and putting all of his time and effort into becoming a marksman.

"Thanks for your question about humanitarian ops," Stark said. "Let's get through this cycle, and then we'll find a place to talk about force structure options—give you some things to think about for when you're a captain or Chief of Naval Operations."

"Neither of those, sir. Not at this rate. I thought for sure I'd do at least twenty, but I'll be out in five."

"This deployment can't be that bad."

Bobby just shook his head.

"You know, Bobby, you have a good wardroom. They're good officers and good role models."

"I know, sir. They're great. They're not the problem."

"Don't give up, Bobby. Tough times call for good people to rise to the occasion. We'll do some good for these people on Socotra, people who've never heard of us and won't ever see us again. But we'll be helping them. It's a good feeling. That's one of the many positive things we get to do in the Navy. You'll learn from this experience—what to do and what not to do. And as you rise in the ranks, you'll look after those behind you."

"Thanks, sir."

"My pleasure, Ensign. It's been awhile since I've been on a Navy bridge. Can you show me around?"

Fisk showed Stark each of the bridge stations in turn, interrupting their conversation now and then to issue course changes and speed commands to the helm.

"We didn't have one of these when I was in," Stark said, pointing to a high-tech screen.

"That's the VMS navigational display, sir. We can preset coordinates based on the navigator's recommendations and then see how closely our actual course has aligned with the original track."

Stark narrowed his eyes as he tried to read the display. Something stood out. "We're operating in a box at this point?"

"Yes, sir. Since earlier this evening, when all the ships arrived just north of Socotra after an eighteen-hour transit, each of the ships has been assigned a box that they're required to maneuver within until we re-form tomorrow at zero eight hundred for the final leg to the anchorage point outside Hadiboh."

"Can this display zoom in and out?"

"Of course, sir," said Fisk, reaching down to adjust the screen.

"While we're in this operational box, you're deciding on the track we follow, right?" Stark asked.

"Uh, yes, sir."

Stark brought up the reason for his visit. "May I borrow your flashlight to look at the deck log?"

"Of course, sir. Looking for anything specific?"

"Just curious, Bobby, about the night last week when the ship picked up me and the other *Kirkwall* survivors."

"I was the conning officer that night. The captain had me pulling double duty."

Stark read through the times and course and speed corrections, especially at the beginning, then went to the chart table. "QM1, do you still have the marked-up charts from the night I was picked up? Here's the exact time."

The quartermaster returned a few minutes later and handed him the requested chart. Stark, though out of practice, made some calculations and then straightened.

"QM1, all of these times and data points are correct?"

"Of course, sir. We double-check everything."

"I thought so. Thanks." Stark rejoined Fisk near the window and spoke softly. "Bobby, can you tell me why the captain didn't order flank speed immediately after you received our general hail for emergency assistance?"

"We recommended flank speed, sir, but the CO ordered us to proceed at trail shaft. Eventually, the other officers argued the case to him and he changed the order."

"Why would he have ordered trail shaft in the first place?"

"You'd probably get a better answer from OPS or CHENG, sir."

"I'm asking you. What the hell was the captain thinking?"

"He's very concerned about fuel efficiency, sir."

Stark shuddered as he considered what would have happened if the captain's original order had been carried out. Then he looked back at the VMS screen. "Is there another VMS screen?"

"Yes, sir," Bobby said hesitantly. "In the captain's quarters above his rack."

Stark manipulated the trackball and zoomed out from the intended ship's track to display a track that followed two three-quarter circles separated by a long shaft of two parallel tracks.

"Interesting track. What do you call it?"

"The, uh, . . . cock 'n balls track. Sir, do you want me to delete the track and the current course?" he asked.

"No, keep it there, Bobby. Keep it right there," Stark said.

DAY 15

Mar'ib, 0401 (GMT)

Mutahar's desk at his estate had three phones. He was talking on one of them when his chief security officer knocked softly and entered the room. Mutahar interrupted his conversation immediately and hung up the phone. "What is it?"

"Faisal. We cannot reach him."

"Why not?"

"His ship left Mukalla two days ago."

"So? He has a satellite phone on his ship, does he not?"

"We tried."

"What is the ship's destination?"

"It reported no destination."

Mutahar stood and placed both hands flat on his ornate desk. Anger darkened his eyes. "Get me the admiral right now."

USS *Bennington*, off Socotra, 0423 (GMT)

"RSO, DATT. Radio check." Stark depressed the button on the radio Golzari had given him. The defense attaché, in his blue coveralls and wearing a ball cap with the ship's crest, was standing on the starboard bridge wing.

"DATT, RSO. I read you loud and clear, over." Golzari responded from one of the cruiser's two RHIBs as it was being lowered, giving a wave to Stark. C. J., wearing a yellow life vest sat beside him.

Stark returned the friendly gesture with his fingers touching the rim of his ball cap in an informal salute. "RSO, DATT. Good luck. DATT out." The Motorola radio had a range of up to five miles, well within the target zone.

The *Bennington* was at anchor three miles off Hadiboh. Most of the humanitarian operation would take place within a quarter mile of the town itself, so Stark and Golzari would be able to speak at will except for a period later in the morning when Air Boss was going to take Stark along in his helo during its surveillance mission.

A semicircle of Yemeni ships sheltered the cruiser and the accompanying supply ship from possible danger. Beyond them were a few fishing boats, but nothing else of note showed within sight or on the radar. The aid workers were huddled on the deck waiting their turn in the RHIBs. Ten had joined the ambassador and Golzari in the first RHIB. At this rate, Stark calculated, all of them would be ashore within ninety minutes. Supplies were being offloaded on the shore from the *Mukalla Ali*, a small roll-on roll-off ship.

The flurry of activity and the high-noon sunshine on the rippling water reminded Stark of his first day at sea as a newly minted ensign on the last remaining U.S. battleship making its final deployment. When the ship pulled out of Norfolk, it passed one of the new Aegis cruisers—perhaps even the *Bennington*. Now, it was the cruiser's last deployment on its final mission. He hoped the *Bennington* would carry out this mission better than its last one.

"Commander, you ready to fly?" Air Boss looked eager to get in the air.

"Ready."

"We'll fly Batwing 57—check with our aircrew for a helmet with a mike that actually works. We'll fly to the east and north. Batwing 58 is scheduled to take off two hours after us for the west."

"Good. Are you armed?"

"Four Hellfire missiles and an M-240 7.62-mm machine gun. Around here, it's always better to be armed, although it took a lot of convincing to get the captain to agree."

"It seems he needs a lot of convincing to do a lot of things."

Air Boss grinned. "He does. But we have a way around that for emergencies, like when we sped up the night we took you and the others aboard."

"How'd you do it?"

The lieutenant commander swiveled his head to ensure no one overheard. "OPS has a friend at Fifth Fleet. We've only done it a few times, but we can gin up orders to move the captain along."

"Otherwise he'll take action like a snail?"

"Pretty much."

"I see. Thanks for keeping me in the loop, Boss. The secret's safe with me. Remember, the only rules you shouldn't follow are the stupid ones."

"I like your style, Commander. Care to join us for the rest of the deployment?"

"With or without the captain?"

"We can only do so much, sir."

"I'm trying to help, Boss. I suggested to the XO that we post more watchstanders and get a few more shooters on the deck. I don't want what happened to my boat to happen to this ship."

Fifteen minutes later, Batwing's pilot and copilot watched as an air crewman escorted the crouching Commander Stark to the rescue station seat and buckled him in. A few minutes later the OD issued the "green deck" command, granting permission for the helicopter to launch. The 53-foot rotor blades spun up to speed, powered by 3,600-shaft horsepower, and twenty-two thousand pounds lifted off the deck with four souls aboard and reported its status to the Combat Information Center.

Hadiboh, Socotra, 0610 (GMT)

The humanitarian operation's hillside base camp was on the inland side of Hadiboh, on a slight rise with a clear view of the crescent-shaped stretch of coast where the locals beached their fishing boats and where the cruiser's RHIBs were landing people and material. The RHIBs raced back and forth shuttling people from the ship, which was clearly visible at anchor out in deeper water. A narrow paved road led from the beach up to the town of nine thousand. Few of the stone buildings still standing after the earthquake had more than a single story. Functional vehicles were few, although rusting pickup trucks dotted the town, their tires and windows long since removed for other purposes. To the east were the mountains of Socotra. Golzari assigned his two assistant RSOs and two Marines to stand watch from the two tallest rooftops.

Under the shelter of a small tent at the edge of the base camp Ambassador C. J. Sumner was looking at an oversized diagram of the operation. Bill Maddox stood to her left. To her right, Special Agent Damien Golzari stood with his back to her in order to watch for potential threats. Several Highland Maritime Defense personnel were nearby to protect Maddox.

"I see you've decided to set up within sight of the Chinese archway," commented Maddox. "Rubbing it in their face, C. J.?"

"No more than they'd rub it in ours. I know they're just itching to get their hands on that oil offshore."

"I don't have much choice in that, C. J., unless you can think of another option the U.S. government would approve."

She frowned at him. "There are always options."

"You have an idea?"

She shrugged noncommittally. "I'm not sure. Let's get this set up first. We can talk tomorrow once things are rolling along here."

Golzari strolled around the open-sided tent, satisfied that the ambassador was safe for the moment. C. J. paid no attention to him as she leaned over the table and scribbled on the drawing, modifying where key people and supplies would be located to make the process more efficient.

"For a place so far off the map, this island has a lot of legends connected to it," Golzari said, his eyes moving constantly as he monitored the camp.

"Really?" C. J. said, without looking up from her diagram.

"According to local legend the Apostle Thomas was shipwrecked here and converted the island's population."

"It didn't stick, then." She erased some names on the paper and moved them to a different sector.

"Marco Polo visited here, too. He thought the locals were witches who could conjure up storms to destroy invading ships."

Sumner stopped working and straightened to look up at him; in flat soles, the ambassador was nearly a foot shorter than Golzari.

"Is this idle chitchat, or is there a point?" She put her pencil between her teeth and crossed her arms.

"A little of both. I haven't seen much out of the ordinary on this island—aside from the Chinese, of course. But out there . . ." he tilted his head toward the *Bennington*.

She took her pencil out of her mouth and tossed it on the diagram. "He has a way of finding trouble, doesn't he?"

"I'm more concerned that trouble has a way of finding him." Golzari shrugged as if to shake a nagging doubt, then turned his attention to her diagram.

"I'm intrigued by this plan, Madam Ambassador."

"Go on."

"The setup you've designed is a semicircle centered on your tent. To the right you have the emergency hospital tents, in the middle you have the tents where the medical personnel will sleep, and to the left the construction workers. Back behind the semicircle you have boxes for the supplies we'll use for construction."

"So?"

"If I didn't know any better, I'd say this was a perfect design for an orchestra. The violins here, the timpani and percussion back there, the woodwinds and brass over there. And that would put you—here—as the conductor."

She laughed, amused to be found out by her bodyguard. "Huh, well, it seemed reasonable and organized."

"It is. It's a model of efficiency. It also makes my job much easier. I know where everyone is and my men are perfectly positioned in the taller buildings on both sides of us."

"You're familiar with classical music, Agent Golzari?"

"Yes, of course. But when I play the piano I prefer jazz. Like Brubeck."

"How do you feel about Chet Baker?"

"I once stayed at the hotel in Amsterdam where he died."

"I have a friend who likes Chet Baker. You two have quite a lot in common."

A reflection from the *Bennington* caught Golzari's tireless eyes as the first of the ship's two helicopters launched.

Batwing 58, 0632 (GMT)

The three crew members in Batwing 58, west of Socotra at ten thousand feet, watched the traffic patterns of the ships below. None seemed to be headed toward Hadiboh, although there was an enormous ship slowly making its way east-southeast past Abdul Kori Island. The ship was escorted in a clear pattern by half a dozen dhows. Already low on fuel, Five-Eight took photos and then headed back to the *Bennington*.

USS *Bennington*, off Socotra, 0723 (GMT)

The XO rolled her eyes and issued the CO's latest directive: all officers and chiefs not on watch were required in the wardroom at twelve-thirty, where officials from Socotra would explain the local culture, customs, and port requirements those going ashore would need to know. This was, of course, irrelevant. No one would be allowed ashore here.

Bobby had the watch as force protection action officer on the bridge while WEPS manned the Combat Information Center as tactical action officer;

the rest of the officers and most of the chiefs were either in the wardroom or on their way. Bobby watched as one of the ship's RHIBs approached, carrying three locals wearing life vests straight out of an old coastal rescue photo. Instead of the single-piece flotation devices modern mariners wore, these were little more than a series of tissue-box-sized Styrofoam pads strung together with rope. He stifled a snicker.

Hadiboh, 0724 (GMT)

Golzari left Ambassador Sumner with one of the Highland Maritime Defense personnel, a former beat cop like himself, while he took a walk along the shoreline where the *Mukalla Ali* was unloading construction supplies. He noticed one of the RHIBs returning to the ship. Using his binoculars, he saw three men in the boat who, judging by their clothing, were neither ship's crew nor aid workers.

"*Bennington*, RSO. You have an inbound RHIB with three passengers. Who are they, over?"

"RSO, *Bennington* FPAO," Bobby replied. "Three passengers are port authority and cultural liaison meeting with the captain and officers about the area, over."

"FPAO, I should have been advised of anyone expected to approach the ship. Don't let anyone board yet. Get the captain to turn them back until I can check them out."

"RSO, I will advise the captain immediately, over."

"FPAO, advise ASAP. RSO standing by."

Golzari scanned the coastline and caught sight of an SUV on another hill, far from any buildings. Four men surrounded the SUV, and another with binoculars stood a few yards away, also watching the small boat pull alongside the warship. Golzari focused the lenses on him and could see that he was a tall, bald Somali. His stomach muscles clenched when he realized that the man was Abdi Mohammed Asha, and that Asha was now peering through his own binoculars directly at him.

Golzari yelled into his wireless. "All units, this is the RSO. We have a target on the hill three hundred yards west of my position: five individuals, one white SUV. Marines to remain with the ambassador and aid workers. Highland Maritime, proceed to the bottom of that hill. Sniper—take out that engine block."

Golzari sprinted past the shacks and rusted vehicles toward the hill where Asha and his men were standing. His earlier inspection of geographical maps of the area had told him that the hill had a cliff on one side; there was only one way for Asha to leave his position. He heard the sharp cracks of two rifle shots and knew that the Marine sniper had taken the white SUV out of commission. Half a dozen mercenaries were running as fast as he was, vectoring on the bottom of the hill. He could see Asha and his five men scrambling for cover, just as he and Stark had done in the ruins of Old Mar'ib.

Golzari called for two of the mercs to join him and ordered the others to break off in teams of two and spread out. He wouldn't make the same mistake the pirates in Old Mar'ib had made.

When Golzari and the other teams had closed to within a hundred yards, AK-47 fire erupted from the hilltop. The only structures nearby were a small stone house and a shed; a couple and several children ran out of the house at the sound of the gunshots. Golzari ordered one team to use the shed twenty yards away as cover and had his own team turn over an old oil drum to use as a step up to the roof of the house. One by one they climbed up, dropped to a prone position, and set the barrels of their weapons along the roof edge. Golzari directed the third team to support his left flank.

He saw two of Asha's men bolt from the vehicle and charge at the team of Highland mercs off to the far left. The mercs dropped to the ground and trained their weapons on the oncoming attackers, who advanced firing. One went down, then another. The mercs were cool customers, he thought. Stark had hired the right people. That left only Asha and three others.

USS *Bennington*, off Socotra, 0725 (GMT)

When the captain didn't answer his call, Bobby raced to the CO's cabin one deck below, holding onto the railings midway down and letting his legs fly over the steps. His rapid knocks got a response.

"Come!"

Bobby entered the stateroom and said breathlessly, "Sir, RSO just called in concerned about the three men coming aboard and said he hadn't been informed and needed to check them out."

"RSO? The embassy guy? I don't think so, mister. This is my ship. What the RSO doesn't realize is that we do this all the time. These are just some locals who want to try to sell us trinkets. Shouldn't you be on the bridge, Ensign?"

"Yes, sir, but the RSO said . . ."

"Is the RSO your commanding officer, Ensign Fisk?"

"No, sir," *but it wouldn't be a bad idea.*

"Then get back there. I need to get to the wardroom and greet our local dignitaries."

"But, sir, this is a force protection issue in coordination with an embassy-led humanitarian operation. We are required to comply, sir."

The captain pulled himself to his full height of five feet six inches. His face was growing dangerously red. "How dare you question me."

"Sir, I am not questioning you, but there is an immediate force protection concern issue raised by the RSO. I will not allow them to board until they've been vetted."

"*You* won't allow them on *my* ship?" The captain was spewing saliva in his rage. "You're relieved of duty." In his peripheral vision Bobby saw three sailors who had emerged from one of the shacks in response to the shouting.

"No, sir. I'm going to tell the XO and sheriff not to let them board until the RSO has checked them." Bobby turned his back to the captain and was about to head below toward the wardroom when the captain shouted to the sailors, "Stop him!"

Bobby felt a hand grab his khaki cloth belt. Two other pairs of hands took him by each arm. He struggled to pull himself free. "Let me go! This is an emergency!"

"Hold him here until he cools down." The captain smirked at Bobby. "Your career was very short, Ensign. You won't be a problem to any other captain, I promise you. After I greet our visitors below I'm putting you off the ship. Let the embassy RSO on the island help you." The captain proceeded below.

A minute later Bobby felt the sailors' grips begin to relax. He stood perfectly still until the first sailor released his grip on Bobby's belt, then wrenched his arms out of the hands of the other sailors and bolted away from them toward the wardroom two decks below and half the ship's length away.

The three visitors sat directly across from the XO, OPS, CHENG, and the command master chief as the other officers and chiefs settled into chairs around them. The youngest of the three, a man whose face was dripping sweat, sat quietly, understanding little of what was said in this room where the Navy officers ate.

His best opportunity would come when the captain entered. He planned to wait for that.

Batwing 57, off Socotra, 0731 (GMT)

The patrol sector east of Socotra was mostly quiet, though the helo's occupants saw numerous small and large fishing boats. A cluster of ships to the north, just over the horizon from Hadiboh, caught Stark's attention. At the center of the cluster was one of the offshore support vessels that routinely plied these waters, though it was one of the larger ones he had seen. Closer inspection revealed two smaller OSVs nearby, each towing half a dozen skiffs. He also noticed a helicopter on the deck of the large OSV. The helicopter's rotors began to spin.

"What's that ship's speed and heading?" he said into the mike, shouting to be heard over the sound of the Seahawk's rotors.

"Three knots and heading into the wind," Air Boss, the mission's pilot, responded.

"How far are we from Hadiboh?"

"Thirty nautical miles."

"Boss, I need to talk with the TAO."

"Stand by, Commander. Go."

"TAO, DATT. Be advised we may have some pirate mother ships and skiffs approximately thirty nautical miles north of you. They also have a helo about to take off."

"DATT, TAO. Understood. Will advise the CO immediately."

"Roger that. Boss, can we get a closer look?"

"I'd love to oblige, Commander, but we need to refuel. We're taking photos of the ship cluster now and relaying them back to the ship."

USS *Bennington*, off Socotra, 0735 (GMT)

The XO had been watching the three men closely while she waited for the captain to arrive and get this ridiculous meeting under way. The youngest man, who was sweating profusely, was playing with a piece of metal on his primitive life vest. His eyes met hers. She saw him unscrew the safety cap and pull the lanyard.

The XO pushed away her chair and dove over the table in courageous desperation, knowing as she slid across the polished surface that it was too late.

"Bomb!" she cried out, hoping a last-second warning would save some of her shipmates.

The young man stood and yelled, "Allahu Akbar!" as the four five-hundred-gram bricks of TNT concealed in his life vest caused a percussive explosion that ripped apart half of the men and women in the wardroom. The captain, coming down the passageway toward the wardroom, was slammed against a bulkhead by the blast.

Batwing 57, 0737 (GMT)

Batwing 57 circled the *Bennington* once at two thousand feet before making its landing approach. Connor settled back and looked down at the starboard side of the 10,000-ton cruiser just as smoke and flames shot from two portholes like water out of a fire hydrant. The deck of the great ship bulged upward. Those portholes could only have been the wardroom.

"Holy fuck!" Air Boss yelled through the headphones.

"It's the wardroom, Boss. Gas explosion from the galley?" came the copilot's voice.

"We aren't landing until we find out."

USS *Bennington*, off Socotra, 0739 (GMT)

Bobby ran into one of the sailors making his way down from the helo deck.

"Some kind of explosion, sir. It's bad!" the sailor shouted. "Whatever just happened below buckled our deck."

Bobby got on the STC-2—the internal ship's phone—and told the bridge to have the quartermaster send out damage control parties.

The quartermaster's voice boomed immediately from the loudspeakers: "All hands, this is the bridge, we have an explosion of unknown cause. Damage control teams report immediately to officers' country."

The confusion began in earnest as Bobby reached the VIP quarters. Damage control was trying to break through the hatch that led to officers' country—the place where he slept, ate, studied, and, along with every other junior officer, complained. Two corpsmen rushed by carrying the blood-covered captain. Bobby couldn't tell if he was dead or alive. At the very least he was unconscious and bleeding from head and torso lacerations.

"One, two, three!" the big boatswain's mate commanded as the work party pulled the hatch away and tried to force their way inside. Collapsed bulkheads and galley equipment blown off its moorings blocked the way. Flashlights exposed the dark reality of burnt materials and body parts beyond. A few faint groans could be heard over the sounds of metal settling.

Bobby was close enough to catch the stomach-churning odor of what remained of his friends. Desperate to get inside, he turned around and raced back to the quarterdeck, turning on the deck outside and heading aft to get to officers' country from the rear hatch. The same devastation reigned there. The field was clear through the bathroom and showers, but after that all was darkness and debris. He knocked vainly on the few stateroom doors that hadn't been twisted or blown away. No one answered. They had all been in the wardroom.

Suddenly realizing that he was one of only a handful of functioning officers left on the ship, Bobby returned to the bridge to coordinate emergency procedures.

Hadiboh, 0741 (GMT)

Damien Golzari was about to take a shot at one of Asha's men when he saw the explosion in his peripheral vision. Instinctively he turned his head to the right and saw fire and smoke burst from the starboard side of the cruiser. At almost the same time he heard a cry from the shed twenty yards away. One of the mercs must have been hit.

Asha and his two remaining men were covering themselves well behind the SUV. Golzari could find not an appendage to target.

"Orders, sir?" asked the merc to his right, his gun still trained on the vehicle.

Golzari would not let Asha slip away again. "You two stay here. When I tell you, I want you to lay down suppressing fire. I'm going to advance. When I'm within twenty yards of their position, start firing into the air."

"Roger that."

Golzari eased down from his perch and made his way to the shed. One of the mercs was down and breathing heavily but gave a thumbs-up indicating that his wound wasn't life threatening. Golzari joined that team and told the remaining shooter his plan. He caught the eyes of the third team covering the left flank and signed to them what he intended to do. Palm suppressed—wait. Finger pointed to himself and then two wiggling fingers toward the hill—he'd charge them. Pointing to the mercs, he depressed his thumb several times—lay down suppressing fire. Pointing to the left team, he instructed them to get up and follow him.

Golzari peeked around the shed once more, imprinting a mental photograph of the terrain and trying to identify the best route. He estimated the range to be less than eighty yards. He'd need about twelve seconds of fire to make it to the enemy's position.

He took several deep breaths. "One. Two. Three. Now!" The three mercs opened fire as Golzari, taking out a pistol for each hand, began the run of his life.

Batwing 57, 0743 (GMT)

"When can we land, Boss?"

"Not until I get a 'green deck' from the bridge; the TAO has asked us to stand by until they're sure of what's happening, Commander. It had better be soon, though. We're almost out of fuel."

Three minutes later the bridge authorized green deck and Batwing 57 settled on the pad. Connor Stark and the Air Boss were on the bridge within seconds, listening as Bobby Fisk explained to them and to WEPS, who joined them temporarily from the CIC, what he thought had happened: the three local envoys, or at least one of them, had detonated explosives in the wardroom and had killed or seriously injured every officer and chief on the ship with the exception of themselves and Batwing 58. "What do we do, WEPS?" he asked plaintively.

WEPS responded immediately, "We put out a message to Fifth Fleet and await arrival of a new command crew."

"That could take a day or more, WEPS," Air Boss said. "What do we do until then?"

"We defer to the senior line officer present," WEPS answered. He turned to Stark: "Commander Stark, that's you. What are your orders?"

Stark paused, looking at the impossibly young men and women who now constituted the *Bennington*'s senior personnel. They were in their twenties, barely out of school and suddenly without the command structure that had governed their lives over the past few months. Their youthful faces had suddenly aged with the loss of their shipmates and the realization of their vulnerability and their new responsibilities.

"Get the message to Fifth Fleet," he ordered. "Air Boss, I need to know if we can recover Five-Eight or if they need to land on Hadiboh. I'll contact the RSO and advise him of the situation and then contact the Yemeni Navy. WEPS, get back to the CIC and resume TAO duties. I want you to find out what the helo we saw is doing. I'll be here on the bridge with Ensign Fisk. I want some eyes out on deck for small boats, and I mean *really* small boats. I saw only one of the RHIBs when we landed. Where's the other one, Bobby?"

"Hadiboh, sir."

"Good. Contact them. Have them round up as many civilian medical personnel as they can get on the boat. Let's get help for this crew."

"Aye, sir." Bobby grabbed a radio on his way to the bridge wing.

Stark took the handheld-radio from his go-bag. "RSO, what's the situation on the island, over?" Nothing but static. "Golzari, respond, over." Static. Stark knew that a professional like Golzari wouldn't have turned off his handheld for any reason unless he was involved in an attack. With the situation going to hell here, Stark's responsibility was to the ship; he had to trust Golzari to take care of whatever was happening in Hadiboh.

Hadiboh, 0748 (GMT)

Golzari ducked his head and charged up the hill. The other team was coming up on his left. Eleven of the twelve seconds he had estimated remained.

He had never been the fastest runner at the federal law enforcement training facility in Georgia, but he was the quietest. Someone there once called him the Panther because he could move so silently. It was another trick he had learned from his father's former Savak bodyguards. It didn't matter if you were fast as long as they didn't know you were coming.

Nine seconds now.

Golzari blocked out the sound of the suppressing fire, shutting down unnecessary sensory input to his brain so he could focus on the target. He saw no one as he ran. Asha and the others kept themselves out of sight.

Six seconds.

When the bodyguards taught him how to be a sharpshooter they instructed him to remain calm, to use long, slow breaths, and to fire on the exhale. A racing heart would cause the body to move slightly and throw off the shooter's aim. Almost to the SUV now, he forced himself to breathe evenly.

Three seconds.

He and his father and the bodyguards had returned to Iran in secret once after the Revolution to visit a dying relative. They disguised themselves as simple merchants and took a dhow across the Persian Gulf from Jebel Ali. The Iranian town they visited was no larger than Hadiboh, but it did have a Revolutionary Guard post. On the final night of their three-night visit, he and the bodyguards came across a local teenager beaten bloody by Islamic radicals, who continued to kick him and spit on him as Golzari and his guards approached. There was no one else in the alley. The radicals told Golzari and the bodyguards to move along, that they were dealing with this homosexual teen as he should be dealt with. Instead, the bodyguards shot the radicals at close range, then picked up the teenager and helped him on his way. Golzari understood that if his family had stayed in Iran, he might also have been a victim of this Islamic extremism because of his similar sexual orientation. At that moment he had reached a decision that changed his life. Those who tried to force fundamentalist Islam on the population must be stopped, and those too weak to fight against them must be protected. The Somali pirates, just like those Iranians, were brutal, murderous bullies. And they would be stopped. And of course he thought of Robert—always of Robert.

As he reached the hilltop, all his senses switched to full receive mode—vision, hearing, touch, smell—every bit of information he could gather was important.

Two of the Somalis popped their heads above the SUV. Golzari came around the left side of the vehicle, raised both weapons, and fired eight rounds, felling the two before they could respond.

The only man standing was Asha himself, who raised his hands to show that he had no weapon. Apparently he had left the fighting to the others. Golzari pounced on him and swung the butt of his pistol across Asha's forehead. Asha tried to throw a punch, but Golzari deflected it with one arm as he brought the butt down again, closer this time to the center of Asha's head. The unmistakable crack of a skull being split echoed in the air. Asha fell, helpless but still conscious.

The mercs had closed in behind him now. Golzari holstered one pistol and reached into his pocket for his digital voice recorder. He spoke to Asha in Arabic. "Did you kill John Dunner?"

Asha said nothing.

"Abdi Mohammed Asha, listen to me carefully," Golzari said, pointing his pistol at Asha's temple. "Answer me truthfully and live. Did you kill John Dunner in Antioch, Maine?"

"Yes."

"Why?"

"I have an agreement."

"An agreement with who?"

"I am to return to Somalia and take control," Asha said.

"Who is the agreement with?" Golzari said, shaking his prisoner.

Asha grinned. "There was an American. A very powerful American. I never met him."

"That's not good enough. Who *did* you meet? Who did you work with?"

A mile away, a party of Chinese observers had watched the entire battle and shipboard explosion unfold through high-powered binoculars. Mr. Hu, wearing his usual black pants and a pastel green shirt, ordered his men to deal with the situation, then got into a black Land Rover and was driven away from the scene.

Golzari grabbed Asha's shirt collar and lifted him to his feet, already planning the best way to get the Somali back to Washington to extract more information from him. As Golzari turned toward the security personnel to issue recovery orders, Asha's head exploded, spraying the agent's face with blood, pieces of bone, and brain matter.

"Down, down, down," one of the mercs screamed.

Golzari released Asha's body and dropped to the ground, trying to determine if any of the blood was his own.

"Sniper," Golzari realized. "Where is he? Did anyone get a make?"

"I've got him," one of the security personnel called out. "He's about three hundred yards to the west and just got in an SUV heading back over the hill."

Back to Chinatown, thought Golzari.

USS *Bennington*, off Socotra, 0813 (GMT)

"Bridge, TAO."

"Go ahead," Stark said.

"Inbound ship and slow-moving aircraft that we're still trying to identify. Coming in from zero-one-zero degrees."

Stark looked at the navigational chart. "Air Boss, where was that cluster of ships?"

"Right here. It would be coming from zero-one-zero."

"Bobby, are our SM-2s ready?"

"Sir, we're empty."

"What do you mean we're empty?"

"We don't have any missiles. No SM-2s. No Tomahawks. No Harpoons. When Fifth Fleet disapproved us for Persian Gulf escort duty with the carrier, they had us transfer all our missiles to other ships."

"That's just great," Stark said. Then, thinking quickly, "Boss, does Five-Eight have the same number of Hellfires as Five-Seven?"

"Same load. I made sure of it."

"Does Five-Eight have enough fuel to intercept that aircraft?"

"They're still twenty minutes out, but they can push it to twelve. It'll burn more of their fuel and they'll be riding fumes, but I think they can do it—at least before I can get Five-Seven fueled back up."

"Direct them to intercept that aircraft. I'm pretty sure it's the helo we saw spinning up on the OSV's deck. I want Five-Eight to see if there are small boats ahead of it as well. The night I went in the water I heard a helo, and it wasn't one of ours. I couldn't figure out how they were running remote-controlled boats when no other ships were in sight, but it makes sense if they were running them from a helo."

Hadiboh, 0817 (GMT)

Golzari and the others returned to the operations site carrying the wounded Highland security officer. "Gunny, SitRep," he said, suddenly tired as the adrenaline that had pushed him up the hill toward Asha left his system.

"All accounted for. Our teams are still in position in the buildings," said the gruff Marine.

"Ambassador, Abdi Mohammed Asha was there. He's dead."

"He was going to attack our operation?" she said. "Thank-you isn't enough."

"That isn't all of it."

"What do you mean?"

"Asha confirmed that he killed John Dunner and said an American was involved, too."

"Who?"

"He died before I could find out," said Golzari. "Right now, though, we have to find out what happened on the *Bennington* and figure out how to get our people out of here."

Golzari turned on his handheld radio, checked his watch, and looked in the direction of the ship. Wispy smoke was still trickling from the wardroom portholes.

"DATT, RSO." No response. Maddox and Sumner waited anxiously for Stark to respond.

"DATT, RSO," Golzari repeated.

He tried one more time. "DATT, RSO."

"RSO, CO. Message heard. Out." It was Stark's voice. He did not respond as the defense attaché. He responded as the ship's commanding officer.

What the hell is going on out there? Golzari tried to piece together the little bits of information he had. The "local dignitaries" carried by one of the ship's RHIBs had been allowed to board even though he had told the officer on the bridge to turn them back. There had been an explosion on the ship. Asha had placed a small force on a nearby hilltop, almost certainly as part of an attack on the humanitarian operation. The Chinese seemed to be involved. And now this cryptic message from Stark. "Bloody hell," he muttered.

"What is it?" C. J. asked. "Do you know what's going on?"

"It's worse than I thought, ma'am. Commander Stark has apparently taken command of the *Bennington*. He would do that only if the command and senior staff were unable to perform their duties. By his message, he's informing us that that has happened, and that things are so serious that he doesn't want to violate any op-sec—operational security—over an open radio. He also doesn't want us asking more questions at this point. The entire command structure of the ship must have been taken out in the explosion. This is getting more and more serious."

"How much more serious could it be?" Bill Maddox asked.

"Mr. Maddox, if you and your senior staff were suddenly gone, would your organization be in a position to respond quickly to a new crisis?"

Maddox and Sumner finally grasped the gravity of the situation. The *Bennington* had been effectively decapitated. It was now both far more vulnerable to another attack and completely unable to protect the people ashore. Only a few untried Yemeni Navy ships stood between them and whatever was coming next.

USS *Bennington*, off Socotra, 0820 (GMT)

"Bobby, I want open comms with the TAO at all times from here—no phone, understood?"

"Understood, sir. Five-Eight is now ten miles out and reporting fifteen minutes left of fuel."

"TAO, where's that incoming aircraft?"

"Still coming in slow at less than thirty knots."

The time was fast approaching for Stark to make his first two command decisions. "Boss?"

The lieutenant commander anticipated the new CO's question. "Five-Eight can get there. She can't make it back."

"How much fuel time does Five-Seven have?"

"We landed with twenty-five minutes remaining."

"I want you up now."

"Sir, with only twenty-five minutes of fuel I'll have one pass at best."

"Boss, I give you my word that Five-Seven and all souls on board will return with a few gallons to spare. What I'm planning will have you up and back within fifteen minutes. I know that's cutting it closer than the books say. I need to know if you can do it."

"Yes, sir."

"As soon as you're up, we'll bring in Five-Eight. Five-Seven will intercept that incoming aircraft, determine intent, and then contact me for instructions. Got it?"

"Aye, sir."

"Go. Bobby, I'm a little out of practice on this stuff so I'm going to rely on you. How long would it take for us to pull up the chains and get under way?"

"Twenty, sir."

"How long if I gave the command right now to cut the chain?"

"Five."

"Cut the chain."

Connor stood by the 1MC, cleared his throat, and looked at his watch.

"All hands, this is Commander John Connor Stark. Effective twelve twenty-two hours, I assumed command of the USS *Bennington*. The ship has temporarily lost most of its command staff, but it hasn't lost you. Damage control teams are to continue rescue and recovery efforts in officers' country. I know we're shorthanded. Civilian medical personnel are now aboard and rendering assistance to our wounded. Everyone must step into the roles of your chiefs and officers. We have incoming platforms over the horizon. We will not run except forward into battle."

Stark looked down at the deck and the ship's crest before continuing. "Crew of the *Bennington*, our motto is Vigilant and Victorious. If we have been short on vigilance, we will not be short on victory. All hands, battle stations. CO out."

"All ahead two-thirds, steer course zero-one-zero," commanded Stark.

"All ahead two-thirds, aye, steer course zero-one-zero," Bobby relayed to the helm.

"RSO, CO, over," Stark called through the handheld radio.

"RSO, go ahead, over."

"I'll lose you in a minute. I just wanted to let you know we have something to take care of, over."

"RSO, understood. Godspeed CO. Out."

Stark nodded. He could trust Golzari to take care of the embassy staff and aid workers while the *Bennington* was out of the area.

"Sir, Five-Seven is requesting green deck."

"Green deck is authorized."

Five-Seven emerged from the aft superstructure and paralleled the ship on the starboard side. Air Boss saluted the bridge, then accelerated ahead. Two of the Yemeni 134-ton *Bay*-class patrol boats came up to the damaged cruiser on either side. The ship to port carried the Yemeni admiral.

"All stations report manned and ready," Fisk told the CO.

Stark focused his attention on the horizon, where he could now see the ship headed toward them, still twenty-five nautical miles away.

"Ensign Fisk, request our Yemeni escorts maintain course and speed abreast of us." Stark could only hope the escorts *would* remain, if only as a show of united force against the unknown enemy.

Stark picked up the ship-to-ship radio microphone. "This is the USS *Bennington* to the three ships thirty nautical miles north of Hadiboh, Socotra. You are on course to a security area. You are directed to reverse your direction immediately, over."

When the speaker returned nothing but static, Stark repeated the hail. This time there was a response.

"This is the merchant ship *Suleiman* to U.S. Navy warship," came a voice in broken English. "We do not recognize your authority in this region."

"*Suleiman*, this is *Bennington*. If you do not reverse course immediately, we will be forced to fire on you," Stark responded.

Silence.

"Bridge, TAO," WEPS called from the Combat Information Center. "Five-Seven reports twelve small inbound boats, six manned, six unmanned. Distance ten nautical miles and closing rapidly."

"Understood." Stark's face showed grim determination. It was the *Kirkwall* sinking all over again. Well, not this time. He didn't intend to let another ship and crew sink beneath him. And he was damned if he was going to allow terrorists, pirates, or whatever they were to be victorious against a U.S. Navy ship and all it represented.

"*Suleiman*, this is your final warning." He replaced the ship-to-ship mike. "Conn, steer course zero-eight-zero. Report—are both 5-inch guns manned and ready?"

"Yes, sir."

"TAO, this is the captain. Advise the gun crews to commence firing at the small boats."

"Aye, sir . . . message relayed. Fire will commence now."

The aft 5-inch fifty-four came alive first, then the forward mount, both firing sixteen rounds a minute, shaking the 10,000-ton ship with each recoil. Only a lucky shot would take out one of the fast boats directly, but if shells landed close enough they'd capsize.

"This is *Suleiman*. Stop firing."

"Tell me why, over."

"We have women and children."

"Then tell your boats to turn around."

"Bridge, TAO. Five-Seven is in proximity to the unidentified helicopter. No response from it despite repeated hails."

Stark saw one of the small boats explode from a good shot. Seven more were still inbound.

"TAO, CO. Direct Five-Seven to take out the helicopter with their Hellfire." Stark and Bobby watched a moment later as Batwing 57 went in for the kill. A smoke trail flew from its side toward the *Suleiman*'s helicopter, and a micro sunburst appeared in the sky to their port quarter. The helo fell from the sky in flames.

"TAO, CO. Convey to Five-Seven, BRAVO ZULU. Return to ship immediately."

The four unmanned remote-controlled boats veered off wildly without direction from the master controller in the helicopter.

The crew manning the portside M-2 .50-caliber machine guns now took their turn as the three manned boats pulled within a mile of the ship. One by one the small boats fell victim to the firepower of the *Bennington* and the Yemeni ships.

"Conn, all engines ahead two-thirds. Steer course," Stark paused to read the compass heading, "three-five-five. Make your heading for that ship. Ensign, what do you call your VBSS teams?"

"Hessian 1 and Hessian 2, sir."

Stark took the ship-to-ship radio back and switched to channel 46, the prearranged channel to communicate with the Yemenis.

"Admiral, this is Stark. We intend to board the main ship. Request that you and your ships stop and search the other two."

"Commander Stark, I copy. We will begin searching. I was just informed that Ali may be on one of the ships." The Yemeni ships picked up speed to intercept the two smaller OSVs. Stark prayed that Ali was not on the *Suleiman*.

"Ensign Fisk, order both VBSS teams to prepare for a noncompliant boarding. I'll join the Hessian 1 boat. Make sure one of them brings my Beretta." He offered an encouraging smile and pat on the shoulder to the young ensign who represented the future of his navy and his country. In the midst of battle, Connor Stark realized that they had indeed again become his navy and his country.

"Aye, sir!"

"TAO, CO. Order forward mount to fire three shots across the bow of the *Suleiman*."

Stark waited a few seconds for the first shell to hit the water before returning to the open mike. "*Suleiman*, this is *Bennington*. Heave to and prepare to be boarded."

"*Bennington*, stop your attack or you will all die." The voice, with an Arabic accent, not a Somali one, spoke with slow and deliberate coldness.

"Bridge, TAO. *Suleiman* is increasing range, but she can't do any better than she's doing, according to our recognition books."

"TAO, CO. Forward mount is authorized to fire one shot at the *Suleiman*'s stern. I will buy all of them a beer at the next port if the first shot takes out her propulsion." The first shot landed near the stern, but still close enough to damage the propellers. The ship slowed.

"Bobby, the bridge is yours."

Bobby looked oddly disappointed for a junior officer who was receiving command of a U.S. Navy warship. "S-sir," he stuttered, "I haven't completed my surface warfare quals yet."

Stark had seen nothing to make him doubt Bobby's ability to take over the bridge. Had he perhaps hoped for something else? Then he realized what it was. "TAO, CO. Report to the bridge to assume temporary command. Bobby, I seem to have forgotten that the VBSS teams don't have officers. You are to take the Hessian 2 team and follow up on Hessian 1."

"Aye, sir." Bobby's grin went from ear to ear. "We'll see you there!"

With Five-Seven having returned to *Bennington* to refuel, Hessian 1 and Hessian 2 lacked air cover and were far more vulnerable to gunfire. Stark called to the target over the radio. "*Suleiman*, prepare to be boarded. Drop your weapons and gather on the stern of your ship, over."

"Go to hell, Americans," came the sharp reply.

Both RHIBs were still two hundred yards away when Stark ordered them to hold up. The *Suleiman*'s deck suddenly swarmed with men, many of them armed. The sharpshooters on the RHIBs methodically shot down every one of them who was carrying a gun. Stark commanded the boats to proceed. More men emerged as the boats got nearer. Some leapt into the water while others went aft holding their hands behind their heads.

When Hessian 1 arrived alongside, two of the team members threw a rope ladder over the transom of the *Suleiman* and climbed aboard, paving the way for their new CO. Stark joined them, his 9-mm pistol in his right hand.

Stark called for four men to follow him as he made his way to the bridge. They met brief resistance as they rounded one corner, but a Hessian with a Remington 870 shotgun easily cleared the way. When they reached the wooden door to the bridge, Stark motioned for his men to stand back and fire through it. Afterward, Stark pushed the shattered frame through and carefully looked around the bridge, his pistol still at the ready. There were three bodies lying on the deck. One was a Somali who must have been standing in front of the door when the volley came through. A second Somali seemed to have been shot at close range, possibly prevented from escaping. Stark recognized the third man, a Yemeni. And in the corner lay Ali, bound but unhurt.

Connor carefully walked toward the third man, keeping his pistol trained until he was sure the man had no weapon. Faisal was lying on his back, alive, his legs covered with blood. "Get the medical kit," Stark said to one of his sailors as he knelt beside the injured man. When their eyes met, Stark found himself momentarily unable to speak to the man responsible for the blood on this deck and in the wardroom of the *Bennington*; the blood of many others was on his hands as well—the *Kirkwall*'s crew among them.

"Faisal. I didn't want it to be you. Your father is my friend. How could you do this?"

Faisal said nothing. He neither turned away nor closed his eyes. He simply stared into Stark's damp eyes, his own eyes blazing with hatred.

"How many people have you killed? And Ali. Why did you take him? For what?"

"For my country! We must free ourselves from Americans and Ali's ideas of progress. We will live by sharia law and grow strong and righteous." His strength ebbing, Faisal whispered, "I have failed. I will die now."

"No, Faisal," Stark said steadily. "I am going to return you to your family. Your father will know what you have done and will decide your fate." Out of the corner of his eye, Stark saw Bobby Fisk enter the bridge, pistol ready, his arm close to his body and arm bent at a forty-five-degree angle.

"No!" Faisal said, showing the first sign of fear. "You cannot do that. Give me my gun, let me . . ." he tried to reach for a nearby AK-47, but Stark shifted the weapon beyond his reach.

"We are not finished yet. Who were you working with? Tell me."

Faisal refused to answer.

Stark shrugged. "You *will* tell me—now or later." As Stark began to rise, Faisal's right arm swung upward. Stark saw a glint of metal. Just before the knife plunged into his abdomen, a shot rang out. Faisal's hand was blown backward as the knife flew across the bridge and fell harmlessly in a corner.

Stark turned to find Bobby Fisk in the classic pose of a marksman, left arm extended, his right hand wrapped around and supporting his left. The pistol was still pointing at Faisal.

"Pistol team at the Academy, huh?" Stark asked with a sigh of relief. "Just how good were you?"

Bobby didn't take his eyes off Faisal. "I was okay, sir."

"How okay?"

His eyes still on Faisal and his pistol unwavering, Bobby answered, "Standard Pistol intercollegiate champion two years in a row."

"Nice shot. Thanks," Stark said. "Tie him up," he said to another VBSS member, who pulled plastic cuffs from his belt.

Faisal propped himself up on one elbow. "I have failed. But they will not," he taunted.

"What do you mean? Who?" Stark shook him roughly. "What do you have planned?"

Faisal said only, "My family will not succeed," before closing his eyes and sinking back on the floor.

"Faisal," Stark came close enough to whisper in his ear, still wary that the handcuffed Yemeni might try something. "What your family will do to you is far worse than anything I could do."

"No. They are weak, like their American friends."

"You're wrong." Stark turned to Ali, still tied up in the corner and trying manfully to control his shaking. "It's okay now, son," he said as he untied the boy's bonds. "Your father will be overjoyed to see you." He helped Ali to stand and turned back toward his team. "Invite the Yemeni admiral to come aboard. Both will go back with him."

With one arm still around Ali, Stark made his way to the deck to greet the admiral, who returned his salute with respectful gravity. When he had finished telling the Yemeni the details of the last half hour, he motioned toward Faisal and Ali. "Please take them both to their father, Admiral. I'll follow later. Bobby," he said to the young ensign, who had holstered his weapon, "have you ever scuttled a ship before?"

"Intentionally, sir?" he asked with a grin.

"Once everyone is safely off the ship, scuttle her."

"Aye, sir."

Stark looked back from the RHIB returning him and his team to the *Bennington* in time to see the admiral leaving the ship with Faisal, Ali, and the surviving Somali pirates. A strip of duct tape blocked Faisal's mouth; another strip covered his eyes.

Once back aboard the *Bennington*, Stark went immediately to the bridge to meet with what remained of the senior personnel—Fisk, WEPS, six pilots from the Lost Boys detachment, and the first-class petty officers who were now the senior officers in their respective divisions.

"Welcome back, sir!" WEPS said.

Stark nodded. "Thanks. Conn, make a course for Hadiboh, and please don't put us on a sandbar."

"Aye, sir!"

Then he looked around the bridge. "Congratulations, everyone. You all did a first-rate job. Please extend my appreciation to your divisions. It was their professionalism that allowed us to get the pirates responsible for this attack. Ladies and gentlemen, I need a status. WEPS, damage report?"

"Most of the damage was contained in officers' country. Thirty-two officers and chiefs are dead, including the two culinary specialists who were in the galley. We have thirteen wounded, including the CO. The civilian doctors have stabilized most of them, but two have more serious injuries. The docs said we should at least get those two off the ship to Hadiboh. Power and water are out in that section. We've secured officers' country."

"Did we get a response from Fifth Fleet?"

"They acknowledged our initial message about the attack, sir. We're standing by."

"All right. I'll draft the after action report. Air Boss?"

"Both helos are on the deck. Some damage to the hangar from the explosion, but the fuel lines are secure. We should have both fueled up and ready to go in about six hours. Five-Eight did see something to the west they need to report."

One of the pilots stepped forward with a photograph. "It's a supertanker, sir. We've confirmed that it's the *Katya P.*, the one taken by pirates several weeks ago. According to our intelligence specialist the ship never made contact with its owners."

"I'm listening."

The intelligence specialist stepped forward. "Sir, the photo shows six dhows accompanying the tanker, three on each side, in a clear formation."

"Where? Show me." Stark took him by the arm to the chart table.

"Right here, sir." The specialist pointed to a spot just west of Socotra. "They were headed at eleven knots on a course east by southeast."

Stark didn't need someone to explain the implications of that course and the unusual formation.

"I need a navigator." A quartermaster first class cautiously stepped forward.

"No need to hesitate, QM1. The job's yours." She turned immediately to the charts. "Sir, are we going back to Hadiboh?"

"Not yet." He looked around the bridge. "Ladies and gentlemen, we have another unexpected task ahead of us. Conn, make course zero-nine-zero. The new NAV here and I will provide a longer-term track later. For now I want the crew to take some time to themselves. Was the chaplain among those killed?"

"Yes, sir," answered Bobby.

"Tell your men and women we'll grieve later, but we will honor our casualties by the actions we take now. By my estimate, we'll be in action again tomorrow morning. Air Boss, I need you to deliver a couple of messages when you evacuate the two seriously wounded crewmembers to Hadiboh. Then I want you to rejoin us east of the island."

Hadiboh, 0924 (GMT)

Golzari read the message from the *Bennington*'s new commander aloud, finishing with: " . . . therefore, I am taking the ship to protect U.S. assets and lives. XOXOXO, Stark."

"Is that last bit code, ma'am?" the British-educated Golzari asked the ambassador innocently.

She snorted. "Yes, it means that despite what's happened he's still maintaining his sense of humor—and still being a pain in the ass."

DAY 16

USS *Bennington*, South of Socotra, 0200 (GMT)

As the sun rose behind the ship, Stark sipped at a fresh cup of coffee and decided he ought to nominate the new NAV for a commendation. The timing was exactly as he had hoped. The ship was proceeding at full speed and the second helicopter was just lifting off the deck. The ship had slowed just long enough to launch the helicopters and the two RHIBs, which were now well ahead of them. The oil platforms were within sight. Twenty nautical miles astern of the *Bennington* was a new friend.

He reread the note from C. J. that had come back on the helo. Golzari had stopped the attack and taken Asha, but a Chinese marksman had assassinated the Somali pirate before Golzari had finished questioning him. So it was indeed the Chinese who were behind this.

The radio suddenly crackled with a desperate voice. "This is Maddox Oil Platform 3 to anyone. We are being approached by seven ships approximately twenty nautical miles from our position, heading two-six-five degrees. Is anyone out there, over?"

"Sir, do we respond?" asked Fisk.

"No."

Bobby was confused by Stark's terse—and callous—response. Someone calling in with an emergency should at least know that help was on the way, shouldn't they?

A minute later the platform called for help again. Still no response from the captain. Several more calls, increasingly plaintive, came in over the next ten minutes.

"Sir?" Bobby couldn't stand it anymore.

"It's okay, Bobby. This is all a ruse. I sent a message yesterday to Mr. Maddox, and he spoke to his people on the platforms. They're following our instructions right now."

"Ambush, sir?" Bobby said hopefully.

"Just a little payback. No need for the pirates to know that help is nearby. They think they took out the ship's command yesterday and that we can't respond. Let's prove them wrong, okay? Maybe it'll be one for the Academy's history books."

"If that happens, I hope they spell our names right."

"I don't think Bobby Fisk will be a problem. But everyone misspells Connor."

Bobby grinned and relaxed a bit. "I'm glad you're on our side, sir."

When the *Bennington* negotiated the waters between the platforms and Socotra twenty minutes later, the massive ship was clearly visible on the horizon. Its dhow escorts were still too distant to be seen by the naked eye.

Stark squared his shoulders. "It's showtime, folks. Bobby, order the RHIBs to proceed and execute Foxtrot Tango. TAO, CO. Advise Batwing 58 to move to Battle Position One. Advise Batwing 57 to move to Battle Position Two."

At his order Batwing 58 descended from nine thousand feet to five hundred in a dizzying spiral, fired a Hellfire at each of the first four dhows, and raked the other two with its machine-guns.

Batwing 57, half a nautical mile ahead of the *Katya P.*, likewise descended and hovered above the ship, facing the superstructure while flying in reverse, a testament to Air Boss's flying skills.

Saddiq and the pirates looking out the bridge windows at the helicopter had taken the *Katya P.* as a trophy. It was about to become their grave.

"Say hello to the night," Air Boss said, quoting from the 1980s movie *Lost Boys*, the namesake of the *Bennington*'s helicopter detachment. He fired one Hellfire directly into the pilothouse, then rejoined Batwing 58 to help reduce the remaining dhows to splinters.

"U.S. Navy warship, U.S. Navy warship, this is the People's Republic of China Navy destroyers *Harbin* and *Shenzen* responding to distress calls from a supertanker and the oil platforms. We are fifteen nautical miles from the tanker and will be landing forces on the oil platforms to protect them. Do not interfere with our assistance."

"We're in a shit-storm now, aren't we, sir?" Bobby asked, his eyes as big as saucers in his round face.

"At least we created this one. Hand me that ship-to-ship." Stark took the mike and sipped more coffee before speaking. "Chinese Navy ships, this is USS *Bennington*. Thank you, but we require no assistance from you. India Navy ship *Talwar*, we respectfully request your battle group's assistance in protecting American and Indian citizens on the oil platforms, over."

"USS *Bennington*, this is Capt. Jayendra Dasgupta in INS *Talwar*, currently closing your position. We are available to assist you as requested."

"*Talwar*, this is *Bennington*. I thank you very much for your assistance. Chinese Navy ships *Harbin* and *Shenzen*, we have indicated our ability to restore security to the area. We respectfully request that you move off and return to your convoy duties, over."

"*Bennington*, this is *Harbin*. To avoid a U.S.-initiated incident, move away immediately while we secure the platforms. This is your only warning, over."

The bridge was silent as its occupants awaited Stark's response. Stark shook his head to clear it. He, like most of the crew, had been awake for more than a full day. He felt momentarily faint and put his hand on Bobby's shoulder for support as the five other sailors on the bridge watched.

"I hope you don't mind helping an old man, Ensign Fisk."

"Not at all, sir. We're all in this together . . . Captain."

Stark smiled at him. "If I have this right, we have about half a minute. Give me your assessment, Ensign."

Bobby brought up his binoculars and saw the two Chinese destroyers veering to port to block the *Bennington*.

"They must have been listening to our bridge-to-bridge and other transmissions. They've watched us and waited for the right time to outnumber us. The Indian ships are still out of range, so that time is now."

"Very good, Ensign. So what do we need?"

"A carrier strike group would be good right about now, but all of our ships are in the Gulf or off Korea."

"You're right. And the Chinese probably know that."

The TAO called up to the bridge. "CO, we now have several aircraft behind us, approximately ten nautical miles and closing fast."

"Sir," Bobby said. "The *Talwar* class only has one helo. Who else is out there?"

Rather than answering, Stark clicked on the bridge-to-bridge radio. "Indian Navy Ship *Talwar*, this is USS *Bennington.* On behalf of the Indian citizens working there, we formally require immediate assistance from your strike group in securing the oil platforms from foreign incursion."

"USS *Bennington*, this is *Talwar*. We have transmitted this incident to the *Viraat* Carrier Group, which is operating east of us and should arrive shortly to assert India's protection of its citizens and to assist you, over."

Stark looked at Bobby and smiled. "One carrier group made to order, Ensign."

He clicked on the mike again. "*Harbin,* we assume you are aware of the very kind offer from the Indian Navy. I ask you again to return to your convoy duties. This is *your* final warning, over."

After a long pause, the radio crackled. "This is People's Republic of China Navy ships *Harbin* and *Shenzen*. We are returning to antipiracy patrol in the Gulf of Aden, out."

Stark grinned at the others on the bridge. "Well, wasn't it nice of them to offer to help?" Then he turned serious again. "Okay, everyone, we still have a problem. According to this radar, the *Katya P.* is still on course for the platforms, and it's almost certainly carrying a load of explosives. If it hits a platform, an environmental catastrophe on the scale of BP's oil spill in the Gulf of Mexico will result. It's up to us to stop it. There's an auxiliary steering station aft in that ship. Ensign Fisk, get a team ready to board and work with us."

"Sir, we don't have any bomb experts on board."

"Bobby, Batwing took out their bridge, and I hope most of their people. It's up to your team to take out anyone left. Just get to the aft steering compartment, swing the rudder hard to starboard and secure it, then get out of there."

"Sir, she's only fifteen miles away from the platforms. Even a rudder shift might not be enough."

"Do it, then get back here ASAP for the next step."

"Aye, sir." The ship's phone rang before he could leave the bridge. Bobby hung up the phone and looked at Stark in consternation.

"What is it, Ensign?"

"That was Engineering, sir. We've been burning fuel fast. We're almost out."

"How much do we have?"

"About thirty minutes at this speed."

Stark pressed his fingers to his temples. In the chaos of the past day he had neglected to ask the most basic of ship operation questions—one that even the *Bennington*'s CO knew to ask—how much fuel did they have?

Within a few minutes of the RHIBs coming alongside the *Katya P.*, their VBSS teams had rappelled up each side and retaken the ship. They found a few dead Somali pirates in the ruins on the bridge, but otherwise the ship was deserted. They increased the ship's speed and turned it hard to starboard as ordered.

As the *Bennington* approached the tanker a nautical mile away in a port-to-port passing, Stark turned the ship 180 degrees to allow the VBSS teams to reboard. Bobby was out of breath when he got back to the bridge.

"Mission accomplished, sir. Ready for whatever's next."

"Ensign Fisk has the conn," Stark announced. "You ever hit anything, Bobby?"

"Uh, only a channel marker, sir. But this is my first deployment. Why do you ask? Uh-oh," he exclaimed when he realized his CO's intent.

"All hands," Stark called over the 1MC, "proceed immediately to the port side of the ship and stand by for collision to starboard." The collision bell sounded as the crew complied.

The *Bennington* pulled up even with the oil tanker, then moved closer and closer as the few people remaining on the bridge watched in fascination.

"What's the distance, Conn?"

Bobby shouted, "Two hundred feet," as he steadied the range finder.

"Call out every thirty feet. Helm, steady on course at one-five knots."

The *Bennington* passed the tanker's superstructure.

"One hundred seventy feet . . . one hundred forty feet . . . one hundred ten feet." The *Bennington* was now dangerously close to touching the tanker, and a vortex began developing between the two ships. The cruiser was nearly at the bow of the tanker. "Eighty feet . . . fifty feet . . ."

"All hands, brace for collision!" Stark called out. "Right standard rudder, starboard engine ahead one-third, port engine ahead full! Bobby, get the hell in here."

Bobby dove in from the bridge wing just in time to hear the sickening sound of metal on metal, far louder and more painful to his ears than hitting the channel marker had been.

"Helm, stick us to them. Right full rudder. Bobby, get a damage control report from the bow. Make sure our landing was soft enough."

"Aye, sir."

Slowly, the whale of a supertanker turned, the *Bennington* acting as a giant tugboat. The Navy ship shuddered and began to lose way as one of its great screws stopped churning.

"NAV, how are we doing?"

"Projected course now due east of the platforms. We're in the clear, sir."

"Keep us with her, helm. All right, we need fuel, and I need ideas, no matter how crazy they sound."

"Sir?" Bobby Fisk chimed in. "I read something in *Proceedings*," referring to the monthly publication of the 140-year-old Naval Institute, "about a procedure where a Military Sealift Command ship was refueled by a tanker. I asked BM1 Garcia in my division about it when I was working on my quals, and he told me that it works only with the newer tankers. Older tankers burn heavy fuel oil that's incompatible with our engines. I checked the registry, and the *Katya P.* is only two years old, which means she has multifuel burners."

"And?"

"Garcia's a qualified rig captain, and we can do a stern-to-bow transfer instead of the traditional UNREP."

"Make it happen, Ensign."

A few minutes later, Stark watched from the bridge wing as Hessian 2 motored toward the tanker. Ensign Fisk and a boatswain's mate sat huddled together over a naval ship technical manual trying to figure out exactly how they would do what the ensign had just told the CO he could do.

Hours later, when the tanker was well clear of the platforms and the *Bennington* had enough fuel to continue its mission, a crew took control of the *Katya P.* to return it to its owners. Back on the bridge, Bobby Fisk asked his skipper a nagging question about the engagement.

"Sir, we never got verification of the *Viraat* Carrier Group. Shouldn't they have arrived by now?"

Stark laughed. “I’ve been waiting for you to ask. How much of your naval history do you remember from the Academy, Ensign?”

“Sir?”

“Battle of the River Plate, 1939.”

Bobby searched his memory. *South America . . . early World War II, before Pearl Harbor . . . Got it*! “The German pocket battleship *Graf Spee* was in a neutral port—Montevideo—and three smaller British ships—*Achilles, Ajax,* and *Exeter*—were waiting for her to come out. The *Graf Spee* was going to engage, but then the British ships contacted a larger strike force over the horizon and the *Graf Spee* intercepted the message. Instead of coming out, the skipper scuttled the battleship.” Relieved that he had managed to pull that out, Bobby swore to read more naval history in the future.

“What about the British force?” Stark asked.

“It didn’t exist. They were false messages sent out to deceive the *Graf Spee*. It worked . . . just like today.”

“Just like today,” the captain said. “Almost. We had help from two Highland Maritime ships and their helos.”

“But how did the Indian ship know to do that?”

“Be grateful to Ambassador Sumner. She worked it out with the Indian ambassador. I spoke with the Indian naval attaché a couple of days ago in Sana’a before he boarded the *Talwar*, and he agreed to step in and help if we were outnumbered. Fortunately, he had studied the *Graf Spee* incident as well.”

“They helped us, sir. Do they get something in return?”

“Oh, yes. They become very important partners in a strategic resource. Bobby, you have the bridge. I’m going below to check on the wounded.”

DAY 18

Hadiboh, 1112 (GMT)

Two days after the Battle of Socotra and the defeat of Faisal's pirate fleet, the USS *Bennington* was again on station off Hadiboh. This time it was tied up to the newly arrived LPD-17, the *San Antonio*, which was there to assist the cruiser, provide a new command staff, and relieve Commander John Connor Stark so that he could return to his assigned duties as defense attaché.

The humanitarian operation was a beehive of activity. The conductor had handed off the baton to her concertmaster, the consul general, while she attended to more immediate duties. The conductor's tent had been enlarged to accommodate a table with three chairs and two rows of folding chairs lined up behind it. At the table sat Yemen's foreign minister, India's ambassador to Yemen, and Ambassador Caroline Jaha Sumner. In the folding chairs were subordinates furiously taking notes. Well behind the chairs stood Bill Maddox, Connor Stark, and Damien Golzari, watching the event but not taking part in it.

"Gentlemen," continued Ambassador Sumner after the initial introductions and diplomatic dances had been completed, "allow me to reiterate my deep appreciation for the people and government of Yemen, whose navy courageously deflected an attack here a few days ago. It speaks well of their intent for stability in the region and the lengths to which they will go to pursue what is right. You have our gratitude and admiration. We are here today to sign an agreement that few of us thought possible even a few days ago, but we have seen in recent days what cooperation among our nations can mean for each of our peoples. This agreement has three primary provisions.

"The first is that Yemen selects India and the United States to produce the oil in the fields south of Socotra. The platforms there have now been sold to the Yemeni firm Mar'ib Oil . . ."

"Thanks a lot, Connor," Maddox whispered to his old friend. "That was one hell of a quid pro quo. Mutahar asked my firm to assist with some construction projects. It will be one of the largest construction partnerships in the region."

"Consider it payback for that double date our freshman year."

"Second," Sumner continued, "a portion of the wealth generated by the oil will be used to build and operate a new medical facility for the people of Socotra and to hire and train personnel to protect the unique environment of the island, a world treasure that from this moment will always be treated as such.

"Third, Yemen agrees to allow the Indian and U.S. navies to develop a small port and airfield on the western side of Socotra, at a position to be determined at a later date, specifically for the purpose of fighting piracy in the Horn of Africa."

"Nice, Connor," Maddox again whispered. "I'm sure the Chinese loved that move."

"You don't see their archway anymore, do you?" Stark returned softly.

Golzari, standing on Stark's other side, said in an undertone, "Commander, by any chance do you play chess?"

"I've played once or twice," Stark answered.

"We'll have to play sometime."

"Why? You've realized that you'll never beat me in a shooting or fencing match, Golzari?"

"On the contrary, old man, I just want to make sure you have a chance for a best of five."

"We'll see. This all may have to take place in jail. I get the sinking feeling that a few things I've done here are going to bring me up in front of another court-martial."

"When are you going to tell me about the first one?"

"Best three out of five, Agent Golzari, will earn you the right to that story."

"I look forward to it. And if I lose?"

"I'm running short on whiskey," Stark suggested.

"It's a deal. I'm stopping by to see a sick friend in the U.K. on my way back to Washington tomorrow. I'll find something you'll approve of—in case I lose, of course."

"It's always best to plan ahead, Agent Golzari."

After the ceremony, C. J. strolled up a nearby hill with Connor as Golzari followed ten paces behind.

"Thank you, Connor. This agreement may not be what the White House expected—or wants—but it's a good one."

"Why thank me, C. J.? You worked out the deal and got the president to approve it."

"Because we figured this one out together and you facilitated it. I couldn't have done it without you and your connections. The Yemenis love you more than ever now, and owe you a huge debt too. And the Indians—the ambassador and the naval attaché couldn't stop talking about you. You made India a player here and bumped the Chinese in the process. You have some new and very powerful friends there."

"I may need them, C. J., depending on how this all works out."

She shook her head. "This isn't Canada. You did things the right way this time. I leave for Washington the night after tomorrow to get the answers to some big unanswered questions. I think I can fix things for you there. For now, please accept this," she said, offering him an envelope.

"Can I open it now or do I have to wait until Christmas?"

"If you want to stay here six more months on active duty, be my guest and wait."

He opened it to find a modification to the orders he had received just two weeks before. He was now officially off active duty. A second faxed page was his honorable discharge from the Navy.

"I figured you might want to frame the real thing. It will be forwarded to you in Ullapool."

"Thank you, C. J., but there's one item of business left—the American Asha said was behind all this. Damien suggested that it may be Eliot Green."

"There's no doubt in my mind," she replied without hesitation. "That's the only way this makes sense. He's been manipulating events from the start."

"You knew? I'm the only one who hadn't figured it out, I guess. I need two more favors from you, C. J."

"You're so high maintenance."

"Let Golzari and me handle Green and the rest."

"Done. That's one favor, Connor. What's the other?"

"This is a special favor for someone." He whispered something into her ear.

"Agent Golzari, look over there—flying elephants!" she called out, pointing to the sky.

Golzari turned his head instinctively, then, recognizing the utter impossibility, turned back just quickly enough to see Ambassador C. J. Sumner kiss Commander Connor Stark on the cheek.

DAY 19

Mar'ib 0747 (GMT)

Stark and Mutahar entered the abandoned stone house in the desert several miles from the Yemeni's luxurious estate. Inside, the naked body of his firstborn son rested in an awkwardly arched position with a crate bracing his lower back. His hands and feet were tightly bound by shackles secured to the stone walls. Two days of feces and urine caked the floor beneath him. His teeth and the cheap, blood-stained pliers that had been used to remove them were scattered about, and the skin from his fingertips had been burned away to forever remove other means of identification. The flies had come for him, and as each touched down on his body he winced with no means to swat them away. His torso jerked with his inaudible whimpers begging for a drop of water or for the torture to end.

Mutahar's face was expressionless as he gazed on the son he had loved.

"He is ready to answer questions," said one of Mutahar's security officers. "Commander Stark did not lie to you."

"He never has," Mutahar reprimanded the security agent. "Connor, he is yours."

Stark knelt beside the helpless Faisal. Any sympathy he might have had for Mutahar's son had been destroyed by the deaths Faisal had caused and the destruction he had nearly accomplished. "Your crime of piracy is evident, Faisal. But you were not just a pirate, were you?"

Faisal shook his head.

"What was the purpose of your piracy?"

He answered through swollen lips, "It was the only way to fight the West, by attacking their ships. I wanted my ships to control the Gulf of Aden and beyond, and my fleet to be greater than my father's."

"That's not enough. Tell me more. Why were you working with Asha and al-Ghaydah?"

"A man named Hu. He is Chinese," Faisal whispered. "When Asha's warlord was killed, they protected him and used him in America. Then they had the Americans bomb his warlord's killers. They were going to put him in power in Somalia, and he would give them access to ores and other resources there." Faisal coughed, a plea for water.

"Did you conspire with al-Ghaydah's family?"

"Yes, yes. I had worked with al-Qaeda first. When I was young, I helped bomb the American ship in the harbor. I worked with them and with Ahmed al-Ghaydah's family and Hu to rid Yemen of the West and its allies."

Mutahar stepped forward. "Am I an ally of the West? And our family?" he asked.

"Yes," Faisal cried. "You worked for them and let them come here. You treated one as a brother! I wanted to stop the Western ships coming through the Gulf of Aden. Al-Qaeda was to start riots in the port cities when people began to lose their work; al-Ghaydah's family would do the same in their district. We were trying to create disorder. I would bring order from that chaos."

"And you would be the new leader of Yemen?" Stark asked.

"Yes."

"What would Hu get?"

"The oil."

"But you were going to destroy the oil platforms with the *Katya P.*"

"Yes. But the Chinese had brought equipment to Socotra to rebuild them."

Mutahar rubbed his face and looked once more on the body of his son, who struggled to meet his father's gaze.

"What was al-Amriki's role?" Stark asked.

"He gave us information—about the embassy, about the ambassador, and the military adviser. He was working with Hu. I never met him."

"What do you know of him?"

Faisal paused. The security officer pulled his shoulder and Faisal screamed.

"Al-Amriki is a powerful man in Washington," he immediately yelled. "He ordered the Navy ships away from here. He ordered weapons away from the cruiser to make it helpless."

"Does he work in the Navy? In the Pentagon?"

"No. He works for your president."

Stark and Mutahar looked at each other.

"Do you know his name?" Stark asked.

"No, but Asha told me it was a color."

"A color?" Stark paused. "Green," he said. "Just as Golzari thought."

"I know that name, Connor. Is he not President Becker's chief of staff?"

"Yes. I knew him once. This doesn't surprise me." He looked down at Faisal. "Please end this, Mutahar. I have what I need. I did not want it to come to this."

"Nor I, my brother."

"Father?" Faisal called out weakly.

"You are done with him?" Mutahar asked.

"Yes, I must leave immediately to attend to some matters."

"As must I."

Stark and Mutahar embraced; then the father bent down on one knee and whispered into his son's ear. "You shamed our family. You lifted a sword against my brother Connor, the man who once saved your life and who has never lied to me or disrespected me, my house, or my country. You planned to lift a sword against your own family and your country. You must never be allowed to tell anyone of this. You have brought this upon yourself. You are no longer my son. You are alone in this world."

A few days later a new beggar appeared on the filthiest street of Sana'a. His tongue had been cut out and his right hand and left foot had been amputated in accordance with Quranic law governing *hirabah*. The passersby who threw him an occasional scrap of food would never know the wailing beggar's name.

DAY 22

McLean, Virginia, 0323 (GMT)

Eliot Green turned off the outside lights to avoid attracting insects and stepped onto the deck off his study for a late-night smoke. Summers in D.C. were miserably hot and humid, but having a house right on the Potomac River helped. Furious that Sumner and Stark had foiled him again—just as they had in Canada—he made plans to cover his tracks in the affair. Some money had to be returned, and some planned major purchases had to be deferred as a result. It was an inconvenience, nothing more.

Sumner hadn't provided the details yet, but somehow she had succeeded in getting the Yemenis to sign an oil agreement. He slapped his hand on the deck rail in anger, then stubbed out his cigarette. When he opened the door to go back inside, he found himself facing a man standing in the shadows with a gun pointed at him. Eliot Green feared no one in Washington, D.C.—until this moment.

"Sit down, you fat, malevolent bastard," commanded a second voice from the far wall, out of reach of the dim light coming from the hallway.

Eliot Green, who never obeyed anyone, obeyed now. He began to sweat. "I have money."

"How nice for you," said the second voice.

"What do you want?"

"Answers," responded the first voice.

"To what?"

"Your role in Yemen," answered the second man, still hidden at the other side of the room.

Green heard a click, then a recording. The voice he heard was clearly that of a man in pain, but the words were muffled.

"Al-Amriki is a powerful man in Washington. He ordered the Navy ships away from here. He told me that he had taken weapons away from the cruiser."

A second voice sounded from the recorder. *"Does he work in the Navy? In the Pentagon?"*

"No. He works for your president."

"Do you know his name?"

"No, but Asha told me it was a color."

"I know your voice," Green said to the man standing out of sight.

"You should, Eliot." Stark stepped forward.

"You look older, Stark."

"And you look guilty, Green. Illegal use of military assets to assassinate a Somali warlord, conspiracy in the murder of Dunner's son, conspiring to kill a U.S. ambassador and military personnel, treason. Shall I continue?"

"You have lies from a man clearly undergoing torture. You've got nothing."

"Actually, I have quite a lot. Thanks to my friend here, I've learned that a Chinese firm made deposits into an Antiguan account that belongs to you. The payments coincide nicely with some interesting dates—the day Tomahawks landed on a certain warlord in Somalia, the day the attacks were made on Ambassador Sumner and the defense attaché, and others. The Chinese firm's payments also coincide with payments made to the al-Ghaydah family and suspected terrorists in Yemen. Nice group you've tied yourself to."

"What do you want?" Green snarled. "You know you can't touch me."

"C'mon, Eliot, you know the D.C. playlist: 'What did the president know and when did he know it?'"

Green scoffed at the questions. "What did the president know? Shit, he knows what I tell him. And that's only as much as I let him know or he wants to know."

"Which was it for Yemen?"

"He wanted to know."

Stark snorted. "Nice. So you destabilize Yemen, help the pirates, create an incident, get the United States out of there, and make the Chinese seem like the nice peaceful people they are. And you get a whole lot of money from the Chinese. Did the president know about killing C. J. Sumner?"

"Yeah, he agreed to it. But he didn't like it. She was his favorite mistress, after all."

"His what?"

Green burst out laughing. "You didn't know? After all this time? I thought you had half a brain, Stark. Hell, how do you think she saved you from a dishonorable discharge after your little escapade in Canada?"

"C. J.?"

"You've spent all this time with her in Yemen and she didn't tell you?" Green was getting his confidence back now. "She couldn't stop the court-martial, so she used the relationship she had developed with Becker when he was in the Senate. There's more. I'm the man who knows D.C.'s best-kept secrets, Stark. Walk away with your friend and your guns now, and I may even share a few more with you."

"Go to hell, you bastard."

Green reached for a cigarette but stopped when he heard an unmistakable metallic click.

"Put your hand back where I can see it," commanded the first voice.

"What's next?" Green sneered. "Are you going to have someone arrest me?"

"No," Stark replied.

The first man stepped forward from the shadows. Green didn't recognize him. "Who the hell are you?"

The man reached into a pocket and pulled out another pistol, this one specially made for the Soviet Spetsnaz.

"You can't shoot me," Green said incredulously.

The man spoke with a hint of a British accent. "That's true. I can't. Unless it's in self-defense," Golzari said. "But no one can trace this gun anyway."

"Do you know the story of General Rommel?" Stark asked. "How he died? He was given a choice: a predetermined public trial and the Nazis' destruction of his family or a dose of cyanide. Same choice, Green. One bullet. It's easy."

"I don't have a family. You lose."

"Ah, but what *do* you have? Power? You'll be discredited; the president will drop you rather than further taint his administration. Hell, with this recording we just made of you implicating the president, that'll be a moot point because he'll be impeached before the next election. You'll go to jail. Money? That'll be gone with your legal fees if the government doesn't take it first. Reputation? After a long and nasty trial you'll never have a job again. Not to mention the Chinese, who probably won't be happy when all this comes out. What would they do to keep you quiet? You have nothing, Green. *You* lose."

Green thought it over, his mind churning to come up with some way to save himself. He always had before. But not this time. He had no chance to escape.

All his precious contacts would fade away if a crack opened in his glass house of power. He'd have no one, no money, no power. Shit. Stark had won.

Green opened the desk drawer and slowly pulled the pistol out as Golzari took a stance that demonstrated he would drop him at the first sign of a wrong move. Green brought the barrel up to his face and stuck it in his mouth. "Huck hue," he snarled, glaring at Stark instead of his accomplice holding the gun.

"Really, Green? Those are your last words? They'll go down with 'I have but one life to live for my country.' I'll remember your words and cherish them."

"Huck hue!" Green grunted louder, then pulled the trigger. His lifeless body dropped backward into the high-backed leather executive office chair, which rolled a few inches across the study floor.

Golzari, wearing latex gloves, handed Green's laptop to Stark and was checking Green's desk for more evidence when the two men saw the lights of a car outside.

"The police couldn't have been called this quickly," Stark whispered. He made his way to the study's closet and slipped inside, leaving the door ajar. The digital recorder was still on; he held his gun at the ready. He motioned Golzari to go out the door leading to the deck.

The front door clicked open. No one had rung the doorbell. Stark heard footsteps coming down the hallway—at least two people. As they appeared in the doorway, the dim hall light revealed that both were Chinese. The one Stark assumed to be the leader motioned to the other, who went around Green's desk and used a flashlight to examine the bloody mess in the office chair. They spoke again in muted Chinese and began looking around the room. They were searching for something—the laptop maybe?

Stark slowed his breathing and raised his gun, preparing to emerge from the closet. He waited until the one behind the desk was bent over sifting through the drawers and then opened the door wider, keeping his gun trained on the leader.

He had taken two steps out of the closet when the man behind the desk noticed him and reached for his weapon. As stealthily as a panther, Golzari slipped up behind him and put the Russian pistol to the henchman's head.

The other Chinese man, the one closest to Stark, said something, and the man obediently pulled his hand back from his holstered weapon.

Stark stepped slowly to the right, keeping both men in view as he maneuvered to a position where his back was to the rear wall of the house and he could see all the way through the study's entrance to the front door.

"Who are you?" he asked the leader.

In the semidarkness he thought he saw a smile on the man's face.

"No one of concern to you."

"You are of concern to me if you had an appointment with Green."

"It would be best if you allowed us to go on our way."

"Why?"

"Green is dead. My business with him is finished."

"What was your business with Green?" Stark kept his eyes moving between the two men and the front door, ready for sudden movement from either direction.

"You are interfering," the leader said, and again said something in Chinese. This time the man behind the desk didn't react.

A shadow crossed the deck, and Stark retrained his pistol toward the double doors leading outside. The second man made a move for his gun, and Golzari shot him in the arm. The double doors swung open and another Chinese man burst into the room. Stark shot him, missing the center of the torso where he had aimed. The man lived but dropped his weapon.

The leader simply stood there, immobile and uncooperative.

Golzari heard police sirens in the distance. Most likely a neighbor had heard the shot when Green killed himself and reported it.

"Our business is done. Get out now," Stark told the leader, who motioned to his men and left the house. When they were out the door, Stark retrieved the computer from the closet where he had stashed it and followed Golzari out the back door.

On the way to his car a few streets away, Stark turned off the digital recorder and slipped it into a pocket, intending to have a friend at one of the intelligence agencies identify the voice and translate the man's words.

"Hu?" Golzari asked.

"That's my guess."

"Why'd you let him go?"

"We got what we wanted—for now," Stark responded.

Golzari shook his head in disgust. "Well, that went bloody well. Do you even believe in the law?"

"I believe in justice."

Camp David, 1423 (GMT)

C. J. sat directly across from President Hamilton Becker in the informal office at the presidential retreat in Maryland.

"It's so good to have you back, C. J. I wish I could come around this desk and take you in my arms."

"You asked to see me, Mr. President?" she said coldly.

"C. J., this Hadiboh Accord you got us into. We didn't exactly get what we wanted, did we? The United States had no intention of entering a partnership with India."

"If it hadn't been for Commander Stark, we wouldn't have anything at all, sir."

"Stark. Yeah, I have a report here that Eliot and the chair of the Senate Armed Services Committee put together yesterday that cites a number of issues involving him: assuming command of a U.S. Navy ship without authorization, attacking local merchant ships, attacking innocent Somali fishing dhows and killing innocent people, attacking a Chinese-flagged ship, participating in unauthorized joint operations . . . the list goes on and on."

"Tear it up."

"What?"

"Tear it up. Now."

The president reared back in surprise. "You can't tell the president of the United States what to do, Miss Sumner."

"I damn well can, Hamilton. And there's more. Here's what's going to happen. First, you're going to get Helen Forth's resignation."

"I won't do that without checking with Eliot."

"Second, you're going to announce tomorrow that you have decided not to accept your party's nomination for reelection at the convention in two weeks."

"What the . . ."

"Oh, and you're going to push the party damn hard to nominate John Dunner at the convention."

"But . . ."

"But nothing. I'm doing this to make sure you don't ever get the chance to do again what you did in Yemen. I know all about Green's role in the attack on the *Bennington*, and I know that you knew about it. I have recordings to prove it."

The president was paralyzed, shocked into immobility.

"You'll read this statement," C. J. said, tossing a typewritten page on the desk before him. "It's simple and direct—like the one Eliot forced John Dunner to sign. Yes, I know about that too.

"Third, I will be your point person on Capitol Hill in getting the Senate to ratify the Hadiboh Accord. It's a good agreement, and it's going to happen.

"Oh, and fourth, you will recall this person to active duty," she handed him a slip, "in command of a destroyer—now."

"I can't do that, C. J., I'm . . ."

"You're the commander-in-chief, at least for now. Act like it. Finally, you and I are finished. I wish to God we'd never started. You're not the man I believed you to be. Maybe you never were."

"C. J. . . ."

"You and Eliot Green planned to kill me, humanitarian aid workers, and the crew of the *Bennington*. I have stated four demands. Comply with them or be impeached, tried, and convicted. Understood?"

"Let me get Eliot in here. We can work all these things out, C. J. I promise. He'll be here soon. He'll handle all of this to your satisfaction."

"Eliot Green isn't coming in today. It's time you learned to make your own decisions, Mr. President." C. J. walked out to meet the newest member of her new protective detail, Agent Damien Golzari.

EPILOGUE

THREE WEEKS LATER

USS *LeFon*, Norfolk, Virginia, 0420 (GMT)

The captain of the newest warship DDG-125, the USS *LeFon*, was admiring her dayroom when a knock sounded on the door. "Come." One of her new junior officers entered carrying a shoebox-size carton. "Yes . . .?" She eyed the red nametag on the summer white uniform. "Ensign Fisk, is it?"

"Yes, ma'am. I just reported aboard."

"Please, come in. Where was your last billet?"

"USS *Bennington*, ma'am."

"The . . ." She raised her eyebrows, then smiled warmly. "Welcome aboard, Ensign Fisk. It's a pleasure to have you on my ship."

"Thank you, ma'am. I was ordered to give you this on reporting." He raised the box, which had a card taped to the top. The blond commander nodded toward her right arm, which was in a sling. "Set it on the chart table, please." The box made an interesting gurgling sound as the ensign complied. She lifted off the card and opened it.

> *This bottle may not be as good as your coffee, but keep it in your desk for when you really need it. You always deserved this command, Jaime. And keep an eye on young Ensign Bobby Fisk. He'll stand by a good skipper through the thick of it. I can only imagine what he'll do for a great skipper like you.*
> *—Connor*

Ullapool, Scotland, 1620 (GMT)

It was drizzling again as he walked toward the pub. It always seemed to be drizzling in Ullapool. He was still clean-shaven and close-cropped from his active-duty assignment, and men he knew well passed him without recognizing him. Connor chuckled and decided that perhaps he didn't need the beard and ponytail after all.

For the twentieth time since leaving Yemen a few weeks before, he pulled the folded fax from his pocket and focused on the only two words on it that mattered: "Honorably discharged." Rain droplets splattered across the page as he folded it back up and slipped it into his coat pocket.

He entered the pub. Nothing had changed. His friends were predictably at the dartboard, at the table in the corner, and on the bar stools. Glasgow's team was fighting it out with another rugby team on the television. As he walked in, the lively chatter fell to a dull murmur and then complete silence as the crowd turned to him—much as they had weeks before when two naval officers had come to take him away.

He slowly approached the bar and set his large olive-green seabag on the ancient wooden floor.

"The same, Mack," he said to the confused bartender.

At that moment, red-haired Maggie made her way out of the kitchen with an armload of plates. She alone recognized him.

ACKNOWLEDGMENTS

This work would not have been possible without the support of family, friends, colleagues, acquaintances, and others. To anyone whose brain I picked to see if a character, a line, or a plot made sense, thank you for sharing your thoughts and expertise. I also drew inspiration from the U.S. Naval Academy Brigade of Midshipmen. As of this writing, I have been in the classroom with 910 students. In his musical *The King and I*, Oscar Hammerstein wrote: "If you become a teacher, by your pupils you'll be taught." No truer statement has ever been written. Thanks to all of you, especially the Class of 2009, who were plebes on my first day teaching.

My wife, Kate, read the book as it was initially being written and offered a multitude of suggestions. I am indebted to her for her patience and perspectives.

The boys from the "Ink and Drink" read and critiqued the first draft. Temple Cone, Tim Feist, Marcus Jones, as well as Ed Naro and John Williams ripped it apart and then drank my beer.

If the "Lost Boys" come across as the unsung heroes of the book, it's because of my great respect for helicopter pilots, particularly those with whom I served: Neal Barham, Eric Bondurant, Dustin Budd, Jason Burns, Margaret Ewers, John Mikols, and Matt Somerville. Then there are the surface warfare officers and sailors, especially Wade Barnes, Brion Bennett, Matt Bucher, Dick Curtis, Rich Durham, Patrick Gatchell, Kim Himmer, Casey Mahon, Greg McIntosh, Todd McKinney, Todd Stengel, and Kevin Sullivan--and too many others to name here. No characters in the book bear any resemblance to them, but they all represent the finest Navy in the world and the commitment with which they perform their jobs every day at sea.

For the character of the nameless captain of the USS *Bennington*, I simply removed every positive character trait I observed in Capt. Daryl Hancock,

USN, one of the finest officers and individuals I've known and under whom I served twice overseas. The *Bennington*'s captain is the antithesis of Daryl Hancock.

The publishing side would not have been possible without the extraordinary team at Naval Institute Press, from its director, Rick Russell, who took a chance, to expert editors Adam Kane, Marlena Montagna, and Mindy Conner, and the marketing team of Clair Noble, Judy Heise, and George Keating. My appreciation also goes out to my publicist, Jen Richards, and Barbara Esstman, who provided editorial advice with an early draft.

In the interest of advancing the storyline, I ask the reader to suspend some disbelief. For example, it would be implausible for someone not selected for command or even in the Navy (as in the case of the character Jaime Johnson) to be given command of a warship.

Secretaries of the Navy name warships. Since I'm not a secretary of the Navy, the only way I can name ships is through this and potential future novels. The Navy cruiser *Bennington* is so named because Connor Stark is the fictional descendent of Revolutionary War Maj. Gen. John Stark. I spent the better part of my senior year in college writing a paper on John Stark; naming a ship after one of his battles seemed appropriate and, with some exceptions, is in line with the general naming convention of the *Ticonderoga*-class cruisers. The destroyer at the end of the novel is named the USS *LeFon* as a small tribute to the late Captain Carroll "Lex" LeFon, USN. Some knew him as a leader and mentor in the Navy. Many more of us became devotees of his wit, wisdom, and inspirational literary prowess as the milblogger Neptunus Lex.

Finally, a portion of the net proceeds of this work will go to Horses for Heroes (www.horsesforheroes.org) and other veterans organizations. The warriors these organizations support are the real-life heroes. Please support them. Thank you.

ABOUT THE AUTHOR

Claude Berube has worked for the Office of Naval Intelligence and on Capitol Hill. An officer in the Navy Reserve, he deployed with Expeditionary Strike Group Five in 2004–2005. He is the co-author of three non-fiction books and has taught at the United States Naval Academy.

The Naval Institute Press is the book-publishing arm of the U.S. Naval Institute, a private, nonprofit, membership society for sea service professionals and others who share an interest in naval and maritime affairs. Established in 1873 at the U.S. Naval Academy in Annapolis, Maryland, where its offices remain today, the Naval Institute has members worldwide.

Members of the Naval Institute support the education programs of the society and receive the influential monthly magazine *Proceedings* or the colorful bimonthly magazine *Naval History* and discounts on fine nautical prints and on ship and aircraft photos. They also have access to the transcripts of the Institute's Oral History Program and get discounted admission to any of the Institute-sponsored seminars offered around the country.

The Naval Institute's book-publishing program, begun in 1898 with basic guides to naval practices, has broadened its scope to include books of more general interest. Now the Naval Institute Press publishes about seventy titles each year, ranging from how-to books on boating and navigation to battle histories, biographies, ship and aircraft guides, and novels. Institute members receive significant discounts on the Press's more than eight hundred books in print.

Full-time students are eligible for special half-price membership rates. Life memberships are also available.

For a free catalog describing Naval Institute Press books currently available, and for further information about joining the U.S. Naval Institute, please write to:

Member Services
U.S. Naval Institute
291 Wood Road
Annapolis, MD 21402-5034
Telephone: (800) 233-8764
Fax: (410) 571-1703
Web address: www.usni.org